THE PSICLONE PROJECT

THIRD IN THE PSICLONE SERIES

SIMON STANTON

www.simonstanton.com

CONTENTS

PROLOGUE

Michael settled back in the chair. He, Anna and Eric all sat in the Head's office, cups of tea or coffee in hand, biscuits at the ready. The Head herself sat behind her desk. Michael cast a quick glance at the Head. She showed little sign of her recent kidnapping and escape from almost certain death at the hands of Marshall, Bullock and Singh. He admired her fortitude. He'd always regarded her as an office-based political animal, but now he saw the clear signs of someone who had seen close action. Tonight, he suspected, had not been her first time in battle.

The last few hours had been dramatic and tiring. They had finally located his three former colleagues at a rural farmhouse where they had held the Head captive. Michael and Eric had attacked the farmhouse and had fought the Three. Michael had freed the Head and in the battle had shot and killed Evan Bullock, but Marshall and Singh had escaped.

As they sat and reviewed recent events, the Head had finally agreed to divulge her full understanding of the project which had resulted in Michael's team becoming powerfully telepathic. The story would also explain the events which had led to three of the team (Vince Marshall, Evan Bullock and Julian Singh) becoming renegades who returned now, three years later, on a violent blood-lust for revenge.

'It's important to understand,' said the Head, 'this story is part fact and part conjecture. Over the last three years, I've pieced together some parts of it which I didn't know at the time, but I suspect the entire story has never been fully understood.'

'Why not?' asked Eric. Direct as usual, thought Michael, but it was a question which needed answering.

'When Michael came to join MI5 we were on the final countdown to the 2012 Olympic Games. After that, other events took over. We understood as much about the project as we decided we needed. Perhaps now is the time to reassess that decision.'

Michael bit into his custard cream.

'The story starts when Captain Sanders and his team arrived at a research facility. The camp was a Ministry of Defence property and used for projects run jointly with external suppliers.'

Michael swallowed his mouthful of biscuit as quickly as possible so he could interrupt.

'No. Sorry. It starts earlier than that.'

'Your team's involvement in what was known as the Psiclone Project began at that point,' said the Head.

'Yes, it did,' said Michael, 'but before that, certain key events took place and certain individuals came to our attention. I think we'd understand everything better if we started earlier.'

'And where do you suggest we start?'

'Our first surveillance mission in Afghanistan, in Kandahar City,' said Michael.

He held the Head's gaze. Perhaps she was reviewing those earlier events, maybe deciding what she should confess and what she might prefer to keep secret.

'Yes,' she said, 'you're right. That mission was a key event. It was a military operation, but MI5 had a close interest in the surveillance target, so I was running Command and Control for the operation from here, while Captain Sanders and his team were on the ground in Kandahar.'

ONE

The imposing facade of Thames House, the headquarters of MI5, concealed all manner of secret activities, few more secret than those hiding on the first floor. The Operations Directorate occupied almost the whole of the first floor and was the area from which all active operations were monitored, controlled and directed. Hi-tech Command and Control rooms were the centres of activity for each operation. Each was equipped with a dazzling array of large wall-mounted display screens and smaller screens on the huge central desks and numerous peripheral workstations. These rooms were where MI5 personnel worked alongside their military counterparts with hi-speed communications links to other agencies (foreign and domestic) and to the data and communications network of GCHQ, the government's intelligence and surveillance agency.

Command and Control Room 4 was fully operational. The light in the room came from the wall mounted displays and the numerous flat-panel displays adorning the single large rectangular desk which occupied the centre of the room. The room was bathed in the light of maps, photographs of individuals, scrolling displays of information and status updates. At the head of the table was the Head of Section. A stern and forceful character, she was admired, respected and feared in equal measure by most who worked for her. Commonly referred to as Ma'am in her presence, and 'the Head' out of hearing range, she ran the largest and most active Operations Section.

'Do we still have an open link to Sparrowhawk?' she asked. At times the code names seemed almost infantile, at others they were crucial. Whoever Sparrowhawk was, and even the Head didn't know, ensuring his security and anonymity were vital. She looked up at one of the big screens, the multiple windows showing maps and satellite images of the southern areas of Afghanistan. One image was a grainy, black-and-white picture, obviously taken from extreme altitude. A pulsing yellow dot showed Sparrowhawk's location. She could only imagine the focus and dedication it must take to operate under cover, in the midst of the enemy.

An analyst answered the question. 'Yes, Ma'am. Comm's link is open and active.' The analyst was hidden somewhere in the dimness of the rear of the room.

'Any sighting of Nightingale?' Another code name, another person putting their life on the line, another anonymous individual who needed protection in exchange for vital information. Sometimes she thought of this as a game, but the deadly nature of this game never escaped her. She fought down the nerves. She knew she had a reputation for being hard and calculating, a reputation she fostered, a reputation that often masked anxiety and uncertainty.

There was the tapping of keys before the analyst replied. 'No Ma'am. Sparrowhawk says no sign of movement.'

Eyes looked at clocks. It was still five minutes before the scheduled rendezvous time, before another piece of the jigsaw might fall into place. Might. There were never any guarantees. Nightingale may yet decide not to risk his life after all, he might not actually have the information he promised, he might even be hostile and luring enemy forces to Sparrowhawk's location. Every alternative presented risks, every risk needed mitigating.

The Head looked across at the Military Liaison Officer, the Army (in this case) officer responsible for communicating directly with the soldiers providing support for the operation. He wore his uniform shirt and trousers and a worried expression. They were the boots on the ground, the men with guns who'd do the shooting if it came to that. If it came to shooting then everything would have gone very badly wrong. If all went well then Nightingale would turn up as planned and tell Sparrowhawk exactly where and when the meeting would take place. The soldiers would go in and install covert surveillance devices and listen to the meeting, then melt away, leaving no-one suspecting the meeting had been overheard. The pieces were always moving on the board, a board that could never be fully seen, and often even the board moved. But it was a game she played well, with focus and intelligence, and above all, patience.

'Is your team ready?' she asked.

'They are,' answered the Liaison Officer, 'but if it all goes pear-shaped they're too far away to rescue Sparrowhawk.' The Head said nothing to this. The team of soldiers were supposed to be too far away, they weren't there to rescue

Sparrowhawk, their mission came next. Their time would come.

'Are all GCHQ resources online?'

'Yes Ma'am,' answered another analyst. 'They're patched into our communications, they have translators ready for real-time translation to English, intelligence analysts ready to evaluate any information we get.'

Somewhere in Kandahar, Afghanistan's second-largest city, two people would meet and talk in what they would assume would be a safe and secure environment. Face to face they'd expect their conversation couldn't be intercepted, and they'd talk about arrangements for terrorist actions in the UK. With luck they'd mention names of people in the UK, they'd mention names of people in Afghanistan. If all went to plan this operation would uncover who was planning the action, when it was being planned for, and (most importantly) who in the UK might be involved. Names, even suggestions of names, would tell MI5 who to focus on, who to keep in the sights of its surveillance and intelligence gathering.

'Can we get any better aerial surveillance?' the Head asked, looking at the images on the big screen. This was one area where she felt exposed.

'No Ma'am,' someone replied from the dim edge of the room. The images came from a drone courtesy of the US Air Force, but the drone's primary function was communications, not surveillance. The images from the drone's cameras were a bonus, it could show the general area where the meetings would take place, but it couldn't show them the movement of individual people. The Head felt almost blind. Limited hearing, insufficient vision, not ideal, but she'd had to deal with worse.

She thought at least these days they had the capability

for remote surveillance, to provide soldiers on the ground with immediate updates, to whisper directly in the ear of someone thousands of miles away to tell them danger lay around the next corner. In earlier years, in Northern Ireland, they'd had no such facilities. She'd had to play the game from a distance, relying on soldiers who were out of reach.

'Two minutes,' someone called out. The level of conversation dropped, eyes focused on screens. The Head half closed her eyes. For her, the most important screen was in her mind. She let the pieces of the jigsaw settle, others still moved, not yet fixed in place. The picture was always in motion, there were always gaps and uncertainties. She could feel her shoulders stiffen, always a sign she was over-thinking things. A deep and slow breath helped her relax a little.

A voice jerked her out of her introspection. 'Sparrowhawk reports movement in the street.' The atmosphere in the room took on a new, tenser feeling. Instinctively people looked up at the big screens, but there was nothing to see there. An eerie silence fell over the room, like a crowd holding its collective breath at the moment an athlete makes a game-winning play.

'Specify,' said the Head, forcing herself to keep her voice calm and even.

A pause. 'He says cars moving, people shouting.' She ran through possibilities in her mind; locals on the move, enemy movement but ignorant of Sparrowhawk's presence, enemy movement moving in on Sparrowhawk.

'Is he compromised?' she asked, ready to consider changes to the plan.

A longer pause. 'Not yet, no-one's moving towards his position.'

Whoever Sparrowhawk was he would have little chance to escape. If Taliban or Al Qaeda forces knew who he was or where he was they would already have him surrounded. She hoped this was just a case of locals being vocal.

The Head resented not having a live audio feed from the agent in the field, she much preferred hearing what was happening. She was no field agent and had no desire to ever go into the field, but hearing events live gave her a more visceral sense of what was happening and how to respond. Sparrowhawk did, however, have a small device, probably similar to a smartphone, and could send short text messages.

'Sparrowhawk says he thinks they've got Nightingale,' someone said.

'Shit,' said someone else, quickly followed by a muttered apology. The Head had thought the same response. In the game, they had probably lost a key piece, a valuable asset had been taken off the board. In real-life, somewhere out there, a real living human being was probably about to be murdered.

The Head's attention focused on her significant asset, Sparrowhawk. Plans might need to change quickly. The game could change quickly. It could be a marathon chess game one minute and a boxing match the next.

'Can Sparrowhawk get out?' she asked. He was an asset she was keen to keep intact.

Another pause, longer, longer. 'He's sent one word,' the analyst said, 'he says "running."'

The Head noticed the Liaison Officer looking across at her, but now was not the time to bring the soldiers into play. Sparrowhawk would have to look after his own escape. She looked across at the liaison officer.

'Can your team still carry out their surveillance?'

The man drew a breath before answering. 'They can,' he said, carefully, 'but I'd advise against it.'

The Head fought back the temptation to comment on the unsolicited advice. She needed information, not guidance.

The man continued. 'If we don't know exactly when this meeting is happening there's a chance they'll gate-crash the party.' He didn't add the other risk, that they might instead be hiding for hours waiting for the meeting, with the ever-increasing risk of discovery.

She knew that, of course. And she knew he had to decide whether the mission was worth the risks to his men's lives.

'Understood, but I'm not sure we can afford to walk away from this,' she said.

Decision time. The Olympic Games started in two months' time. MI5 knew there were threats from various domestic terrorists planning actions against the Games. They knew at least one of those threats was serious, well provisioned, and had support from some very well resourced overseas players. They just didn't know the exact identities of either the foreign or domestic players. There was an enemy out there, somewhere in the world, people who were plotting to hurt and kill innocent civilians, people who were adept at operating from the shadows and covering their tracks. There were soldiers out there, men whose lives she might risk. It was one thing to risk a chess piece in a game. She found it quite different to risk people's lives.

Focus, intelligence, and patience.

'Send your men in,' she ordered.

GCHQ, Cheltenham, May 2012

A SENSE of energy pervaded the briefing room. Even though there were only five of them in the room Anna could feel a sense of excitement bubbling under the calm and professional demeanour of each of those present. She checked her hair was still tied back. Her hair was thick and black and smooth and set off her olive skin and slim features. It reminded her of the feeling in a crowd at a concert in the moments before the main act came on. As the most junior of the analysts, having only just graduated from the final phase of her intelligence analyst training programme, Anna was keen to see how real intelligence operations worked. Did Olympic athletes feel this way, stepping onto the track in front of a cheering crowd?

For just a brief moment she allowed herself to wonder what her university classmates would be doing this afternoon. Most of the top achieving mathematics graduates had been snapped up by the big banks or consulting firms, some by research institutes. Anna hadn't told her friends where she'd be going, only saying she'd be working for a small enterprise doing some interesting things in data mining.

The Government Communications Headquarters, GCHQ, was not exactly a small enterprise. The main facility was a huge circular building on the outskirts of Cheltenham. Often called the Doughnut, the building stood out as the most visible feature in this part of Gloucestershire, South West England. It wasn't small in terms of people, either, over five thousand people worked at the site, a unique blend of communications and IT specialists, intelligence analysts, mathematicians, linguists, cultural specialists, and more.

Today was special. Today was the most special day so far. Today Anna Hendrickson started work on her first real mission as intelligence analyst support. She looked around the room. She knew Wayne Browning, a senior analyst, and she vaguely knew Kingston Smith, another analyst. Smartly dressed, darker skin than Anna, straight black hair, Kingston had a kind of somewhere-Asian look to him. Browning moved with a kind of teenage awkwardness to him.

The team leader entered the room, a laptop tucked under his arm, obviously finishing a conversation with someone who then disappeared down the corridor. She thought he looked surprisingly young and wondered if he'd started shaving yet.

'Good afternoon,' said Brian Delaney as he sat down at the table. He opened the laptop and tapped some keys, the computer's display appeared on the wall mounted monitor.

'We can do introductions later, we need to cover the mission details first,' said Delaney. Everyone opened their notebooks and made ready to write down the key information.

Delaney began the briefing. 'We know there are credible threats to the London Olympic Games. We already have surveillance on high priority domestic activists. At least one group is believed to be in contact with well-funded and well-resourced foreign backers who are planning to provide materials and funding for a large-scale attack.'

Windows of information appeared on the screen; names, identities, a few blurred photographs, maps. People started scribbling furiously in their notebooks. Anna wasn't sure which of the information was relevant, so she hastily wrote down some of the names and details from the screen.

Delaney continued. 'One group is believed to be

working through a contact currently in Afghanistan. This person, we believe, is about to make contact with the representative of their backer at a meeting in Kandahar. MI5 have an ongoing operation with MI6 and with Special Forces to determine the exact location and time of the meeting, and to then provide audio and video surveillance of the meeting.'

Delaney paused to let people finish writing their notes. 'Once the Special Forces unit has deployed their surveillance equipment we'll be plugged into their feeds. We need Arabic to English translation, real-time correlation with our current intelligence databases and immediate analysis of voice and facial recognition data.'

He paused again to let it sink in. Anna took a breath as she finished her notes. This was "it." This was as real as it got, supporting soldiers on the ground, uncovering information which would prevent a large-scale terrorist action in the UK. She imagined this would beat anything her colleagues were doing in banking this afternoon.

'When does the mission start?' asked one of the other analysts.

'It's already started,' said Delaney, which caught most people by surprise. Anna stared at him, wide-eyed. 'MI6 have an agent in Kandahar who's due to make contact any minute with an informant who will reveal the precise time and location of the meeting, which is expected to be this evening. They need us online and ready as soon as we get back to our desks.'

Anna thought now would be a good time to ask a really insightful question, but she was still stunned by the immediacy of the situation. She'd assumed she'd have a day or two to do research, to prepare, to ask advice from other analysts about how to deliver her little piece of the operation. She made a mental note never to make such an assumption again, but that was about all she could do, her mind seemed to be going blank in a very worrying way.

Anna listened closely to the rest of the briefing. Delaney explained what little they knew about the people involved, the communications arrangements, and the role each person would have during the operation.

The meeting ended and everybody made to leave the room. She and Kingston sat close to each other in one of the main open-plan office areas, perhaps she could ask him, but still no coherent thoughts would form.

As they walked along the corridor towards the office area Kingston looked back at her and smiled. His smile turned to a frown, perhaps sensing Anna's growing sense of panic.

'First live operation?' he asked.

'Yes,' she said, almost having to force the words out.

'It's scary the first time,' he said. Fortunately her lack of coherent thoughts or the ability to speak meant she wasn't in danger of firing back any sarcastic replies. 'But once it starts and you get involved in the work, you'll forget about being nervous.'

She tried to say something, but all she could do was approximate a smile and sort of squeak.

'What's your field? Maths or languages?' he asked.

'Maths,' she managed to say, clutching her notebook even tighter.

'Me too,' he said. 'Just approach this the same as any maths problem.'

'But there are soldiers involved,' Anna said, starting to voice her real concern. She realised, in a moment of self-realisation, it was the reality of the situation she was struggling to deal with. Only now did she think there were soldiers who might shoot people, and other people who might shoot back, and people might get killed, and if she made a mistake and the operation failed there were terrorists who wanted to kill lots of people.

'They won't be shooting at you,' Kingston joked. Anna didn't respond to the humour. He stopped and let the others walk passed. Anna stopped too.

'I'm Kingston Smith,' he said, holding out his hand. Anna shook hands. It was their first formal introduction.

'Anna Hendrickson,' she said.

'Anna,' said Kingston, 'just remember that you're not running the whole operation. You and I are just small parts of a much bigger operation. There are other people who will make the big decisions, all we need to do is what we're good at and what we've been trained to do. We don't need to do anything more. We don't have to save the world, we let other people do that.'

Anna took a deep breath and exhaled sharply, and managed a smile at Kingston, a genuine smile. She did feel better, a little more in control. They walked through the heavy glass doors into the office area and took their seats at their desks.

Anna put on her headset and dialled the numbers on her comm's unit (nothing with so many buttons could be called just a "telephone.") The system connected her with the conference call for the operation. She could hear the hubbub of conversation between the analysts involved and the other specialists. She used her keyboard and mouse and brought up on her multiple monitors the various programs she'd need. Anna had been assigned to voice and facial recognition, feeding images into the vast artificial intelligence systems running on warehouse-sized computers. She felt a thrill of excitement as she thought how much computing power she had in her control, and what she was about to use that power for.

She thought about saying "let battle commence," but thought better of it. People died in battle, and she didn't feel ready for that just yet.

TWO

D octor Tobias Morrow stood at the window of his laboratory. His reflection caught his attention. He wondered when the man in the reflection had put on that much weight, or when his hair had got so thin. He wasn't sure the small round glasses looked appropriate anymore, too John Lennon now rather than distinguished academic.

From his vantage point he could look down at the paved and landscaped area between the main office block and his specialist research building. He could see his friend and ally walk out of the main building and into the afternoon sunshine. It was only a short walk along the footpath to the doors of the research building. Morrow had sensed his friend had finished in the management meeting, and so Morrow had summoned him.

He thought of the other man as a friend, but that probably wasn't the best word. Ally would be a better word. He relied on the man's counsel and support and influence over the directors and senior managers. He enjoyed the man's company, but to call him a friend implied a closeness which did not in truth exist. Morrow did not want anyone close to him. He liked his isolation, he felt safe in it, he did not need anyone feeling they could share it, or even intrude on it, unless invited.

Morrow let his mind extend outwards. In many ways it was still a strange experience, he could feel his mind expanding and extending. He had wondered how he would describe it to someone who had never experienced it (not that he had any intention of telling anyone about it,) but had decided it was a unique experience, it wasn't "like" anything.

He could sense the other man entering the building and making his way up to the fourth floor. He could, if he wanted, reach into the other man's mind, communicate with him directly, sense his thoughts. If needed he could compel the other man to act, but that would be crude. Far better to encourage someone to act, and then leave them to work under their own motivation. Telepathic control of another individual could be tiring, requiring a huge focus of concentration.

Telepathic communication was also extremely useful. He had sensed from the other man that something had happened in the management meeting which had caused concern. He could do without such distractions. He had so much to do, so much required his energy and attention, he did not need the distraction of dealing with managers.

Presently the doors to the laboratory swept open. In walked an older man, dressed as a gentleman, elegant in a suit which though not ostentatious was no doubt expensive. Yves Falcone was one of the few managers Morrow had any time for. True, Falcone was a non-executive director, not a manager, but Morrow had no time for the distinctions between grades of management. So long as they carried on managing the business and left him alone he had no problem with them. Now, however, he suspected something had changed, and at least one of them now thought 'managing the business' needed to include Morrow's operation. That would need to be stopped.

'Yves,' said Morrow, smiling and extending his hand. The gentleman shook his hand and returned the smile. Morrow had always thought Falcone looked the part of a gentle-man, a gentle grandfather figure, but he always had the impression Falcone would happily smile and shake your hand as he stuck a knife in you. Falcone had the air of someone who valued politeness and good manners, even when stabbing a friend in the back, even if only metaphorically.

'Tobias,' said Falcone, his smile fading, 'we need to talk.'

'I thought as much, come into the office.' Morrow led the way out of the laboratory area and into a small office. It had no external windows, just a glass wall between it and the laboratory, and was very much a functional room, no personal items were to be seen, no certificates, no photographs. Morrow's attention had become more and more focused, to the exclusion of absolutely everything else in his life. They sat, Morrow behind the desk, Falcone in front.

Morrow resisted the temptation to simply reach into Falcone's mind and find out what the man wanted to talk about. It was not only tiring but Morrow still considered in some cases it was, in a way, rude.

'Tell me, what concerns you, Yves?'

'I've been in a meeting of the Operations Board,' said Falcone. 'The Director of Operations made it very clear, he expects all scientific discoveries made by PanMedic to be fully exploited and generate the maximum profit possible.'

Morrow thought about this for a moment. Inwardly he

sighed. This was exactly the problem large companies created, and the kind of problem he could do without. PanMedic had all the facilities and benefits of a large and well-resourced pharmaceuticals company. As one of the chief research scientists it provided him with all the equipment and people he needed to carry on his research, and just recently his research had uncovered something very special. Whilst he had to admit PanMedic might feel it had some claim over the drug which released telepathic ability, Morrow felt no inclination to share it. He had other plans, much bigger plans, plans which could not accommodate the petty profit-driven priorities of ambitious managers. 'And?' he asked.

'He expects a full inventory, a full audit of all projects, all resources being used, and an analysis of the profit generated from them.'

Morrow considered this for a moment more. He didn't know the Director of Operations personally, but had been in several meetings with the man. Morrow thought the man could have made an excellent serial killer, he had a cold and ruthless streak and totally lacked any kind of compassion or interest in people. Morrow knew the man would probably engage IT specialists, possibly from outside the company, to hack into every database inside PanMedic and find out who was doing what and how much profit they were (or weren't) generating. Morrow had no intention of letting this manager delve into his activities. He had a very special project under way, and any interference would be most unwelcome.

'This could be most unfortunate,' he said to Falcone. 'I don't want this man meddling in what we're doing.'

'I didn't get the impression he was offering it as a choice,' said Falcone.

'I think it's more important than ever that we acquire the

means to protect our activities,' said Morrow. 'I like your idea of creating a unit of soldiers we can control, dedicated to protecting us and our project.' Morrow had fallen into a habit of calling it 'our' project, as though he shared the ownership and direction. He did not. It was his project, and anyone else involved was simply a means to an end. But it seemed polite.

'That might not be achievable in time to stop the Director,' said Falcone. 'He seemed quite focused. My contact in the military projects division might well be able to find a suitable group of soldiers, but there is no guarantee he can do it quickly.'

'Be that as it may, we need to press ahead with that plan. Have him make the necessary preparations. As soon as he can identify a suitable group of soldiers I want to begin their preparation.'

'And the Director? What do you want to do about him?'

'Ask him to come and see me, tell him I have a project that will be of particular interest to him.'

Falcone frowned. 'The Director might not be so easy to control. He's made his intentions known publicly, he won't back down, can't back down, not even if you influence him directly.'

'Leave that problem to me, Yves,' said Morrow. 'However, I do want you to contact your man in security, we might need him to arrange for our Director to meet with some misfortune.'

Morrow could see Falcone physically recoil at the suggestion. They'd discussed it before, through his contacts in the military projects division, and through contacts he'd made when working in Africa, Falcone could reach out to some very unsavoury individuals who, for a price, could make certain problems go away. Falcone had the capacity to make these arrangements, but Morrow sensed he still lacked the motivation to go through with it. If Morrow couldn't directly control the Director, he was quite willing to take more serious actions.

Morrow got up and wandered around the desk until he stood behind Falcone. He put a hand on Falcone's shoulder, a seemingly friendly gesture, then put his other hand on the back of Falcone's neck. Morrow let his thoughts expand through his hand and made a direct mind-to-mind contact with Falcone. He let go and his mind surged through the physical contact. He needed more control over Falcone, he needed to be able to compel the man to follow orders, no matter what his moral objections might be.

As his mind overwhelmed Falcone's he imposed his will on the man, his thoughts surging through Falcone's mind. For minute after minute he stood there, Falcone's eyes closing, his head slumping forwards. When he'd finished he took his hands off Falcone. He'd let Falcone rest for a while. Morrow would also need to rest, but he would do that later. First he'd need to make sure Falcone would arrange direct access to his military contacts. Morrow had a measure of control over them as well, but he needed to strengthen it. Leaving people to work under their own motivation was all well and good, up to a point, but for the serious things he might have to control people totally and completely. These people would be useful to him, for now.

HONG KONG, May 2012

LEE JOON-HO SIPPED at the champagne as he stood at the

panoramic window and looked out over the sparkling lights of Hong Kong island. From the suite on the upper floors of the office block he could see across the harbour to Kowloon, the mainland. Music drifted through the room. He assumed it to be music, he found the western sound discordant and bland, so he paid it no attention.

Joon-ho was average height but a slim build. He could afford whatever he wanted, but the deprivations in his childhood had robbed him of any chance of a muscular physique. In some ways his childhood was a world away, in other ways it was still so close, and yet he had gone so far to escape it.

One of his aides interrupted his reverie, gesturing for him to meet another guest. Smartly dressed men and elegantly dressed women filled the room, indeed the entire suite, all rich and powerful in one way or another. Waiters circulated with trays of drinks as introductions were made, relationships forged, deals begun. Joon-ho had come here with an intention, and his first move must be to keep his purpose hidden. The moth must come to the candle.

'Mr Joon-ho, may I present Mr Li,' said the aide. Mr Li inclined his head, a bow of acknowledgement. Joon-ho returned the gesture, and both waited for the aide to retreat. For a brief moment he regarded Li, a short and rotund man, someone who obviously did not hold back in enjoying whatever pleasures he chose to purchase. Li was one of the many wealthy people in the room. Most had acquired wealth through legal and legitimate means, and some also through less legal enterprises. Joon-ho had little interest in how they had acquired their wealth. With people like Li he was only interested in the man's money, his motivation, and his discretion.

'A pleasure to meet again, Mr Li,' said Joon-ho. Perhaps

Li knew that Joon-ho's sole purpose at attending the party was to meet him, perhaps he did not know this, it didn't matter. The performance was everything.

'Likewise,' said Li, never a man to use an excess of words.

'Are you in Hong Kong for long?' asked Joon-ho, 'the Dragon Boat festival is a spectacle not to be missed.' Joon-ho knew full well Li only planned to be in Hong Kong for another two days, and would then leave for Dubai where he would attend meetings at the Middle East offices of his finance business.

'Another week,' said Li, 'perhaps next year for the boats.'

How easy it would be to rush things. How would the Americans put it? "Cut to the chase?" How like them it would be to "put all their cards on the table." The cards of most value were the cards not shown, the cards held back, the cards not yet dealt.

'A pity,' said Joon-ho, 'I have arranged to stay long enough to see the festival this year.' He had not.

There was a silence, and Joon-ho relaxed, he liked the silence. The longer the silence went on, the more people wanted to fill it.

'I find Hong Kong too busy,' said Li.

'Perhaps, but it has its uses,' said Joon-ho.

'Indeed, there is much business to be done here.'

Another silence. Joon-ho could almost feel Li's need to speak first about the topic which concerned them both. Let him speak first, let him break the silence, let him play the first cards.

Li turned and looked out of the windows. 'It is a useful place the British built here,' said Li.

'The British had an influence on the founding of Hong Kong,' said Joon-ho, 'but that influence is fading.'

'Some would wish that influence would fade more quickly,' said Li.

'World events are turning against them. Forces are ranging against them, forces they will submit to in the fullness of time.'

Again a silence. The moth approaches the candle, but will the moth circle the candle? Or will the moth fly away into the dark?

'Perhaps those forces could be encouraged to push harder,' suggested Li.

'I am sure they could. There are those who are helping push, and I am sure there are those who are wanting to help,' said Joon-ho.

Li looked at Joon-ho. 'We must talk again,' said Li, 'before I leave.'

Li turned and walked away, quickly lost in the shifting body of people. Joon-ho let him go. The moth had made an orbit of the candle. Another, more private meeting would allow them to talk more openly, where arrangements could be made.

The aide reappeared, walking briskly, a mobile phone in his hand.

He bowed quickly and held the phone out to Joon-ho. 'I apologise sir, but the call is urgent.' Joon-ho took the phone and the aide bowed again and departed.

Joon-ho looked at the phone and confirmed the "call" had come via the custom app', a piece of software which used triple encryption and employed multiple routes and carriers for the call, making it impossible to trace or intercept.

'Yes?' he said tersely into the phone.

The voice on the other end spoke English, but the heavy Arabic accent caused Joon-ho to listen more closely. He moved to the far edge of the room, away from the noise and the people.

'Again, say it again,' he said sharply.

'The meeting in Kandahar might have been compromised,' said the voice on the phone. 'Our people caught the owner of the warehouse talking to someone.'

'Who? Who was he talking to?'

'Unknown, he has refused to say,' said the voice.

Joon-ho paused for a moment. Plans were advancing quickly. He needed to start the next phase on schedule, delays would be difficult to accommodate. He looked around to make sure no-one was close enough to hear him.

'Cut the man's fingers off.' There was a pause as the other voice spoke, then Joon-ho replied. 'No, cut his fingers off first, then ask him who he was talking to and what he has said. Make it clear what you will cut off next if he refuses to answer.'

'And after?' asked the voice.

Joon-Ho beckoned to one of the hovering waiters. The man walked forward, the tray of drinks seeming to glide through the air ahead of him.

'Wait,' snapped Joon-Ho into the phone. He put his empty glass on the tray and took another, motioning with his eyes for the man to leave. His drink replenished he returned to the matter of the call.

'When you are sure you have everything, deliver his head to his family.'

'And the meeting?' asked the voice.

'We cannot change the plan now, the meeting must go ahead. Your man must still attend the meeting.'

'There is a risk that others might already know about the meeting.'

'We must assume they do, and they will take steps to

intrude on the meeting,' said Joon-ho. 'Your man must be ready, and must be able to spoil their plans.'

'He will be.' The call ended.

Joon-ho looked out again across Hong Kong island. They said the world was changing. They had no idea how much it was about to change.

THREE

The lorry coughed and spluttered as it trundled along the empty road, little traffic passed through this run-down suburb of the city. Most of the buildings were warehouses and workshops, many abandoned, all were tired and dirty. Smaller side streets led away from the main road, dwellings scattered along their lengths. In the fading light of the early evening few people were outside, and those who were paid no attention to the dirty, bearded pair in the front of the lorry.

The lorry lurched as the engine coughed and a cloud of diesel smoke erupted from the exhaust. The passenger shouted some curse at the driver, who ignored him. The lorry, the driver and his passenger, the street, the buildings, all had seen better days, but not for a long time. The driver seemed focused only on the road ahead, his passenger fiddled with his keffiyeh, his cotton headscarf, trying to straighten it. As he untied it the scarf fell over his face, and he cursed. Neither paid any attention to the warehouse building as they drove passed.

Unseen by anyone watching were the four men in the

back of the lorry; soldiers, dressed in black combat cover-alls, cradling their submachine guns, black helmets and black nylon bags at their feet. Captain Michael Sanders was the commanding officer of the unit. Typical of Special Forces he was average and unforgettable. Average height, average build, average brown hair, the kind of man who never stood out in a crowd. He looked at each of the three men in his unit, one sitting to his side on the bench running the length of the cramped space, the other two sitting facing them on the opposite bench. Sanders sat next to Sergeant Vince Marshall, a big athletic man with black skin and a piercing gaze. Across from them were two others; the slim and wiry frame of Lieutenant Julian Singh, his tanned good looks and smooth talking a result of his Egyptian birth and elite British education, a far cry from the youthful and unkempt blond Corporal Evan Bullock.

The atmosphere was hot and uncomfortable, and despite the careful preparation to make the lorry only look like a wreck it still managed to leak diesel fumes into the compartment. The four soldiers paid no attention to the fumes. Each pair shared a small video monitor, and they all focused on the images. A miniature video camera had been hidden under the side edge of the lorry, giving the soldiers a view of the buildings on the right side of the street.

A loud bang-bang resounded on the partition separating them from the cab. The soldiers hunched down over the monitors. As they passed one particular warehouse they examined it carefully through the video monitors. Each soldier focussed on a pre-agreed aspect of the building; one looking at the buildings either side, another watching the front edge of the roof, another the windows, and the fourth the doors and the open area in front of the building.

Within moments they had passed the building. They straightened up, and the four looked at each other.

As the commanding officer, Michael Sanders looked at each one in turn, inviting an opinion. He turned first to Marshall. 'Looks okay to me,' said Marshall.

'Nothing there to worry about,' said Bullock.

'Clear,' said Singh.

Captain Michael Sanders twisted the control on the top of the radio unit clipped to the front of his jacket and pressed the transmit button. Through his earpiece he heard the beep which signalled a successful connection to the communications network.

'Echo Base, this is Ghost One, comm check,' said Sanders, his voice picked up by the throat mic'.

After a moment's pause came the reply, played through the earpiece of each of the four soldiers. 'Ghost One, Echo Base, comm check confirmed.'

In that moment the entire communications system had been confirmed as working. The small personal radios carried by each soldier linked to the larger unit in the black bag at Julian Singh's feet. The shoe-box sized multi-function device relayed voice and video in a fully encrypted stream of digital data up to a range of ten miles. The US drone aircraft circled eight miles above them, remote piloted from a US Airforce facility somewhere in the United States. The drone relayed the signal to the Joint Military Communications Network satellite, and from there through the British military's communications network and into the MI5 network. From there they could be fed intelligence and analysis from MI5, from GCHQ and from any other source MI5 chose to connect to. A miracle of modern digital technology it gave the soldiers almost instant access to intelligence, early threat warnings, and updated information on local activity.

Like all digital technology it was a minor miracle, provided it worked.

Michael transmitted his report. 'Echo Base, the location is quiet. Awaiting orders. Out.'

They had nothing to do but sit back in discomfort and wait. The two Special Forces soldiers in the cab would carry on along the pre-arranged route, watching for any signs of hostile individuals who might be in the area. In about five minutes they would reach the holding point where they'd wait.

Marshall yawned and folded his arms as he leant back. He closed his eyes but a sharp bump in the road had them open again and he offered another profanity. Michael pondered the fact that life for a Special Forces soldier was not a comfortable one, and in a masochistic way he liked that. They lived for the challenge, the thrill of overcoming obstacles and surviving environments most people would run a mile from.

The vehicle came to a stop. The location had been chosen because it was deserted, not overlooked, no-one would question a lorry sitting there, the occupants apparently doing nothing.

'Right,' said Michael, leaning forwards, 'let's re-cap.' It never hurt to go over the plan again, and again. They lived by the 6-P principle, "proper planning prevents piss-poor performance." He continued, 'the warehouse has three main sections.'

'Do we know how many people are meeting?' asked Bullock.

'No,' said Michael, 'intelligence suggests two, but I wouldn't rely on that. We don't know if these people know each other and will get close to talk, or if they're strangers and will keep their distance. We need to be able to listen to a whisper.'

'I can do that,' said Singh. 'The microphones will pick up an ant's fart, but only if I know where the ant is going to be.'

'That's what we're waiting to find out,' said Michael. 'Once we know precisely where they're meeting, and when, we'll get in, set up the mics and cameras and fall back.' He turned to Evan Bullock. 'Evan, you take up position on the roof of the building behind the warehouse. If it goes tits-up I want you to be able to give us locations of the bad guys.'

'And preferably kill them,' said Marshall, 'not us.'

'Fuck you,' said Bullock, sticking one finger up at Marshall. Michael let them get on with it. The banter was part-and-parcel of life in the unit, and in Special Forces generally. Marshall particularly delighted in calling Evan "bollock," an obvious play on his name. Bullock gave as good as he got. No-one stood on ceremony, no-one was better (or lower) than anyone else, but when the shooting started everyone knew their job and was ultra-professional.

And now the waiting began. Much of what they did involved waiting, or lying in a muddy ditch watching some-one, or crouching on a snowy peak waiting. Whatever the mission it usually involved spending long periods of time in somewhere really unpleasant waiting for something to happen. Michael didn't mind the discomfort, he could turn his mind off to that, it was the challenge he enjoyed, pushing himself harder and harder. The challenge wasn't just to push, but to stay in control. Anyone could push themselves to the point they fell apart, the real challenge was to push beyond that point and keep hold of their self-control.

The bleep came through on the earpiece, they each

heard it and looked up. About time, the temperature was rising in the back of the lorry, even as the sun went down.

'Ghost One, this is Echo Base,' came the message.

'Ghost One, receiving,' said Michael.

'Ghost One, be advised, no further intel' is available on your location.' They looked at each other, and almost in unison mouthed the words "what the fuck?"

'Say again, Echo Base,' Michael said. He'd heard the message perfectly well, but it was good practice to confirm things.

'I say again, no further intel' will be available on your target location.'

'That's different,' said Singh. 'Sounds like we're not going to get the detail.'

'How the hell do we cover a meeting if we don't know where or when?' said Bullock. It was an obvious but very relevant question.

Marshall, of course, hit the nail on the head. 'If they can't tell us when the meeting is, how do we know we're not just going to walk into the middle of it?' The frustration in his voice was not disguised, he was never one to hide his feelings.

Before Michael could ask, the message came through their earpieces. 'The mission is GO, repeat, the mission is GO, proceed as planned.'

'This could be awkward,' said Singh.

'Please advise if there is any further detail on the timetable?' Michael asked.

There was a pause, a long pause, which dragged out. Surely saying "yes" or "no" didn't take this long.

Another voice came over the earpieces, a female voice, calm but firm. 'This is the MI5 Head of Section. Our contact has been compromised, but we need to hear what's said in that meeting, it's our only chance to stop significant hostile actions against UK citizens.' The beep signalled the end of the communication.

'Well,' said Marshall, 'that told us.'

'Didn't realise we took orders from them,' said Bullock.

'We don't,' said Michael, 'but we are tasked with supporting them, and this will have been agreed with our Liaison Officer, so if she says "go" then we go.'

'If this goes wrong, I'll have words with her,' said Marshall, without smiling.

Michael banged on the partition with the cab. 'Let's go, boys, we're on,' he shouted.

The engine revved into life and the lorry set off with a jerk. As they bounced down the road the team reviewed their options.

'So,' said Bullock. 'We don't know exactly where this meeting is going to take place.'

'No,' said Michael. He didn't like the sound of this any more than the rest of them, but if it was going to be easy there wouldn't be a need to send in Special Forces soldiers.

'It could be in the warehouse, it could be outside, it could be in the road,' said Singh.

'Correct. And entering through the wrong door could be a signal the location's compromised, we just don't know,' said Michael.

'And we don't know when it's happening,' said Singh. 'We could walk in half way through, or we could be there for days.'

'Basically, yes,' said Michael, his voice remaining flat.

Bullock muttered something. Marshall raised his voice. 'Speak up, I'm not a fucking mind-reader.'

'I said what's so special about this meeting anyway?'

'Don't know, don't care,' Marshall said, shouting to be

heard as the lorry's engine revved. They were accelerating down the straight stretch of road which approached the warehouse. They knew the sign. Each pulled on their helmets, bag of equipment in one hand, weapon in the other. They braced as the lorry turned to the right, now they were off the main road, then a left turn and they were down the back of the warehouse.

Michael pushed in his earpiece, this was what connected him to his team. His contact with the control room and with people who could feed him information was useful, but his contact with the others is what made them a team, a single unified fighting force.

The lorry slowed to a crawl and there came another bang on the partition. Without a word Bullock leant forward and pulled the quick-release on the tailgate. It banged down and one by one they slid from the lorry, landing in a crouching position at the side of the road. Marshall was last out and kept up with the lorry, pushing the tailgate closed. In one step he too was at the side of the road, crouching against the wall at the back of the warehouse.

The driver looked at them in his wing-mirror, then the lorry revved again and accelerated away, leaving them with a farewell cloud of diesel fumes.

Michael pressed his transmit button. 'Ghost One has landed.'

MICHAEL LOOKED AROUND, trying to spot any signs of movement, any indication they'd been seen. As the chugging and coughing of the lorry disappeared into the evening gloom he signalled to his men; Bullock to move to the building opposite, the rest to follow him into the warehouse.

They kept low and moved without a sound. Bullock crossed the narrow dirty road and into the courtyard of the building opposite the back of the warehouse. Within moments he had slipped inside and out of sight.

Michael, Vince and Julian moved into the enclosed yard. Old wooden pallets and broken crates littered the ground, an ancient Lada car sat in one corner, evidence of former residents of Afghanistan. The dust and sand on the ground suggested no-one had been here in recent times. The large, two-storied building showed years of neglect. Most of the glass had gone from the first-floor windows, and the walls had seen one layer of paint after another, each covering the flaking remains of the previous layer, every painted area a different shade of white or grey or yellow. Michael could feel the temperature leaving as quickly as the light. It would be dark soon, and that would make their task more difficult. Vince Marshall had already made short work of the rusted padlock holding the door closed, he pulled it open just enough for the three of them to slip inside, and then pulled it shut.

Michael looked around the dim space of the warehouse. Darkness crept over the city and now only a dim light came through the empty window spaces above them. Many of the windows on the ground floor had been boarded up. Smells floated on the air of fruit that had rotted away years ago, the sweat of working men, engine fumes, all of which had permeated the walls and the flaking paint. The single interior space of the warehouse had originally been divided into three distinct sections. Splinters and rotted planks were the only remains of the large sliding wooden doors which had once separated the three sections. They looked up at a mezzanine floor, the far end of which looked like an office, perhaps once a foreman looked down from there on the workers. Their scant intelligence reported the electricity supply had long since been disconnected, not that they would risk turning on the lights even if they worked.

'This has got "trap" written all over it,' said Marshall.

'I agree,' said Michael. 'Julian, let's set up and get out, I don't want to be here when anybody else shows up.'

'Okay,' said Singh, who drew a deep breath and looked around. 'This isn't going to be easy, they could meet anywhere in here, I'll just cover it as best I can.' He slung his submachine gun around his back, picked up his bag of equipment and walked off into the gloom.

They had a simple mission: set up hidden cameras and microphones to eavesdrop on a meeting, then retire and monitor proceedings from a safe location. Michael had always found the simple missions presented the greatest possibility of disaster, and this time they lacked even basic intelligence. He loved the challenge, the danger and the complexity, the need to be quiet and focused, to be better than the enemy, to win through patience and persistence. If needed though, they would win through controlled violence and aggression.

'Let's see what else is around here,' Michael said.

'Too dark for me,' said Marshall, pulling his night-vision goggles out of his bag. Michael did the same, and in moments he could see the inside of the warehouse as a sparkling green image. He appreciated the benefit of the goggles, the ability to see in otherwise dark environments, but he disliked how they deprived him of all sense of depth, which could be a problem when it came to shooting people.

Michael looked around and to the left. Doors separated them from some other part of the warehouse. The warehouse had more than this single space after all, their intelligence had been incomplete. He held up his weapon and pointed it ahead of him, he could see Marshall doing the same, and as one they moved towards the doors, one careful step after another. Marshall held his weapon in one hand and with the other he reached out to the door handle.

Marshall nodded his head, counting down, three-two-one, and pulled the door open. Michael waited a moment, then stepped forward, his weapon ahead of him, not quite into the doorway. Beyond he could see a large room, crates scattered around, some oil drums, a tarpaulin covering a pile of something unknown.

Marshall gave him a thumbs-up. Michael returned the gesture.

Michael pressed the transmit button on his radio. 'Julian, progress?' They needed to leave the building as quickly as possible. Their safety lay in nobody knowing they were there, security-through-obscurity, a form of safety which could evaporate in an instant.

'I've got microphones and cameras covering as much as I can, but if they sit by the door and whisper we're not going to hear anything.'

'Are you finished?'

'Almost, I want one more microphone in the office, just in case.'

'Copy,' said Michael. 'After that meet us back by the door. Evan?'

There was a pause before Bullock answered. 'Yes boss,' he said.

'See anything?'

'I've got views into the warehouse. I can see you and Vince, can't see the office. No view of the front or the road.'

Michael knew Evan Bullock would be set up with his sniper rifle attached to the tripod, night-vision scope giving him a clear and close-up view of his targets. He felt uneasy at their lack of coverage of the front of the building. Anyone could approach and they wouldn't know it.

'Okay,' said Michael. 'Vince, Julian, let's get out and join Evan. If anyone shows we'll see and hear something.' The set-up was less than ideal, the cameras and microphones might not pick up anything, but someone thought this meeting important enough to intrude upon it.

The other three each acknowledged the order. Michael turned his attention to those monitoring from further afield.

'Echo Base, this is Ghost One,' he said. He knew they'd been listening to their communications, but protocol demanded he gave them an explicit update on their progress and situation.

'Ghost One, we copy,' came the reply.

'We've set up in location one. We'll pull out and monitor from location two.'

'Roger, audio and video feeds are working.' At least the teams back in England were seeing and hearing something from the warehouse.

'Heads up,' came Singh's voice over the radio, sharp and urgent. Michael stopped in mid-stride. Singh spoke again. 'Movement at the front.'

Michael looked at Marshall in the green haze, he could see Marshall looking towards the broken boards of the window closest to him. He could see lights moving outside.

Singh spoke again. 'One vehicle at the front, two getting out.'

Passers-by? Or the evening's entertainment? Michael had no way of knowing. He and Marshall could slip out of the back door, but Julian would be exposed if he tried to leave the upper level.

'Stay where you are,' said Michael. He gestured Marshall

towards the door to the storeroom. 'We're in the ground floor storeroom. Echo Base, I need to hear what's going on.'

As they crept into the store room and pulled the door closed they could hear a door opening at the far end of the warehouse. Two sets of footsteps, two voices.

The warehouse had gone from feeling like a trap, to being a trap.

Michael could only think one thing: Show-time, then realised what a cliché that was.

FOUR

orrow and Falcone were still in Morrow's office as dusk fell. The small office took on a ghostly look as the lights from the main research building filtered through the windows of the laboratory and the internal window. Falcone had rested after Morrow's telepathic 'education,' and Morrow had taken the chance to do work on his computer. He had so much to do, and he never seemed to have enough time to do it all. He knew Falcone would rest for a while, he had subjected him to a substantial telepathic surge. But, these things had to be done.

Falcone had been a supporter of his since Morrow had first been appointed to his role as senior research scientist. Falcone had fought his corner in more than one management meeting, but Morrow had still not dared share the secret of his discovery without also asserting telepathic control over him.

Eventually Falcone came around and seemed unaware time had passed since he and Morrow had last spoken.

'Tobias?' Falcone asked, eventually.

Morrow looked up and stopped typing. Sometimes he

wished Falcone was a younger man, more able to absorb the telepathic energy.

'Do we really need soldiers?' Falcone's uncertainty was clear in his voice. 'I know my contact could find a unit of soldiers, but do we really need to use force in this?'

'Yves,' said Morrow, in the most soothing voice he could imitate. 'If we don't, who will protect us?' The way forward was clear, it seemed to be such an effort to make Falcone see it. For all the power his telepathy gave him, Morrow still couldn't force people to understand something, that phenomenon still had to come from within.

'Protect us from whom?' Falcone asked.

Morrow fixed him with a gaze. 'Imagine for a moment,' said Morrow, 'that the Russians, or the Chinese, or the Americans found out we had the ability to create telepathic soldiers, potentially in vast numbers.' He let the thought hang in the air for a moment. Silence could be very effective, sometimes.

He continued. 'What do you think they would do? Do you imagine they would make an appointment and come around for a chat and a cup of tea.' He tried to keep his impatience out of his voice.

Falcone looked down and was about to answer, but Morrow continued. 'Of course they wouldn't. They would try and take the capability for themselves, and that means you and it means me. They would come for us. They would take us, and they would make us tell them everything they wanted.'

Morrow kept quiet, Falcone was obviously running the scenario through in his mind, and his face suggested he was imagining 'how' such people might 'make' them talk. Morrow had thought about this a lot, and in everything he had been able to discover, nothing had convinced him that the secret service of any government would show them any mercy in getting his secret.

'And then there are people like the Director,' Morrow went on. 'People who would try and interfere, they would try and take control, they would try and use this ability for their own purposes. We can't allow that.'

Eventually, Falcone nodded his head, slowly.

'Yes, I can see our security might need protecting,' Falcone finally said. 'But soldiers? Is there no other way? Must it be violence?'

'I don't want to use violence, Yves,' Morrow said. In fact he had no moral problem with using force. He couldn't use violence personally, he hadn't been in a fight since his earliest days at school, but the idea of having a unit of soldiers capable of using extreme force to protect him felt quite natural. 'And they would only use force as a last resort. After all, using force brings unwelcome attention, which is what we are trying to avoid. But if it comes to it, if there is no other way, but to use whatever means are necessary to protect ourselves, that must be a means I can control completely.'

Survival was of the fittest. Had not Darwin discovered that? Nature was red in tooth and claw.

'But soldiers can be so, limited,' said Falcone. Morrow paused, uncertain what his friend meant by this.

'Explain,' he said.

'If such agencies will go to such lengths to discover what you know and what you can do, would they also not use more technological means of attack?'

Morrow pondered this. He had to admit he had over-looked this rather obvious consideration. He began to feel a degree of annoyance, it was unlike him to miss something so obvious, but he could think about that later.

'Go on,' he said. He wanted to know more about what Falcone had been thinking. He hadn't picked up any of this in his psychic link, but then he had been focussing on dominating the man, not catching up on recent speculation.

Falcone went on. 'As I said, I believe the Director of Operations might well use external consultants to probe into every system within PanMedic. Other agencies might well do the same, and governments have a lot more computing power and expertise at their disposal. If they decided to try and compromise us electronically, I'm not sure there's anything we could do to stop them.'

Morrow noticed Falcone had put a slight emphasis on "we."

'And do you have a suggestion?' Morrow asked.

'If we're making use of our contact in the military projects division, then I believe he also has links with MI5. They are past-masters at electronic surveillance and intrusion, and security.'

Morrow considered this. There were aspects he liked, but there was one huge problem he didn't like at all.

'Yves, I don't want to bring anyone else into the project. We need to keep this as small and contained as we can. The more people we bring in the more I am stretched and the greater the chance that someone will let something leak, and that is the very thing we are seeking to avoid.'

'I'm not sure what else we can do,' said Falcone. 'The only way to secure against state sponsored hacking is to be protected by the best in the world, which is our own government's cyber-security specialists.'

It was a persuasive argument, but it would still mean having to take control of someone else. He needed to maintain a direct telepathic control over anyone and everyone who got close to the project. If it was one more, just one more, then perhaps it might be worth it.

'Very well, Yves. If your man has a contact in MI5 who can help us, then I will need to meet that contact.'

Falcone looked Morrow in the eye, the first time in a while. 'I'll talk to him. I'll let you know what we can arrange.'

MICHAEL AND MARSHALL had managed to get behind the first stack of crates in the storeroom. The old and rotten wood would provide no protection should anyone shoot at them, but it might help muffle the sound of their breathing. It had always amused Michael when TV shows depicted night vision devices as making a high-pitched whistle. Had the producers never thought such a sound would be an instant giveaway to the enemy? The goggles made no sound, but without the depth perception of normal vision it would be easy to move and bump into something and make a sound. Right now, remaining undetected was their best way of staying alive.

Michael had planned to listen to the conversation from a more secure, and more distant location. He had to assume Singh had managed to hide in the upstairs office. Michael had given up asking himself how much worse this could get, in case he found out the hard way. They were trapped. There was no other way of thinking about it, they were trapped.

They heard talking from outside, in Arabic. Moments later a woman's voice came over their earpieces, translating the words into English.

'One is saying they must wait. Two is asking where is he,

One is saying to relax, he'll be here,' the woman said. The participants were named, One, Two, Three, in the order they joined the conversation.

So the meeting involved at least three people. Michael wondered what else their intelligence had missed, but gave up speculating.

'Two is asking how long they give him,' said the woman. She paused as there was more talking from the warehouse. 'One says they'll wait as long as is necessary, but it shouldn't be long.'

Michael thought through their options. If there were only two people outside the storeroom, and if Michael and his team retained the element of surprise then they would still likely have superior force and firepower, especially with Singh and Bullock in elevated positions.

Bullock's voice came over the radio, quiet and calm. 'I have a clear sight of one target,' he said.

Michael made an effort to relax his breathing. They had trained and practised for just this kind of situation, waiting in the shadows, listening, staying unseen and unheard. He felt the cool grip of his weapon, it comforted him.

There was more talking. The woman translated. 'They're talking about the weather.' Her voice had a hint of amusement in it. 'Now they're saying he's here.'

After a short pause Michael could hear things beyond the door, footsteps, the outside door opening and closing. Then a new voice joined the conversation.

'Three is asking if the place is secure. One is explaining it is completely secure.' A pause. 'Three is saying American spies are everywhere. One says they have nothing to worry about from the Americans.'

Michael knew everyone would have had the same

thought: was he hinting they knew there was someone else to worry about?

'Three says the British Secret Service have already arrested one of his men. One says the British are just shooting in the dark.'

There would, Michael thought, be a flurry of activity in Thames House. Whoever One was, he had a connection to someone recently arrested based on evidence from MI5 or GCHQ, and that was a big piece in the jigsaw of the man's identity.

'Now Two is saying they should get on with it,' said the woman.

Another voice joined the conversation. 'This is Echo Base. We can't see the face of Three. It's vital we identify him. Can you point camera four down ten degrees?'

There was no verbal reply. None of Michael's team could risk making any verbal comment. He could only hope Singh would only attempt to leave his cover and adjust the camera if he were confident he wouldn't be seen. But if the camera was in the line of sight of the target's face, then the target had to be able to see anyone adjusting the camera.

Michael heard Bullock's voice. 'I can only see Three's profile, no chance to ID him.'

'Three is saying his people will be ready, but he needs to know the money and the property will be in place.' The woman paused as the other man talked. 'One is saying that everything will be ready on time. He says Three needs to make sure his people stay quiet.'

There was a longer pause before she spoke the translation. 'Three is asking how can he know One's employer can get the money and property in place on time.'

'We have a view of Three's face,' came the voice of Echo

Base. Michael could imagine people working quickly to identify him.

'Two is explaining that the bright light is not to be doubted.' There was a note of uncertainty in the woman's voice. Bright light? A codename? 'Arabic reference to Shining Light, recognised code name of a high-value target.'

Michael instinctively looked at Marshall. In the green light of the night vision goggles he could see Marshall looking back. At least the mission had been worthwhile. Whoever One and Two were, they had a connection to someone already high on MI5's list of bad and dangerous people. This wasn't just an innocent conversation they were eavesdropping on, this was decision-time for dangerous people.

They could hear angry tones in the voices outside. Probably Two shouldn't have used the blatant reference to Shining Light. Everyone knows walls have ears.

'Identification of Three,' said Echo Base. 'Mohammed Arshad, known terrorist with links to active UK cells.' Singh had obviously taken a chance. So far, it seemed he'd got away with it. Now they knew the conversation was between a known terrorist and someone who had links to possibly a powerful backer of terrorism.

'Three is saying he needs confirmation that One and Two's employer has made the first payment. Three's people need to make final preparations. He's nervous that the Secret Service might be watching his people.'

Michael and everyone else listening knew the Secret Service was more properly called the Secret Intelligence Service, or MI6, and wouldn't be watching suspected terrorists in the UK, that was MI5's job. Michael didn't feel the urge to go and correct anyone.

A pause. 'One is explaining that he will ensure all

payments are made on time and that his employer is completely aware of what British Intelligence is doing and is not worried about them, and therefore nor should Three be worried.'

Boasting? Michael wondered. If they were lucky someone might make one boast too many and actually reveal what they knew or how they knew it. More pieces of the jigsaw might fall into place.

Echo Base's voice came on again. 'Probable vocal identification of One. Second name Shaffee, first name unknown. Believed to have arranged funding for several terrorist groups and funded direct actions in UK and Europe.' Michael thought now probably no-one was boasting. These were serious people having a serious conversation. And so far they didn't know that lots of other people were listening in and would make plans to foil whatever these people were planning.

The woman's voice came back on. 'One is asking if Three would be worried if he knew there were British soldiers in the building listening to them?'

The woman's, Echo Base's, and Michael's breathing all seemed to freeze.

MICHAEL FOUND himself caught between the urge to stay still and call the man's bluff, and the impulse to come out shooting, making use of the element of surprise, while it was still theirs. But he couldn't be sure they still had that element, if indeed they ever had. He could hear noises outside the building, at the front, possibly more people arriving.

There was more talking, more Arabic, a loud and

agitated voice, and then the translation through the earpiece. Michael forced himself to breathe, slowly, deeply, he had to stay in control.

'Three is demanding to know what One means.' More talk, then the translation, the woman's voice still calm, just. 'One explains, they are quite safe. He says to watch.'

The man referred to as One spoke louder, loud enough to be heard. He spoke in English.

'Soldiers,' he said, his voice firm, confident. 'We know you are here. We know you are listening. I have many more men here, you cannot escape.' He paused, perhaps waiting for a response.

Michael and Vince looked at each other through the green sparkle of the night vision goggles. They still had the advantage of firepower over the few men inside the warehouse, and they could see in the dark.

One spoke again. 'No doubt you have electronic devices, and others are listening. Can you not talk to each other? Do you need machines to help you talk?'

Michael and Vince almost mirrored each other's openmouthed expression. Michael had the growing feeling they'd been led here, like turkeys to a Christmas dinner.

Michael heard the beep through his earpiece, and Bullock's voice, urgent, stressed.

'Boss,' he hissed, 'there are...'

One spoke again, louder, enough to drown out Bullock's final words. 'Perhaps you don't need your technology anymore.' A piercing buzzing sound, like an electric drill, screamed in Michael's ear. He tore out the earpiece and stifled the urge to gasp. Marshall must have done the same, but in the reflex action of pulling out the earpiece he caught something. One of the boxes banged against the wall.

They both froze. What happened next could determine

whether the situation became a negotiation or a fire-fight. Now was the time for control and patience, with extreme violence as a handy second option.

One spoke, quieter. 'Now we can talk, without your friends listening in, perhaps you would like to come out.'

There was the sound of the warehouse's front doors opening, then footsteps. Light glared under the storeroom door. Someone had turned on the warehouse's lights. The light in their eyes from the night vision goggles was almost blinding. They both ripped off the goggles, blinking, trying desperately to get their eyes accustomed to the light.

There was only a thin strip of light from under the door and around its edges, but clearly the lights were in working order. Any advantages they might have had were now gone. Michael and Vince looked at each other, a deep stare into each other's eyes. Michael lowered his weapon and let in hang by his side, holding it only in his right hand. With some reluctance, Marshall did the same. Michael stood up, pushed open the door, and stepped out.

Despite his racing heartbeat, Michael forced himself to act calmly. If he appeared calm they were more likely to treat him as a calm person. He focused forwards but trying to use his peripheral vision. The more he could see in the first few moments the better he could assess their options.

Facing them were three men, obviously locals, each holding a Kalashnikov AK47 rifle aimed at the two soldiers. Michael saw no point in trying to start a firefight from this position. He kept his eyes on the three men. In his peripheral vision he could see three men standing further back in the warehouse, no doubt these were One, Two and Three, though he wasn't sure which was which. One of them stepped forwards, and spoke. This was One.

'I'm disappointed, I expected more of you,' he said. His

English was good, heavily accented but understandable. He spoke quickly, in Arabic to his three armed men. 'You,' he said, pointing at Vince, 'stand there.' He motioned to a point away from Michael. This man was experienced.

Vince hesitated, doing as he was told but not being too compliant. He took a few steps and stood a short distance from Michael. This gave one of the armed men space to step behind Michael and then Vince, relieving each in turn of his submachine gun, holstered automatic pistol, and knife from the hip sheath.

'Are there any more of you?' One asked. Michael opened his mouth to reply, but One spoke again, 'I'm sure you'll say no, but we'll search the building anyway, and then we'll burn it.' Again he barked orders to his men.

'I think we need to go somewhere more private, where I can ask you some questions.'

His calm and pleasant tone masked an obvious and ominous implication, one which made Michael almost shiver. Going somewhere 'private' with this man would be a one-way trip. Michael knew his team would be of one mind: they'd go out fighting, even against impossible odds, rather than be led away meekly to a gruesome and protracted execution.

Michael's eyes darted around. He couldn't see Julian, and he guessed the three they'd been listening to hadn't seen him when he'd moved the camera, but that had been in the dark. Michael had to trust Julian would move when it was safe to, or when he could use the most surprise and do the most damage. Waiting, it always came back to that, waiting for the right chance. What nerve does it take to wait, knowing your life could end at any moment?

One gestured to the door through which Michael's team had first entered the warehouse. His meaning was clear.

One of the armed men stepped in front and pulled the door open, he motioned with his gun that Michael and Vince should step outside. Michael went first, he could feel Vince close behind him. The Afghan gunmen kept their distance but didn't seem to mind the two soldiers being close to each other. From the corner of his eye Michael could see one of the gunmen to his right. The others were behind and out of sight. He shuffled forwards, not wanting to move ahead too quickly. He needed Vince with him, close to him.

He felt something hard prod him in the small of the back, the barrel of a gun. He shuffled further forward. In the stillness of the evening he could hear a vehicle approaching, a rough engine growling, some part of it squeaking, crying for some oil. He heard One again shouting orders, somewhere behind them. Now two of the gunmen were to the sides and slightly in front. One gunman was out of sight, but they didn't know if the original three were armed. Michael had to assume they were.

Michael was ready for it, expecting it, even if he couldn't know the precise moment it would happen. He could feel Marshall physically close to him, the two of them could react at the same instant. There was no gunshot sound, Bullock's rifle was silenced, but there was a loud wet crack and the man to their right collapsed to the ground in a heap without making a sound. Something warm and wet splashed Michael's face, the man's brains and blood, he assumed. Michael felt Vince move and he had just enough time to see the big man lash out with a knife (who knew where he'd hidden that?) and plunge it into the second man's throat.

The man dropped his rifle (Marshall almost caught it as it fell) and staggered backwards, clawing at the knife embedded in his throat, a gurgling gasping sound coming from the wound under his chin as he fought for breath, just one last breath, trying to scream, desperate to breathe. The man collapsed thrashing around, but now Michael had collected the first man's gun.

Michael and Vince crouched in front of the door and fired into the warehouse, a volley of shots each, the cracking of the AK47s echoing around the street. The third gunman was dead before he had a chance to fire a single shot. At almost the same instant the lights inside the warehouse went out, the others presumably trying to use darkness as a place to hide. In a moment they were moving forwards through the door and back inside the warehouse. They could see the figures of the original three retreating into the gloom of the warehouse, but from somewhere above came the distinctive clattering of a silenced MP5SD submachine gun as Singh killed one of the three.

Michael felt himself relax for a moment. The situation had the feeling of familiarity about it. This was what they trained for. Hours and hours in darkened rooms, practising moving together, locating targets and shooting them whilst avoiding hostages or bystanders. This was now their territory, this was the game they played to win.

Before he could say anything Michael saw a figure make a break, heading out from behind a pile of crates and towards the front door. Michael aimed the AK47 and fired a sustained burst. None of this 'double-tap' nonsense, keep shooting until the bastard falls over and stops moving - a crude but effective tactic. There was gunfire from outside, at the back, Bullock had found his own action. For now they had to find the remaining enemy, they didn't have time to creep around and play hide-and-seek.

Michael could see Vince moving forward, the AK47 pointed ahead of him. They were used to using their

Heckler and Koch HK-MP5SD submachine guns, but had trained to use just about any firearm. It would be pointless capturing a gun and not knowing where the safety catch was. Ahead of them was the pile of crates, the only hiding place they could see.

A sudden movement and a figure ran from behind the crates towards the steps leading to the mezzanine floor, and straight into a burst of almost silent gunfire from Julian Singh. The silenced submachine gun (the team used the silenced version of the HK-MP5, far more discreet) hissed and spat out the stream of bullets, killing the man instantly. He had no time to make a sound, simply collapsing on the spot.

'It's me, Bullock, coming in,' shouted a voice from the back door. Evan Bullock jogged in, sniper rifle slung across his back, cradling his submachine gun and Michael's and Vince's lost weapons. 'Thought you might need these,' he grinned.

Things were starting to look up, the team was back together, all they needed now was to re-establish communications with Echo Base.

There was the sound of another vehicle and shouting, from the rear of the building.

'Shall we leave, gentlemen?' Michael asked.

'So soon?' grinned Julian, 'I was just getting to like the place.'

Marshall pulled open the front door, just enough to look outside.

'Once more unto the breach,' said Julian, the quip lost on the others, even Michael, as they sneaked out, crouching, four black-clad figures sliding out into the Afghan evening.

FIVE

The four of them spread out along the wall, crouching, staying low and in the shadows. Michael looked along the road spreading out to either side. They had moonlight but no streetlight, something that could work to their advantage, but they would have to move quickly. There were voices, shouting, coming from behind them, or possibly from one side, Michael couldn't tell. There had been so much gunfire there was no doubt they would have attracted a lot of attention. They could only hope people wouldn't want to rush towards the sound of guns.

Close by there was the sharp sound of a window breaking. Michael turned to see Singh pulling an object out of a derelict looking car parked nearby. The object was smooth and black, out of keeping with the state of the car and the warehouse and the neighbourhood. Singh put the object on the ground and fired a short burst of bullets into it.

'Fucking radio jammer,' said Singh, 'I knew it had to be close.' Singh pushed his earpiece back in. Michael did likewise and almost immediately heard the reassuring beep as their contact with the comm's network was re-established. No doubt the jammer was something One had brought with him, but that had to mean he came knowing Michael's team would be there. It seemed in the game of cat-and-mouse the key piece of information they were lacking was that they were the mouse.

'Echo Base this is Ghost One,' said Michael. He caught himself holding his breath as he waited for a reply. He didn't have to wait long.

'Ghost One, we copy, what...' came the reply, but Michael spoke first, cutting off the man.

'Mission is compromised. Area is hostile. Need directions to rendezvous site alpha,' Michael said. As he spoke he became aware of the sound of vehicles approaching.

'Contact, left and right,' said Marshall. He and Bullock raised their weapons as a large and slow-moving lorry lumbered towards them. He turned and saw Singh, covered behind the car, aiming at a pickup truck approaching faster from the opposite direction. Michael took up a position close to Singh, crouching by the rear of the car, his weapon levelled at the truck.

A voice came through their earpieces. 'Proceed north,' it said. 'Far side of the building, then continue east.'

'We're moving,' shouted Michael, and that's when the shooting started.

The usual Rules Of Engagement only authorised them to fire when fired upon, or if they were in immediate life-threatening danger. Michael viewed this as immediate, and life-threatening. He fired first, and the others joined him in an instant. A volley of fire at each approaching vehicle, shattering the windscreens and bursting the tyres. There were shouts and screams from each vehicle. The lorry swerved sharply to its left and crashed into the side wall of the warehouse.

The pickup truck kept coming, shots being fired by someone lying covered in the rear of the truck. The four of them now focused their fire on the vehicle, the hissing and spitting of their silenced weapons creating a strange sound in the air, mirrored by the cracks and bangs of the bullets piercing the vehicle's bodywork while the shots from the truck reverberated off the buildings' walls. The gunfire from the rear of the pickup truck ceased and the vehicle stormed passed them unchecked. Michael didn't know if the driver was alive or dead, all he cared was their way was now clear.

'On me,' he commanded and set out into the street. The four of them jogged across the street, backs to each other so they each faced outwards and covered a quarter of their circle. On the far side of the road a low wall bounded an open space, and beyond that a basketball court, evidence of the American presence and influence in Afghanistan. Beyond the court was a low single-story building, western in design and construction, but tired and neglected. The building was enclosed by a wall on either side, making their most direct route to the rendezvous site through the building, rather than around it.

They were quickly over the wall and across the space and as they approached the building Michael saw the front door was old and flimsy. Marshall reached it first and wrenched it open, he and Michael peered into the darkness inside, waiting to see if anybody was waiting for them. Before they could make their next move there came the sound of more vehicles, news had apparently spread. Two more vehicles were approaching, both Toyota pickup trucks, old and tattered but still fast and nimble. No doubt their occupants would be fast and aggressive, clearly time was running out.

Michael led the way, he slipped through the door, aiming his gun ahead of him. The building must have been built as some kind of community centre. It looked out of place in this part of the city. A corridor stretched out on either side, doors led to rooms. The lights were off, the building sat in its own silence and darkness. The end of the corridor opened into a larger space. There was movement, muttered voices, the unmistakeable sound of women hushing children, desperately pleading with them to be silent. He had to find a way through the building and time was against them, but he was also keenly aware these people were not part of the fight.

'These are civilians,' said Michael to his three team-mates. He wasn't sure, but he thought he heard one of the team reply 'So?'

The gunfire erupted without warning, the shots deaf-ening inside the building. Single shots from pistols punc-tured the silence closely followed by screams of terrified civilians. Muzzle flashes lit the room casting momentary ghostly shadows across the walls. Instinctively the team each dropped to a crouching position and returned fire, short sharp bursts, controlled, aiming at the sources of the pistol shots. Their silenced weapons made almost no sound from the bullets, but the actions of the guns, the mechanical workings, clattered and rattled.

More shots from behind, shouting, louder now, male voices, strong and commanding, their pursuers were closing in. Michael felt the tension rising in his body, and he fought it down. Control was everything, his training had prepared him for this, but still, people firing live rounds added a certain piquancy to the proceedings.

'We need to get out of here,' Michael shouted. He peered around the corner into the open area. Soft seats circled the room, what could have been pool tables occupied the centre. On the far wall were fire escape doors. Even here health and safety had to be a priority. More shots rang out, pistol shots, followed by a burst of fire from his team.

'This way,' he called. He fired a longer burst of fire towards the far end of the room, aiming higher up the wall, intending the resulting shower of plaster and debris to cause anyone there to keep under cover. He dashed to the fire door, aware of the next man behind him, from the shape it had to be Bullock. He lashed out at the door with his boot and it burst open, wood and glass crashing out into the street beyond. At that moment there was an outpouring of machine gun fire aimed at them, wood and glass and plaster erupted around them as the bullets tore apart the building's weak construction.

Glancing left and right Michael and Evan Bullock dashed to the far side of the street beyond, a gun battle raging now inside the building. The machine-gun fire from Marshall and Singh was inaudible, but their pistol shots sounded weak compared to the heavier guns ranged against them. If the others were resorting to their sidearms they must be running low on ammunition.

Even above the cacophony of gunfire he could hear men and women screaming, scared for their lives. They hadn't come here to hurt innocent people. In the eeriest way the shooting stopped, and there was silence, a moment of silence which stretched out and out.

The explosion blew apart the side wall of the building, the deafening percussive bang shook everything and sent Michael and Bullock crashing to the ground. Michael forced himself to look up and around, he couldn't let anyone take advantage of this and close in on them. Michael's head pounded like he'd been drinking rough cider for a week, but he pushed himself up into a crouched position, scanning around, weapon aimed forwards. Bullock was also quickly up, the smoke blowing across them obscuring their vision but also camouflaging them. Debris continued to rain down and Michael heard bangs and crashes as pieces of brick and timber landed, his hearing was returning.

The sound of gunfire once again cracked inside the building. Michael could see shapes moving in the smoke in the mouth of the crater opened in the side of the building. Black-clad figures, submachine guns held forward, firing silent bursts into the building as they backed out into the street. Bullock and Singh had made their own exit from the building. Michael couldn't help but wonder how many civilians they had caught in the blast. Bullock must have used a grenade to blast through the wall, and grenades had a habit of being indiscriminate in who they killed.

'Come on,' shouted Michael, 'we've got a bus to catch.' The four of them regrouped and jogged down the street, Marshall and Singh jogging backwards ready to fire on any pursuers, Michael and Bullock facing forwards ready to counter any new threat.

Another dull and thundering pickup truck lurched around the corner fifty yards ahead of them, a figure leaning out of cab window firing single pistol shots at them. Michael and Bullock stopped dead, Marshall and Singh shoved into the back of them. The truck had swerved to a stop, side-on to them, the driver firing from the safety of the cab, another figure peering over the side wall of the rear of the vehicle. The four soldiers split up, two to each side of the street, one in each pair facing and firing at the vehicle, the other in each pair covering the street behind them.

Sure enough, shots rang out from the vicinity of the now burning building. Michael looked across the street at Bullock, the long rifle now in his hands. A single sharp crack, dry like a snapping twig, and Michael saw the figure in the rear of the pickup truck slump backwards out of view, his pistol falling to the ground. Michael fired another burst, aiming at the cab. The driver returned fire, perhaps luck was on his side tonight, but there was another sharp crack from Bullock's side of the street and the firing from the truck ceased. Maybe luck hadn't been on the man's side after all.

'Forwards, gentlemen,' said Michael, loud enough to be heard over the shooting, 'we have a ride.'

Within moments they had thrown the bodies of the two dead men out of the pickup truck. Michael drove, the others in the rear of the truck, lying low and ready to fire. The truck might have been old but the engine and transmission were in good order, and within moments they were out of range of those pursuing on foot. Michael doubted their respite would last long, no doubt others were already being contacted by radio or telephone and being told where to set up intercepts or roadblocks.

The voice over the earpiece guided Michael through the streets. The rendezvous site was five miles from the warehouse, it would have been a long and hard fight to make the escape on foot. As they approached the rendezvous site, which was simply a pre-agreed spot at the side of a main road, two lorries thundered out from the right into the road ahead of them, stopping sharply, blocking the road. Michael braked hard and stopped, barely fifty yards from the roadblock. A third lorry dashed out of a side road on the left, swung around sharply, heading towards Michael's team but on the other side of the road. There was a voice in Michael's ear, but the sound of tyres and engines and now gunfire drowned out the words.

Michael took a moment to see men jumping out of the two lorries ahead of them and firing at them, a larger force than they had ammunition to fight. This new third lorry was almost level, and in his rear-view mirror Michael could see his team moving to take a position to fire as the truck came level. A new and unmistakable sound joined the fray, the heavy banging of the General Purpose Machine Gun mounted in the rear of the third lorry, firing into the men and vehicles of the roadblock ahead. The GPMG battered the surprised and now frightened men who scattered, seeking any cover they could find as the machine gun dismantled their vehicles and those still inside in a blizzard of shrapnel and smoke and blood.

As it drew level the driver of the new lorry leant out of the window, and with a huge grin and an unmistakable Scottish accent called, 'do any of you chaps need a lift? We're going your way.'

The team lost no time in abandoning their requisitioned pickup truck and boarding the new lorry. The machine gun fire ceased for the moments it took them to jump inside and resumed fire as the lorry set off.

The two soldiers in the back of the lorry, operating the machine gun, gave the team the thumbs up. They'd stopped firing and now just watched for any new threats as the lorry charged down the main road heading back to Kandahar International Airport.

Michael sat down against the back wall of the cab. How close had they come to disaster? Had they overheard enough? Had they stopped whatever terrorist action was being planned? Had it been worth the risk? Had it been worth the civilian lives that had no doubt been lost?

Anger mixed with relief. They'd had close contact with the enemy and survived, again. His team had been professional and effective, again. He looked at his men. He was proud of them.

'Echo Base, this is Ghost One,' Michael said.

It was only a moment before he heard the reply. 'Ghost One, this is Echo Base. What is your situation?'

'Ghost One, rendezvous complete. EndEx.' End Exercise. Mission over.

He pulled his earpiece out, sometimes he didn't need it to feel connected to his team, and at the moment he didn't want or need to talk with Echo Base. The interesting questions which needed asking and answering would come later.

———

CAMP BASTION WAS the base for the International Security Assistance Force, the coalition of armed forces securing "peace" in Afghanistan. Home to thirty thousand troops and civilians it was an expanse of barracks, offices, hangers, sheds and other buildings.

In a whirlwind of noise and dust the helicopter dropped out of the night sky and settled onto the landing area at Camp Bastion. The ground crew ran forwards to secure the aircraft, and the engine noise dropped as the pilot shut down the engines.

The side doors slid open and the four black-clad figures climbed out. They were in no hurry as they carried their helmets and weapons with them, heading for the fence which separated the helicopter operations area from the rest of the compound. A guard pulled open the gate and the four walked through, leaving behind the fading noise of the helicopter's still spinning rota.

Michael led the way as they headed back to their barracks. Some of the buildings were temporary modular units, others were substantial buildings, reflecting the more permanent role of Camp Bastion. The size of a large town, it had all the charm of a multi-storey car park. UK Special Forces had their own area of the camp, towards the outer edge, with access to a dedicated helicopter service area. Michael ignored most of his surroundings as thoughts whirled around his mind.

Some might view the mission as a success, but Michael was coming to view it more and more as an unmitigated disaster. Their intelligence had been lacking to begin with, but had then gone from lacking to inadequate to simply wrong. What had started as a straightforward surveillance mission had turned into a full-on engagement with the enemy, for which they had not been prepared or provisioned. Even worse, worse than the usual lack of information and unexpected contact, was the enemy had known they were coming. The enemy had been prepared and had been waiting. It had been a set-up, a trap from beginning to end. They had escaped, but more by luck than skill, and that gnawed at his professional pride.

But there were darker thoughts at the forefront of Michael's mind. He could feel the anger brewing, and he fought to keep it in check. He reached their assigned accommodation building, pulled open the door and went inside, heading for the briefing room. The building was empty, the other soldiers barracking there were out on assignment. He walked into the briefing room and dumped his equipment on the floor by the wall. They'd return their weapons and kit to the Quartermaster soon enough.

The room was plain and functional. Cheap plastic chairs surrounded a simple table. Bare strip lights cast a harsh white light across the room. Narrow windows ran around the top quarter of the wall while an air-conditioning unit hummed as it kept the room cool. Like all things in the Camp the room was adequate, but could never be called pretty.

He heard the others come in and dump their kit, Velcro tearing and zippers being pulled undone as the men discarded their jackets and webbing. When he heard the door close he turned around to face them.

Before he could speak, Vince Marshall started. 'What the fucking hell was that?' he said, not shouting but the anger evident in his voice. 'Sorry boss, but that was a fuck-up from beginning to end.'

'The intel' was incomplete, and some of it wrong,' said Michael, forcing himself to keep a calm and even tone.

Again, Marshall got in first. 'No, that was a fuck-up. That was a trap. Whoever that "Head of Section" is, she sent us into a trap.'

Michael maintained eye-contact with Marshall. 'The Military Liaison Officer would never have agreed to our deployment unless there was an obvious need,' he said firmly. He could feel the tension in his chest, the heat rising, but now was not the time to get drawn into a shouting match.

'I have to agree, boss,' said Singh, always the calm voice of reason, 'whatever the need, whatever the state of the intel', someone missed the fact that that was a trap, clear and simple.' Singh pulled out a chair and sat down, stretching out his legs.

Singh was right. Marshall was right. Whatever the objective of the mission, whatever the gaps in their intelligence, it had been a trap, and no-one had known anything about it.

They had been lucky, that was clear, but luck was never a justification for bad decisions.

'We'll get to the bottom of this,' said Michael, 'we'll review the mission and the planning.' He had too much energy to sit. He wanted to run, to go out into the evening air and just run and burn off energy. He'd have to wait for later to do that.

Bullock sat on one of the tables, swinging his legs. 'But who's going to review MI5?' said Bullock. It was a fair question. Their mission review wouldn't include MI5's decision to request the meeting, nor would it consider their intelligence gathering, despite that having been the greatest failure.

'We'll review the mission,' Michael repeated. He focused again on Marshall. 'And we'll discuss your use of extreme force, to the point of endangering civilians.'

'No problem,' said Marshall, with only the very slightest hint of a sneer. 'I've got no problem with what I did, they boxed us in, I got us out.'

'How many civilians were killed by your grenade?' Michael demanded.

'I didn't stop to count, on account of the people shooting at me,' said Marshall. He wasn't going to back down.

The door opened and cut their conversation short. In walked Lieutenant-Colonel Stephen Clifton, Theatre Director of Special Forces, Afghanistan. Lieutenant-Colonel Clifton was the senior officer in charge of all UK Special Forces operations in Afghanistan. Units from all the various branches of UK Special Forces deployed to Afghanistan reported to Clifton, providing a single coordinated command structure for the soldiers "in theatre."

The four all looked over at Clifton as he walked in. Neither Bullock nor Singh stood, none of them saluted.

Special Forces had a very relaxed approach to military etiquette.

'Good evening gentlemen,' said Clifton, his accent and manner were refined, his thinning grey hair swept back, all betraying his public school and Cambridge University education and his Sandhurst officer training. 'Looks like you had an entertaining evening.' He grinned at them. Clifton might have been the product of the very best (or at least, the most expensive) public schools and university, but he was an experienced soldier who'd served his time in the field. The men under his command respected his experience and appreciated his understanding of their role in the Army. Michael could imagine Clifton on horseback, dressed for the fox hunt, or ready for the polo match. He could also imagine him in battle kit, lying in a bomb crater, being shot at and shooting back.

Marshall grinned at him. 'It had its moments,' he said. Michael wondered just how much Clifton knew.

'Good,' said Clifton, 'glad to see you're not just topping up your sun-tans. We'll start your debriefings in half an hour.'

'We'll look forward to that,' said Singh.

'Yes,' said Clifton, 'it seems various people are keen to see your mission reports. Special Forces Directorate want their copy, Special Forces Development wants to see a copy, and MI5 have asked for one.' His raised eyebrows suggested how seriously he took that last request.

'Are you going to give them one?' asked Bullock, grinning at the more than obvious double-entendre.

'We'll see, son,' said Clifton, 'but your trip this evening has garnered all sorts of attention.' With that Clifton left the room and closed the door behind him.

'They should tell MI5 to sod off and mind their own

business,' said Marshall. Michael had to admit, Marshall was right on that point.

'They probably will,' said Michael. 'They'll keep saying a copy's in the post. I'm just curious as to why Special Forces Development would want a copy. They never get involved.'

MINISTRY OF DEFENCE BUILDING, Whitehall, London

MAJOR LIAM TURNER sat at his office desk in the Ministry of Defence building in Whitehall. The sun was already up, and outside the commuter rush was getting into full flow. Turner was used to early mornings and made a habit of getting as much done as he could before 7am, before the usual early-morning flurry of emails began. His trim physique was the result of self-discipline and early-morning runs, ever since he moved to Whitehall he had been determined to maintain his fighting fitness.

Turner's office could have been straight out of a stately home. The gorgeous rosewood coffee table and chairs in the middle of the room could have accommodated an Earl and his guests. The large and ornate desk could would have sat comfortably in a Victorian gentleman's office, had it not been for the telephones and computer.

He tapped at the keyboard, and the computer screen on his desk displayed the next mission report in the queue. He was looking for something, but today it seemed he couldn't quite keep in his mind what he was looking for.

Yves Falcone had another project he needed resources for. Falcone had a number of projects underway for which Turner had provided one kind of input or another. As the

Head of UK Special Forces Development it was Turner's role to seek out and evaluate anything which might give his soldiers any edge or advantage. His brief was broad, and he evaluated weapons, communications systems, training programmes, diets, boots and more.

Falcone's focus was, of course, drugs. PanMedic made various drugs his soldiers used, everything from pain killers to antibiotics to poisons. From time to time Falcone had come to him with a more esoteric request, but this latest one was the strangest by far. If only he could remember the details. Turner knew he'd met with a scientist from PanMedic, a fascinating individual, whose name seemed to have slipped Turner's mind. His memory of the meeting was equally vague, almost like a half-remembered dream.

Turner did know he needed to identify a suitable unit of soldiers who could be assigned to the latest PanMedic research project, and it was to this end that Turner spent his time scrolling through mission reports, looking for just such a unit.

There was a knock on the office door and in walked Miss Harrow, his PA, carrying Turner's customary cup of tea. She placed the china cup and saucer on the large and impressive desk, not too close to Turner's keyboard and mouse.

'Did you not sleep well?' she asked, frowning at him. Sometimes she fussed a little too much, but he'd come to rely on her counsel and efficiency, so he overlooked her motherly tendencies.

'Not last night,' he said. He had no intention of trying to explain his sometimes foggy thinking this morning. At this moment he merely wished she'd leave so he could focus. She regarded him for a moment longer and then left the office. She always judged well when to pry and when to leave-be.

As the door closed he focused again on the screen. There was another project he needed to find resource for, but somehow that just kept slipping from his mind. Falcone's project was the one which seemed more important, much more important. He felt an urgency, something pushing him, a curious feeling. He dismissed the introspection and returned to the task at hand.

A new line of information appeared in one window on his computer, a new mission report had arrived. He clicked on the relevant entry and brought up the details in the main window. He skimmed the detail, and something inside him told him he needed to pay attention.

He scrolled back up the screen to reread the report. This time he read it carefully, word by word, reading the detail of the report, and reading between the lines.

This seemed perfect. A lone Special Forces unit, coming to the end of their assignment in Afghanistan, no immediate plans for redeployment, a recent mission which seemed to have been botched in every regard. He could make it look like he was doing people a favour by getting this particular unit out of the way of the Special Forces Directorate. The senior commanders wouldn't want this unit or news of their mission to be too prominent for a while. If the subject of bad news couldn't be hidden, sometimes it could be quarantined.

It seemed he had found what he was looking for, what Falcone was looking for. He felt a sense of satisfaction.

Turner started to compose three messages. The more difficult message would be to the Director of UK Special Forces, asking (but stating it more as a fait accompli) that this unit be reassigned to a Special Forces Development project. While some might like to see this unit sidelined for a while there were still questions others would want answering about their recent mission. Turner needed to avoid making too much of a fuss, he would prefer the unit be reassigned quickly and quietly.

The next message was to the Theatre Director of Special Forces in Afghanistan. He would be the one to tell the soldiers they would be returning to the UK, and would not be immediately deployed to a new mission. Turner needed to make sure the soldiers themselves didn't make a fuss, didn't start asking questions of their own. The sooner he could get them back to the UK and moved to the project's facility the better.

The final message was to Falcone, informing him he'd found a suitable unit of soldiers and that his project could begin. Turner couldn't shake the feeling that somehow, he thought, Falcone probably already knew.

SIX

The Head skimmed the report displayed on the computer screen. Most of the staff from the previous night's operation had gone home, leaving the Command and Control room quieter and less frenetic. A small staff remained to make sure Sparrowhawk made a safe escape and the military operation was all wrapped up. It had a sense of an almost-empty house after the party had finished, and just the clearing-up remained.

She finished the report and closed the document. It had been messy, but in the mess and chaos something was hiding, she could feel it. She'd played this game often enough and for long enough to know the most important clues were never in the reports or the official communications. Clues hid in dark corners, in quiet places. She had to seek them out, drag them into the light and examine them carefully. This was where the adrenaline of action morphed into the slow and (frankly) boring work of on-ongoing surveillance.

She looked up at the main clock on the wall. The scheduled conference with the GCHQ liaison was due in another minute. With so much of their enemy's communications being conducted by electronic means, GCHQ was a vital resource. It had an unparalleled capability to intercept communications and extract the relevant pieces from a sea of information.

She reached forwards to the keypad for the conference call facility and pressed the appropriate button. In a moment she was joined to the call with their GCHQ liaison officer.

'Good morning,' came a voice from the hidden loud-speakers in the room, giving the voice an almost other-worldly quality. 'This is Geraint Evans, Section Leader.'

'Good morning. Have we had confirmation from Sparrowhawk?' Typical of the Head, no introduction, no small talk, straight to the most important issues.

Another voice came over the speakers. 'Brian Delaney, team leader. A transmission was received from Sparrowhawk confirming he had reached a secure location.'

'Good. Have you positively identified the key players from the meeting?' the Head asked.

'Yes, we have,' said Evans. 'As first thought, the key participant was Tariq Shafee, a well-connected financier of various extremist and terrorist groups. Shafee has been linked to funding bombings, shootings and kidnappings across Europe, the Middle East and Asia.'

The Head looked up at one of the big screens on the wall of the Command and Control room. It showed a grainy picture of a man, the image-compression suggesting a picture taken with a telephoto lens. Details of the man scrolled in another window on the screen. Something irked her, like a mental itch she couldn't scratch. She made a note, and dismissed it. Patience was a virtue, even when interrogating one's own thoughts.

Evans continued. 'Shafee's companion in the meeting is a known employee of his, basically his fixer, details on screen now.' Evans paused to let the Head skim the details of the other man. It didn't surprise her to see he had been a nasty, violent individual. 'The second key participant was positively identified as Mohammed Arshad, a graduate of the Afghan training camps under the Taliban, an active participant in various terror attacks, the Americans have twice targeted him with drone strikes, so far without success. Arshad has direct links with known sympathisers in the UK.'

'Has there been any reaction from Arshad's contacts in the UK?' asked the Head.

'No,' said Evans, 'it's all gone quiet, your boys silenced Shafee and Arshad, I think the whole operation is shut down.'

The Head pondered this for a moment. She let it slide that he'd called the soldiers "her boys," they were nothing of the sort. There was something not quite right, something out of place, she knew it. Then it came to her.

'Why was Shafee there?' she asked. 'Shafee must be high up the food-chain, why did he attend this meeting and not some subordinate?'

The question was met with silence, which she took as confirmation it was the right question.

'We know that Nightingale was taken,' said Evans, 'I would infer they got from him that he'd given away details of the meeting. Shafee must have decided to personally take charge of trying to capture the soldiers.'

It was plausible, but to the Head's mind, something still didn't fit. There was a piece missing, or a piece out of place.

'Someone else was referenced,' said the Head, not quite as a question.

'Yes,' said Delaney. 'There was a reference to "daw' satie" - roughly translated as 'shining light.'

'Who does that refer to specifically?' said the Head.

'Unknown,' said Evans. 'The name has been logged before, and from what little intelligence we have on this individual our inference is it is someone also influential and well-funded. We believe this person also provides resources for a range of terrorist activities.'

'What else do we know?' asked the Head.

'Almost nothing,' said Evans. 'Pieces of intelligence imply this character has funded a wide range of terrorist groups responsible for a great many killings, but there is no clear ideology behind it. We have no intelligence at all on this person's identity or motives, only the vaguest idea of the scale and reach of their influence.'

A light started to come on in the Head's mind. The pieces were beginning to fit better.

'Shafee was not the financier for this operation,' she said, 'he was acting on behalf of this Shining Light, the ultimate directing force. Shafee had let the meeting be compromised, and he was ordered to make amends. He tried to do this by not only foiling our plans for surveillance but by capturing the soldiers.'

'With respect, Ma'am,' began Evans, 'that is supposition.'

'Of course it is,' she said sharply, 'it is a hypothesis intended to include and explain all currently known facts. Shining Light is a fact that must be included in our understanding of this issue.'

'But the soldiers killed Arshad,' said Delaney, 'they killed this network's link to activists in the UK.'

'They killed that link,' said the Head. 'We've no evidence Arshad was the only link, just as we've no evidence that Shafee was the only intermediate financier.'

'And yet the comm's traffic between Arshad's contacts in this country have dropped significantly,' said Evans.

'We've cut off one head of the Hydra,' said the Head, 'we've not slain the beast.' Was the bigger picture not obvious to these people? She wondered if sometimes they were too close to the detail to appreciate the context.

'We'll continue to monitor Arshad's known associates,' said Delaney, 'just to see if they become active again.'

The Head sat back in her chair, contemplating. No, this wasn't over, something else was still going on. She still felt they were missing something.

'The communications have dropped,' she said. 'Something is going on, something is happening, and I want to know what.'

'Their communications might have dropped because their leader has been killed. They've no funding, no direction, nothing to talk about. No-one to talk to,' said Evans.

'I agree,' said the Head. 'That is possible. But it is also possible that communications have dropped because one or more of them have gone dark prior to engaging in hostile acts. I want surveillance stepped up, as deep and intrusive as possible. If someone like this Shining Light is involved then killing low-level players like Arshad is not going to stop anything, all we've done is kill the one person we knew to keep under surveillance.'

'It's hard to listen in when people aren't talking,' said Delaney.

'Listening is what you're supposed to be good at,' said the Head. 'Show me you can listen to whispers, show me you can find out what's going on.' She ended the call.

ANNA MADE sure she was in work early the next day. Even though it had been late by the time they were told the mission had ended and were stood down she had a sense this wasn't over.

Her desk was in one of the big open-plan areas within the outer ring of the Doughnut. The two concentric rings and the landscaped lawn in the centre gave the building its distinctive shape and name. The outer ring was home to several areas of open plan office space, large stretches of desks and computer workstations. Wall-mounted monitors gave views of ongoing surveillance activities, current threat-assessments and team assignments.

Anna's desk was towards the inner side of one area, so she had only a limited view of the panoramic windows and the world outside. Her world was one of computers and data and analysis, turning snippets of information into useable pieces of understanding. Other people would assemble those pieces into jigsaw-like pictures of the geo-economic-political-religious world. Motivations blended with the movements of money, the strength of religious factions clashed with the preparedness of armies, rising and falling food supplies mirrored bull and stag stock-markets; and they all meshed together into one massive ever-changing breeding ground for revolution and conflict. Anna's world was the world of these snippets.

One of the big monitors on her desk showed a list of intercepted emails, another window showed the results of a program she had running to find patterns in the times of the emails. She stared at the monitor, feeling less than completely engaged. A movement in her peripheral vision caught her attention.

Brian Delaney stood there, beckoning Anna to join him, Kingston Smith and Wayne Browning were already standing with Brian. Anna stifled the impulse to ask "who, me?" She locked her computer workstation, picked up her notebook and joined the others.

'I need to brief you and the team,' said Delaney, turning towards the door and motioning them to follow him. The butterflies in Anna's stomach took flight again.

Minutes later the original team were assembled in the meeting room, the other two analysts whom Anna did not know had joined them. Anna felt excited again, hoping this would lead to something more interesting than analysing email dates and times but also feeling it vindicated her suspicion that something was still going on.

'I had a call a few minutes ago,' Delaney began, 'with Geraint Evans and with the MI5 Head of Section.' Anna made a note to look up Geraint Evans and see who he was.

Delaney continued. 'MI5 believe that the terrorist activity is continuing, even though their soldiers killed the three people present at the meeting in Afghanistan.'

'Why do they believe that?' asked Wayne Browning.

'No idea,' said Delaney, with a hint of despair in his voice. 'They believe other individuals may be involved and that the financing may still be in place.'

'But didn't the soldiers also kill the terrorist with links to activists in this country?' asked one of the other analysts.

'Yes, they did,' said Delaney. 'However, MI5 believe that with the financing still in place other activists will carry on whatever was being planned.'

'So what do they want us to do?' said Browning, 'beyond what we're already doing?'

Delaney paused as if trying to find the right words to explain. 'The UK activists linked to Mohammed Arshad have mostly gone quiet. There's been a steep drop-off in their communications.'

'All communications?' asked Kingston.

'Mainly,' said Delaney. 'We will check, but first indications are they've pretty much stopped using email or social media or any of the usual communications channels.'

'So, again,' said Browning, 'what do they want us to do?'

'They want us to monitor the communications of these activists,' said Delaney, his expression betraying the fact he'd essentially contradicted himself.

'They want us to monitor the communication of people who've stopped communicating?' asked the so-far quiet analyst.

'Yes,' said Delaney.

Anna thought it did sound like a contradiction, but it stirred an idea in the back of her mind. It made her think of something she'd been reading recently, a New Scientist article about astronomy. Why would it make her think of that?

'With respect,' said Wayne Browning, 'it is a bit ridiculous. We can put surveillance on them, in case they communicate, but if they're not talking it's going to be hard to listen to anything.'

'I have to agree,' said Kingston. 'We can intercept any communications they do make, but if they're quiet then there just won't be much to intercept.'

The idea crept closer to the front of Anna's brain. She thought she knew what it reminded her of, but it wasn't something she felt she could share with the group. It was only a vague idea, better to explore it back at her desk and get the facts straight before speaking out.

'I know, I know,' said Delaney, 'but the Head of Section was quite insistent. She's firmly of the opinion they may have gone dark prior to starting some kind of action.'

Delaney paused, and let the idea sink in. He said, 'it is possible.'

It was possible, and everyone around the table knew that it was possible, but it still didn't offer a way of intercepting communications which weren't being made.

'It's a bit like looking in the proverbial dark room for the black cat that isn't there,' said one of the analysts.

'But the cat is there,' said Anna, before she could stop herself. She became very painfully aware of the moment's silence that followed, and the five pairs of eyes staring at her.

'How do you mean?' asked Delaney, in a calm voice. Anna was pleased his voice sounded genuinely inquisitive. The problem now was she'd spoken, and she couldn't take back what she'd said. Like it or not (and she didn't) she was, for the moment, centre-stage.

'In the idiom,' she said, 'the contradiction is looking for a cat that isn't there, the facts that the room is dark and the cat is black are irrelevant.' She paused. No-one spoke, which she took to be a good thing. 'But in our case the cat, the terrorists, are there. It's just their pattern of communication has changed.'

'So what are you suggesting?' asked Browning.

'How do you find a black hole?' asked Anna, meaning it as a rhetorical question, so she quickly continued. 'Like the cat, you can't see it, because it's black, so astronomers see it by its effects on neighbouring stars.'

'True,' said Kingston, 'and how does that apply to our situation?' It wasn't a dismissive question, Anna saw it as a perfect question to set up her explanation.

'These people won't have known that Arshad has been killed. Someone must have told them, and must have told them to stop communicating.' There were nods around the table, her idea was finding favour. 'We can track the pattern of their final communications, and that will establish their chain of command.'

'Like it,' said one of the analysts, smiling.

'We can also analyse the patterns of communication between the second and third level contacts of the ones who were connected to Arshad. If the primary contacts are communicating offline, sooner or later a lower-level contact is going to pick up the phone for the next communication. We can track the activity of the network, infer what the primary contacts are doing.'

The people in the room were writing frantically in their notebooks. Anna decided that now was probably the best time to stop talking.

'Excellent idea,' said Delaney.

'It's more than an idea,' said Browning, 'it gives us a strategy.'

'It does,' said Delaney, 'and I'll report back to Geraint that we have a way forwards. I'll let him talk to MI5 and tell them yet again we have a way of pulling the rabbit out of the hat.'

As the meeting ended and people made to leave, Anna realised Kingston was smiling at her. She was sure if it hadn't been so public he'd have given her a thumbs-up.

DESPITE THE STRESSES of the previous night, or maybe because of them, Michael had slept well and now needed breakfast. Their accommodation unit provided them with one room for sleeping (Michael had slept despite Bullock's snoring,) a toilet-and-shower facility shared with the other teams resident in the unit, several briefing rooms, and a common room for eating and (in theory) relaxing.

Michael was the first into breakfast, the harsh white of the strip lights mixing with the brightening morning sun. Breakfast was a minimal affair of toast and a mug of tea, there was always tea available. He put three slices of toast in the toaster and pushed the lever down. It was quiet in the common room, pleasantly quiet. The team frequently rose together, showered together, breakfasted together, but this morning Michael was happy with some time alone, some time to reflect.

He took a slurp from his mug of tea. It was still almost scalding hot, but his time in the Army had taught him to gulp his tea down, to do otherwise always to risk losing it to someone with nimble fingers and a bigger thirst. The events of the previous night still troubled Michael. He could accept (just) the woeful lack of intelligence, they rarely had full and complete information. There were serious questions to be asked about why they were ordered in when it turned out to be a trap, but those were questions for those higher up the food chain.

The actions of his team troubled Michael more, particularly the actions of Vince Marshall. Michael knew Marshall could be aggressive, sometimes violent. They were trained to be aggressive and violent, but they were also trained to look out for civilians and to avoid drawing innocent people into their violence. Marshall had been reckless. Worse, he had been reckless with innocent people's lives. Michael had avoided making a point of this when he gave his account of events in the debriefing. He'd wait for later when he could have a word with Marshall alone, just to make sure the two of them were clear on each other's position.

The toast popped up at the same moment the door

opened. Bullock walked in, wearing nothing but his khaki boxer shorts.

'Toast!' he said. 'Brilliant. Thank you very much.' He strode towards the table, reaching out for the toast.

Michael picked up the three dark slices of hot toast. 'Officer's privilege, do your own.' They both grinned.

Singh and Marshall soon joined them, both a little more dressed than Bullock.

'Make way,' said Marshall, heading for the food table, 'hungry bastard coming through.' Within minutes the four of them were guzzling large mugs of tea and shovelling down several rounds of toast each.

'So what was that bollocks about Special Forces Development getting a report?' said Bullock, crumbs tumbling out of his mouth.

'Who cares?' said Singh, 'just more paperwork for someone to do.'

'I don't know,' said Michael. 'It's odd, I've not known them ask for a copy of a mission report before, at least not that quickly.'

'Maybe our fame is spreading?' said Bullock.

'After the noise you made last night I'm surprised they didn't hear it in London and simply want to know what that fucking bang was,' said Singh, grinning at Marshall.

A silence settled over the room, and everyone was aware of it. Michael also looked at Vince Marshall. He could feel the heat rising inside again, and it wasn't from the tea. He hadn't wanted to bring this up now, not in public. Maybe the moment would pass.

'Hey, don't blame me,' said Marshall, his tone becoming less jocular, 'I just did what I had to do.'

Michael had an uneasy sense the moment wasn't going to pass, not now.

'I don't think that wall needed a grenade to get through,' said Singh.

'They pinned us down,' said Marshall, his voice now louder, 'I got us the fuck out of there. I don't remember you complaining last night.'

'That was a building full of civilians,' said Michael, forcing himself to keep his voice calm and measured. He didn't need a stand-up argument between the four of them, not now, but he needed to make the point.

'The building was also full of bad guys shooting at us,' said Marshall. Michael was glad Marshall spoke his response, rather than shouted it. 'Sorry boss, but we were cut off. Civilians or no civilians I needed a way out, and I got one. End of story.'

Michael drew breath to respond, but the door opened, and in walked Lieutenant-Colonel Clifton. He stopped halfway through the door, picking up on the tension in the room.

'Hope I'm not interrupting,' he said, and carried straight on, obviously not caring if he was interrupting. 'Need you in the briefing room.' He looked at Bullock. 'Preferably fully dressed.' Clifton left the room, closing the door behind him.

Putting their Special Forces training to good use the team demolished the remains of their breakfast in moments. After a short pause to allow Bullock to pull on a pair of trousers and a t-shirt the team joined Clifton in the briefing room.

The five of them sat on the cheap plastic chairs in a loose circle, looking something like a therapy group. Michael had a momentary thought that perhaps a round of group therapy wouldn't be a bad idea. He quickly dismissed the idea. He couldn't imagine Marshall going all touchy-feely.

'I've had a communique from UK Special Forces Development,' said Clifton, sounding hesitant.

Michael was curious, he'd not heard Clifton sound this way before. He found himself leaning in slightly, eager to listen to what Clifton had to say next.

'It seems,' said Clifton, 'that you're being assigned to some special research project.' Michael looked at the man and at his team and they looked back at him, and they all turned to look at Clifton.

'Research project?' asked Michael. 'What exactly does that mean?'

'Actually, I've no idea.' Clifton seemed to smile a touch at this point.

'Researching what, exactly?' asked Singh.

'Can't tell you any more, sorry.'

Bullock turned to Michael. 'Boss, this doesn't make sense.'

Clifton answered before Michael could. 'I really don't know any more, but this has come from the Head of Development, and it's sanctioned by the Director of Special Forces.'

Michael was lost for words. The Director didn't typically get involved in operational assignments, not once they were in theatre, and he'd never heard of a team being taken off operational duties and put onto any project for the Development division.

'Sorry, but we have to challenge this,' said Michael. 'We're on operational duties, they can't just take us off and sideline us.'

'Out of my hands,' said Clifton, 'your orders have come through, transport's arranged back to the UK.'

'Come on boss,' said Bullock, in an almost pleading tone

of voice. 'What happened last night wasn't our fuck-up.' He cast a glance at Clifton. 'Sorry. But it wasn't.'

'Is this because of what went wrong last night?' asked Singh.

Clifton sighed. 'I genuinely don't know. I have your orders, but I have no information about why those orders are the way they are.'

Marshall leant forwards and opened his mouth to speak. Clifton raised a hand to silence him. 'I can tell you this,' said Clifton. 'Last night was a fuck-up of almighty proportions, and there are going to be a lot of people having to answer a lot of uncomfortable questions. You could make a fuss and join in the mud-slinging that is about to happen.'

'Or?' said Michael.

'Or you could just keep your heads down, put up with this project, let the dust settle, and before you know it you'll be back on operational duty, and everyone will have forgotten about last night.'

The team looked at each other, and looked at Michael. Giving in and keeping quiet was not in his nature, it wasn't in their nature, but neither was playing politics.

'Looks like we've got a choice,' said Michael to the team, looking at each one of them in turn. 'We either go home and play soldiers for some other unit for a bit, or we stay here sat on our arses and play the blame-game. I know which I'd rather do.'

'Politics isn't my scene,' said Singh, almost immediately.

'Testing some shit for the Development division sounds dull, but we might get our hands on some new kit,' said Marshall.

'I'm not staying here to carry the can for someone else,' said Bullock.

Michael turned to Clifton. 'Looks like we're going back to Blighty for a while.'

Just for a moment Michael wondered if this was a good deal, or if they'd just made a pact with the devil?

'Good stuff,' said Clifton with a grin. 'You'd better get packing, your flight leaves in two hours.'

SEVEN

Lee Joon-ho sank back into the leather seat of his limousine. The chauffeur navigated the streets of Kowloon, heading for a destination further along the coast. He closed his eyes, shutting out the traffic and bustle of the busy Hong Kong afternoon and giving himself some clear mental space. So many pieces were in play in this game, he had to move carefully. This was a game played with people, and people could be unpredictable, some more than others. This game called for subtlety, careful timing, and above all patience. But it also called for boldness. The game did not always go according to plan, and when it didn't, he needed to adapt, to be creative.

His meeting with Mr Li was important, and as he'd hoped he now had a private meeting with Mr Li, time and space to discuss things. The events of the previous night had been unfortunate, and now new arrangements would need to be made, a test of his adaptability and creativity. He also needed to ensure certain key people kept their nerve. He looked at his watch, almost time.

Using the secure app on his phone he selected the contact and dialled.

'Is everything ready?' The man on the other end spoke without announcing himself. Joon-ho sometimes had to concentrate to understand the man's thick Russian accent. 'Will your man have things ready?' Could nothing stop this man worrying?

'My man came to an unfortunate end last night,' said Joon-ho. He paused. The Russian would no doubt react, probably most emotionally.

'Is the mission compromised?' demanded the Russian. 'We must replan, things cannot continue if there have been setbacks.'

'It was a setback, nothing more. I expected some involvement from government agencies. My man confirmed such an involvement, and put an end to it,' said Joon-ho. The best plays, Joon-ho thought, were when the actors played their roles with focus but focused only on their own role. If the actor started trying to manage the scenery, problems were sure to follow.

'And your man?' asked the Russian.

'He sacrificed himself for the good of the mission.' A barefaced lie, but Joon-ho had no moral issues with lying, or manipulating people, or killing them. 'I have to make some alternative arrangements, but everything else will proceed as planned. As must you.'

'If government agencies were involved then they must know about the plan,' said the Russian. 'We must abort, plan for another time.'

'There is no need to do that,' said Joon-ho, using the most soothing voice he could effect. He preferred to give orders to this man, but at this time orders would likely be unproductive. 'The agency in question did not know about the plan, they only knew about one individual. That individual has been silenced and that agency has no further connection with us. The plan must proceed on schedule. Timing is everything.'

'But they will be alert, they will be ready for something,' said the Russian.

'They will try and be ready for anything but will know nothing. Our people in England will be ready as planned, there is no change to the plan or the timetable.'

Silence. Joon-ho waited. The Russian would decide whether to continue or not. If he didn't it would present a significant problem, his skills would be most difficult to replace.

'And the consignment?'

'I will deliver it personally,' said Joon-ho, almost smiling.

Another silence. 'Very well. But if there are any more problems then I will disappear.' The line went dead.

Joon-ho put away his phone. He knew full well the Russian couldn't hide from him. If he chose to, Joon-ho could have men find the Russian within hours, and he believed the Russian knew that. A little fear for one's own safety could be such a motivating factor.

He looked out of the car window. Smart and clean buildings sat juxtaposed with smaller, darker dwellings, some were older, dating from Hong Kong's colonial past, some were modern, even futuristic. The buildings all sat in marked contrast to the street scenes from his childhood. North Korea had been a harsh and unforgiving environment. Survival had only been for the fittest, or most ruthless. Starvation had been everywhere. Since his escape he had come to understand how the sanctions imposed by the West had caused the hardships endured by his family and his countrymen. For all anyone else knew he was an orphan from a rural South Korean family who'd fled to Hong Kong to seek his fortune. He did not parade his past for the amusement of others.

The car stopped. The chauffeur opened the door and Joon-ho walked to the front door of the building. Mr Li's office hid in a small and unimposing building, modern, with clean lines and a set of shallow steps leading up to the smoked glass door. The doors swept open as he approached, and the aide to Mr Li greeted Joon-ho with a bow.

Joon-ho was soon sitting in Mr Li's office, a most informal room, with a small and functional work desk, the rest of the furniture was easy chairs, low tables. All high quality and no doubt extremely expensive.

Mr Li smiled as he sipped his tea. Joon-ho regarded him carefully. The amateur would be tempted to rush into business, but still, he had to take his time. Mr Li had to come willingly, he couldn't be persuaded to join.

'I believe you will be in England?' said Mr Li, 'For the Olympic Games?' He said it in an almost mocking tone.

'I will,' replied Joon-ho. 'I have close ties to some of the Chinese financiers of the previous Games.'

'I imagine the English government would be most concerned at the prospect of any kind of violent assault on any of the athletes or audiences.'

'I am sure they are,' said Joon-ho. 'And for good reason.'

'How so?'

'Tensions in parts of the Middle East are rising, various groups are becoming more active, and more ambitious. The Games present a target some would find hard to resist.'

'Surely an assault on such a target would be suicide. Or would that not be a concern?'

'There are those who would mount such an assault, especially if they believed it would bring them martyrdom and eternal glory.' Joon-ho sipped his tea. He had a story to tell, a story he needed Li to believe, and the key would be in how convincing he could be.

'Do they have the resources to mount such an assault?'

'I do not know,' said Joon-ho, lying, 'but I imagine there are people who would provide them with sufficient resources. Resources to make a damaging impact on the host country.'

'How damaging?'

Joon-ho paused, searching for the right words. 'Hosting the Games is a matter of international pride and prestige. A country's economic welfare is tied to such pride and prestige. A sufficiently damaging assault would not only devastate the Games but would also devastate the host country.' He left the point hanging in the air, giving Li time to take in the words and make suitable images in his mind.

'I am sure such resources would be costly.' Mr Li was making the right suggestions.

'They would be. And I imagine anyone providing such resources would be grateful of any offer to share such a cost.' He had made the offer, without being so rude as to voice it out loud.

'How do you imagine they might show such gratitude?' asked Mr Li.

'If a key western economy were to fall, particularly if it also toppled the economy of any Middle Eastern country implicated in such action, then key Asian concerns would be well placed to step in and capitalise on such a situation. The profits would naturally be shared by those who had shown support.'

'Then I am sure anyone looking for such support would share tea with someone able to provide such support.' Mr Li raised his teacup. Joon-ho inclined his head towards Mr Li, and the deal was sealed, the offer had been made and accepted.

All that remained was to put the plan into action, quickly.

———

ANNA STARED AT THE SCREEN, hardly seeing the lists of emails or the spreadsheets. She could feel the tension in her throat getting tighter and tighter. Why did she say that? Why did she speak up in the meeting? Now everyone was expecting her to work some kind of miracle and trace people who'd become invisible. Maybe she should have kept quiet. It would have been so much easier just to come back and analyse the lists of emails, do what other people told her to. She'd never been scared to voice an opinion in tutorials at university, and she had thought this would be similar, how wrong she had been.

What scared her the most was the prospect of not delivering on her big idea and then being relegated to doing only the most menial analyst jobs. Everyone had applauded her for her insightful thinking, for her creative solution to the problem. All she had to do now was devise a way of putting her idea into action, and this is where the problem lay. She had not the slightest idea how. It had seemed so easy in the meeting when it was all theoretical. Now she actually needed to do the job it seemed a lot more difficult. Doubtless, the other analysts would be working on the problem too, but how embarrassing it would be if she were the only one not to deliver any results.

'I said I was wondering if you were telepathic,' she finally heard someone say. She looked around and realised Kingston was looking across the desk at her. She thought he had a friendly face, and his smile did start to make her feel a little more relaxed, but only a little.

'I'm sorry?' she said.

'You've been staring at the screen for ages,' he said. 'I was wondering if you were trying to operate the computer by telepathy.' He smiled. She nearly smiled.

'No,' she said, not fully realising his humour, 'no, just thinking.'

'That's a lot of thinking. Anything wrong?'

'No,' she said, shaking her head slightly, 'nothing wrong. Just thinking.'

'That was a good idea you had, in the meeting,' he said.

Anna had no reply to this. She just stared at him. Having a spontaneous idea hadn't been a problem. Being insightful and creative on demand was her problem.

'Any idea how you're going to do it?'

Her mind seemed to have slowed down. Where usually thoughts and ideas popped into her mind almost on demand, now there was just a mental tumbleweed, blowing through her brain.

'If I had to guess,' said Kingston, leaning slightly closer and lowering his voice a touch, 'I'd say you have no idea how to actually solve this problem, and you're worried that you'll be the only one not to have anything to show Delaney.'

Anna realised she was staring at Kingston with her mouth open, and she hoped she hadn't been dribbling. She nodded her head, very slowly. If her mind had been working properly she would have been amazed at his insight. She might also have guessed he spoke from experience.

Kingston continued. 'When I first started here I had a problem I was working on. Delaney was expecting me to come up with some brilliant idea. I hadn't a clue what to do.'

Anna continued to stare, she couldn't think of anything intelligent to say, or anything unintelligent. 'Do you know by what brilliant technique I solved the problem?' Kingston asked.

Again, Anna shook her head slowly. Kingston wheeled his chair closer to Anna, leaned closer to her, and said quietly, 'I asked someone for help.'

She sat back, eyes wide, not sure whether to laugh or disagree. Her tension started to disappear like air whistling out of a balloon.

Kingston moved back a bit and dropped the whispering voice. 'This is a collaborative environment, we work best in teams. There are very few superstars here, very few Lone Rangers. If you have a problem, ask someone for help, you'll be amazed how generous the people around here will be with all their amazing brain power.'

Now Anna smiled properly, and found she could relax, at least more than she had been. 'So who should I ask?' she finally asked.

Kingston grinned. 'Oh, I don't know. There's possibly a really smart analyst knocking around somewhere, probably not far away. Might find one really close by, if you thought about it.'

Anna frowned for a moment. She thought through the people she knew. Several were language or cultural specialists, they probably wouldn't have an answer. She didn't want to go and ask Delaney or Browning, asking them would just seem like admitting defeat. Her startling intellect seemed to be taking the morning off.

'Wouldn't care to give me a clue, would you?' she asked.

Kingston's smile dropped into a mock-wounded expression. 'I'm wounded,' he said, 'that you overlooked the most obvious.'

Then the obvious finally dawned on Anna, and she beamed a big wide grin at Kingston. 'Ah,' she said. Anna made a play of putting on a serious look. 'Kingston, do you have any suggestions as to how I might track the apparent non-communication of these individuals.'

'Well, it's funny you should ask,' he said, 'but yes, I do have an idea, and I will tell you.'

Anna reached for her notebook and pen and sat poised waiting for Kingston's suggestion. He spoke. 'Sleimann back-bit and non-bit regression,' he said. Anna wrote it down, guessing at the spelling, and then frowned at Kingston.

'Look up the details,' he said, 'it's a bit of an obscure theory, but I think it will do the job, you'll just have to work through the mechanics of applying it to our data.'

It was obscure an obscure piece of work, Anna had never heard of this particular theory, but she set to work searching the Web for relevant papers and journals. She was soon in her element, sketching out the basics of the theory, doodling ideas about how to apply it, writing snippets of computer code to use the theory to analyse spreadsheets of data. Before long her screens were filled with windows of spreadsheets and code and lists and graphs.

Engrossed in her work, Anna had lost track of time, but at some point she became aware of somebody standing next to her desk. She looked up. Brian Delaney was standing watching her.

'Sorry,' he said, 'didn't want to interrupt. I need to give an update to Geraint. Any progress?'

Anna sat back in her chair and nodded towards the screens of information. 'Yes,' she said, 'I've been working with Sleimann's theory, it seems to do the job. We can work out how the message to stop communicating was spread, how that correlates to known but unexpected face-to-face meetings. I think we can identify at least ten in the group who got the message from Afghanistan.'

Delaney grinned. 'Oh, marvellous,' he said. 'I'll let Geraint know. He's got a catch-up with the MI5 Head of Section, he'll be delighted to report this to her.' He walked off, and Anna relaxed, relieved he'd been pleased with her progress but also relieved she hadn't been asked to give any updates in person. She'd had enough stress for the moment.

'Well done,' said Kingston, 'at this rate you'll start to get a good reputation.' She looked across at him, but he was already back working away at his own computer.

Anna wasn't sure she wanted a reputation. Surely people with reputations got asked to do more things, more difficult things.

TURNER, too, stared blankly at a screen. The monitor looked out of place on his grand office desk, but he couldn't do without his connection to the electronic side of the military. He blinked, as he realised he'd been staring at the report without reading it. He focused on the words. The report confirmed the unit of soldiers had boarded the plane and had departed Camp Bastion, and were now on their way back to the UK. He allowed himself a smile of self-satisfaction. He'd had to call in some favours to get the unit's reassignment authorised, but they were now committed to his Division. Once assigned to him he decided which project he put them on.

He sat back, and the grin left his face. He had a portfolio of development projects he ran on behalf of the UK Special Forces Directorate. It was Turner's job to seek out and evaluate anything which might give UK Special Forces any kind of advantage in their operations, and to then recommend to the Director any resources which ought to be formally adopted. Beyond that brief directive he had free reign to run whatever project he saw fit. He had one particular project sitting on the shelf, waiting to be started. He'd been wanting to start this project for some time but had always lacked a suitable group of soldiers. Now this unit of soldiers would be ideal candidates for the project. He felt the growing temptation to have them start work as soon as they got to the project's facility. The more he thought about it the more it made sense. He could have them fully up to speed on the project by the end of the week. There would always be another group for His project. But there was the problem. It was tempting, but He could be very persuasive. Turner thought about it for a moment, it had been a while since he'd met Him, and yet what he'd agreed to do for Him still seemed so important, so vital.

Now he came to think about it, he couldn't remember exactly what the other project was. His project, Morrow's project, should be his highest priority. Turner couldn't quite remember why it mattered so much, but there was no doubt it did. The more he thought about it the more clearly he saw, the soldiers could only be assigned to Morrow's project. He clicked with his mouse and checked other documents. The transport had been arranged, the project facility had been prepared, Captain Conway had been briefed and was expecting them. He felt satisfied he'd done everything he needed to.

Turner also had the other matter Morrow wanted taking care of. Morrow had called earlier that morning and given him the details of what needed to be done. It had seemed so simple when He explained it, but now Turner thought about it, it didn't seem quite so straightforward. No matter. It needed to be done.

Turner picked up his desk phone and dialled a number. The woman who answered had an unmistakable voice. The edge to her voice was almost her calling card.

'Major Turner,' said the Head as she answered his call, 'this is an unexpected interruption.'

'Always,' he said, partly in jest. 'I'm sorry to hear about your recent operation, it seems things didn't quite go according to plan.'

'Bad news about secret operations seems to travel quickly, and widely.'

'I make it a point to stay up to date, particularly with any problems my chaps might be having,' said Turner. He felt a temptation to digress into small talk, a rare pleasure, but he disciplined himself.

'I take it you want something?' asked the Head, changing the subject.

'Of course. I have a project and we're dependent on a civilian supplier. I'm not convinced that the supplier's IT security is all it should be. I need your help securing their IT systems.' No point in beating around the bush, so to speak.

'You have people who can do that,' said the Head. 'People who are considerably less busy than I am.'

'I do have people,' Turner said, 'but for this particular project I'd like to make arrangements slightly less formal.' Before the Head could question this he added, 'and I think it's a project that you'd find particularly interesting.'

'I'd love to,' said the Head, 'and when the Olympics have been and gone I'll be only too happy to help.'

Turner spoke quickly, before she could end the call. 'It won't wait. I don't want to go into details here, but this is something that could be of benefit to you, and like I said I'd like to keep this off the official books. It could be win-win.'

'Sorry,' said the Head, 'my to-do list is full. As you pointed out, we've got our own challenges to deal with.'

'Yes,' said Turner, 'and this project could have provided a solution to the problem your team had. It could have secured them against any kind of communications interruption, and more.' It was a balance, he felt it keenly, how to tell her enough to be tempting, but not enough to enable a decision.

'Tell me more,' she said.

'It's not so easy to describe,' he said, 'but you only have to see it to understand.'

Turner endured the moment's silence on the phone, and he knew he'd piqued her interest. 'I'll send someone to take a look,' she said. He could hear a hesitation in her voice. Surely she was considering taking a look personally. Turner knew he had to get her to visit in person, He had been quite clear in that. She had to meet Him.

'This isn't something I can share with anyone else, not until you've seen it and understood what we're doing.' He thought for a moment he might have pushed it too far. He couldn't risk scaring her off, nor could he risk letting her fob him off with excuses. There was another silence. The temptation to say more grew stronger, to try and persuade her further, but he knew he had to remain silent. He had to give her the space in which to speak and to commit herself.

'I can't afford to be away from the Office.' "The Office" was MI5's nickname for Thames House.

'You don't need to be,' said Turner. 'Come to my office, I can tell you enough here to convince you. I'm sure you can afford to walk across to Whitehall for an hour.'

'This had better be worth it, Liam,' she said and ended the call.

Turner paused to congratulate himself, then he pressed the keys to dial Yves Falcone. He had to report success and to make sure Morrow would be ready for when the Head came to call. Turner had no doubt he could persuade her to take a trip to PanMedic's facility, but when she first called into Whitehall he had no doubt Morrow would want to be part of the conversation, in spirit if not in body.

EIGHT

SHROPSHIRE, ENGLAND

T he minibus swept up the main road, passed green field after hedgerow after woodland. The landscape was more interesting than the weather, which was iron grey and drizzling. The windscreen wipers squeaked on every upward stroke.

In the two-and-a-half-hour journey from RAF Brize Norton the squeaky wiper had gone from annoying to irritating to a symbol of the team's predicament; making a vague noise about an unhappy situation. They'd tried to engage the driver in conversation, mainly to try and get him to give a clue as to where they were going, but he didn't seem the talkative type, and they soon gave up.

Michael stared at the hills in the distance. They were coming into Shropshire, the county which bordered Wales. They weren't far now from the Brecon Beacons and the hills where almost all UK Special Forces went through the rigorous and gruelling selection marches.

Less than an hour before they'd skirted the south side of Cheltenham and Michael mused how close they had been to the GCHQ building, the place from which the flawed intelligence had originated for their ill-fated mission. Now he had a sense of almost coming home. The cold and seeming never-ending Beacons was where he'd done his selection exercises, covering longer and longer distances with ever heavier loads against almost impossible deadlines. Cross-country running had always been a passion, and the pain of the fatigue was something he could compartmentalise. He hadn't minded so much even when one of the supervising staff had surprised him and ordered him to lie in a cold and wet ditch for half an hour. He knew it had been a test of stamina, and whether he'd put up with more discomfort without question.

He'd always borne in mind the advice he'd been given by a colleague who'd been through Selection a year or two before; don't come first, don't come last, don't get noticed. Now he and the team were in very real danger of being noticed, for the wrong reasons. There was never going to be any point in trying to argue it wasn't their fault, or that someone else was to blame. Someone had fucked up, and now someone (but not necessarily the same someone) was in danger of taking the fall.

As they turned off the main road and through a village, Michael noticed the name, Bishop's Fort. It wasn't a place he knew, although he'd seen it on maps of the area. He became curious, he wasn't aware of any Army facility around here, certainly not any Special Forces barracks in this particular locality. The quizzical looks on the faces of his team-mates showed they too had noticed they'd turned off a familiar route and into unfamiliar territory.

After a few miles they turned off the road onto a narrow track. The old and rusty sign had said something about private property but had given no clue as to where they were going. The track was narrow and in need of some attention, weeds growing out of cracks in the Tarmac. The vehicle hit at least two pot-holes.

'I've spotted at least three surveillance cameras,' said Singh, a glint in his eye.

After another minute they came to the fence. It was easily nine feet high, topped with coiled razor-wire. Beyond the fence sat a hut, perhaps home to a security guard, but the darkened windows obscured anyone inside. A tall lamp-post stood to one side of the road passed the gate, half a dozen large CCTV cameras sprouted from the post and covered every aspect of the road and the gate and the gate-house. The big sign, white and clean, made it clear this was Ministry of Defence property and that soldiers beyond the gate would use lethal force against trespassers.

The driver seemed in no hurry to perform any action to open the gate, no-one came out of the gatehouse, there was no intercom through which to announce their arrival. Michael assumed the cameras were verifying the registration of the vehicle and perhaps performing facial recognition on each of them. After a few moments the gate started to open, sliding to one side, rattling and clanking as it went. Once the gate had opened the driver drove slowly into the compound beyond.

The roads inside the compound were in better repair than the track approaching it. The compound itself seemed quite large, the road split left and right, there were one and two-storey buildings, a few people trotted quickly between the buildings, shoulders hunched against the drizzle. The driver stopped outside one of the single-storey buildings.

Marshall pulled open the side door of the minibus and they each climbed out, stretching aching limbs, glad to feel the fresh air and the rain, an improvement on the stale air of the vehicle.

'Good afternoon, gentlemen,' came a voice. They turned around and marching towards them—almost literally—was a man in combat fatigues. Michael wasn't sure if he saw the suggestion of a limp in one leg, but guessed the man was a similar age and build to himself. The man was lean, dark-haired, and wore a tired look, like he'd not slept properly in months. 'Captain Conway,' said the man, his voice leaning towards being friendly, and making no attempt to salute or greet them formally.

The team didn't return his greeting but stared at him. Michael could imagine the ferocity of Marshall's stare, but didn't turn around to look.

'I suggest you get your things stowed in your accommodation,' said Conway, 'it's this one here.' He gestured to the building they stood in front of. 'I've got a couple of things to take care of, after that we'll have a chat and get you started.' With that he marched off.

'I don't make snap judgements,' said Marshall, he heard Bullock mutter 'yes you do,' Marshall ignored it and said, 'but he's a tosser.' Michael had a sinking feeling their time here could pass very slowly. Michael had been pondering the point that no-one had specified how long they'd be here, or what the duration was of this "project." Perhaps Conway would enlighten them. Michael reminded himself the less hope he had, the less chance there was of disappointment.

The accommodation was almost identical to that they'd had at Camp Bastion, except this was a bricks-and-mortar building rather than a temporary module. One single room with four beds, one full-length locker each, a toilet and shower room, and a small communal area. Michael couldn't imagine they'd do too much relaxing and chatting in front of a log fire, not here.

Singh shut his locker with more force than perhaps he'd intended. He paused.

'I've got to say it,' he said and got the attention of the others. 'But the more I think about it, the more I think this is a mistake.'

'Yep, me too,' said Bullock.

Marshall said nothing, but his expression demonstrated his agreement.

Michael sighed. He thought his team's compliance had been too good to be true.

'This has all been a complete fuck-up,' said Michael. 'But we agreed, the only way to avoid being caught in the shit-storm of blame that's going to happen is to just keep our heads down, get on with this "project," whatever it is, and get put back on operational duties.'

'We weren't to blame for what went wrong,' said Marshall. 'It was that MI5 Head of Section, she made a bad call. She should carry the can for it.'

'Someone should,' said Michael, 'but people like that only get where they are by being very good at not taking the blame for things. I don't want to mess with her or any of the other political-types.'

The others were silent. His reasoning had obviously made some kind of sense to them. None of them had any time for politics, they were soldiers, they did their jobs and followed orders.

With almost perfect timing a young man arrived at the door. Dressed in jeans, trainers and a heavy waterproof, it was clear from his posture he was a civilian.

'Captain Conway asks that you join him for a briefing,' said the young man.

'We'll be with you soon,' said Michael.

'Captain Conway asks that you join him for a briefing.

Now,' repeated the man, obviously a civilian who, in this place, had authority. The four soldiers looked at the young man, who confidently returned their gaze.

They followed the man down the road to another building, and into a small meeting room. Again, the room was similar to the one they'd been in only hours before, in Afghanistan. The military, and whoever ran this place, seemed to waste no money on interior design or pleasing decor. Conway welcomed them and bid them sit. The young man left, closing the door behind him.

'Let's get to business,' said Conway. 'I'm sure you have lots of questions, first and foremost is what kind of project you've been assigned to and when you'll be finished with it and back to operational details.' His words were met with four nodding heads. Michael recognised the mark of a trained negotiator, this man knew how to put his audience at ease, something usually done ahead of breaking bad news or preparing to manipulate the audience.

'This facility is a joint exercise between the Ministry of Defence and a private contractor who supplies a range of resources to the British Army.'

There were four intakes of breath, but Conway held up his hand. 'No, I won't tell you the name of the contractor. You won't recognise it, and it doesn't matter. What does matter is that the Army needs to get the most out of each and every soldier. There are fewer soldiers in the Army now than at any time previously, we need every advantage we can get. This facility is one where we test anything that might give us, give you, an edge. Here we test weapons, armour, training methods, medicines, IT equipment, anything that makes you better or more effective. This particular project is one of a number evaluating the use of drugs which increase stamina and endurance.'

Conway paused, no doubt expecting questions. The four soldiers looked at each other.

Michael asked the question. 'What kind of drugs?'

'Drugs already licensed and approved for use, but trying them in new combinations to find one which has a significant boost in an individual's stamina and performance. You're the next group to get one of the combinations. We'll get you to do some basic stamina drills, timed marches, the usual, then give you an injection of the drugs and do the same again, measure any improvement.'

'Sounds bollocks to me,' said Bullock. Everyone looked at him. 'Sorry, but it does. We're soldiers, not Guinea pigs.'

'I have to agree,' said Singh, his voice more calm and level than Bullock's. 'This isn't what I signed up for.'

'Me neither,' said Marshall. 'I'll test any new weapons you've got, but I'm nobody's lab' rat.'

Michael looked at Conway to see how he'd react. His face showed no emotion, no reaction.

'You have a choice, gentlemen,' said Conway. 'I have seen the report of your last mission. You can go back to your barracks and face the music, that is one option. But in your case, they'll be playing the funeral march. You'll be lucky to get away with being put on guard duty, you'll likely be Returned To Unit, they'll certainly split up your team to keep you quiet.'

Being Returned To Unit, removed from Special Forces and returned to the regiment from which they came, was the worst punishment possible. It would spell the end of any career in Special Forces, and would likely mean only limited promotion prospects in whichever regiment they returned to.

Conway continued, before any of them could argue with him. 'I'm not going to try and justify what happened, or say who was to blame or who should be held accountable. But it's very simple. You're here. You can stay here and follow orders, or you can demand to return to your barracks.'

'I say we return,' said Bullock.

'And do you really think,' said Conway, 'that whichever civil servant made a mistake is going to give you your chance to explain things and tell everyone how they got it wrong?'

Silence.

'Do you really think they're going to volunteer to give you a "fair hearing,"' the sarcasm in his voice was clear and obvious. 'Do you think they want you running around telling everyone what you think went wrong?'

More silence.

'Wise up, soldier,' Conway snapped. 'You've been shafted, so put your pride away, keep your head down, and salvage what could yet be a promising career.'

The silence that followed was almost stifling. Everyone looked at Conway, but each sneaked a quick sideways glance at the others. Who was going to speak first?

'Is it safe?' asked Singh. 'This combination of drugs, is it safe?'

'Yes,' said Conway, his voice back to calm and reasonable. 'As I said, they're drugs already in use, we're just testing different combinations.'

'How long will we be here?' asked Michael.

'A few weeks,' said Conway, 'by which time there'll be another crisis somewhere in the world which needs your skills and everyone will have forgotten about the other night. And next time you won't need lorries to come and rescue you, you'll be able to run all the way back.'

'And leap tall buildings?' asked Singh with a smirk on his face.

'I'm not offering you super-powers,' said Conway, 'just

more basic physical stamina and endurance.'

Michael looked at each of his team. 'I don't like this any more than you do,' he said, 'but I like the idea of career suicide even less. Anybody want to leave here and go and play politics?'

There was no reply.

'Guess we'll take your medicine then,' said Michael, 'even if you're not offering super-powers.'

———

THE TEAM HAD SPENT the rest of the day running around the road which circled the inside of the compound's perimeter, then working out in the gym. After the flight from Afghanistan and transfer by road it felt good to do some physical exercise. They'd eaten in the compound's mess, a large canteen area on the other side of the site. There were men and women in a mix of military and civilian clothing, some more casual than others. The team kept to themselves and no-one seemed bothered about trying to make friends with them.

Their "work" had started in earnest the next morning. Michael had no great love for gym-work, he preferred being outside, but Conway had explained they needed a basic set of measurements of their individual performances, which would be compared to later. They'd spent the morning doing push-ups and pull-ups, sprints up and down the length of the gym, while civilians with stopwatches and clip-boards wrote things down.

Despite his best efforts, "lab-rat" was how Michael was beginning to feel, and he could only imagine Marshall and Bullock particularly would be feeling it more. He hoped they'd keep it together and just get on with it.

Conway had disappeared soon after they'd started the gym work, he seemed to be a man who always had somewhere else to be. He'd so far given away nothing about his own history. Michael had no idea which regiment he was with or had been with, or what his experience had been.

The team stood waiting to be given their next exercise. The young man they'd met first approached them.

'Your next exercise is a timed march, in full kit,' he said. 'Be ready outside your unit in half an hour, a lorry will take you to the starting point.' The man walked off.

'What is he?' Marshall asked. 'Message-boy? Special gift: giving messages.'

Inwardly Michael felt pleased they'd be going outdoors, a chance to burn off some energy, and a chance to be away from people who wanted them to do something other than what they'd been trained for.

They were ready on time. Their kit had been waiting for them in their room, an issue each of Number 8 dress; Multi-Terrain Pattern trousers, shirt, lightweight jacket and windproof smock. All that was missing were the Tactical Recognition Flashes, the insignia on the right arm showing the wearer's regiment. Their kit had no TRF. Michael had the sense they were starting to operate outside the regular structure of the British Army, and this made him uneasy.

They only stood outside their accommodation building for a minute or two before an Army lorry appeared. Conway sat in the back and dropped the tailgate for them. Michael noticed Conway had no TRF either.

Inside the back of the lorry they found a rucksack for each of them. As the lorry set off, Conway explained.

'Simple exercise,' he said, 'you've all done it before. Rucksacks with a standard weight, timed run over a twenty-mile route, rough terrain. You'll carry one of these each.'

He handed them each what looked like a small digital watch on a black Velcro band.

'GPS trackers. It'll log your location so we know which route you've taken,' said Conway.

'So we don't cheat,' said Bullock.

'You can cheat if you want,' said Conway. 'This isn't Selection, there's no pass or fail, we just measure the route you take and how long you take to do it. We'll do the same in a week when you've had the drug and see if there's any change in performance.'

'And you do this for a living?' said Marshall. Michael couldn't be sure if Marshall had meant to be so dismissive, but that was how it had sounded.

'We all play our part,' said Conway, 'the only reason you use any of the kit you do is because we've tested everything out there and found the best available.'

They each strapped on the GPS tracker, and endured the frosty silence, like children in the aftermath of a parental argument.

Presently the lorry stopped, and they jumped out. They were at the side of the road, at the foot of the hills. A path led from the roadside up the green and rocky side of the hill and into the mist.

Conway pulled out an Ordnance Survey map of the area. He pointed out their route.

'The lorry will be here waiting for you,' was all he said. They said nothing as they set off, and were soon surrounded by mist, the road and lorry now out of sight.

'You reckon he's ever actually seen any active service?' said Marshall as they marched up the hillside.

'The only action he's seen is polishing a chair,' said Bullock.

Michael said nothing. He thought it was possible

Conway was a career desk-jockey, familiar only with the administrative side of the Army, but he wasn't entirely convinced. Soon enough the speculation stopped and they carried on in what Michael found to be a very pleasant silence. They marched strongly up the hill and joined a path which ran along the top of the hill and across the ridge to the adjoining hill. The terrain was challenging, loose rocks and small holes in the path would make short work of the ankles of anyone failing to exercise caution, but this was the terrain they were brought up on. This was where each of their Special Forces journey had started.

From time to time as they marched Michael reflected on his own journey, on his love of cross-country running at school, to joining the Army, to officer training at Sandhurst, to entering Selection for Special Forces' work. His was a different journey to Marshall's. He knew Marshall had escaped from the east London estates of his childhood, joined the Army and saw active service in the Infantry. Their paths had been very different, until they joined Special Forces, where they all became equal.

The twenty-mile march wasn't a challenge for them, especially since there was no clock to race against, and it was daylight, but they pushed themselves none the less. The final part of the route took them back towards road-level, and a path that descended gently down the final mile.

Marshall spoke, his words unexpected and unprompted.

'I'd do it again,' he said, perhaps feeling the need to make his point in some final way. 'If it came to it I'd do it again, cut through civilians to escape.'

Michael didn't slow his pace, he wasn't going to have a face-to-face argument. If Marshall wanted to make his point then he'd have to do it on the move. He said nothing.

'I'm not going to get killed just because some bad-ass

wants to put civilians between me and my way out.'

'Protecting civilians is what we're supposed to do,' said Michael. Neither Singh nor Bullock chose to join in.

'Normally,' said Marshall, 'on the whole, but not when they're between me and my way out with some arsehole shooting at me.'

'So the means justify the ends?' Michael challenged.

'If it means I live, yes,' said Marshall.

'If we don't care about civilian lives then we're no better than the people who use them as shields, or obstacles.'

'That's philosophy, I don't do philosophy,' said Marshall. 'All I know is how to do my job and how to stay alive.' Michael wasn't sure how much to push it. Marshall wasn't going to back down, that much was clear. Perhaps they just needed to put the operation behind them, the grenade thing being just one part of a mission which had gone wrong in so many ways. They'd learn from it, they always did. Michael decided the real crime would be if Marshall did the same thing again.

As they reached a break in the bushes lining the path they could see the lorry, with Conway standing talking to the young man, the two of them looking at the laptop the man held. Conway and the man turned to watch the soldiers approach. Marshall had stopped talking. At least he seemed to prefer to keep this discussion away from spectators.

'Welcome back,' said Conway. 'Time to go, it's time for your first administration of the drugs.'

THERE WAS A SHORT, sharp knock on Turner's office door and without a pause Miss Harrow opened it, and the Head strode in, not waiting to be announced. Turner stood in the middle of the room, waiting. He nodded at Miss Harrow, who retreated and closed the door.

The Head extended her hand first, and they shook hands. Turner considered her for a brief minute, his old sparring partner, his mentor. He caught himself thinking about the past, about things that could have been, and quickly put the thoughts away.

'Liam,' she said, her voice softer than usual, 'it is good to see you again.'

'Rosalind,' said Turner, shaking her hand, 'we always seem to leave it too long.'

'We do,' she said, 'and this time is no different. I am short on time, so I'm afraid we'll have to do the chit-chat another time. You've got ten minutes to convince me this is worth looking at.'

Turner beckoned to the chair in front of his desk, and he sat down in his chair. He had the sudden sensation there were three of them taking part in this conversation. Turner recognised the presence of Morrow, He was here, in Turner's mind. Turner locked away all thoughts that weren't to do with the matter at hand. Some thoughts would never be for His attention.

'I'll be as quick as I can,' said Turner. 'The Special Forces unit you were involved with the other night, I can tell you they are now part of a project being run by my division. This project will equip them with a communications capability which would have defeated the electronic jamming they encountered.'

He paused. She did not. 'Sorry, but we've already got a number of electronic counter-measures. The error the other night was to not foresee the need to use them.' He'd antici-pated this response, and prepared for it.

'What this team are about to get is a communications

method that would have cut through that jamming, through any kind of jamming, would work through barriers that defeat normal radio communications, underground, underwater. It's a quantum leap beyond anything any other armed force has currently.'

'Bold claims, I need specifics.'

Turner could feel the tension in his mind, a silent mental urging from Morrow to divulge as little as possible. How could he convince this woman to commit if he couldn't share anything with her? It would be like playing poker with only one card in his hand.

He sat back in his chair and deliberately dropped his 'confident negotiator' posture. Perhaps honesty was the only card he needed to play. Had his internal conversation with Morrow had words, Morrow would have said "share nothing," and Turner would have replied, "trust me, I know how to handle her."

'I have a dilemma,' he began. 'I have something I know will fascinate you, and you will want to take full advantage of. However. I have no data I can show you. I'm not the scientist responsible so I can't explain it in any meaningful way. I have none of the project participants here so I can't demonstrate it to you. But I know, if I make claims bold enough to intrigue you, you're just as likely to think I'm exaggerating and dismiss it, and that would be a tragedy.'

She thought for a moment. 'So what do you think I should do?'

'I imagine you've seen the cartoon, the king on the battlefield, sword in hand, telling the machine gun salesman he's too busy to see any new invention. What would the king need?'

'To see the machine gun in action.' Her answer was the obvious one, the only one, the one he needed from her.

'I can show you the machine gun in action, but not here. You'll have to risk one morning to see it in action.' He stopped talking. Her next response would signal success or failure.

Finally, she spoke. 'I need to have some idea what this project is.'

Success, he thought. Anything other than an outright refusal signalled success, she was now just negotiating the terms of her visit. But there was still danger. At any moment she could lose interest. It was worth taking a risk. He could feel the presence of Morrow recoil at the idea, so he spoke before He could intervene.

'All I can tell you is that it involves a drug. It's manufactured by PanMedic, a long-term supplier of drugs and medicines to the military. Doctor Tobias Morrow is the scientist in charge, he can show you everything. But the project is at risk.'

'How so?'

'Their IT systems are not adequately secured. There's an increasing risk a foreign agency will learn what they've developed and will have no trouble hacking into the PanMedic systems and simply taking all the project data. That's why I need your help to secure the project, while there's still an advantage there to be had.'

She held his gaze. He could feel Morrow's reaction to Turner sharing so much, but he had said what he needed to, enough to entice her. Turner knew this woman, he knew she had to be left to make her own decision. He'd said as much as he could. It was crunch time.

'Very well,' she said. 'One morning. To meet this Morrow and see everything.'

'Absolutely,' said Turner. 'He'll show you everything you need.'

NINE

Michael and the team had been taken to a new room in a new building. Far from looking like any medical facility the room looked more like a hotel lounge. The room was carpeted in dark blue, and four armchairs circled a low coffee table. All that was missing was a television and a fireplace. The team took a chair each and sat.

The young man (whose name Michael still did not know, but wasn't interested enough to ask) had accompanied them and now stood watching as four nurses, two men and two women, entered the room, one of them carrying a tray of hypodermic syringes and phials of clear liquid.

'The medical staff will give you one injection each of the drug,' said the man. 'You'll be given half an hour just to make sure there's been no reaction, after which you'll have another session in the gym.'

'What do you mean, reaction?" asked Bullock. Michael saw Singh roll his eyes. This wasn't the time he wanted any of his team talking about reactions or side-effects. Michael simply wanted this over with, quickly.

'With any medication, even over-the-counter headache tablets, there's always the chance, a very small chance, of an allergic reaction,' said the young man. 'Once we're comfortable you've had no reaction it will be time to do some exercises.'

The man headed out of the door. As he did Marshall asked, 'it's not like I care, but what's your name?'

'Philips,' said the man without pausing as he left.

Michael watched with interest as the four nurses gave them each an injection in the arm. The male nurse attending him muttered the usual warning, 'sharp scratch,' but Michael felt almost nothing as the needle went in. Within minutes the nurses had finished and had left the room. Michael had a sense of unease as the last nurse closed the door behind her. It wasn't the drug that concerned him, it was the "experimental" part of it.

'If my arm drops off I'll sue,' said Bullock.

'Oh grow a brain, Bollock,' sighed Marshall. 'There again, if you grew a brain the drug really would have worked miracles.'

'Oh fuck off,' said Bullock, and yawned. Michael sensed himself feeling tired. Not drowsy, not sleepy, just tired like he'd been on a long run. He looked over at Singh and saw his eyes were already closed. Marshall was breathing deeply and Bullock had already started to snore.

Michael had the vague sense that maybe he ought to be worried by this, but sleep had taken him before he could have another thought.

THERE HAD BEEN much fussing over them when they woke up. Philips said they'd been out for about half an hour.

Michael felt like he'd just woken from a light sleep. He felt refreshed, cleansed, but Philips insisted the nurses take pulse and blood pressure readings and a blood sample from each of the team, just to check for any tell-tale signs of a reaction.

Each of them reported the same; they'd slept and now they felt fine. The moment Philips showed a sign of suggesting that perhaps they weren't ready to continue, the team, almost as one, insisted they were fine and ready to do the gym session. They didn't wait for Philips to agree, they simply went back to their accommodation unit, got changed, and headed straight for the gym.

When they got there, the PE instructors were waiting for them, so perhaps Philips had relented. Michael felt a twinge of disappointment on being told their next round of exercises were all gym-based, he would have much preferred another outdoor march. He resolved to put in a good performance in the gym, with the aim of getting back outside as soon as possible.

The first round was press-ups, Michael and Marshall, as many as they could in one minute. Michael had no doubt Marshall would win, but he would never voice such a belief. He'd make Marshall work his hardest for any victory. The PE instructor stood next to them, stopwatch in hand. On his "go" Michael and Marshall dropped to the press-up position and started pumping. For his size Marshall was strong and fast, but Michael was lighter, it was going to be a test of stamina, who could push themselves the furthest, keep going through the pain?

'Stop,' said the instructor, and they lay face to the mat, gasping for air.

'Not bad, for an old man,' gasped Marshall, looking across at Michael.

Michael could feel the burning in his chest and in his arms. He fought it back to speak. 'Who are you calling old?' Marshall and Michael were the same age, to within a few months. He certainly felt like he'd pushed himself harder than usual. Had he pushed himself because of the drug, really? Or were they just expecting to work harder? Michael couldn't tell, he certainly didn't feel any superhero-like surge of strength.

Marshall got to his feet, not with his usual bounce Michael noticed. Marshall extended his hand to Michael. 'Come on, old man, I'll give you a hand.'

Michael grasped Marshall's hand and hauled himself to a standing position. For a brief moment he had the strangest sensation. It was so strange he could hardly describe it, a kind of tingling in his hand (obviously from the physical exertion) but also a sense of being bigger, sort of being able to hear more and see more and sense more and just having a bigger presence in the room. He dismissed it, perhaps just a moment of light-headedness brought on by the injection and the exertion. He looked at Marshall, who had an almost quizzical look on his face, and Michael wondered if he'd had the same experience, but dismissed the idea.

'Well done, gentlemen,' said the instructor, 'dead heat, and the same performance as last time.'

'So much for getting any super-powers,' said Bullock.

'Go on, then, super-Bollock,' said Marshall, 'show us how it's done.'

Bullock's and Singh's performance was no better than the others and no better than before. Michael was pleased no-one had suddenly turned into the bionic man, but equally he was concerned. Did they know this drug would enhance stamina? Or was it simply scientific speculation? Were they just four in a long line of Guinea pigs, each trying a different concoction until someone happened across one that worked. He didn't feel convinced it was the best or safest approach, but for the moment this was the job they were paid to do.

'Chin-ups,' said the instructor, indicating the high bar. Again, Michael and Marshall went first.

'You've no chance, pal,' Michael heard Marshall say.

'Want to bet?' said Michael.

Michael noticed quizzical looks on the faces of the other two and the instructor. He didn't think they'd said anything particularly out of the ordinary. As Marshall prepared to jump up and grab the bar and begin his attempt, Michael saw Singh and Bullock whispering to each other, no doubt having a little wager on who would win. Michael was confident with this exercise. Marshall was stronger but significantly bigger and heavier, and in this task that weight would be an issue.

Through sheer determination Michael beat Marshall's performance by two chin-ups in the thirty seconds and was happy to see a grinning Singh shaking hands with an annoyed-looking Bullock. He noticed, though, that each seemed uncertain as their hands parted.

'Sprints,' said the instructor, interrupting Michael's musings.

They all made their way to one end of the sports hall, ready for the timed sprints to the far end and back.

'Loser buys the beers,' Michael said.

'Where is the bar?' said Marshall, as he walked towards what had been agreed as the start line. Marshall had his back to Michael, yet his voice sounded close, crystal clear. Michael put it down to the odd acoustics in the sports hall.

Now that he thought about it, he hadn't seen one. 'Good point, where is the bar?' asked Michael.

Singh and Bullock looked at each other, then at Michael.

'What made you think of drinking at this time?' said Singh.

'I admire your enthusiasm boss,' said Bullock, 'but maybe we should get the day job done before we find the bar.'

Michael was starting to feel confused like he was taking part in half a conversation.

'Vince said "loser buys the beers,"' said Michael. Vince Marshall nodded.

'No, he didn't,' said Singh.

'Nope, muscle-man didn't say a word,' said Bullock.

'Can we focus on the exercises, please?' said the instructor, with more than a hint of annoyance in his voice.

Again, their performances were good, on a par with their previous time in the gym, but no-one excelled, none of them out-performed themselves. Michael was the last to run and took little notice of his time from the instructor. His work done, the instructor walked away to confer with his colleagues.

'So have I,' said Bullock, surprising everyone.

'So have you, what?' said Marshall.

'Julian said he'd seen better, I said so have I,' said Bullock.

Michael looked at each of the three. Things were making less and less sense, and he was starting to suspect something was not right.

'Julian never said a word,' said Michael.

'I did,' said Singh, 'I said I've seen better, Evan said so had he. We both spoke loud enough to be heard.'

'Sorry mate,' said Marshall to Singh, 'but you never said a word.'

'What is this?' said Michael. 'Is everyone starting to whisper half of each conversation?'

'I think that drug's making us deaf,' said Bullock, grinning. None of the others were grinning, not even smiling.

'I think that drug has had some kind of effect,' said Singh, 'and I'm not sure I like it.'

'Me neither,' said Marshall.

Allergic reactions were one thing, Michael thought, but any kind of reaction that impaired their speech or hearing could easily make them unfit for operational duties. This was exactly the kind of thing he'd feared, and he needed to get this under control as soon as possible.

Making an effort to speak loudly, Michael called over to the instructor. 'Where's Captain Conway? We need to see him. Now.'

CONWAY STOOD in the meeting room facing four angry-faced soldiers. There was a look of thunder and rage on the face of each of them, and for the first time in a long time he felt genuinely worried. He'd faced battle, he'd faced the enemy, but always from a position of being able to shoot back. At this moment he felt exposed, unable to do anything but talk, but he had little to say.

'I don't know what you mean,' he said, 'what has it done to your hearing?'

The four talked at once, each trying to make himself heard and understood. Conway held up his hands.

'Please, one at a time,' he said.

'Your drug has done something to our hearing,' said Marshall before anyone else could speak. 'We're hearing half conversations or something.'

'Too fucking right,' said Evan Bullock, looking at Julian Singh, who hadn't spoken.

Michael Sanders turned round to look at Marshall. 'Yes, I do,' said Sanders.

'Please, one at a time, this is making no sense,' said Conway, exasperated. He was ready with the protocols for allergic reactions, overdose, emotional reaction to increased performance, emotional reaction to no result, but he had no preparation for this, whatever it was.

'It's not making any sense to us,' said Singh, 'so you need to find out what this drug has done to us.'

Conway was at a complete loss, he had no explanation. He'd been told nothing about any effects on hearing, or making people talk in half conversations. Perhaps the drug had induced some kind of hallucination? Or disorientation? God-forbid it had induced some form of psychosis.

'Bullock's right,' said Sanders, 'you didn't tell us the whole story.'

Conway looked at Bullock, who hadn't spoken, or if he had Conway hadn't heard him. Then he looked at Sanders, and back to Bullock. Whatever was going on he had no idea what it was, or how to explain it.

'I'll report this,' said Conway, 'but in the meantime, you've got another march to complete.'

There was an uproar from the soldiers.

'No,' said Sanders, firmly, in a way that everyone could hear. 'We're not doing any more until we know what's going on, until we know what this drug has done to us.'

Conway looked at them and recognised a losing position. He sighed.

'Very well,' he said. 'Go back to your accommodation, get showered. I'll report this and let you know what they say.'

'Why not just get "them" down here?' asked Marshall. Conway wasn't sure at the moment he wanted anyone else meeting these men. They were too angry, and he had to admit he couldn't blame them.

'I will speak to my Commanding Officer,' said Conway, 'who has a direct line to the scientists in charge of drug safety.' He held his hands up to prevent any argument. 'I will come back with whatever they say. In the meantime, please, go and get showered, you're stood down from any further evaluations until we know what's best to do.'

Conway turned and left the room, trying not to look like he was rushing. He exited the building and headed back to the facility's main administration building. He was glad it was on the other side of the compound, it gave him time to think, to compose himself.

He wasn't exactly sure what he was going to report. There was no discernible problem. They could hear properly, that much was obvious, but they were talking in half sentences or imagining things being said which hadn't actually been said. He would, however, contact Major Turner directly, report what he could, and take it from there.

Turner hadn't told him much about this project, only that the drug was a combination of off-the-shelf drugs. He'd said this unit was temporarily stood-down from operational duties but other than that they were battle-ready soldiers, fully fit and active. Turner had said the drug could be a bit unpredictable, and he'd warned it would likely make them drowsy for the first hour after taking it. He'd also said Conway was to keep the soldiers going no matter what. That now seemed a lot easier to say than to do.

MICHAEL STOOD in the team's mess room, waiting for the kettle to boil. They'd showered one at a time. He couldn't remember the last time they'd done that. They worked as a team, they slept together, they shat together, they showered together. But something was different. Whatever had happened had made them each nervous, and Michael had to admit it might have started to make them distrustful of each other.

Coming to this place had seemed like the least worst option, but now he was beginning to regret the decision. This place, whatever it was, wherever it was, had started to feel like a form of limbo. They were outside the usual structure of the Army, cut off from the outside world by razor wire fences and armed guards who may, or may not, be military. Their only contact with anyone outside was an officer who reported to some unknown superior.

Conway had said he didn't know what was happening, but Michael wasn't entirely sure he trusted the man. Maybe Conway knew full well what the drug did. There again, it was possible Conway was as much in the dark as the rest of them. Did anyone know what the drug did, or what it could do?

A worrying thought wandered into Michael's mind. What else might the drug do? Had they yet experienced all its effects?

His thoughts were interrupted when the kettle boiled. He threw a tea bag in a mug and poured on the water. He picked one of the milk jiggers, tore the top off and poured the milk into his tea. He had never been fond of the milk out of the little plastic containers, but putting up with such hardships was part and parcel of life in Special Forces.

As if summoned by the smell of tea, the door opened

and Marshall entered. Without thinking Michael put the tea bag into another mug and poured on the water.

'Thanks,' said Marshall, and for the first time Michael realised he heard Marshall's words perfectly clearly, without Marshall having opened his mouth or moved his lips. He'd never thought of his team-mate as a ventriloquist. Could this be a part of what was happening?

'You're welcome,' said Michael. Marshall's eyes narrowed, and he looked closely at Michael's face.

'Do that again,' said Marshall.

'Do what?' said Michael, 'I'm only making you one mug of tea.' Michael became conscious of his mouth moving, of the air moving through his throat and the words being formed by the movement of his mouth and tongue and lips.

'No,' said Marshall, 'do that speaking without moving your lips thing.'

'I will if you will,' said Michael, slowly, not sure if Marshall was working up to some form of practical joke.

'I didn't do it,' said Marshall, 'you did. You said "you're welcome" without moving your lips.'

'You said "thanks" without moving yours,' said Michael.

Bullock and Singh joined them, almost pushing passed each other to get into the room first.

'Boss,' said Bullock, urgently, 'this is just so...' but Singh cut him off.

'Whatever's happening,' said Singh, 'is just getting weirder. Bollock-brain is starting his own ventriloquist show.'

Michael was slightly taken aback. Marshall often called Bullock "bollock-brain" or some other play on the man's surname, but Singh rarely used it. In fact, it took a lot to get Singh rattled, but now he seemed very rattled.

'No I'm not,' said Bullock, sounding more like an indignant school-boy. 'You're the one who's doing the talking without talking thing, and if you think I'm going to sit on your knee with your hand up my arse...'

Michael stopped the exchange. 'No-one's going to shove their hand up anyone's arse.'

'If Conway shows his face I'll do more than shove something up his arse,' said Marshall.

'Look,' said Michael, firmly enough to get everyone's attention. 'Something really weird is going on. We don't know what, but let's keep it together.'

'So what is going on?' asked Singh, 'whatever it is it seems to be between you and Vince,' nodding at Marshall, 'and between me and Evan.'

'I don't know,' said Michael. 'I don't know if it's done something to our hearing or our speech, and I don't know why it's affecting us in pairs.'

'Why this pairing?' asked Singh. Singh was often logical and analytical. Michael hoped his return to a more measured and logical frame of mind might help keep tempers and anxieties under control. He put tea bags in two more mugs, poured on water and added milk. Perhaps if they each had a mug of tea to sup on there'd be less talking and less wild speculation. Making the tea gave him a vital few moments to think.

'I don't know,' said Michael. 'I've been going over what we've done, but we've all been in the same places, done the same things, eaten the same food. I can't find anything we've done or you've done that's been different.'

'Okay,' said Singh, turning to Marshall. 'Do it. Talk to Michael, do the ventriloquist thing.'

Marshall started to protest, but Singh urged him to just try.

Marshall looked at Michael. Michael heard Marshall's

voice, as clear as ever. He heard him say, 'if Conway comes back in here I'm going to tear his head off.'

'Crude,' said Michael, 'and would probably get you court-martialled.'

'Go on,' said Singh, 'say something.' Michael and Marshall both turned to him.

'We did,' they said in unison.

'You do it,' said Michael to Singh.

Singh and Bullock looked at each other, and a few moments later turned back to face the others.

'Nope, you never said a word,' said Marshall.

'Oh yes we did,' said Bullock, 'we said...'

'It doesn't matter what you said, the fact is Vince and I didn't hear it,' said Michael. 'But you did.'

'It's a trick,' said Bullock, 'it's got to be some kind of trick.'

Michael desperately wanted it to be a trick, but an explanation was creeping towards the front of his brain. He didn't like it, couldn't believe it, but it wouldn't go away.

'So,' said Singh, 'whatever weird shit is going on is between you and Vince.' His expression made it clear he didn't want any sarcasm from Vince Marshall. 'Vince, go over there,' he motioned to the other side of the room.

Singh looked around, then picked up a torn and battered magazine lying on the floor next to one of the chairs. He leafed through it and handed it to Michael.

'Boss,' said Singh, 'if you could read anything from that page, but read it in your ventriloquist voice.'

Michael wasn't sure, partly because he thought he knew what Julian was trying to demonstrate, and he hated the idea it might work.

Michael read from the magazine, saying the words without moving his mouth. Now he focused on it he found it an odd sensation, but somehow quite easy. 'The London 2012 Torch Relay will begin in a few weeks' time, and is expected to draw large crowds as it…'

'Now,' said Singh. 'Vince, what did he say?'

'He was telling me about the Torch Relay for the Olympics,' said Marshall.

'Yes,' said Michael, 'I was.' He turned the magazine to show them the page.

They all exchanged worrying glances. Michael didn't want to say it, probably none of them did, but it was the only explanation.

'So you heard him speak,' said Singh, 'but we didn't, and he read something you couldn't have known about, so you only know what he was reading because of what he said to you?'

'Yeah,' said Marshall. 'I don't get what you're saying.' Michael wondered if Marshall did get it. The man wasn't stupid, he could be quite insightful at times.

'There's a word for talking without words and hearing what someone says even when they're not speaking out loud,' said Singh.

'No way,' said Bullock, 'no fucking way.'

'Telepathy,' said Michael, finally naming the elephant in the room.

'Telepathy,' said Singh. 'It's the only explanation.'

Michael looked at each of his team, not knowing what to say next. It was ridiculous, it was bizarre, it was beyond believable. They were soldiers, they dealt in simple things, rational things. Telepathy belonged in the realm of science fiction and movies, it had no place in the real world, it had no place in their world.

'It can't be,' said Marshall, walking back to the group.

'That's just too weird, there has to be some other explanation.'

'Of course,' said Singh, 'of course there's another explanation, a rational one, a sensible one. Tell me what it is.'

'Well I don't know,' said Marshall, harshly, his frustration becoming apparent. 'You're the brainy one, you explain it.'

'I can't. The boss is right, though, telepathy's the only name I can give it. It's the only thing that fits.'

'It can't be,' said Marshall, 'they can't give us a drug that turns us into mind readers, that's just not possible.'

'If it was just one of us experiencing it we'd never be able to prove it,' said Singh, 'but it's all four of us.' He pointed to the magazine. 'We can demonstrate it, we can do it on demand. I don't like it, probably none of us do. But find me a better explanation, a rational explanation, and I'll gladly take it.'

'We can't tell anyone,' said Bullock, sounding ever so slightly desperate.

'Of course we can't,' said Michael. He looked at this team, not knowing how they were going to deal with this. He knew how they'd cope with an armed enemy, with hostile environments, with mental and physical challenges beyond most people's capabilities, but this went beyond anything they'd dealt with before.

'We can't tell anyone unless you want Conway and his mad scientist friends to come down and cut your brain open,' said Marshall.

'Not helping,' said Michael.

'One question,' said Singh. 'Why in pairs? What's the connection between you two and between me and Evan?'

'There's nothing different,' said Michael, 'no-one's drunk anything or been anywhere.' He reached for one of the mugs on the table. Singh too reached for the mug but caught Michael's wrist.

'That's my tea, drink your own.' His words trailed off as he and Michael looked at each other, both wondering what they'd experienced. Michael recognised the sensation, even though it had been only momentary.

'What?' asked Bullock. 'What's wrong?'

'Say something,' said Singh to Michael, 'say it without speaking, say it to me.'

There was a moment's silence. Singh turned to the others. 'He said he didn't care whose mug it was.'

'I did,' said Michael, almost smiling. 'Touch,' said Michael, 'it's about touch. Vince, you pulled me up from the floor, we touched hands.'

'And we shook hands when we bet the boss would win,' said Singh to Bullock.

'This is just getting too fucking weird,' said Bullock, taking a step back.

'No, he can't,' said Michael.

Bullock looked almost scared, shaking his head. 'Who can't?' he asked.

Michael said, 'Julian can't. Vince asked Julian if he could hear him. I could, Julian can't.'

Michael turned to Vince Marshall. 'Shake hands with Julian? Prove a theory?' Michael asked.

Cautiously, Julian Singh stepped forwards and shook hands with Marshall.

Michael heard Julian ask, 'Can you hear me now?'

'Oh yes,' came Marshall's wordless reply. The three of them looked at Evan Bullock.

'No way,' he said, 'no fucking way. I'm not having anyone crawling inside my head.' He turned and walked out, leaving the door open behind him. They heard the front door of the building open, then close again.

'You don't think he'll try and leave the compound, do you? asked Singh.

'Probably not,' said Michael. 'But if Conway doesn't come back with a decent explanation then we may all leave.'

Marshall walked to the door.

'Leave him,' said Michael, 'he'll come back.'

'I'm not worried about Bollock,' said Marshall, 'I want to find Conway.' He walked out and left the building.

Michael and Julian looked at each other.

Michael heard Julian's words, even though he knew no words were spoken out loud. 'This is another fine mess you've got us into.'

TEN

Michael was still in the common room with Julian when Bullock returned. He went straight into the dormitory room and shut the door. Michael felt a sense of relief that Bullock had returned, at least if he was in the dorm' room he wasn't likely to try anything stupid.

Singh had gone back to reading his book. All Michael could do was sit and think through their options, but he found he was just going over and over the same few. No new thoughts presented themselves.

The front door of the building opened. Michael and Julian looked up as Vince Marshall charged in, a look of anger still emblazoned on his face.

'No luck looking for Conway?' asked Singh, not entirely seriously.

'No, he's pissed off,' said Marshall flicking the switch on the kettle and putting tea bags in mugs. 'I see you're still here.'

'Yes,' said Michael, 'and Evan's in the dorm' room.'

'Why?' asked Marshall, 'have you sent him to bed for

being a naughty boy?' They all laughed at this. At least they were retaining a degree of humour.

'I looked at the front gate on the way passed,' said Marshall. 'Lots of cameras, lots of guns, if you look closely enough. They seriously don't want anyone leaving here.'

'I think for the moment we're stuck here,' said Michael. 'If we want to leave then we'll have to do it formally. Any attempt to go AWOL could be a big mistake.'

'I agree,' said Julian. 'I think if anything truly bad were going to happen, we'd know it by now.'

As if on cue the front door opened again, and in walked Conway. Michael could tell from his steps he was cautious, like walking into the lions' den. Michael could feel Marshall starting to tense.

'He's a superior office, Vince,' said Michael, 'let's not do anything rash.'

'Good suggestion,' said Conway. 'Is Corporal Bullock here?'

Bullock must have been listening because the door to the dorm' room opened. Bullock slid out and into the common room. Keeping to the edge of the room he moved round to the chair in the corner furthest from the others and sat down. Michael had never seen the man look so nervous or unsure of himself, but he could understand it.

'I've spoken with my superior officer,' began Conway, 'and he's conferred with the scientists responsible for the drug. They repeated they've never seen any harmful effects from the drugs, nor from this particular combination of the drugs.'

'So what's happening to us?' asked Marshall.

'No-one knows. Apparently, the scientists did see occasional odd behaviour in some of the rats during one of the experiments...'

Marshall cut him off. '"Odd behaviour!" Why weren't we warned about this?'

'Warned about what, exactly, Sergeant?' said Conway. 'The rats were fine, physically, but it's hard to ask a rat what it's experiencing.'

'He doesn't know,' said Michael, making an effort to be silent. Marshall looked at him, confirmation he'd heard Michael's words. 'I don't think we should share our conclusions.'

Michael looked at Singh. 'He's in the dark, I don't think we should say anything to enlighten him. Not yet.'

'I agree,' came Singh's silent reply. Michael inferred from the changing expressions on Singh's and Bullock's faces they'd also communicated silently.

'My orders,' said Conway, 'are that you're to continue with your evaluation exercises and to assess if whatever you're experiencing has any effect on your battle-readiness.'

'I'm not playing lab-rat for anyone,' said Marshall, out loud.

'I'm not suggesting you do, Sergeant,' said Conway, reinforcing the difference in rank, perhaps the only shield he had to hide behind. 'No-one here is a lab' rat. This is not a laboratory. Everyone in this facility is either a member of Her Majesty's armed services or is working for a private contractor supplying to the armed forces.'

'And what are we supplying?' asked Marshall.

'You're here, like all the other soldiers who come here, to help make our armed services even better. It's just that, in your case, something slightly more unusual has been observed.'

'You can say that again,' snorted Bullock. 'This is just downright weird.'

'Yes, it is. But my orders, and therefore your orders, are

unchanged. You're to continue with the exercises to evaluate any change in your performance.'

With that, Conway left, closing the door behind him.

'He's no idea, has he?' said Singh.

'Nope, none,' said Marshall.

'I have to say,' said Michael, 'all this does leave us with an interesting question.' He paused. 'Is this skill,' he paused again, still not able to use the word "telepathy," 'something we can use? Is it an advantage?'

'There's only one way to find out,' said Singh, 'and that's to play at good little lab-rat and carry on with the exercises.'

'Maybe we should just pretend we can't do this,' said Bullock, surprising everyone. 'Maybe if they think nothing's wrong then in a couple of week's we'll be out and back on active duty.'

'Nice idea,' said Singh, 'but I think the cat's out of the bag.'

'More like the genie's out of the bottle,' said Marshall.

'Interesting choice of idiom,' said Singh. At Marshall's look of curiosity, Singh continued. 'Genie derives from the Arabic, Jinn, a supernatural spirit of great power. The word Jinn can mean a spirit hidden from the senses of mortal men.'

'I thought genies lived in bottles,' said Marshall, perhaps deliberately missing the point.

'In more recent mythology, yes,' said Singh, 'but it still means a being of great power and with the ability to stay hidden.'

'Isn't the genie under the control of whoever rubs the lamp, or something?' said Bullock.

'Depends on which myth you believe,' said Singh, with a smile. 'But in this case, we are soldiers, we still follow orders, so to a degree, yes, we are under the control of whoever's released this genie from the bottle.'

'Julian's right,' said Michael. 'For now, we carry on, follow our orders, see what happens, and see if we can make use of this.'

'Oh I think if there's a use for it in our work, we'll find it,' said Singh.

'You can bet on that,' said Marshall.

'Ah,' said Bullock in surprise, his eyes widening, and for the first time in a while, smiling. The others looked at him. 'Betting,' he said, as though it was obvious. It was not. 'Well think about it, if I can hear you and you can hear me and no-one else can, we'd clean up at poker.'

'No,' the others said, almost in unison.

'No,' said Michael, 'we do nothing to draw attention to ourselves. I don't want anyone else finding out about this outside Conway's chain of command, and certainly not anyone outside the military.'

'But it's a good point,' said Singh. 'Not the poker, but using it in that way. Imagine, battlefield communications that can't be blocked or intercepted.'

Marshall hummed to himself. 'You can hide right next to someone and give a full verbal report without them hearing a thing.'

'So this might turn out to be a good day after all,' said Michael.

'What day is it?' asked Bullock. 'Just wondering.'

It was a good point. With everything that had gone on, with all the travel and changes in location, Michael had lost track of the days.

'Saturday,' said Singh, 'I believe today is Saturday.'

'So,' said Michael, 'our choices are we either make a break for it and try and get out of here.'

'Bad choice,' said Singh, 'very bad choice.'

'Or we raise this up the chain of command and demand that Conway's superiors come here and talk to us,' said Michael.

'Not much better,' said Marshall, 'sort of puts us back to where we were before we came here, playing the blame-game. But if things get any worse, that's our next option.'

'Or we get on with things, and see how deep the rabbit hole goes.'

The other three nodded, slowly.

'Okay, Alice,' said Marshall. 'But if we meet any Mad Hatters or talking cats, then I'm out of here.'

TURNER PACED AROUND HIS OFFICE. He tried not to come into work over the weekend, but this was a special circumstance. Morrow had insisted things move as quickly as possible, and so the soldiers were now in the PanMedic facility and had already been given the drug.

The computer screen on his desk showed the image from the hidden surveillance camera, an image from the common room in the PanMedic facility. Sanders and Singh sitting on one side, Bullock sitting on the other, Marshall standing, and Conway standing in the door. He didn't need to sit and watch it, but he'd turned up the volume so he could hear it as he paced.

He heard Conway explaining that some strange behaviour had been seen in rats. Turner smiled. Morrow had first observed some of his test rats behaving strangely, it was only later experimenting which showed the behaviour was due to mind-to-mind communication. Conway made the point the rat behaviour wasn't itself significant. It was a good point. How would you tell if a rat was telepathic?

His circuit of the office brought him back to the desk. He watched the soldiers' faces. They exchanged glances, expressions changed, and Turner recognised the tell-tale signs of people communicating telepathically. It took an effort to communicate that way and not betray it through facial expression. He watched Conway leave and resumed his pacing and listening.

The more he listened to them, the more he relaxed. This was a most delicate time. There was a very real chance the soldiers would simply be scared or confused by what was happening and withdraw from the experiment, either by demanding to leave or simply by refusing to take part in any activity. He wasn't sure what would be done if that happened.

He listened to them speculate about how they might use their new abilities, and he smiled. If the soldiers were beginning to look on this as an opportunity, as a strength, then it would be more and more likely they'd stay, and become stronger.

And what a strength? They would make an incredible fighting force for Special Forces Development to deliver. He started to think through various operational scenarios where their abilities would be an asset. Of course, if he had more of the drug he'd be able to create more of these soldiers. Perhaps he could create a new Special Forces regiment, of his own, a dedicated telepathic fighting force.

'Liam.' He heard the voice, and almost by instinct turned around. No-one was there, of course. The voice was in his mind. It was His voice. 'Liam,' the voice said again. 'It seems our candidates are coming along nicely.'

Had He been in his thoughts all along?

'You must stay focused, Major Turner,' He said. 'These soldiers are for our project, so our focus must stay on our project.'

The voice said 'our' project, but Turner knew it was His project.

'But they could be so powerful,' said Turner, out loud. 'I could do so much with these soldiers.'

'I know, Liam,' said Morrow's voice, 'I know you could, but they are for our project, and they must remain just for our project.'

Turner felt something. It was hard to describe, impossible to describe. He could feel someone else's thoughts in his own mind, pushing deeper and deeper into his psyche. Turner thought, for a brief moment, there was something else he should be doing or thinking about, but even that thought faded, and there was only Morrow and His project.

'Does Conway suspect anything?' asked Morrow's voice.

'No,' said Turner, 'I've told him nothing, he's just following orders. Conway's just the babysitter.'

'Good, be sure to keep it that way. Captain Conway is useful in that role, but he would become a liability if he knew anything more.'

'Captain Conway knows to follow orders and not ask questions,' said Turner.

'It is nearly time for the next phase,' said Morrow. 'You must make arrangements for me to visit the facility.'

'You?' said Turner, with more surprise than he intended.

'Yes, I need to visit the soldiers. I need to meet them. I need to shake each of them by the hand and introduce myself to them. Once I have control of them, we can begin their training.'

MORROW HEARD the last of his team close the door to the laboratory behind them, and he knew he was alone. Alone physically, but he could always feel the connection to the people he had established control over. It felt like being in a quiet room but always hearing a whispered conversation from another room. He couldn't hear the words, but he knew the conversation was there and could join in if he chose to.

With a little effort he could tune in to one conversation or another, and get a sense of who was there. He could sense each of the people over whom had control. He got an impression of the reluctance Falcone was feeling as he made preparations to get the Operations Director to come and see Morrow, and began to pave the way for more direct action if the Director was too stubborn, or too troublesome.

It wouldn't take much to change focus, and pick up on Turner. He caught impressions of conversations with Conway, reassuring the man, but making an effort to avoid providing any detail. Turner's thoughts flicked to the need to be ready to bring the MI5 woman to see him. He let his attention defocus again, and the ideas and impressions and senses all faded into the background. There were others there, a distant and muted choir of telepathic voices. They were all doing what he needed them to do, none needed any particular attention, not at the moment.

He stood in the middle of the room, breathing in the air. There was something about the smell of the laboratory he connected with. He yawned. The number of psychic connections was tiring, but there needed to be more. He had to agree with Falcone, reluctantly, they were at risk of being hacked by some aggressive agency, either state-sponsored, private sector, or organised crime. They needed to be protected, and who better than GCHQ. But this would mean he would have to take control of Falcone's MI5 connection. She, apparently, was their gateway into the world of GCHQ.

Falcone had warned him that Turner had said she was a formidable character, head-strong and focused. Morrow resigned himself to needing much more mental energy to control such an individual. There was a risk if he exerted only partial control she might rebel. Since she would have to be told the nature of the project she would realise he was trying to exert telepathic influence and she would turn against him. That would present a very dangerous situation. His only option would be to ensure he took complete control of her as soon as possible.

And then there were the soldiers. It had seemed a good idea to have a unit of telepathically controlled soldiers, who would follow every order without question. A unit dedicated to the protection and security of Morrow and his project. But now he thought about how much mental energy it might take to control such people. He knew little about the military, about soldiers, but he knew enough to suspect Special Forces soldiers were, well, special. Especially strong, especially resilient. Each of them would be a challenge to subdue and control, never mind four of them.

His telepathic control was strong, but perhaps not strong enough, not yet. He had been reluctant to take this next step. Each step had come at a price. As his telepathic control became stronger, as his thoughts could extend further, as he became more connected to other people's minds, he felt more and more distant from the real people in his life. True, those people were few, but now he seemed isolated even from them.

Now that he thought about it, he realised he hadn't left the laboratory in days, perhaps weeks. There was a small shower room, and he'd had a camp-bed set up at the back of one of the store-rooms. He'd not slept at home for longer than he could remember. He'd almost forgotten he had a home outside this place. He focused, tried to remember. An apartment, somewhere, he could picture it, just. But there was no-one else there. Once, there had been someone, there had almost been someone. Sonia, he had met her at university, but somehow she had faded from his thoughts, from his life.

'Enough!' he shouted, to himself. He realised he was sinking into a well of self-pity, and that wouldn't do. He walked over to one of the workbenches and opened the small desktop refrigerator. He took out a phial of clear liquid and set up a hypodermic syringe from the box next to the refrigerator.

Without hesitation he injected himself, pressing the plunger in a smooth action. He knew that within minutes he'd feel like sleeping, as the drug took effect. He'd need to go and lie down.

The thought came to him quite unexpectedly. If he spent so much time here, why did he not just have the company convert some of the storage rooms into a small apartment for him, then he could properly live here? He'd never have to leave. He would be properly protected. He could have them surround the research facility with a fence of its own and secure the walkway from the main building, then it truly would be his own fortress.

Perhaps, to this end, the Operations Director might be of some use. Maybe he would be better off making a greater effort to control the man than to have Falcone's contact arrange an accident. Too many accidents might start to draw attention, and that was something Morrow wanted to avoid, at all costs.

As he walked to the storeroom and his camp-bed he

thought about what he needed to do the following day. His plan was ambitious, his goals were big, very big. He would need the soldiers to protect him while he worked to put all the arrangements in place. There was much to do, and it would take time. This was very much a marathon project, not a sprint. He would need all the resources PanMedic could afford him, and therefore he would need the full co-operation of the Operations Director. But that would be for tomorrow.

Within minutes, Morrow was lying on his bed and slipping into a dreamless sleep.

JOON-HO'S HONG KONG office was, as was Mr Li's, unremarkable. He did not need to advertise his wealth or influence. Indeed it suited him to avoid drawing attention to himself. His office was a moderate size and comfortably furnished, but there were no priceless antiques, no valuable paintings. His most valuable possession was his computer system which allowed him an untraceable connection with his network of contacts, associates and supporters.

He used his mobile phone to make the call. Like the desktop computer, it ran software custom made for him by some very talented, and very expensive, Chinese developers. The software split the call across an ever-changing combination of routes and carriers, encrypted using a random cycle of different encryption mechanisms. Few people had devices equipped with the software and thus able to receive his call. His Russian accomplice was one such person. Joon-ho selected the Russian from the short list of available contacts.

'What is happening?' asked the Russian. Joon-ho

noticed the man's accent got thicker the more nervous he became, which made Joon-ho wonder how nervous he would have to become before he became completely unintelligible.

'Everything is proceeding according to plan,' said Joon-ho. 'The consignment will be ready for final delivery on time.'

'How will it be delivered? If your man was compromised then the route of safe passage can't be considered safe anymore.'

'No, it can't,' said Joon-ho, maintaining a calm and even voice, intended to keep the Russian calm. The last thing he needed now was for the man to lose his nerve. 'But as I explained before, I will deliver the consignment personally. I will use my contacts and my status to ensure the consignment is delivered without impedance or interference.'

'Where will you pick it up?' asked the Russian, 'I doubt you have it with you.'

It was a stupid statement. For a "technical expert," the man could be remarkably ignorant. Fortunately, Joon-ho would not have to put up with him for much longer.

'No, of course not. The consignment is stored safely. It will be delivered to me in Croatia on Tuesday, and I will deliver it from there to England.'

There was a pause. 'But you are due in England on Tuesday. What are you going to do? Fly it to England?'

'Yes.'

Silence. The Russian let out an explosive laugh. 'You cannot be serious, you cannot take something like that on an aeroplane and land at an English airport and simply drive it away.'

'That is exactly what I am going to do,' said Joon-ho, his voice never wavering. 'I have assurances from ministers of the British government I will not be bothered by their customs people and my personal effects will be transported, without interference, to my hotel. My personal effects will include the consignment. The government has even offered to arrange the transport and provide a police escort.'

The Russian laughed again. 'Only you could get the British government to deliver the mechanism of their own downfall.'

'Precisely. And I will deliver you safely in the same manner.'

Joon-ho thought he heard the Russian begin to choke on another laugh. Perhaps the man was now unsure whether to laugh or swear. He waited for the Russian to say something. He was in no rush to provoke the man. If the Russian felt in control of the conversation he was likely to feel more in control overall, and less likely to lose his nerve.

'You will send your plane for me? And fly me to England?'

'No. You will meet me in Croatia. You will confirm for yourself the consignment is in good order and is ready. Then you will accompany me to England, where the British government will escort you, and me, and the consignment to the hotel, and where they will guarantee we will not be checked or searched or questioned.'

Joon-ho had made sure that, over the years, he had been seen as a financial supporter of the Beijing Olympic games, and a supporter of London's bid to host the subsequent games. He had cultivated relations with various government ministers and demonstrated how several of his companies were investing significant sums of money in providing services and facilities for the London games.

When it came to the final meetings to hand over responsibility for the Games' legacy from the previous host country

to the next, Joon-ho was assured of his invitation to partici-
pate. He was also assured of the highest level of VIP treat-
ment, and that included being able to enter countries
without the need to meet any customs officials.

'And how will we leave afterwards?' asked the Russian.
This was good. If the man was asking about arrangements
afterwards then it meant he was comfortable with all the
arrangements before.

'The same way. The British government will close all
borders, ground all planes, but it will be keen to expedite
the safe departure of key VIP guests. The government will
have their police ensure our safe departure just as swiftly as
they arranged our arrival.'

'And then?'

'We will land in one of the Russian states, from where
you, along with your payment, will be free to go wherever
you choose.'

The next question was perhaps the most important of
all. This was where the final phase of his plan began or
came to a grinding halt. Despite all the hundreds of millions
of dollars he had spent, the years planning the operation,
the years cultivating relationships and making arrangements, it all finally came down to one simple question to
one rather ignorant man.

'We are about to do something which will change the
world. Are you really ready to do this?' asked Joon-ho.

There was no hesitation. 'I am ready. The West has
embarrassed Russia too often, insulted us, spread lies about
us, and all the time the Americans have spread their own
empire further and further. I can't wait to deal a fatal blow
to the British government. As they fall, so will the
Americans.'

Joon-ho hardly listened to the little speech. In one way it

was good the man was so ignorant, he was all too ready to believe what was about to happen would mark the beginning of a new Russian age. It would, of course, achieve no such thing, but as long as this man believed it, that was all that mattered.

'Very well, then,' said Joon-ho. 'I will send you the details for Croatia.' He ended the call.

He sat back in his chair and closed his eyes. It was beginning.

ELEVEN

The Head looked out of the window at the futuristic blue and grey steel and glass structure of the PanMedic research facility. The Land Rover Discovery was a comfortable vehicle, and the chauffeur was smooth, but she'd expect nothing less from an MI5 trained driver. She and Turner had each occupied themselves with their mobile phones, engaging in email conversations and keeping in contact with their respective offices.

Now they were almost at their destination she put her phone away. She needed this meeting to take as little time as possible, and again she wondered why, other than her friendship with Liam Turner, she had agreed to come here. Turner, no doubt, had various projects which could use MI5 or GCHQ help, all he had to do was pick up the phone to the relevant Head of Section. She was Head of an operational section. This was, strictly speaking, outside her remit, but he had been insistent and had said enough to intrigue her. It certainly wasn't how she intended to spend her Sunday, but on reflection a drive out into the Hampshire countryside was probably a better way to spend a Sunday morning than being stuck in Thames House in the middle of London.

The driver presented his credentials to the security guard on whose signal the big metal gate started to slide aside. They drove into the car park, straight into the bay reserved for them. As they exited the vehicle a smartly dressed woman approached them, ID badge slung around her neck.

She introduced herself as Vicky McClure, Deputy Director of Operations. The Head thought she looked young for such a senior position, but also held a quiet admiration for the determination and focus it must have taken to get there. They entered the main building, signed in, took possession of their visitor ID passes and were escorted down corridors to another set of doors.

ID badges were required to open the doors and from there they walked outside, to the walkway leading from the main building to the smaller of the two buildings on the site.

'This is our specialist research facility,' said Vicky McClure. The Head noted the element of pride in her voice.

'What happens here that's more special than in the main building?' asked the Head.

'The main facility is focused on research into drugs for the mainstream medical markets, investigations into various illnesses and so on. The specialist centre focuses on research for more unique applications,' said McClure.

'You mean military?' said the Head.

'Military,' confirmed McClure, 'work for other government agencies, contracts for various private customers, specialist medical research.' The Head made a mental note to ask later what constituted "specialist medical" research.

It was only a short walk to the security coded doors

leading into the facility. From there they took the lift to the fourth floor. As the doors opened the Head looked out into a futuristic laboratory. It was dimly lit, benches equipped with items of technical equipment she didn't recognise, but it still smelled like a laboratory.

As they stepped into the hi-tech world a short, balding man in a white lab' coat approached. His spectacles were folded and sat untidily in his jacket pocket and his thinning grey hair was swept across his head in an untidy comb-over. The Head thought he looked every bit the caricature of the mad scientist.

The man offered his hand for the Head to shake.

'Good morning,' he said in a soft voice with a slight touch of a west country accent. 'I'm so glad you could come, I'm Doctor Tobias Morrow.'

The Head took his hand to shake it. As she did he smiled and shook her hand slowly. He didn't speak, but did look at her eyes, almost as if expecting her to say something or do something. She noticed his eyes narrow, and he shook her hand more slowly. For a brief moment his eyes dropped to look at their joined hands, as though something was wrong with her handshake.

She let go and pulled her hand back. The man looked quizzical and was now acting strangely, and she had the sense that unless things turned around very quickly she would be making an early exit, friendship with Liam Turner or no friendship.

'Major Turner was most insistent I see this project,' she said. 'I suggest we get on. I don't have long.'

Morrow took them into his office and closed the door as Turner and the Head sat in the chairs facing the desk.

'I will be brief,' said Morrow, 'but permit me to give you just a little background information.'

He continued talking as he turned his computer screen for them to see.

'We were experimenting on varying combinations of off-the-shelf drugs, looking for combinations which would increase stamina and endurance.' He tapped some keys on his keyboard and the screen displayed a video. It showed the stereotypical laboratory maze with rats running around.

'I admit it's hard to see from this video, but we saw behaviour which was hard to explain. Rats would find the food in the centre of the maze, then other rats who had not been in the maze before were introduced to it, and after a few moments with the first rats the new ones went straight to the food.'

He paused for a moment. The Head thought it was interesting, or at least would be interesting for a scientist, but so far this was nothing that would justify her time or involvement.

'We couldn't explain the behaviour, so we gave the drug to some human volunteers,' said Morrow. 'We thought we knew what the behaviour was, but it was too incredible to believe, too extraordinary. We had to be sure, we needed hard evidence.'

'Straight from animal experiments to human trials?' asked the Head.

'The benefits of using off-the-shelf medications,' said Morrow. 'These drugs are already licensed and sold commercially. We're not doing drugs trials, simply observing the effects of different dosages.'

He tapped more keys and up came video of two people, both in white lab' coats, facing each other across a desk. The nearest person had their back to the camera, the furthest one was facing the camera. The person nearest picked up a playing card from the deck on the table in front of her. The camera, and Morrow's small audience, could see the card, the five of clubs.

'Five of clubs,' said the man facing the camera.

The next card, the man named it almost straight away. And the next. And the next. Morrow tapped a key and stopped the video. He looked at the Head, perhaps waiting for a response.

She looked at him, expecting more.

'I'd expect more,' she said. 'That could have been staged in any number of ways. In and of itself it demonstrates nothing, and proves even less.'

'What they were demonstrating,' said Morrow, 'was direct mind to mind communication. The one reading the cards said the name of the card to the one facing the camera. No words were spoken out loud.'

The Head looked at Morrow, holding his gaze. After a while, she looked at Turner. To her surprise, he returned her gaze. She had expected him to look away in embarrassment, at least a flicker of the eyes in another direction.

'Liam, you can't seriously tell me this is what you brought me out here to see?' she said, her voice sterner now.

'It is,' he said. For a moment she thought he was going to offer no more explanation, but he did. 'It is extraordinary. It is almost beyond belief. And like you, I required a lot more convincing.'

'Then convince me,' she said, 'and quickly, because I'm ready to leave.'

'And there we have a problem,' said Morrow. The Head didn't deviate from holding his eyes, but in her peripheral vision she did catch Turner turning sharply to look at Morrow.

'Yes, I thought you might,' she said.

'The two subjects you saw are currently at our military

projects facility overseeing the next phase of this project, which makes staging a demonstration here and now rather difficult. I had assumed you wouldn't want to take the drug and experience the effect for yourself.'

The Head didn't answer. She could feel herself tensing, a sure sign her patience was almost exhausted.

Morrow continued. She expected him to start rushing into an explanation, and then into pleading for her interest, then begging. To her slight surprise he remained quite calm. 'The next phase of the project, which Major Turner is most ably assisting with, involves the unit of soldiers you worked with the other evening.'

It was the Head's turn to shoot a sideways glance at Turner. Morrow might have security clearance for PanMedic's military projects, but he certainly wasn't cleared to be told about MI5's active anti-terrorist operations.

'The project?' she asked. This was starting to sound more than just the exploration of a curious scientific anomaly.

'Yes,' said Morrow. 'I've called it the Psiclone project, the ability to clone, or at least produce examples with almost identical features, numbers of soldiers with psychic abilities, soldiers who can strike like a whirlwind. It's a pun.'

'Yes, I get the phonetic play,' said the Head, she had no time to debate how clever his word usage was, even though she could dispute the similarities between a whirlwind and a cyclone.

'The soldiers are here,' said Morrow, 'back in the UK, at our military projects facility, currently being given the drug. I have observed them myself. They are now manifesting their telepathic ability.'

The Head stared at him. Morrow's claims on their own were fanciful. But if Turner had allocated an operational team of Special Forces soldiers to the project, and if those soldiers were, right now, becoming telepathic. She could hardly bring herself to speculate on such an outlandish idea.

'Think of the advantages a unit of telepathic soldiers,' said Turner. 'Communications safe from any eavesdropping, secure against any disruption. Communications which can work underwater, underground, which will work over any distance.'

Morrow shuffled in his chair. 'To be honest, we haven't yet established the operational range of the communication. It certainly works over several hundred metres, but we haven't firmly established the maximum distance. We've still some work to do.'

'Liam, if it were anyone else who'd brought this to me I'd be making a formal complaint by now,' she said. 'Extraordinary claims demand extraordinary proof. This claim is beyond extraordinary, and yet you've offered me not the slightest shred of evidence.'

Morrow drew breath, but she cut him short. 'No. Demonstrations on video count for nothing. You've shown me nothing I can evaluate. I make decisions based on my experience and on the data to hand. I have no experience of this kind of claim ever having been valid, and you have presented no data. There is nothing here I can invest in. There's nothing here I can even believe in.'

'Everything you say is true,' said Turner. 'And we're not asking you to believe.'

He paused, perhaps to give her opportunity to object. She chose silence.

'For the moment I can only give you my word that this is something I have invested in because what I have seen has convinced me, as Head of Special Forces Development, there is something here of significant military potential. We will, shortly, be able to provide you with evidence I am confident you will find convincing. However. In the meantime the project is vulnerable. PanMedic's IT security is good, but it is not bomb-proof. There are government and commercial entities who would take a very close and very active interest in this research, if they found out about it. At the moment, they would have little trouble hacking into PanMedic's computers and taking anything and everything they wanted.'

'And that's what you want me to arrange?' she asked, looking from one to the other.

'Yes,' said Morrow.

'It is,' said Turner. 'I think it's clear why I couldn't go through the normal channels to engage MI5's or GCHQ's assistance in securing the project. If you can invest two weeks to secure the project, here and at the military facility, I'll make sure you're provided with all the demonstrations you need to believe it was a worthwhile investment.'

She pondered this. It was a convincing argument, but only because of who was making it. If they were right in what they were claiming—she could hardly believe she was evening thinking it—then a unit of Special Forces soldiers who could communicate telepathically would be a powerful asset.

'Very well,' she said. 'Two weeks. I'll have GCHQ assign a senior IT security specialist here, and another specialist at the other facility.'

Turner and Morrow nodded their agreement.

'After that,' she said, 'I expect a full and convincing demonstration, or I will withdraw all support. I need to be fully focused before the start of the London Games, I won't spend any time beyond that on something which has only potential and no actual benefit.'

'In two weeks,' said Turner, 'I will show you just what a unit of the most powerful soldiers in the world can achieve.'

The Head considered him. She knew he wasn't a fool. Morrow couldn't have convinced him through theatre or trickery. Yet the claim was so outrageous it couldn't be true. And yet. She couldn't help but wonder about the uses to which she would put such a unit of soldiers. One use came immediately to mind, but she would have to wait.

Morrow paced around the laboratory. He'd made sure that none of the staff would be in today, even though it was Sunday. He hadn't wanted anybody else here for the Head to talk to. He had needed to be in complete control of that encounter. Despite his control, it had not gone according to plan. As he walked he thought through options and scenarios.

Within minutes of Turner and the Head leaving, Yves Falcone had emerged from the lift. He'd made sure Falcone was in the building, waiting to be summoned after the meeting had finished. He couldn't raise the motivation to smile at Falcone. He tried to contain his emotions, they didn't help him think.

Falcone frowned. 'Did that not go according to plan?' he asked.

'No,' said Morrow, 'not entirely.' He continued pacing. Falcone stood leaning against one of the workbenches and watched him pace. Eventually, Morrow explained more. 'I brought her here on your suggestion,' he said, the accusative tone clear in his voice. He would be more careful in future before taking Falcone's advice.

'Because we need what she can do for the project,' said Falcone. 'Now you control her she will provide the security we need. Everything else can carry on as planned.'

'And there is the problem,' said Morrow. 'I don't control her. I can't control her.' Falcone's eyebrows raised.

The burning sensation started to rise in his chest, and he fought down the anger. He needed to remain focused.

'There is an aspect of the phenomenon I did not explain to her,' said Morrow. 'I don't believe I've mentioned it to you. It's called the omega variant.' He paused. 'I call it the omega variant.'

Falcone said nothing. Morrow went on. 'We saw it in the rats originally, and I speculated it might also be seen in humans, but until now we've not seen an actual case.'

'She's able to block you?' asked Falcone.

'No,' said Morrow, as though it was a ridiculous suggestion. 'Not exactly. No, her mind is strong, but she would never be able to mentally block my telepathic control. No, she is an example of the omega variant, a genetic anomaly which seems to give some people a natural immunity to telepathic control.'

'So you will never be able to control her?' Falcone asked.

'No. So now we have someone who knows about the project, and who is expecting to be told a great deal more and whom I can't control. This presents a very real risk to the project, to everything I'm doing.' Morrow resisted the urge to say that this was Falcone's fault.

'Surely all we need from her is to secure our IT systems against external intrusion?'

'Yes, that is all we need from her. But that is not all she is expecting from me. She is expecting a demonstration, to be convinced telepathy is real, to know everything about the Psiclone project. After that, she will know everything and I will have no direct control over her, none at all.'

'Is that necessarily a problem?' asked Falcone. 'She could hardly discuss it with anyone else inside MI5, she'd never be taken seriously. Turner can make sure that she keeps the project to herself.'

Morrow took a deep breath. Falcone, it seemed, did not appreciate the scale of the problem.

'She is strong-willed, she will no doubt want to use the soldiers for her own ends. Turner does, but I can keep him focused. I wouldn't be able to keep her from interfering. She could start to become a significant problem.'

'I must be clear on something,' said Falcone, his voice becoming sterner. 'There can be no drastic solutions employed with regard to this woman.'

Morrow stopped pacing and looked at Falcone.

Falcone continued. 'She is protected by armed guards, she works for the state's anti-terrorist and surveillance organisation. Should any harm come to her there would be the most intense investigation, they would find who was responsible. There would be the most extreme consequences.'

Morrow had to admit Falcone had a point. The Head was probably someone who was better contained than removed. The consequences of trying any more drastic solution could be catastrophic. How he wished he hadn't taken Falcone's advice on this matter. Surely they could have found private contractors who would have secured the project?

'We will have to make her think she is included,' said Morrow, 'but keep her away from the more sensitive parts of the project.'

'Deception, rather than anything more serious,' suggested Falcone.

'Quite so. By the time she discovers there is anything more than just these four soldiers, the project will be too far advanced for even her to interfere.'

As THE LORRY grumbled its way through the country lanes and into the hills, Captain Richard Conway looked at the mist covered slopes. He always tried to be grateful for what he had and tried hard to resist the temptation to pine over the things he'd lost. He'd had his time marching hard over hills and across rivers, proving his physical toughness and his mental resilience. He'd served Queen and Country, defending the realm, fighting for freedom and democracy. It had seemed less romantic when he was sheltering behind a crumbling wall in a forgotten corner of Iraq, enemy bullets slowly dismantling it around him.

He loved being out in the country, but the damp weather played havoc with his lungs. He'd much preferred his time at the Division's development facility in Cyprus. The warmer weather and drier air were much more comfortable, yet he always felt an affinity for the imposing Welsh hills and mountains. The bomb blast had put an instant end to his time as a fighting soldier. The shrapnel wounds to his legs had been bad enough, but it was the blast damage to his lungs that had effectively crippled him.

The lorry banged through a pothole in the road and jerked him out of his reminiscing. He focused again on the things he had. He was still a serving soldier, working alongside the best soldiers in the world. The British Army; best trained, worst equipped, they said. They were sometimes right. At least here, in the Development Division, he could play his part in remedying that. He could test and evaluate all manner of resources which might give his soldiers an advantage, which might improve their craft of soldiering.

Soldiering. Surely that didn't include whatever these soldiers were doing? Turner had explained it to him, about the side effect of the drug, about what looked like a limited form of mind-to-mind communication. It still seemed too far-fetched to believe, but Turner believed it. Conway had seen it, and couldn't explain what he'd seen the soldiers do, so all he could do was follow orders, whether he liked it or not. He didn't like it.

The lorry pulled over to the side of the road and stopped. In moments the driver had left the vehicle, got into the car which had been following them, and disappeared down the road. Conway drew a breath and sighed. There was no point putting it off. He jumped out of the cab of the lorry and banged on the side as he walked to the rear of the vehicle.

'Good morning, gentlemen,' he called. They'd started to get out of the lorry by the time he reached the rear. Three of them were standing there, Bullock sat in the back of the lorry, dangling his legs out.

He pulled a map out of his inside jacket pocket.

'Right, two things to go through,' said Conway, keeping his voice low, as though any of sheep in the surrounding fields might be enemy spy-sheep. 'I've been made aware of your "new abilities." I've also been instructed to make clear the need for absolute secrecy around this.'

'Secret's sort of what we do,' said Marshall.

'This is more than just operational security,' said Conway. 'It's very possible you've developed a skill that would be extremely valuable to any armed force. Imagine if a foreign government found out what you could do.' He let the thought hang in the air for a moment. 'If any hostile force discovered what's happening it could put us all in very real danger. Not just you, but any of the civilian contractors associated with this project, with this facility.'

'Is that why you got rid of the driver?' asked Marshall.

'I think we get the message,' said Michael Sanders. Conway was sure he did, but he wasn't so sure about Corporal Bullock. 'You said two things to go through.'

'Yes, the second is this morning's exercise.' He unfolded the map and they gathered around him to look. 'You'll proceed in pairs, one pair will have a map and will navigate to this location.' He pointed at the map. 'The second pair will set off in that direction,' he pointed to the path behind them which disappeared up the side of the hill and into the mist. 'The second pair will continue for an hour. Every quarter hour make a random change in direction. Give no information by radio to the opposite team.'

'Then what?' asked Singh.

'Then you'll switch off your radios, and the first team will, if you can, communicate without radios with the second team and direct them to this point here,' he indicated another point on the map. 'Here you will rendezvous at exactly the same time. I'll be listening on the radio to make sure there's no using proper communications.'

'"Proper" communications?' said Marshall.

'I have my orders,' said Conway, 'you have your exercise. Once this is over maybe we can all get back to proper soldiering.'

Conway regarded the four men. He wasn't sure whether to envy them or pity them. Of course they were lab' rats. Given what had happened to them, what else could they be?

'Comm check,' he said. Each pushed in their earpiece

and pressed the connect-button on the radio unit clipped to their jackets. Conway heard the beep in his ear as each radio became active.

Conway gave the order and Michael Sanders and Evan Bullock set off, map free, up the path. Within a few minutes they had disappeared into the mist and were gone. He nodded to Marshall and Singh and they set off, taking the path heading in the opposite direction. They walked away from him and had soon rounded a corner and were out of sight.

What if all this nonsense about telepathy was true? What would become of those four men, he wondered? They'd never be allowed to return to normal duties. What would become of any of them? This wasn't the sort of project the Army would ever allow to become public, some secrets had to be kept, no matter what the cost. For the first time since that fateful day in Iraq, he felt a pang of fear.

TWELVE

Michael pushed in his earpiece and made sure it was clipped securely to his ear. He pressed the transmit button on his radio unit.

'Team two, this is team one,' he said, 'comm check.'

'Team two here,' came Marshall's voice, 'comm check fine on a lovely walk in the countryside.'

'Team zero, comm check,' came Conway's voice, perhaps just making the point that he was monitoring their use of the radio.

As they marched along Michael checked his radio was in its passive mode, receiving only. He checked his watch. Ten minutes until they made a random change in direction.

'So what was that rubbish about proper soldiering?' said Bullock, the edge of an unfriendly sneer in his voice. 'I bet that man's a career desk jockey. The closest he's come to soldiering is the horse shit from the Household Cavalry.'

'He is also a ranking officer,' said Michael, 'so keep the sarcasm in check.' Michael had to confess, he wasn't convinced of Conway's qualification to talk about "proper" soldiering, but he also wasn't convinced the man had spent his career entirely behind a desk. There was something about Conway, but he let the thought go. If it were important he'd work it out later.

After that, they walked in silence. As the path got steeper they put their heads down and marched, just focusing on making progress. Michael checked his watch again. It was time to change course. The path levelled out ahead of them, and to either side was rough grassland.

'Choose,' said Michael to Bullock. 'Left or right.'

'Right,' said Bullock without a moment's hesitation. They turned to the right and headed off the path. Their progress was slower as they avoided potholes and rocks. Clouds drifted across the landscape. Sometimes they had clear visibility ahead of them, sometimes it was just grey, limiting their vision to no more than a few yards ahead. Michael was quite comfortable with the terrain, but not having a map or a destination or any form of navigation was not his preferred mode of travel.

'This really is weird shit, isn't it?' said Bullock, almost at random.

'Yes, I'd have to agree. "Weird shit" is probably the best description,' said Michael.

'I mean, they gave us that drug and now we're Houdini or something.'

Michael suppressed the urge to correct Bullock, but he knew what the man meant. 'Yes, it seems we really can communicate mind to mind.'

'To be honest, I'm still not sure I believe it,' said Bullock.

'Well, said Michael, 'I think this exercise will show if it's real or not.'

'What if it is?'

Michael knew Bullock to be a fierce-some soldier, able to march into battle against almost any enemy. Their current situation, however, would be enough to worry anyone. He knew none of the team would ever confess to worry, let alone fear, but perhaps that machismo could be counterproductive. They were all now in completely uncharted territory, uncertain what the rules were, if any, and completely in the dark as to who might be in control.

'Then I think it's all going to get a whole lot weirder,' said Michael. He checked his watch and turned left. Within minutes the ground began to slope away from them and they started to descend. After another fifteen minutes, they dropped out of the cloud layer and had a better view of their surroundings. Michael didn't think he recognised their precise location, but he could see one of the big peaks ahead of them, on the other side of the valley. They turned twenty degrees to their right and headed in the new direction, picking up a path and picking up speed. Michael had no idea how far they'd travelled.

There was the beep in his earpiece, and they were greeted with Conway's voice.

'Gentlemen,' said Conway. 'Team two, you will direct team one to the rendezvous location, without using radios. You have up to two hours to reach the rendezvous point and you must arrive there together. Take out your earpieces, I will be monitoring the radio channel.'

Michael and Bullock looked at each other, and took out their earpieces, each letting them dangle around their collar.

'Julian,' said Michael, making an effort not to speak out loud. 'Can you hear me?'

'Loud and clear,' came Julian Singh's voice. From the expression on his face, Michael judged that Evan Bullock had also heard the reply.

'First we need to establish our location,' said/thought Michael.

'Tell us what route you took and everything you can see now,' came Vince Marshall's voice. Even in the sort-of-silent way they were communicating, Marshall's voice still had that sonorous quality.

'We travelled fifteen minutes away from the start point,' began Michael.

'In the opposite direction to you,' cut in Bullock.

'Then turned ninety degrees right,' said Michael.

'Had you reached the T-junction in the path?' came Singh's voice. Almost at the same time Marshall's voice cut in, 'was the ground rising or falling?'

From there it descended into chaos. Michael's head became full of the voices of the other three, all talking at once. He tried to make himself heard but as he made his voice louder the others matched it. It seemed that volume wasn't a problem with telepathy.

The noise in his head got louder and louder, to the point where he couldn't make out one voice from another.

'STOP, NOW,' said Michael in a silent voice but with as much energy as he could muster. His command was met with a very soothing silence. 'We need to be disciplined, otherwise we'll just drive each other mad.'

He heard or felt words beginning to form, probably from Marshall, probably some sarcastic retort, but without using words Michael held a clear thought of wanting quiet. The forming words became silent. If he'd had any doubt that their recent experiences had some other explanation, those doubts were silenced along with his team's telepathic words. There could be no doubting it, they were talking to each other by direct mind-to-mind communication. Like most surprises, their reaction had to be simply dealt with, and carry on.

He ran through a summary of the route they'd taken, the valley and the peak they could see. He used his compass to get a bearing on the peak. Within moments Singh's voice came through the quiet.

'We've got a pretty good idea of where you are,' said Singh. 'Head on one-five-zero. You've got an almost clear route to the rendezvous point.'

'When you reach the path, stop walking, or you'll go over the edge,' said Marshall. He gave them directions; take the path, drop down and around the end of the rocky outcrop. He gave them a position to wait at, to coordinate their final approach to the rendezvous point.

From then on, Michael and Bullock marched with a purpose, and without talking. It now seemed too easy, just walking to a point on the map, with no deadline to hit, the only hazard on their route already pointed out to them. He had to think, though. A team of soldiers, with no map, no radio, and no guidance, who needed to meet another team at a specific location at a specific time, would have no chance of achieving it. And yet he and his team would achieve it, and easily. Perhaps what had happened to them had just gone from weird to potentially very useful.

It took forty-five minutes for Michael and Bullock to reach the point where the terrain dropped away from the path. It gave them a natural point of cover, from which they could see the derelict remains of the farm shelter, the rendezvous point. The shelter had probably been last used decades ago by sheep farmers but was now little more than a haphazard pile of stones.

'We're directly opposite you,' came Marshall's voice, 'on the other side of the rendezvous point.'

'Then let's meet,' said Michael. He and Bullock marched up over the edge and towards the rocks. In moments they saw Marshall and Singh approaching from the opposite side.

'Okay,' said Marshall, out loud, as they all approached. 'That seemed easy enough.'

As they arrived at the derelict shelter they saw the brown and green square shape of the remote surveillance camera, balanced on one of the rocks.

'Smile,' said Michael, 'I think Captain Conway wants to take our picture.' Michael pushed his earpiece back in and pressed the transmit button.

'Teams One and Two have arrived at the rendezvous point, at the same time,' he said.

'So I see,' said Conway. Was that a hint of disappointment in his voice? 'Then I think we'll have to judge this exercise a success. Both teams return to the drop-off point. And bring the camera unit with you.'

The radio went dead. It was clear Conway meant they would walk back to the lorry.

As they set off the first few drops of rain began to fall.

'You've got to love the man,' said Marshall.

'Oh, I do,' said Bullock. 'Just a nice walk in the country. I bet he's got a flask of tea with him.'

'He'd better be in a sharing mood when I get there,' said Marshall.

'I'm not sure Captain Conway really wants to share much with us at all,' said Singh. Michael thought that was probably very true. He also wondered with the first exercise a success, what would come next?

MICHAEL COLLAPSED INTO THE CHAIR, mug of tea in hand. The four of them sat in the easy chairs in the common room in their accommodation unit. It wasn't the plushest accommodation, but they had all certainly been in worse places. With no orders regarding the rest of the day, they had time to sit and reflect on the morning's activities.

'Well that was fun,' said Bullock, looking at the rain streaking down the windows.

'Certainly a lot to think about,' said Singh, sipping his tea.

'How so?' asked Marshall. There was a lot to think about, but he was keen to hear Singh's thoughts. Singh more than any of the others, Michael knew, would have been thinking through the implications for the team and possible applications of their new-found abilities.

'We proved that we could navigate over several miles,' said Singh. 'We can operate as one team, navigate together, coordinate activities, all without radio.'

'He's right,' said Michael. 'With a method of communication that can't be hacked, can't be blocked.'

'Well that would have been useful a few nights ago,' said Bullock.

'I can't imagine we're the only ones who've thought that,' said Singh. 'This is Special Forces Development. Using new developments to get a strategic advantage is what they do.'

'So what are they going to do with us?' asked Marshall.

'I would hope,' said Michael, quickly, wanting to say something positive before anyone (Bullock) could get in with some negative sarcasm, 'we'll find out more about what we can do and then start to use it operationally.'

'So what else could we do?' asked Bullock.

'Surveillance,' said Singh. 'You could be standing right next to someone and give a running commentary on what they're doing and what they're saying. One of us can pick that up, and the person you're standing next to wouldn't hear a thing.'

'We could coordinate an attack in complete silence,' said Michael, 'giving each other locations and updates and sightings without making a sound.'

'Poker,' said Bullock, 'or Bridge.'

'NO,' the other three said in unison. Perhaps it was a good thing they were isolated in this facility, no temptations.

'Conway's right,' said Michael. 'For the moment we can't do anything that would draw attention to us. If anyone else got any idea about what we could do it would make us an immediate target for all sorts of really unpleasant people.'

'What I want to know,' said Singh, 'is does this work on other people?'

'What? The drug?' said Bullock.

'No, the communication,' said Singh. 'We know that we needed to touch each other to establish communication. But if we touched someone else does that mean we can communicate with them?'

'Or them with us?' said Marshall.

'Or does it only work with people who've had the drug?' asked Michael. 'I think there's still a lot we don't know.' He didn't voice his next question; did anyone else already know the answers to these questions?

The door opened and Conway walked in. He looked at the four of them and shut the door behind him.

'A successful exercise, gentlemen,' he said. They said nothing in return. 'I've made a report, and the scientists monitoring your progress will evaluate the results. In the meantime, you're stood down for the day.'

'Great,' said Bullock, 'because there's so much to do around here.'

Conway ignored the sarcasm. 'There'll be another exercise tomorrow. It'll be a familiar capture-the-flag kind of exercise. You'll use the simulated ammunition weapons...'

'Great,' said Bullock, again, 'paint-balling.' Michael glowered, not needing to use any non-verbal communication to make his meaning clear.

Conway continued. 'Exactly. You'll be tasked with coordinating your defensive and offensive manoeuvres without radios. We'll see how well you can communicate when things get busy.'

'Busy?' asked Michael.

'Yes,' said Conway. 'My superiors were impressed by this morning's exercise but said it was one thing to communicate when you're in a quiet environment with no interruptions. Now they want to see if you can communicate when people are shooting at you.'

Conway turned on his heels and left the room without another word.

'I think tomorrow we find out what happens if we try and communicate with someone who hasn't had the drug,' said Singh. 'Could be interesting.'

'And we get the afternoon off,' said Marshall.

'To do what?' said Bullock in frustration. 'There is literally sod-all to do around here.'

'He's got a point,' said Singh. 'I'm beginning to think there isn't a bar in this place.'

IT HAD BEEN A STRANGE WEEKEND, Anna thought. The week had gone very well, from that first nervous start voicing her suggestion for tracking the suspects. She'd gone from newly-graduated trainee to fully-fledged member of the team. She'd attended briefings, presented results, developed her approach to tracing silent suspects and shared her developments with other (and in some cases much more senior) analysts.

Saturday had been a welcome day off, and since the rain meant it wasn't a day for going out she'd planned to do some decorating in her new flat. It was only small, and on the outskirts of Cheltenham, on the other side from the Dough-nut. In the end she'd been too tired and had spent most of the time snoozing in front of the television or trying to cook a half-edible risotto.

Sunday lunchtime was where it had really started to become strange. She'd had a phone call from Brian Delaney, who apologised profusely for calling her at home at the weekend, but something had come up and they needed her support. Could she come into work? Now?

Anna had taken a taxi, not wanting to rely on the Sunday public transport service. She also felt she needed to be there quickly and to make a good impression. A well-placed feeling, as it turned out. She'd had a meeting with Delaney and with Geraint Evans. They explained they'd been impressed by her performance, and now had another task for her. It would require two days working off-site, on her own. They'd send a car to take her to the location where she would be working. Was she up to it? Of course she was. Later, she thought maybe she ought to have asked exactly what the task was before agreeing to it.

They had then explained the task, and it didn't seem too onerous, just a little bit cloak-and-dagger, but then what did she expect when she worked for the Government intelli-gence and security service? She'd been given a briefcase and an assortment of CDs and USB memory sticks, all laden with various pieces of software, the tools of her trade.

The car drove slowly along the pot-hole lined road. Although the Welsh borders weren't far from where she now lived, she'd never really explored this part of the country. Apart from the most famous "secret" regiment in the British Army, the Special Air Service, Anna had no real idea of what Army or other military facilities there were in the area.

At the end of the road was the high fence, the cameras, the solid gate which could stop a ten-tonne lorry at fifty miles an hour. She'd not been surprised by the armed guards, this was a Ministry of Defence facility. There were no signs to explain exactly who ran this facility, or what it was for, and Evans had been fairly vague about the whole what-goes-on-there side of things. All she knew was this related to recent activities, very secret, and the facility needed their IT security measures upgrading. Anna was to install various pieces of software to encrypt and secure data and was to report back with any infrastructure upgrades she thought might be necessary.

The car drove through the facility, passed various red brick buildings, and stopped outside one such building. A young man, who introduced himself only as Phillips, met her from the car and escorted her inside. Anna clutched her briefcase tightly as he took her to an office, and to the man sitting behind the desk.

'Ah yes,' said the man, looking up from a paper file he was reading. 'You must be the analyst from MI5.'

'From GCHQ,' said Anna, not wanting to be too pedantic, but some details were important. She regarded the man who had gone back to his file. Anna thought he looked rough in a potentially handsome way, but she didn't warm to him.

'Indeed,' said the man, looking up again. 'I'm Captain

Conway. I've been told you're here to install various pieces of security software that someone thinks we need.' It wasn't, Anna thought, the friendliest of welcomes.

'Yes, that's right,' said Anna. Perhaps the less she said the better. All she needed was to be able to get on. What had started out feeling like an important (she tried desperately to avoid the word "glamorous") assignment was beginning to feel like a job to be finished as soon as possible.

'I believe you need to work on my PC,' said Conway. He didn't move, or give any suggestion he was going to make anything easy for Anna.

'Yes, I do,' said Anna. She braced herself, perhaps better to get things out in the open to begin with. 'And then I need to see your comm's room and the main telephone exchange, and I believe you have some servers next to a project room.'

Conway sniffed, it almost came across as a sign of disapproval. Anna was coming to the conclusion she didn't like Captain Conway. 'Yes, we have.' He stood up and walked out from behind the desk. 'Begin here. I'll have Phillips make sure you're given the access you need.' Without another word he left the office and closed the door.

Anna had thought perhaps she'd start the day with a coffee, but that didn't seem to be on offer. She had no idea if lunch would be offered, but thought perhaps she'd worry about that later.

She sat down and began to examine the desktop PC. As expected, it had all the usual security and anti-virus software installed, so Anna wasn't entirely sure why so much extra security was required. However, she had been given the task, and she would do it as well as she could, not that it seemed particularly difficult.

Her first step was the CD of software to encrypt and protect the data on the computer. She set the software loading and sat back in the chair. She swivelled in the chair, and as she rotated one hundred and eighty degrees she looked out of the windows.

A squad of soldiers jogged passed, dressed in full combat gear and carrying rifles with yellow tags on the ends of the barrels (Anna knew this signified they were firing blanks.) She wondered for a moment where they were going. What were they doing with their Monday morning? Whatever it was, they would probably be doing something more interesting than she was.

MICHAEL HAD LED the team to the quartermaster's stores, where they'd checked out a full set of combat gear each. Now they were dressed in the black combat overalls, black helmets and face masks, black plastic body armour on their torsos, arms and legs. Each of them was armed with what looked like a replica submachine gun, and in effect, it was. The weapons fired a military-grade paintball, achieving almost the same rate of fire as a standard firearm, but inflicting non-lethal injuries. Michael had used these weapons before, and being hit with a shot from one was extremely painful. These might be simulated weapons, but they were in no way toys.

Conway had met them and taken them in the minibus to the combat area at the edge of the facility. Although outside the main facility itself, the area was a square mile of land within the MoD perimeter. The team congregated at their "base." A seven-foot pole stood in a small hole in the centre of the area, from which flew a blue flag. The area was bounded on three sides by brick walls. Stretching out in front of them was the combat area, littered with trees, piles of lorry tyres, brick walls, ditches, and the occasional wrecked car. The land rose in the centre, denying a line of sight to the other side a mile away. As Michael looked around he could see small surveillance cameras attached to trees and brickwork.

'It's a simple exercise,' said Conway. 'Defend your flag, capture theirs. Anyone hit on the head or torso with a paint round is out.' He gestured at the cameras. 'We'll be watching, so anyone hit must leave the area immediately. Cheat, and you forfeit the game. The game ends when one team captures the other's flag or when all of one team has been killed. Any questions?'

'How many on the other team?' asked Marshall.

'You don't have that information,' said Conway. 'But they have radio communication in their team, you do not. Try not to actually kill any of the opposing team. The exercise begins when you hear the signal. Any questions? No? Good.' And with that Conway marched off.

'Anyone would think he doesn't like us,' said Marshall.

'Plan?' said Singh.

'First priority,' said Michael, 'is to establish their strategy. They're unlikely to just sit and wait for us, the big question is how many they'll send to take our flag.'

There was a loud crack from behind them. The three of them turned round to see Bullock had taken the flag pole, put it against the brick wall and stamped on it just below the flag, breaking the pole in two. He'd picked up the length of pole with the flag attached, rolled it up, and stuffed it in his belt.

'Right,' he said with a big grin, 'let's just get their flag.'

'Nicely done, corporal,' said Singh. Michael smiled. Bullock could be an idiot and tended towards the bull-in-a-china-shop option, but sometimes he cut through to the simplest solution.

'That makes things easier,' said Michael. 'Two teams, one down each flank of the exercise area. Keep in touch and report on their numbers and movements.'

'Exercise begins,' came Conway's voice in a thin electronic form. Clearly, the surveillance cameras also had loudspeakers.

'Julian, Evan, that way,' said Michael indicating to the right-hand side of the area. 'Go fast and keep in contact.' Singh and Bullock held their weapons ready and jogged off around the obstacles, keeping close to the brick wall which marked the outer perimeter of the exercise area.

'Right, let's go kill some bad guys,' said Marshall.

'Yes, but no actual killing,' said Michael. He was sure he caught a glimpse of a look of disappointment on Marshall's face behind his mask. They set off, jogging in a semicrouched position, scanning the area ahead with their weapons at the ready.

As they stepped out from behind a burned out upturned vehicle Michael and Marshall saw an open area of ground ahead of them. At the far end, before some bushes was another low wall. Michael nodded to the wall. They needed no words, neither spoken nor silent, they knew how each other worked. They kept low and scurried across to the wall. Michael was about to leave the cover of the wall and head for the bushes when movement caught his eye. He saw two soldiers in standard battle dress leave the cover of the bushes a hundred metres away from them.

'Two of them,' thought Michael, he saw Marshall nod. 'Standard battle kit, heading towards our base.'

'Julian, two of them headed down the centre of the

arena,' thought Michael, 'standard battle dress. We'll deal with them later.'

'Okay,' came Singh's reply. 'Three just passed me, we have them in an ambush. Neat.'

'Our two have gone behind that wall,' came Marshall's voice into Michael's mind. The pair slipped out from behind the wall and into the bushes, moving more slowly now.

The bushes didn't give them cover for long, and beyond that was a jumble of piles of vehicle tyres and oil drums.

'Three down,' came Singh's voice. They were off to a good start. Michael kept a mental note of the numbers. Three taken out already, two on their way to the other end, to be taken care of later. That left five, possibly guarding their flag. Michael guessed that they'd have two at the flag with three establishing a perimeter further out, but that was only a theory for now.

Michael and Marshall stepped out from behind the bushes, at the same moment a soldier stepped out from behind a stack of oil drums ahead of him. Instinctively Michael rushed forward, still in his crouched position, firing rounds at the oncoming soldier. His gun hissed and rattled and banged as it fired the paint-laden bullets, decorating his opponent with wide splashes of pink paint. The man staggered, dropped his weapon, and sank to the ground clutching his chest.

'Contact, Vince,' Michael shouted silently, 'one down.'

'Two on me,' thought Vince in Michael's mind. Michael saw Marshall scurry behind a single oil drum, two soldiers advancing on him, one aiming for Marshall's right the other for his left.

'Aim right,' Michael thought to Marshall. Michael ran forward, firing at the soldier advancing on Marshall's left, catching him in the torso, at least one round hitting the man on the side of the chest, in a gap in his body armour. He heard the man scream at the same time he saw Marshall firing almost blind from behind the oil drum but hitting the approaching soldier.

Michael dashed to the man he'd hit. A shot from one of these weapons in the side of the ribs could be a serious injury. The man was struggling to stand. Michael grasped his hand and pulled him up.

'Are you okay?' Michael asked. Even before the man could answer, Michael felt it. He felt it in his hand, but somehow he felt it with his whole mind. He could feel the contact with the man, he could feel his mind moving through his hand and through the man's hand, touching the man's mind. He got a sense of surprise from the man, a sense which for a moment over-rode the pain in his ribs. Michael focused, and felt his mind rush with more energy through the connection. He could feel the man's thoughts buckle almost as his knees buckled.

Michael had an idea. It flashed into his mind, just a single thought of something that he needed to try.

'What's your strategy?' Michael asked the man, sending his silent words through the connection.

He both felt and heard the man's reply, unsure whether the man actually spoke anything out loud. 'One guarding the flag, two flanking in sniping positions, two men return up the centre to cut you off from the rear.'

Michael made a deliberate effort to speak out loud. 'You're okay, these paint bullets hurt like hell and really disorientate you.' He pulled the man back into a standing position. He turned to the man's comrade. 'You need to get him out of here, he'll be in a light shock to begin with, but he'll be okay.'

Michael turned to Marshall and spoke without speaking. 'Let's leave before he asks what really happened.'

Michael and Vince slipped behind the oil drums from where the two opponents had emerged.

'I heard,' said Marshall, out loud. 'Useful to know how that works.'

Michael broadcast his thoughts so they could all hear. 'Ten in total, five down. One guarding the flag, two flanking in sniping positions, the two that passed us will return to assault us from the rear.'

'How'd you know that?' asked Bullock, his jovial tone clear even in their silent communication.

'I asked nicely,' said Michael, returning the light-hearted sarcasm. 'If we touch someone we can establish a link with them, even control them.'

'That's useful to know. Do we have a plan?' said Singh. There were several ways they could respond. Michael thought for a moment.

'Vince and I will take the two snipers,' Michael broadcast. 'Julian and Evan, take up a position in the centre, forward of their base, intercept the returning pair.' Without a word, Vince Marshall jogged off, heading for the opposite side of the arena.

There would be questions and discussions about their latest discovery, about how to use their abilities to control people, about how far that control might go. Michael knew he'd have to leave those questions for now, they needed to focus on their current exercise and not get distracted.

Michael started to make his way forwards. One of the opposing team should be in a concealed position, forward of their flag. The trick was to discover the man's location without being seen. He crawled up behind a burned out vehicle. He could peep through the vehicle and catch sight of their opponent's base. There was no sign of the man guarding the flag, and Marshall's position was too far away to be visible. He could, however, see movement ahead. Someone was hiding behind a low brick wall.

'Julian, Evan, where are you?' Michael asked.

'Your four o'clock,' came Bullock's voice.

'Your eleven o'clock,' Michael thought to Bullock, 'contact behind the low wall. Shoot at him, I'll get him as he breaks cover.'

Without another word there was the banging and rattling of one of the paint weapons from somewhere behind Michael's position. Paint exploded around the low wall. As expected the man jerked to his feet and scurried to his right, straight into Michael's line of fire. Four shots to the chest and the man was out of the game.

'Target killed,' said Michael. From somewhere over towards Vince's position there was the sound of more weapon's fire. Then silence.

'One more down,' came Vince's voice. 'Idiot broke cover when you shot his friend.'

Michael crouched back behind the vehicle. Their progress was good, but they weren't finished yet. Singh and Bullock had yet to take care of the remaining pair, who would probably know by now that their team wasn't doing so well. Then there was the problem of the one soldier guarding the red flag.

The enemy flag position was a Ford Transit van on its side creating a back wall, and two four-foot-high brick walls on either side. Three oil drums were stacked in front of the position, obscuring the view. The lone soldier guarding the flag was in a strong position, as far as the exercise went. Normally a grenade would be his undoing, but here he would be able to shoot anyone trying a frontal assault.

Michael crept out from behind his cover and keeping low moved slowly to the wall which had shielded his previous victim. From here he had a clear shot at the entrance to the flag position. He daren't try an assault, but if the soldier guarding the flag came out he'd get him.

'We've got company,' came Singh's voice. 'Stand by. I have an idea.'

Michael waited. He was tempted to ask what was happening but knew the better option was simply to let Julian get on with whatever he was doing. He heard the weapons-fire and expected an update from Julian. But still there was silence.

Then he heard Singh's voice. 'Your target will be coming out in a moment.'

From the enemy flag position Michael heard the electronic voice from a radio, the thin metallic voice from the handheld radio unit. Apparently, the opposing team had radios but not earpieces. Someone was communicating with the soldier guarding the flag. Michael stared at the entrance to the flag position, his weapon held ready to fire. He heard another couple of rounds of weapons' fire from behind. Julian, or Evan, had found someone else to shoot at.

The soldier guarding the flag walked out, holding his weapon casually by his side. The man was hit with simultaneous fire from Michael and Vince Marshall. Out of sheer fright and surprise he dropped to the ground, his weapon tumbling away from him. In an instant Michael and Marshall were moving, weapons still held forward, just in case.

They stepped over the groaning soldier and Marshall pulled the flagpole out of its hole.

'Exercise ended,' came Conway's voice from the loudspeakers.

The lone guard staggered to his feet and, muttering curses under his breath, limped away to the edge of the exercise area. Marshall dropped the flagpole to the ground in front of the enemy position. He and Michael pulled off their masks, Singh and Bullock walked out from behind a pile of tyres, weapons and masks in hand.

From the direction of the departing soldiers came Conway. Michael had half expected him to be smiling. The exercise had been a success, surely he would be pleased? But instead he wore his usual half-frown.

'Congratulations,' he said, sounding like he meant none of it. 'It did all look rather easy though.'

'Do you want to play?' asked Marshall, offering his weapon towards Conway. Conway ignored the gesture.

'Perhaps we can devise an exercise where you're being shot at, where you are under some real pressure, see what happens then,' said Conway.

'With limited information, no radio communication and three-to-one odds, I think we did alright,' said Michael.

Again, Conway ignored the comment. 'You'll have another evaluation session in the gym this afternoon.' He turned around and walked away.

'Looks like we're walking back again,' said Marshall. The four of them walked towards the exit from the exercise area. As expected, there was no vehicle waiting for them. Marshall and Bullock marched ahead, exchanging ever more vulgar opinions of Conway.

'I could murder a pint,' said Michael to Julian Singh.

'I know what you mean,' said Singh. 'I've come to the conclusion that this facility is a very boring place.'

'Maybe we need to make alternative arrangements,' said Michael.

THIRTEEN

The Palace of Westminster, the seat of the British Government, was not exactly the best place to review top secret documents, but Turner had managed to find a quiet corner in a meeting room. He was able to sit with the laptop balanced on his lap, facing outwards with no opportunity for anyone to stand behind him. He checked his watch, he had a short time before his meeting with the Minister.

He spent a few minutes skimming through the latest report from Conway, outlining the progress of the soldiers in their capture-the-flag exercise. He looked through some of the videos which had been edited together and read the summary notes Conway had made. Of course, there was no sound on the video worth listening to, which made it all the more impressive.

Turner was particularly intrigued with the clip of Singh staring into the eyes of one of the 'enemy' soldiers, after which the soldier spoke into his microphone and told his comrades they'd won and it was safe to come out. Perhaps he should have been surprised the soldiers had reached this stage of development so soon, but then again they were particularly focused and driven individuals, which was why they had been selected.

Turner snapped his laptop shut, gathered his briefcase and reminded himself where the Minister's meeting was being held. It was at that moment he heard Morrow's voice come into his mind.

'Not now,' Turner almost said. He nearly said it out loud and had almost said it in his mind to Morrow.

'I need to know how they are progressing?' said Morrow, apparently paying no heed to Turner's annoyance at the timing, and seemingly unconcerned whether Turner had time to communicate.

'They are developing quickly,' thought Turner. 'They're able to work together, use their abilities to coordinate and communicate.' Turner was about to say something else but hesitated. He knew as soon as he had done it that He would pick up on the hesitation, as though He could hear it as clearly as He heard words.

'What else, Liam?'

'They've already discovered how to take control of other people.'

Turner could imagine Morrow pacing around his laboratory, hands clasped behind his back as he thought about the implications.

'I need to visit the facility as soon as possible,' said Morrow. 'I need to meet each of the soldiers. I need to take control of them.'

'It may take a little time to arrange a visit,' said Turner.

'It needs to be as soon as possible,' said Morrow, 'it needs to be today.'

'I can't arrange it that quickly,' said Turner. 'It will take at least a couple of days.'

'That's not soon enough, Liam,' He said. 'It is too risky to leave them any longer.'

'What risk?' asked Turner. 'They're inside a secure facility, they're not going anywhere.'

'Aren't they?' He asked. 'They've learned how to control others. How long before they decide to take control of some of the staff at the facility? Or of Conway? They're in a secure facility, but they effectively have the keys to every door they might want to go through.'

Turner thought about this. It did indeed seem a risk. But risk or no risk, the more he thought about it the more he was certain he could arrange nothing today, and probably not even tomorrow.

Morrow continued. 'The genie is out of the bottle, Liam. How long before the genie decides to take over? I imagine they're still thinking about the military applications of their abilities, but how soon before they imagine what else they'll be able to do?'

'So what do we do?' asked Turner. He looked around at the few occupants of the other chairs in the room, none seemed to have noticed him say anything, and he felt more confident he hadn't spoken out loud. 'We could split them up. Hold them in solitary confinement until you get there.'

'That would only work if you could put each in a separate cell. Even then they would be able to communicate. After a day or two in solitary they would be very difficult to approach safely.'

'So what do you suggest?' asked Turner.

'We need to make them think that using their abilities would lead to discovery, with dire consequences,' thought Morrow.

'How would we do that?' thought Turner. 'How would you tell if someone's been subject to a telepathic influence?'

'We don't need to,' said Morrow. 'We only need them to believe it's possible, and they only need to believe for a short time.'

'So we need to convince them that we can do some sort of test and tell if they've controlled someone?'

A woman stepped into the meeting room and stood looking at Turner. She made a point of clearing her throat, loudly. Turner looked up.

'The Minister is waiting, Major Turner,' the woman said and left the room. Turner checked his watch. Damn. He was late for the Minister.

'Yes,' thought Morrow, sounding satisfied. 'Yes, a test. We can tell them that we can test the personnel in the facility.' Morrow was obviously making this up as he went along. Turner stayed silent and let Morrow continue. 'We could have Conway tell them a blood test has been developed, which tests for a protein marker released when someone is subject to a telepathic link. Everyone on the base will have a finger-prick test twice a day, or more.'

'So they'll think that any control of anyone on the base would be discovered within half a day?' said Turner. 'What would we have them believe the consequence would be if they were discovered? There are already those in the facility who know about their development.'

There was a moment's silence as Morrow thought, but it was Turner who had the idea.

'The more people who know the more likely the Minister will find out, and if that happens they become Government property, beyond our power to protect them,' said Turner.

'Very good, Major,' said Morrow. 'Make sure Conway makes that clear to the men.'

'I will,' said Turner.

'And Major, I need to visit as soon as possible. This ruse will not work for long. I need to take control of these men as soon as possible.'

'I'll arrange your visit as soon as I can.' Turner got up and headed for the door. He hoped he'd be able to carry on the conversation as he walked towards the meeting room and the Minister, but all had gone quiet. It seemed, for the moment, Morrow was satisfied with the progress, and with the arrangements he was about to make.

CAPTAIN CONWAY MARCHED towards the accommodation block. While the team had been in the gym for their next round of evaluation exercises, he'd called into the office to check on the progress of the MI5 woman, and had had to ask her to leave when Major Turner rang.

Turner had not, of course, given Conway a huge amount of information, but he had explained a few things, and for a moment Conway had wondered if this "project" was going to end sooner than expected. Now he had time to think about it, he thought it was probably wishful thinking. The project was likely to last the full two weeks, and a cynical part of him suspected it might last longer than that.

There was a rather intriguing new incendiary explosive he'd been made aware of. A small team of soldiers were due the day after tomorrow to begin testing the explosive; that was a project Conway was looking forward to. As he marched he thought about the various scenarios they could run with the explosive, the different ways in which they could test its potential, and discover any pitfalls or drawbacks.

All too soon he arrived at the accommodation block, and was disappointed to find the team had finished in the gym, had showered, and were now sitting down to yet another round of mugs of tea. Perhaps, he thought, there was nothing special about these men after all. Perhaps they were simply hallucinating because of an excess of tea. He wondered, was it possible to get tea poisoning?

He marched into the common room and closed the door behind him. The four soldiers were all sitting. The two facing the door looked up at him, but the two with their backs to him did not look around.

He thought for a moment what to say, but decided quickly not to waste time making any small talk or with any pleasantries.

'I have an update for you,' he said and waited for a response. There was none. He regarded the two with their backs to him. 'I'd appreciate it if you'd at least face a superior officer when he's addressing you.'

Marshall and Bullock shuffled their chairs round to face him, not making any effort to do it quickly.

'I don't mean to be rude,' said Singh, 'but is this going to take long?'

'Why?' asked Conway, 'going somewhere?' He almost smiled.

'As it happens, yes,' said Singh.

Conway's almost-smile faded away, and a frown took its place.

'What do you mean, you're going somewhere?' he sighed.

'We've had a very busy time recently,' said Michael Sanders. 'We were transferred here directly from active duty in Afghanistan. It's been a busy few days here, and a lot's happened.'

'So?'

'So we're going to go into town for a drink this evening,' said Sanders.

'No you're not,' said Conway, fighting the urge to say it any more loudly. 'You have no permission to leave this facility.'

'You can come with us,' said Bullock, that stupid grin on his face. Conway was certain the offer was meant only as sarcasm.

'You're not allowed out of this facility,' repeated Conway.

'Why not?' asked Marshall. His voice was lower and slower than usual, and for a moment Conway thought it made the man even more intimidating.

'Because, as I've explained, it's too much of a risk,' said Conway. 'If any suggestion gets out of what's happening here...'

Sanders cut him off. 'With respect, sir, I don't believe Bishop's Fort is crawling with Russian spies, and I think we can be trusted to act with discretion.'

'Can you?' asked Conway.

'Yes,' said Marshall, not inviting any further discussion.

Conway didn't care, Sergeant's didn't tell Captains when a conversation was over.

'It seems your activities of a few nights ago were anything but discreet,' said Conway. 'So you'll forgive me if I'm not convinced that you can keep quiet and go unnoticed.'

'Captain,' said Sanders. 'To be fair, other than the other night, keeping quiet and going un-noticed is what we specialise in. Going to one pub for a drink and staying out of trouble is not a problem.'

'No. I'm sorry. It is still too great a risk to allow you off this facility,' said Conway.

'So we're prisoners?' said Singh.

Conway suppressed another sigh. He did wonder sometimes if these "special" forces soldiers were worth the aggravation they came with. Their lax approach to discipline might work well for them, out in the field, but it made everybody else's lives more difficult. In some way, regular soldiers were just easier to work with.

'No,' he said, stifling a growing urge to resort to orders and authority. 'You are not prisoners, but you do not have my permission to leave this facility.'

'So you're using your permission as a chain, as a way of keeping the door shut to us,' said Singh. 'So, in other words, we are prisoners.'

'You are soldiers who work within the authority structure of the Army,' said Conway, becoming more desperate to think of a form of logic that would work with these men. 'And at the moment you do not have my authority to leave this facility.'

'But in fact,' said Sanders, 'you are not our commanding officer. We agreed to join a project which you are managing for the Army, but we do not take our operational orders from you.'

Conway stared at him. He could find no way passed this. Turner had been quite clear that they were not, in any way, to be given the impression they were being held against their will.

'There is something else I need to tell you about,' said Conway, now wishing he'd chosen to sit down.

The four soldiers did lean slightly more towards him. Perhaps now he had more of their attention.

'For the few people who know anything about this

project or about your abilities,' said Conway, 'discovery is the greatest risk. There is a concern that anyone who has this ability might be tempted to use it outside the bounds of an exercise or an operation. That would pose a significant security risk, the dangers of which have been made clear.'

Conway was aware he was beginning to sound like a school teacher reprimanding a class of naughty school children.

He continued. 'They've identified a blood test that will show if someone's been subjected to any unauthorised influence.'

'So now they want more blood from us,' said Bullock.

'No, I don't think the blood test is for us,' said Singh.

'Correct, Lieutenant,' said Conway. 'Staff in this facility will be monitored regularly, to make sure you've not subjected any of them to any unauthorised influence.'

'It sounds like someone doesn't trust us,' said Bullock. For once, Conway thought, Bullock had actually understood the situation, but he said nothing in reply.

'It's for your own protection,' said Conway.

'Well if we're safe,' said Sanders, 'then we're safe to be let out. We'll catch a taxi from the end of the road and go into town this evening.' It was said as a statement of fact.

'One of the scientists is coming to see you tomorrow,' said Conway, making sure he got out the next piece of information before anyone moved the conversation on.

'Don't worry,' said Marshall, grinning again, 'we'll be back early and we'll behave tomorrow.'

Conway considered the situation for a moment. It seemed there was no point continuing this discussion any further.

'Very well,' he said, and left the room.

As he walked back towards the office he felt the anger

growing inside. He so much wanted to find a way to be rid of these men. Perhaps if they were stupid this evening they'd be disciplined, or even just re-assigned. But then if they drew attention to themselves it would likely be more than just them who would suffer the consequences. He could only hope that this visiting scientist would decide to whisk them away and experiment on them somewhere else.

AFTER THE RECENT RAIN, the air was fresh and invigorating. Michael had found the confines of the facility becoming almost stifling, even though much of their work had been outdoors. Being outside the gates and the guards felt fresher, he felt refreshed.

To his slight surprise the gate had opened as they approached it, and they'd walked down the road to the main road, where a taxi had been waiting, as arranged. It was a short journey to the outskirts of Bishop's Fort. They each had a small selection of civilian clothing with them in their kit bags, so now Michael felt mercifully free of uniform and weapons and communications devices. For a while he almost felt normal.

They'd asked to be dropped at the edge of the town, and the taxi driver left them with directions to what she said was the best pub in the town, about a mile's walk from where she left them. The road took them passed rows of middle-of-the-century single-storey dwellings, an occasional shop, a house or two dating from much earlier times. It seemed few people bothered going out on a Saturday night in Bishop's Fort.

'Is it just me?' asked Bullock, for no apparent reason, 'or

is anyone else wondering just what the hell else we can do with our "gift"?'

Michael was curious, it seemed no-one wanted to use the word 'telepathy.'

'I think we've all thought about it,' said Singh.

'Because I can see a bright new future in the world of professional gambling,' said Bullock, as though he was the only one in the conversation. 'Poker could just be the start,' he went on. 'No point in games that are only chance, there has to be someone else involved, some measure of competition. Boxing. Can you imagine boxing? Imagine doing this with a boxer, you could have him drop his guard, just a bit, just take a big punch and down he goes, guaranteed. Kerching, payout time.'

Michael was going to interject, but Marshall got in first.

'Not enough excitement,' said Marshall. 'Anyway, win too often in places like that and you'll get noticed.'

'And what would they do to me?' snapped Bullock.

'Ban you,' said Singh, 'then what would you do?'

'I'd start closer to home,' said Marshall.

'How close?' asked Michael, wondering where Marshall was going with this.

'Conway,' said Marshall. 'Imagine if we took control of him. We could make a lot of our problems go away, very easily.'

'You're forgetting the blood test,' said Michael, 'back to your problem of getting caught.'

'But who orders the blood tests?' asked Marshall. 'Conway's the senior army officer in charge of the project. He'd make sure we wouldn't get caught.'

'What you're talking about is mutiny,' said Michael. 'You'd be court-martialled for it.'

'Really?' snorted Marshall. 'You think anyone's going to

stand up in a court martial and accuse any of us of taking psychic control of a senior officer?' Michael had to admit, to himself, Marshall had a point.

'Enough,' commanded Michael, loudly enough to bring the group to a halt. They all turned to look at him. 'We're soldiers in the British Army. We've sworn an oath to protect Queen and country. We follow orders. What's happened is so strange I can hardly believe it, but it has happened, and we have to deal with it. But that doesn't mean we suddenly abandon the chain of command.

'I follow orders,' said Bullock. 'I took an oath and I stick by it. I follow my orders to protect Queen and country. My problem isn't with the Queen. We've been lied to. We've been used. I've got a big problem with whoever's lied to us.'

'Our blond haired buffoon is right,' said Singh.

'Fuck you,' said Bullock, loudly. Michael looked around, but there seemed to be no-one out and about, and for now, they'd gone unnoticed.

'But he is right,' said Singh. 'We have been used, and we have been lied to. My issue is loyalty to those who've lied to us, and who will almost certainly lie to us again.'

'Sorry, boss,' said Marshall. 'But the boys are all right. This is so weird I can't believe it's happening either, but it is. We know it is. We all know it is. But other people know, too. And they probably knew before they gave us that drug. This is way outside normal soldiering, even for us. How safe are we? Really, boss. Do you know we're safe?'

Michael had no quick and easy answer. He knew a quick answer would probably silence Marshall, for the moment, and if he was quiet the others would be too. But he had no answer, and the silence between them was almost painful.

'No,' said Marshall. 'I didn't think so.'

'No-one's suggesting we all just go AWOL,' said Singh. 'But I can guarantee someone, somewhere is thinking of all sorts of uses they can put us to. Why shouldn't we think the same?'

'Because we follow orders,' said Michael, again. 'If we stop following orders then we're little more than mercenaries.'

'I think we'd be very good mercenaries,' said Marshall. 'I think we'd be something really unique.'

'Yeah,' said Bullock, 'and really expensive.'

Michael believed Singh when he said he wasn't planning to walk off and make his way as a telepathic hired-gun, but he wasn't so sure about Bullock. The young man could be impetuous. Marshall was a stronger character, and if Marshall decided to take a different path then Bullock would likely follow. Michael didn't like the way the conversation was going. He started walking again. Maybe if they reached a public place it would stifle some of the conversation.

'And how long do you think you'd last?' asked Michael. 'Before someone like the Americans found out? Or the Russians? Do you think they'd let you out for a drink in an evening? No. They'd lock us up and no-one would ever hear of us again.'

Singh picked up the pace and walked ahead of the group. 'I've got to admit,' said Singh, turning back to look at the others. 'I am curious, about what this scientist wants tomorrow.'

'A progress check on his lab rats,' said Marshall.

'What if he doesn't like what his rats have been doing?' asked Bullock. Michael knew it was the question they'd each thought.

Bullock went on, 'we've been screwed by the people

we're supposed to rely on, now we've been silenced, I won't stand by if they try and bury us.'

Singh stopped. He looked up at the sign hanging outside the pub. The Ox and Cart. They'd arrived at the best pub in Bishop's Fort. Michael's first thought was if this was the best pub, he didn't want to see the others.

FOURTEEN

Despite its less than glamorous appearance, the pub suited them very nicely. It was an old building and had some charm and character. Few of the locals paid them any attention, and they found a quiet corner where they could keep to themselves.

The first two rounds of drinks had gone down very quickly, but after that they slowed down, and relaxed. With people coming and going Michael didn't feel comfortable talking about their current situation, not even in whispers. None of the others raised the topic either, and they spent the night reminiscing, swapping war stories and trying to out-do each other in telling the most obscene jokes they could think of.

By the end of their three hours in the pub, Michael felt more relaxed than he had since before their mission in Afghanistan. He looked around the pub. He always found it amusing that the people in the bar, talking about their farms or their jobs, had no idea that they were in arms' reach of Special Forces soldiers who, only days before, had been in a shoot-out in Afghanistan.

The girl behind the bar had been slightly surprised when Marshall had asked to use a payphone. Michael had listened as Marshall made up an explanation for why none of them had a mobile phone with them. She must have believed him, because she rang for a taxi, arranging it to meet the group in half an hour where they'd been dropped off.

They stepped out into the cool night air and started walking. To begin with they walked in silence, but it wasn't long before Bullock could resist the temptation no longer, and tried to find an even more obscene joke than Marshall's last offering. As usual, Bullock's joke was more obscene, but not more amusing.

After a few minutes there was a metallic jangle as Bullock kicked something. He bent down and picked up a bunch of keys. Five or six keys of various kinds on a single split-ring. The team gathered around and examined the keys.

'Could be anyone's,' said Marshall.

'Best hand them in at the pub,' said Michael, 'they'll probably have an idea whose they are.'

'I'll take them,' said Singh. With a shrug, Bullock handed the keys to Singh.

Singh gasped, and for a moment held the keys as though they were burning hot. Michael thought he was about to drop them, but he held on, staring at the keys.

'What is your problem?' asked Marshall.

'I know who these keys belong to,' said Singh, astounded. 'I can see him. I can know his name. I can see where he is.'

'What are you, psychic?' asked Bullock. Michael, and probably all of them, realised how ridiculous Bullock's question was.

'Seriously, what is it?' Michael asked.

'It's like when I touched that soldier,' said Singh, 'in the exercise, when I touched him and could make him say things. I felt the connection with him. It's the same with the keys, I can feel the connection with them.'

'This just gets weirder and weirder,' said Marshall. 'Let's have a go.' He held out his hand.

Singh hesitated, then held out the keys, and dropped them into Marshall's palm. Marshall looked at the keys, closing his fingers around them.

'Nope,' he said, 'not a thing.'

'I didn't feel anything either,' said Bullock.

Michael's mind was already running through the possibilities of this new skill, and he was beginning to wonder what else they could do. "Weirder" was a good description, he thought.

'You try,' said Marshall, offering the keys to Michael. Michael took the keys.

He felt the connection almost immediately. As Singh had said, it was just like when he had connected with the soldier. He could feel his thoughts extending into the metal of the keys, touching the essence of the man who owned them. He could almost, but not quite, hear the man's thoughts. He knew the man was at home, and home was not far away. He could also see the most important door which the keys opened. How did he know it was the most important? Because he could feel the man's knowledge of which was the most important.

'He's a jeweller,' said Michael.

'And the keys are to his jeweller's shop,' said Singh, 'which is currently unoccupied.'

'Wow,' said Bullock. 'We could...' but Marshall cut him short.

'No, we couldn't,' said Marshall. 'We'd be common thieves if we did that.'

'Maybe not to the jeweller's shop,' said Bullock, 'but that's a really useful skill you've got.' Michael realised that Bullock was looking more at Singh than himself.

'This changes everything,' said Singh. 'This makes us more capable than anyone has suggested.'

'It makes us more powerful,' said Marshall.

'Maybe this is why that scientist wants to see us tomorrow,' said Bullock. Once in a while he did get it right.

'This also makes it even more important to stay out of the limelight,' said Singh. 'If the Americans or Russians got wind of this, they'd cut our heads open and dissect our brains to find out how this works.'

'Evan, take the keys back to the pub,' said Michael. He was keen that neither he nor Julian should handle the keys any more than they needed. He wasn't sure what would happen if they pushed through the connection and his thoughts entered the consciousness of the jeweller.

'You're wrong about one thing,' said Singh, looking at Marshall. 'It wouldn't make us common thieves, it would make us very uncommon thieves.'

'If you can do this, we're becoming super-heroes,' said Bullock, grinning like a schoolboy. Michael realised he hadn't seen as much of Bullock's stupid grin in recent days, and he missed it. Bullock did bring a levity to the team.

It was Singh who brought them back to reality. 'Yes,' he said, 'but we could easily become super-villains. We do need to be careful.'

'We need to get back,' said Michael. 'We still have orders to follow.'

Bullock jogged back to the pub to hand in the keys, the

others set off in the direction of their rendezvous with the taxi.

After a couple of minutes Michael became keenly aware that he was out in front, and the other three were behind him, together. For the first time, he wondered if they were communicating with each other, without him.

Joon-ho sipped the coffee, which he had to admit was not altogether unpalatable. The staff in the VIP suite had gone out of their way to accommodate him and had done an adequate job. He and his team had occupied the whole suite, and had now excluded all airport employees. His armed security team stood guard at every entrance to the suite.

From his armchair he had a panoramic view across the taxiway of Zadar Airport, the Croatian countryside stretching out beyond the black strip of the runway. His private Boeing 737 sat on the far left of the taxiway, the refuelling truck replenishing the aircraft before the final leg of his flight.

He stared at the box. The flight case was black, ironically the size of a coffin. Metal edges and catches gave some detail to the otherwise featureless object. It sat on a wheeled pallet, and he couldn't take his eyes off it. To say the contents of the box had been expensive would have been an understatement. It had taken guile, cunning, a lot of negotiation, and a considerable amount of money to acquire the box and its contents. But the contents were of little use without the man who could make them work. He too had taken negotiation and a lot of money, and was now late. Joon-ho did not like people being late. He worked to a timetable, he ran every day to a timetable. He needed to know what was happening, and when, and what was going to happen, down to the last minute. Details were everything.

The smoked glass door of the suite swung open, pushed by one of his security detail. The man beckoned, and in he walked. Joon-ho recognised the Russian from his photographs, although they had never met before. The man was short, dishevelled, his shirt half untucked, his remaining hair fighting to stay flat on his head. He clutched a black attaché case, holding it as though his life depended on it, which it did.

As soon as he walked into the room the Russian stared at the case, as though he'd never seen it before and it held the most precious gems in the world.

'I must see it,' said the Russian.

Joon-ho had expected the man to be ill-mannered. A polite greeting would have been in order, perhaps an exchange of some meaningless pleasantries. But no, the man was gruff and direct.

Joon-ho said nothing, but rose and walked to the box. He revealed the hidden keypad, entered the code, scanned his thumb-print, and the case unlocked. As though approaching the devil himself the Russian shuffled towards the box. Almost painfully slowly he reached out and lifted open the lid of the box, and stared inside.

'No-one has interfered with it?' he asked, or was it a statement?

'I assure you,' said Joon-ho, 'it has been handled most carefully, and is in perfect condition.'

Without another word the man rested his attaché case on the edge of the open box and pulled out of it a small electronic device trailing a length of ribbon cable. He took the connector at the end of the cable and reached into the box.

There was a click as the connector snapped into position. The man watched the small LCD screen on the device. Joon-ho could see the screen flickering and changing, displaying information, but he couldn't see the detail.

The Russian breathed a deep sigh, and his shoulders relaxed.

'All is in order,' he said. This was no surprise to Joon-ho, he knew everything was in order.

'Perhaps you will relax now,' said Joon-ho. The Russian nodded, unplugged his device and stuffed it back in his case. He collapsed into one of the chairs. 'In a little over two hours we will land in England, and their police will ensure our consignment is delivered safely and without inter-ference.'

'And we will be safe there?' asked the Russian.

'I spoke with their government minister this morning. I insisted on their most capable military bodyguards to ensure our safety. I had his guarantee he would arrange it personally.'

Joon-ho looked at the case. They were getting close now, so very close.

THE GREY-HAIRED LADY sat in the public departure lounge of Zadar Airport and watched through the panoramic windows. She could see the plain white aircraft taxiing towards the end of the runway. Apart from the aircraft's identifying number on the tailplane, it was completely plain, nothing to advertise its owner or its purpose.

She could have been anyone's grandmother, elderly and well appointed, trying to keep up with the times with an open laptop resting on her knees. Closer scrutiny would have revealed the mobile phone connected to the laptop, but the only application visible on the screen was a Sudoku game. The scream of the engines was audible even inside the terminal, and she watched as the plane accelerated down the runway and rose gracefully into the air, banking and cruising out of sight.

With a few taps on the trackpad of the laptop she closed the Sudoku game and shut the lid of the laptop. She unplugged the phone and stuffed the laptop and the cable into her embroidered bag. Slowly, and not very steadily, she stood and wandered over to the window, away from the waiting passengers.

Holding the phone in one hand she tapped icons with her thumb and lifted the phone to her ear. The call was connected within seconds.

She kept her voice low, but this far from the seating area no-one would be able to hear her conversation.

'As expected,' she said, 'the mark had full electronic counter-measures deployed, no surveillance was possible.'

She paused for a moment, listening, then spoke. 'Yes, I have recordings of the signature of the jamming signals, I'll send them now.' She ended the call.

It was all very routine, and all very unproductive. Another surveillance operation, another exercise in futility. Whoever had been in the VIP suite had gone to quite some lengths to ensure there was no eavesdropping. Her MI6 surveillance equipment was state-of-the-art, but so was the jamming system used by the occupant of the suite. All she had acquired was data on the frequencies of the jamming system used. No doubt it would be of interest to someone. She now needed to find somewhere quiet to set up the laptop and download the files to the GCHQ servers.

WAYNE BROWNING WAS COMPOSING an email when the notification popped up in the corner of his computer screen. The email was important, but so was the notification. Normally he'd put the notification in his queue of things to do, and get around to it later. Analysing profiles of electronic communications was unrewarding work. It was grunt work, and it was very tempting to hand it over to one of the junior analysts. Anna Hendrickson was the first name that came to mind. She was a rising star, making a name for herself. He also reckoned it would be slightly unfair, she was a very capable individual, and this particular task would not be the best use of her abilities. Besides, he remembered, she was absent, off on some assignment for Evans.

Given the current concern about potential terrorist activity there was an increased focus on trying to get any lead from any surveillance activity, perhaps he should deal with this first. With a few clicks of the mouse he brought up the relevant files. The surveillance had been a flop, nothing recorded except the profile of whatever electronic jamming had been used.

He was about to close the files and leave the task until later when a thought crept into his brain. Counter-surveillance measures capable of completely blocking an MI6 eavesdropping operation were unusual. The number of different microphones and devices used meant that usually some snippets of conversation were recorded, or some images acquired. But for nothing at all to be captured, this was unusual. Who would be so keen to avoid onlookers that they would use such sophisticated anti-surveillance technology? Who had such technology? Not many people, that was certain.

He brought up the few mission details available, which told him very little. He clicked a few more times with his mouse and subjected the files to the standard array of analyses. Sophisticated signal analysis algorithms, pattern matching routines, and statistical transformations might yield some clues. He waited, watching the progress counter give him the percentage complete. This was going to take some time. He returned to his email.

Finally, after much editing, the email was ready, and he clicked the Send button. He thought about getting another coffee but decided to check on the analysis of the surveillance data. To his surprise the process had finished, perhaps the email had taken longer than he thought. He scanned the results of the analysis. Each anti-surveillance system had its own way of protecting its owner through the transmission of various radio signals designed to scramble and interrupt snoopers, sub-sonic transmitters which masked the voices of those talking to the point where the words were irretrievable. Each system had its own signature, and most were distinct and recognisable.

Browning looked at the data on the screen. He didn't immediately recognise the various details he was looking at, this was a jamming system new to him, although something about it seemed familiar. The more he looked at it the more he thought there was something he recognised about it, but he couldn't put his finger on it.

He picked up the phone and dialled a number.

'Geraint,' he said when his called was answered, 'I need a favour. I've done a basic analysis of an MI6 surveillance op', complete bust, totally jammed.'

'So what have you retrieved?' asked Geraint Evans.

'Nothing,' said Browning, 'it was totally jammed.'

'Totally? That is a bit unusual. Can you send over the profiles? I'd love to have a look.'

'That's what I was hoping you'd say,' said Browning. He clicked with his mouse and within moments the files had been sent to Geraint's workstation.

There were a few moments of silence, punctuated by the occasional 'oh,' or 'hmmm,' from Evans.

'Ah,' said Evans, sharply. Browning sat up straight. 'Yes, I have seen this before,' said Evans. 'The rotation of the base jamming frequency, we've seen this, recently.'

Browning looked on his screen for that particular value, represented as a small chart in the corner of the screen. The shape of it was familiar, and now that Evans drew his attention to it he realised this was the value he had found familiar. But from where?

'This is the same jamming signature as the one used on that joint MI5-Special Forces mission the other night,' said Evans.

Of course it was. The similarity had been lost in all the details and reports that Browning had read and analysed over the last few days, but now that he looked at it, the similarity was clear.

'I'll get hold of the MI5 Head of Section,' said Evans, 'I've no doubt she'll want to know about this.'

THE HEAD WASN'T SATISFIED, she rarely was. The meeting of her Team Leaders had shown some progress in tracking the assorted individuals suspected of having links to Arshad. In one way or another MI5 and GCHQ had kept them under surveillance, monitored their communications and movements. Details of the various surveillance operations scrolled across the monitors on the walls of the Thames House meeting room. As she listened to the reports the Head was forming an idea that these people were planning something, but there was no tangible evidence. It was almost as if they were all getting into just the right position, but the right position for what?

'Have we seen them in possession of any materials?' asked the Head. 'Anything at all?'

'No Ma'am,' was the reply. The Team Leader consulted her laptop. 'None of the nineteen have been seen carrying or moving anything other than super-market shopping or bags of laundry.' Before the Head could ask, the Leader explained, 'and yes, we've had operatives check the bags of laundry, nothing but dirty socks.'

'So what are they doing?' she mused.

'There have been meetings,' said another of the Team Leaders, 'just pairs or threes at the most, they've not been heard to say anything out of the ordinary, they've not swapped messages that we can see, but they've all made slight changes in daily routine. Some have moved across the country.'

'Why?' said the Head, picking up on the fact.

'All outward indications are simply to visit family,' explained one of the Leaders. 'On the surface, everything looks normal.'

'But?'

'But we know they've got links to Arshad and possibly others, and now they're making changes to routine and associations and location, and the lack of communication is suspicious and ominous.' The Team Leaders looked at each other.

The Head pondered this. There were too many

unknowns, too many possibilities, too little evidence. Her experience told her something was happening.

One ventured the unspoken thought. 'We could have them arrested,' she suggested, 'question them.'

'No,' said the Head, slowly, 'they'd all go to ground. We'd never find out what they were planning.'

'Or if there's a second team we don't know about,' said another.

The discussion was interrupted by the ringing of a mobile phone. The Head hesitated for a moment, then pulled out her phone and answered it.

'Is this important?' she said.

'Yes, I believe it is,' came the voice of Geraint Evans.

'Wait, I'll put you on speaker.' The Head put the call through the phone's loudspeaker and set the phone on the desk. 'You're on speaker with my Team Leaders.'

'We've had the results from a routine surveillance mission,' explained Evans. 'The target was protected by a particularly sophisticated anti-surveillance jamming system. The most significant finding was the system had the same signature as that used to compromise your Special Forces unit the other evening.'

Another piece of the puzzle was now in play. But where did it fit? Was it part of the same puzzle? Was this coincidence? She didn't think so.

'Was this individual involved in the Afghanistan meeting?' asked one of the Team Leaders, looking up details on his laptop as he spoke.

'My best guess?' said Evans, 'no, not directly. But I'd be suspicious that he supplied the jamming system that was used, one that he was familiar with and had confidence in.'

'Who was the target?' asked the Head.

'His name is Lee Joon-ho,' said Evans. 'He's a prominent

Chinese businessman, no known links to terrorism, but we know suspiciously little about this man.'

The Team Leaders began furiously tapping at their keyboards to pull up anything and everything any of the security services' databases had on Joon-ho.

'Thank you, Mr Evans,' said the Head. She picked up the phone and ended the call.

One of the Team Leaders began reciting what information he had found.

'Lee Joon-ho. Resides mainly in Hong Kong. Has a range of business interests across Asia, the Middle East and Europe, some developing interests in Africa. Several of his companies were key suppliers to the Beijing Olympic Games. He's on the advisory board responsible for handing over the Olympic legacy to London.'

'I doubt this is coincidence,' said the Head. 'We need to establish what this Joon-ho's role is, who he's connected to.'

'He's due in London,' said one of the other analysts, 'to be a part of the delegation meeting Government officials to do the handover of the governance for the Games.'

'When's he due?' asked the Head, sharply. She was starting to suspect they were only now catching up on events which were very current.

'His plane is due to land in three hours,' said the Team Leader.

THE HEAD CLOSED the door to her office. Some conversations could only be had in private. Her Team Leaders had all the necessary security clearances, of course, but this was a delicate matter. She dialled a number on her desk phone and selected loudspeaker.

Within a couple of moments the Minister answered.

'I hope this is important,' he said in a rather pompous voice, 'I have a lot on.'

'It is important, Minister,' she said, as though she'd call just to pass the time of day. 'I believe Lee Joon-ho is due in the country this afternoon.'

'Yes, he is,' said the Minister, as though not wanting to discuss the matter any further. 'Why?'

'For reasons I'd rather not discuss on the phone, I need to keep this individual under surveillance.'

'Absolutely not,' spluttered the Minister. 'Mr Joon-ho is a personal friend of the Prime Minister, and here at the invitation of the Government.'

The Head closed her eyes. Politics and politicians, they could complicate even the simplest situation

'Minister,' said the Head, struggling to keep her voice calm and pleasant, 'I would not make this request lightly, and in person I will explain everything.'

'I'm sorry, but no. Mr Joon-ho is being afforded every measure of co-operation during his stay. I have assured him of this personally. He's asked for the very best in protection, and I've arranged a detail of SO14 officers to look after him.'

SO14 was the Metropolitan Police unit tasked with close protection of the Royal Family and certain very special visiting dignitaries.

'I very nearly assigned a unit from the Special Air Service,' said the Minister.

The Head was about to end the call when she had an idea. It was a risk, but perhaps one worth taking.

'If you want to demonstrate to Mr Joon-ho that you are affording him the very best in personal protection,' said the Head, 'then there is a unit of Special Forces soldiers I can have assigned. They're trained and ready to go. I can have them operational immediately.'

There was a pause.

'For close protection only,' said the Minister. 'Mr Joon-ho is not to be kept under any surveillance.'

'You have my word,' said the Head, meaning none of it.

FIFTEEN

Morrow remembered the first time he'd visited the special project facility. He'd been fascinated by the cameras and the guards and the guns. Now it was all just a delay and a hindrance. He sat in the back of the car, Tuner next to him, as they waited for the gate to open.

He knew they'd soon be in Conway's office and he'd be able to start making preparations to take control of the soldiers. He'd often thought about taking control of Conway but realised now that not having done so was probably a good idea. Should any of the soldiers be bold enough they might try and connect with Conway, or even control him. If they did, there was a chance they'd realise he'd already had telepathic contact with someone, and that could complicate things. If they had reason to believe they were not the first they might suspect they had been deliberately influenced (they had) and someone had a specific plan for them (he had,) they might also suspect they would not be given a choice over what happened to them (they certainly would not.)

The soldiers were key. He needed a small and capable group over whom he could have complete control. He needed a unit of soldiers who could be his protectors, his bodyguards, and his way of removing any troublesome individuals. He had no doubt that Turner could make the necessary arrangements with the military to have the soldiers assigned to the project on a permanent basis.

The car took them straight to the administration building and a young man escorted them inside and into Conway's office. Morrow thought that Conway looked distracted, and again thought perhaps direct control of this man, or at least the ability to read his thoughts, could be useful, despite the risks. Perhaps later.

'Where are they?' asked Turner. Morrow noted they didn't mess around with all that silly saluting business.

'They're on an exercise,' said Conway, 'in the hills. They'll be back shortly.'

'And how are they?' asked Morrow. He had almost asked "how are they coming along," but managed to stop himself at the last moment.

Conway looked at Morrow, and then at Turner. Morrow noted that he seemed to talk more to Turner than to himself. Perhaps it was a military thing.

'They're coping well,' said Conway. 'They seem to have accepted what has happened and are making the best of it. Today's exercise is a chance for them to work together as a team, using their...' his voice trailed off as he seemed unwilling to use the most obvious words.

'It seems what has happened is truly remarkable,' said Morrow, hoping he wasn't overacting. 'I'd like to see the soldiers.'

'Sir?' asked Conway, looking again at Turner, perhaps asking his permission.

'I think it would help if Doctor Morrow saw the soldiers,' said Turner.

'I'd like to reassure them,' said Morrow, 'explain we've since given the drug to others who've had no unexpected effects and who are all still perfectly fine.'

Morrow didn't think Conway looked particularly reassured but did get the sense the man accepted the logic of allowing a civilian to talk to his soldiers.

'I will take the men individually to meet with Doctor Morrow,' said Turner. Morrow smiled inside. All he had to do was think what he wanted and Turner said it, or did it.

'Very well, the project room should meet your needs,' said Conway. 'Is there anything else I can do for you, Sir?'

'No thank you, Captain,' said Turner. 'If you could show us the room now.'

Conway took them to the project room, a typically soulless meeting room with a table in the middle and six chairs around it. Turner said he had other things to discuss with Captain Conway, and left. Morrow thought it would be good if Turner spent time talking about Army things to Conway, it would make everything seem more normal. He pulled out a chair and sat down, and waited.

Morrow took a deep breath and closed his eyes. It was nice to have some time to himself. It was tempting just to sit and think, but he had too much to do. He let his mind expand outwards. He could feel Turner, he was close. He sensed Falcone and knew he could make contact if he wanted. He let his mind expand further, and became aware of the others. For the moment everyone was working on exactly what they should be, everything was going according to plan.

It took him a few moments, but he noticed there was a presence he didn't recognise. He knew the unique mind-signature of everyone he'd connected with, and yet here was one he didn't know. He focused on this individual. It had a different quality to the others. It was almost like tasting a familiar food and becoming aware of a slightly different ingredient, or looking at a familiar landscape and taking time to notice a new feature.

Then it came to him. One of the curious aspects of this new presence was their location. They were close, very close. They were in the room next door. He allowed his attention to narrow further. He didn't recognise this person because he had not connected with them through a physical connection.

He let his thoughts coalesce around this person. The sensation was almost delicious, it had a refreshing quality about it. He realised, he was now able to connect with someone without having to touch them, without having to be in the same room.

This thought very quickly led to an inevitable, and very important question. Could he take control of them without touching them?

ANNA REVIEWED the list she'd made in her notebook. Almost everything about the security of the room was lacking. To say this was the room housing all the key servers and computers related to the project, there really wasn't much security at all.

There were bars on the windows, but a chain and a Land Rover would make short work of them. The windows were large enough to allow, once the bars were removed, an average sized person to get inside. The lock on the door was a mechanical key-number lock, with a single bolt locking the door. The door itself was a standard wooden door, meaning it and lock would pose almost no defence against someone intent on getting into the room.

The servers themselves were in racks, tall grey cabinets, a dozen computers in each. But the cabinets had no doors on them, nothing to prevent physical access to the machines, and all the USB ports and network connections on the servers were still active. All anyone would have to do was plug in a USB stick with a suitable piece of software loaded to take control of the servers, which is exactly what Anna had done.

She'd spent most of the morning loading what security and encryption software she could onto the computers, but her growing list detailed many things that would need to be done to properly secure the computers and the data they held.

She sat on the unpleasantly dirty plastic chair and stared at the screen of the PC sitting on the lone table. The progress bar showed how far her current program had got, and it showed another few minutes before it finished.

Anna looked up as someone came into the room, only to realise the door had not opened. No-one had come in, yet she was sure someone was there. She wondered if they were behind the racks of servers, but the racks stood against the walls, no room behind them to conceal a person.

The feeling got stronger. For a brief, and possibly insane moment, she wondered if the place was haunted. Anna laughed out loud. Ghosts were a childish fiction, no more real than Father Christmas. The feelings could only be a manifestation of her dislike of this particular task and her desire to be back at the Doughnut with the people she enjoyed working with.

Perhaps it would help if she left the room, left the

machines to get on with their work. She could get a coffee, there had to be somewhere on site for a coffee. She tried to stand, but it just seemed too much effort. Perhaps she was having a stroke? Perhaps she was hallucinating as brain cells died. The thought frightened her. Her brain was her strength, her intelligence and her imagination were what set her apart, she couldn't lose those. Anna lifted her left hand to eye level, and examined it. Then lifted her right hand. If she could lift both hands without trouble then she wasn't having a stroke.

It began to feel like someone was sitting next to her, right next to her, far too close, so close they were touching her. It felt uncomfortable. No, it was more than that, worse than that, it was obscene. She tried to close her mind to it, but the feeling was inside her. Could she think of something else? Of course she could. Her imagination and her intellect were her strengths, she could think of something so completely she would shut out these feelings.

The thought that first came to mind was almost laughable. Fermat's Last Theorem. One of the most famous unsolved (and to many, unsolvable) mathematical problems. One mathematician had found a solution, but it had been deeply complex. Anna had always been fascinated with the idea there was a simple and elegant solution. She began focusing on the problem, thinking through the various possible solutions she'd read about, the ways in which they'd failed, the opinions she'd come across from leading thinkers as to whether the Theorem could ever be solved. She reviewed Andrew Wiles' modern solution and the suggestions from previous centuries as to how it might be solved. Soon enough, the ideas of mathematics and equations filled her mind, and she began to feel at ease, almost at peace.

MORROW REALISED he had actually held his hand out in front of him, such was the strength of his feeling of being close to the person next door. He could almost touch them. He could certainly touch them psychically, he could feel that, but now it was as if he could almost touch them physically.

He felt a surge of telepathic energy building. Now was the time to find if he could take control of someone from a distance, without having to make physical contact first.

It was then he realised he'd lost the sense of being almost able to touch them physically. In fact, his psychic connection had changed. It felt as though he was no longer next to them, whispering to them, but shouting from a distance, shouting through a wall or a window, and they couldn't hear him.

What was this? How had this change happened? He hadn't done anything differently. It was inconceivable the other person could have done something to block him, how could they? No-one was strong enough to block him.

He gasped when it happened. It was like a door being slammed in his face. The psychic connection was lost. No, not lost. It had been broken, and not by him. They had shut him out. Somehow they had erected a psychic barrier and shut him out. He almost swore out loud, feeling a growing anger, wanting to hit something or kick something. Morrow swore to himself he would find out how this had happened, and how to overcome it in future.

He also resolved that when he met each of the soldiers he would apply the full force of his telepathic power on them. He would give them not the slightest opportunity to oppose him or refuse him. No matter how strong they were as soldiers, they would not be able to defend themselves against him. He was so close now to completing this phase of the project, nothing was going to stop him.

ANNA WALKED SLOWLY BACK to the administration building. It had only taken a few minutes in the fresh air for her to stop shaking. She still couldn't explain what had happened, but she had no doubt whatever was going on in this place was something she wanted nothing to do with.

Her work was finished. She had loaded all the security software she could. She had made copious notes about what else needed to be done to enhance the security of the IT systems and their data. Now it was time for her to leave. She couldn't wait to get back to Cheltenham, to the Doughnut, to her familiar world, the world where she belonged.

As soon as she got to the offices she would phone Evans and tell him she'd finished and she was ready to leave. She hoped with all her might that she would never have anything to do with this place, or what went on here, ever again.

THE WIND on the hills had been chilly, but nothing was as frosty as the atmosphere in the back of the Ford Transit van. The four of them sat in silence as the driver made his way along the country roads back to the project facility. In previous times the team would have been noisy, trading jokes or insults, discussing the upcoming or previous opera-tion, or idling away time with crude banter. Today, they were silent. They avoided each other's gaze and each other's thoughts.

The morning's exercise had gone well, and initially Michael had been pleased. Each of them had been driven separately, and blindfold, from the facility to a drop-off point. With no map, no compass and no radio they had to meet together at a particular point at a given time. As they started the exercise and communicated telepathically they seemed to make good progress, giving each other updates on landmarks they could see, finding common bearings, orientating themselves with the few details they'd been given about the rendezvous point.

It would have been a complete success, had Bullock been able to avoid showing off. But he hadn't. He couldn't. He couldn't resist the temptation to boast, to gloat. Always like a kid who'd got away with some minor wrongdoing, he couldn't avoid boasting. He'd denied doing anything wrong, he'd argued he'd worked within the rules of the exercise, he'd argued the exercise had had no rules, and finally he'd confessed.

Bullock had connected telepathically with his driver. He'd discovered where Marshall and Singh were to be dropped. No wonder they'd made such good progress. They'd cheated. It was true that no rules had been made clear, so strictly speaking they hadn't broken any. But the point of the exercise was to test their ability to navigate solely by using their silent communication. In this they had failed. They knew they could connect with people and compel them to speak, this was nothing new. Michael had to almost pinch himself. He was now telling himself that psychic control of another person was nothing new and nothing worthy of testing.

It was then that the silence had set in. Michael had been

tempted to say something, but once the driver arrived he chose to stay silent. He had, for a brief moment, considered having a telepathic discussion, but decided he didn't want to risk a telepathic shouting match. So he said nothing, and neither did the others. At least, they didn't say anything he could hear.

Once back at the accommodation building they quickly relieved themselves of their battle kit, showered and dressed in civilian clothes. Without speaking they all knew what they needed next; tea. Bullock got to the kettle first and had soon started providing steaming mugs of tea.

Soon enough, the four of them were together in the room, mugs in hand. This time, Michael took the initiative.

'I know we completed the exercise,' he said, looking at Bullock, 'but you cheated.' Before Bullock could reply, he carried on, 'and don't tell me there were no rules, you know full well what the exercise was for.'

'To be fair, Boss,' said Marshall, 'whichever way you want to try and cut it, we completed the exercise as given. We used our abilities and we showed what we could do. If it didn't show exactly what someone wanted then they should have designed a better exercise.'

Michael didn't say out loud that he had to agree, very reluctantly, with Marshall's reasoning.

'They've done this to us. I don't know if they knew this was going to happen...' said Marshall.

'They knew,' said Bullock, almost under his breath, but not quite.

Marshall went on. 'Now they want to know what we can do. They have no idea what we can do. We could be unbelievably powerful, soldiers like no-one has ever seen before.'

'Yes,' said Michael, 'soldiers, soldiers who still follow orders, soldiers who are still part of the chain of command.'

'Maybe,' said Marshall. Michael didn't like his tone or his implication. 'We'll see what they want to do with us.'

'Apart from that,' said Michael, 'involving someone else like that risks being discovered. You know what Conway said about the blood test.'

'If it's true,' said Singh, 'maybe we'll find out if their blood test is for real.'

'What if it's not?' asked Bullock.

'All bets are off,' said Marshall.

'No,' said Michael, as firmly as he dared. 'We need to stick together.'

They were interrupted by Phillips barging in. The man stood there and regarded the four of them for a moment.

'Captain Conway needs to see you,' said Phillips, looking at Michael.

Phillips and Sanders left the room. The others waited to hear the outer door close, then looked at each other.

'Is there any chance we can get him on board?' asked Singh. Silence was the answer.

Marshall spoke. 'I doubt it,' he said. 'The boss has a pole up his arse about being a good little soldier-boy. I think he thinks whoever's done this is going to look after us, that everything's going to turn out alright.'

Singh asked the more poignant question. 'If we could get him back on-side, would you want to?'

'No,' said Bullock, as an almost automatic response. 'Vince is right, he can't see what's happening, he can't see what we're able to do.'

'He can't see all the things we could do,' said Marshall. 'We need to stick together, whatever they've got planned for us.'

'All for one, and one for all, eh?' asked Singh.

Marshall looked at him with a piercing stare. 'It was

called the Three Musketeers for a reason,' he said, emphasising the word 'three.'

CONWAY STARED out of his office window. A squad of soldiers jogged passed, feet moving in unison. They had been sent here to test a new design of boot, a far cry from Turner's project. Conway didn't like the four soldiers, he wasn't sure what was going on, and he definitely didn't like what was happening with them.

Turner had left, saying he had other people to talk to while he was here. Morrow had stayed in the project room, waiting for the four soldiers to be taken to him. Phillips had gone to find Captain Sanders, he'd be taken to Morrow first. Perhaps after this the four soldiers would be gone, but somehow Conway couldn't believe it would be that simple. When was it ever that simple?

The ringing of his desk phone snapped him out of his daydreaming.

'Conway,' he said, answering the phone.

'Captain Conway,' said the voice on the phone, 'this is Captain Garrett, Special Forces Directorate.' Conway knew the name, although he didn't know Garrett personally. Garrett wasted no time in explaining what he needed, and what was about to happen.

Conway put down the phone and allowed himself a smile. He took a few moments to relish this latest and unexpected development. Sometimes, it seemed, things really could be that simple.

He marched out of his office and towards Sanders' unit's accommodation building. As he turned the bend he saw Phillips walking towards him, accompanied by Captain

Michael Sanders. Conway took a breath. This could either be very easy, or it could get very messy.

'Captain Sanders,' said Conway as he approached the pair.

'Captain Conway,' Sanders said in return. 'I believe you want to see me.'

'I did,' said Conway, 'that is, the reason I need to see you has changed. Phillips, that will be all.'

Phillips gave a questioning look but departed without saying anything. Conway waited until the young man was safely out of hearing range.

'You and your men have been reassigned,' said Conway. 'I've just had a message from Special Forces Directorate, I need to arrange a briefing for you and your men, immediately.'

'Reassigned to what?' Sanders asked. Conway hoped the man wasn't going to argue or put up any resistance.

'Get your men together, get them ready to move out immediately after the briefing,' said Conway, trying hard not to smile. He had to remain professional, this was just business. 'Bring them to my office as soon as they're ready.'

Sanders didn't reply, but turned around and marched back towards the accommodation building. Conway did an about-face and marched towards his office, trying not to run, or even jog. This was almost too good to be true, he didn't want to jinx it by being too enthusiastic.

As he approached the admin' building Turner came out of the door, perhaps looking for him.

'Where's Captain Sanders?' asked Turner. 'He's to be taken to see Doctor Morrow.'

'I'm afraid there's been a change of plan,' said Conway, not stopping but walking passed the Major and into the admin' building. Turner followed him into Conway's office.

'What change of plan? I haven't authorised any change,' said Turner, his voice more forceful now.

'I'm sorry Sir,' said Conway, standing beside his desk. He resisted the temptation to sit, he was addressing a senior officer. 'I've had word from the Special Forces Directorate, the unit has been reassigned. There's an immediate operational need for them.'

'They can't do this,' blurted Turner. 'Those men are assigned to my project.'

'And the Director of Special Forces has seen fit to reassign them, Sir,' said Conway.

'We'll see about this,' said Turner, pulling out his mobile phone and dialling as he stormed out of the office.

Once Turner had gone, Conway sat in his chair behind his desk. Perhaps now they could all get back to what they were supposed to do here, proper soldiering. None of this weird shit that Morrow had brought in. With any luck, those four soldiers would go on another operation and become someone else's problem.

TURNER WAS FURIOUS. As he stormed out of Conway's office he dialled the number for the office of the Director of Special Forces. He doubted the Major General would take his call personally and was taken aback when the man himself answered the call.

'Turner,' said the Major General. 'I thought you'd call.'

'Sir,' began Turner, but the Major General was ready.

'Don't, Turner, I know the unit was assigned to you, but there's an operational need.'

'Sir, these men need to remain under medical supervision,' said Turner. He needed to find a reason why the soldiers should stay at the facility.

'No, they're not listed as under medical supervision. They've been on exercise and they're currently deemed ready for operations.'

'Yes Sir,' said Turner, thinking frantically how to explain his need without revealing what was actually happening with the soldiers. 'They are fit, but...'

The Major General gave him no time. 'I've been updated by MI5,' said the Major General. 'Head of Section Garvey has explained the need for a close protection operation and these soldiers have a possible connection with the target, they're the best unit for the job. They're assigned to it.' The last sentence left no sense that it was a debate.

'Sir,' said Turner, as an acknowledgement. The Major General ended the call. Turner stopped walking. The Head had taken his soldiers? How dare she? How could she? She knew that these soldiers weren't ready to be let out, not yet. He had to stop himself. In fact, she didn't know that. All she could know was what he had told her. All she could know was a unit of soldiers were here and were developing telepathic abilities.

He looked at his phone. He would speak to Rosalind Garvey later. He had to tell Morrow. For all he knew Morrow had already picked up on what was happening. He turned around and marched towards the project building. It took him only moments to reach the building and to find Morrow still sitting in the project room.

Morrow stood as he entered. 'Shall we begin?' asked Morrow, looking passed Turner, likely looking for his first soldier to control.

'There's been a change,' said Turner. 'The soldiers are being transferred to operational duties.'

'You can't let them,' said Morrow, sounding almost like a child having a favourite toy taken away.

'It's out of my hands,' said Turner. 'It's been sanctioned at the highest level, there's nothing I can do.'

'You have to stop them,' said Morrow, sounding more forceful. 'We can't let those soldiers out. It's not safe.'

'I know,' said Turner, staring Morrow in the eye. 'But there's nothing I can do. I can't stop them.'

'I need to see them before they leave,' said Morrow. 'Just one short meeting, just a quick meeting, but I must see each of them before they leave.'

'I can't,' said Turner, trying to make the man understand. 'This is the Army, they have their orders. I have my orders. I can't stop them, not unless you want the Director and his staff down here with Military Police all asking questions about what we're doing.'

'I don't care who comes down here,' said Morrow, with a calm that Turner found almost chilling. 'Can you imagine how dangerous those men are? They have full telepathic ability, but no-one to control them. I can't control them. Can you imagine how much damage they could cause?'

'Yes, actually, I can,' said Turner.

JOON-HO LOOKED out of the window of his private Boeing 737. It was by far the easiest way to travel, and the most secure. He could take his personal security staff with him, and ensure there were the fewest opportunities for anyone to eavesdrop on conversations, or pry into his affairs in any way. He watched as the sea below got closer and closer. Their destination airport was close to the coast, far enough out of London to be away from the main centres of focus of the British security apparatus, but big enough to accommodate his aircraft. He could see the Kent coast stretch away as they approached the mainland, and then they were over the ground.

Within moments the plane bounced and juddered as the wheels connected with the runway. The engines roared briefly on reverse-thrust and the plane slowed as it approached the end of the runway. He could see the airport terminal building, and to one side were the vehicles awaiting his arrival. Two black Mercedes limousines stood waiting, as did three minibuses, and behind them were two Ford Cargo lorries. A smaller car stood to the side of the lorries, and beside them waited a man and a woman. Joon-ho expected them to be the Government representatives. Now they would see if the Minister's promises held up.

The Russian sat opposite him. Joon-ho couldn't be sure if the Russian had ever flown in an aircraft like this. Perhaps he had only ever flown on scheduled flights, crammed in with screaming kids, fat Americans, and over-friendly cabin staff. Joon-ho relished his privacy, his large leather seat, the crew who would only approach him if he summoned them. As the aircraft came to a halt he prepared himself.

As soon as the crew had the door open, Joon-ho was walking down the steps, the Russian following like an attentive dog. The man's insecurities would serve him well, he would be unlikely to risk saying anything unguarded, or to leave Joon-ho's protective company. The waiting man and woman approached. The woman smiled and offered her hand to shake.

'Good afternoon, Mr Joon-ho,' said the woman with a well-rehearsed smile, and expression devoid of any genuine warmth. 'I'm Felicity Wilkinson-Brown, private secretary to the Minister.' Joon-ho shook the woman's hand, briefly. He noticed she made no attempt to introduce the man. Joon-ho made no attempt to introduce the Russian.

'I am grateful for the arrangements you have made,' said Joon-ho. In his peripheral vision he noted the vehicles approaching the sides of the aircraft, and the cargo doors swinging open.

'The Minister apologises for not being here in person to greet you,' said the woman. Joon-ho waved away the apology. He was glad the Minister was not present. It was easier to deal with underlings.

'I have the Minister's assurance,' said Joon-ho, 'that my staff will be given your fullest co-operation, and there will be no delay in setting up my suite at the hotel.'

'Indeed,' said Wilkinson-Brown, 'your effects will be taken there immediately, as will your staff. We have vehicles ready to take you there.' She gestured to the waiting limousines.

'We will go there directly,' said Joon-ho, looking sideways at the Russian. 'My staff will follow once my effects have been unloaded.' He started to walk to the limousine, as expected the Russian stayed close.

'Of course, sir,' said Wilkinson-Brown.

'The Minister also promised the highest level of security would be provided.'

'Indeed, a team of the best Special Forces soldiers has been assigned to ensure your personal security, they will protect you.'

Joon-ho stopped and looked at the woman. 'My personal staff will ensure my safety, your men are only there to prevent anyone from approaching my suite or interfering with my staff.'

'Yes, of course, sir, I understand that,' said Wilkinson-

Brown. Joon-ho resumed his walk to the limousine. The driver walked to the rear door and opened it for Joon-ho.

Before he entered the car he looked back at the aircraft. The first load of flight cases was being unloaded. He again looked at the woman. 'The Minister assured me my personal effects would be delivered directly to the hotel, with no interference, from anyone.'

'Of course, sir,' said the woman. 'They'll be loaded directly into the lorries and delivered straight to the hotel. Your staff will supervise this, I'm sure.'

Joon-ho climbed into the limousine and sank back in the leather seat. The Russian climbed in afterwards, but still appeared tense. As the car pulled away Joon-ho looked at the flight cases being pushed towards the waiting lorries. It was now he would discover if the Minister was true to his word, if his equipment would be unhindered by any inspection from Customs officers, if no-one would look in that case.

SIXTEEN

Michael led the team into Conway's office. It wasn't big and with five of them in the room it was cosy. Conway closed the door behind him. Michael found himself behind the desk so he took the liberty of sitting in the chair. Conway didn't object. Michael could feel the anticipation between his team-mates. Something was happening, and he got the impression Conway didn't know what it was, which could only mean something new and unexpected.

'I've been told,' said Conway, 'that you'll be given a short briefing now by video link, then you'll leave to make preparations.'

'Preparations for what?' asked Marshall.

Conway didn't answer but squeezed passed the others to get to the keyboard and mouse on the desk. He clicked with the mouse and the video-conference software started up on the computer. An image came up on the screen, a modern looking office, a stern looking woman sitting behind the desk.

'We're ready now,' said Conway.

'Thank you, Captain Conway,' said the woman. Conway stepped back so that the three soldiers could stand behind Michael and all get a view of the screen. 'My apologies Captain Conway,' said the woman, 'but the briefing is for this team only. I have to ask you to leave.'

There was an awkward silence as Conway left his own office, and shut the door behind him.

'We don't have long, so I'll be quick,' said the woman. 'I'm the MI5 Head of Section running the operation in Afghanistan you were a part of the other evening.' Michael could feel the others exchanging glances behind him. 'I am also aware of the project you are involved in there at the facility, and of the "abilities" you have developed.' Her emphasis on the word 'abilities' spoke volumes.

Michael was trying to keep track of all the questions forming in his mind, though he doubted there'd be time now to ask them.

The Head went on. 'This afternoon Lee Joon-ho landed at an airfield in Kent.'

'Oh God,' murmured Marshall, 'it's going to be a babysitting job.'

If the Head heard the comment, she ignored it. 'Joon-ho is an influential Chinese businessman and financier. He was a key player in staging the Beijing Olympic games and he's here for a formal meeting of Chinese and British Government officials and key commercial figures for a handing over of the Olympic legacy.'

'With respect,' said Michael, 'how does this involve us?'

'This morning we tried to eavesdrop on Joon-ho, but he'd protected himself with total electronic jamming. The signature of the jamming signal was an exact match for the jamming used against your operation the other night.'

Bullock let out a low whistle. Singh said something about the coincidence being 'interesting.'

The Head continued. 'Since your operation in Afghanistan, individuals in the UK suspected of being linked to the men you killed have ceased almost all electronic communication between themselves. This can only be a deliberate effort to avoid our eavesdropping on them. They have also changed their routine behaviour and some have started moving to other parts of the country.'

'So arrest them,' said Bullock. Michael knew that Singh would be rolling his eyes at this.

'A simple solution, but unfortunately we are constrained by the rule of law, we can't just arrest people for not using the Internet or for going somewhere new.'

'You suspect they're mobilising for an operation,' said Michael.

'That's our suspicion, yes,' said the Head. 'Joon-ho's arrival and his use of the same jamming system is too coincidental to ignore, especially as he's now here.'

'Surveillance?' asked Michael.

'No,' said the Head, 'not officially. It's been made clear that Joon-ho has political connections at the highest level. He's a guest of Her Majesty's Government, and there is to be no surveillance or monitoring of him at all. Your mission is to provide security and protection.'

'Why us?' asked Marshall. 'Or is that a silly question?'

'Your abilities give you a chance to effect surveillance of a different kind,' said the Head. 'If you can acquire any information from him or from any of his staff to indicate what he's doing or if he's connected with anything untoward then I can use that to petition the Minister to sanction more regular surveillance.'

'His staff?' asked Michael, 'I take it he's not here alone?'

'No, Joon-ho has an entourage with him. He has his own security staff who will provide close protection security. He also has his own business and administrative staff, and I would expect within that team is someone who will oversee the provision of full electronic counter-measures.'

'So where is he?' asked Singh.

'Hampshire,' said the Head. 'All the delegates for the meeting are being hosted at Mountfield House. You'll leave immediately for a detailed briefing and planning session, and from there go directly to Mountfield. I expect you'll be there by 9 pm tonight.'

'No rest for the wicked,' said Marshall.

'No,' said the Head, 'there isn't. Captain, we don't have a shred of tangible evidence, but everything suggests there is a very significant terrorist action being planned. Joon-ho fits the bill for the kind of individual who has the resources and the connections to finance that scale of operation, and his presence here is too coincidental. We need to know if he's involved, and if he is, what exactly he is involved with. Keep me updated.'

The screen went blank, and the call was ended. Michael felt relieved. Whatever the new assignment had in store for them, it would be a welcome change from their current circumstance.

'Well,' said Bullock, 'it's got to be better than being holed up here.' No-one disagreed with him.

'I'll tell you what else is too coincidental,' said Marshall, Michael turned around to face him. 'She ran that operation the other night. All of a sudden we're whisked off operational duties and holed up here, we're given that drug and weird shit starts happening. No sooner can we read minds and control people then she pops up again and hey, she's got a mission for us.'

'You mean she's behind it?' said Bullock.

'We don't know that,' said Michael, 'this isn't the sort of thing MI5 get involved in. This is a military facility.' He'd never known his team be this paranoid before, and he didn't like it.

'Military and civilian contractor,' said Singh, 'the drug is from an external supplier.'

'Whatever her role, we have a mission, and we will follow orders,' said Michael, trying to maintain a belief that military discipline could keep his team together.

'We can also find out just how useful our new "abilities" can be in a real operation,' said Marshall, using air-quotes.

'So is she behind all this?' asked Bullock, again.

'Who cares?' said Michael, 'it's time to go. Anyone want to say a fond farewell to Captain Conway?'

'Fuck off,' said Marshall.

'That's a no then, is it?' said Michael.

THE LIMOUSINE SWEPT up the drive of Mountfield House. The Georgian mansion boasted manicured lawns, landscaped gardens, and lots of privacy. A magnificent ornamental flowerbed formed the centrepiece of the circular driveway in front of the house. The tall broad trees further away provided a picturesque barrier between the grounds and the main road. The two roads into the grounds gave the security services complete control over who was allowed in, and who wasn't.

Lee Joon-ho hardly noticed the grounds or the building. He'd seen more impressive buildings in many countries. At one time he'd owned a more substantial property, and older. He thought it typical of the British to capitalise on their past, and slightly ironic that even though they didn't know it the past was all they would have. Joon-ho meant to deprive them of their future.

The Russian, on the other hand, was staring out of the limousine window like a child on his first visit to a theme park. Joon-ho could see him staring at the armed police at the front gate, surely as a Russian he would be used to seeing armed police, and the man's eyes nearly popped out when he first saw the house. Joon-ho was coming to the conclusion that despite it being bad form to kill a business associate at the end of a deal, perhaps it would be better to relieve the world of this irksome individual. Joon-ho did not relish the prospect of having this man around any longer than strictly necessary.

The car stopped in front of the house and a smartly dressed servant pulled the door open. Two men in smart business suits stepped forward. One was older and reeked of establishment, the other was middle-aged and held himself like an employee, a wage-slave.

'Mr Joon-ho, it is a pleasure to meet you, sir,' said the older gentleman, offering his hand to shake. Joon-ho shook it with the least amount of contact that would be polite. 'I am Sebastian Wellington, on behalf of Her Majesty's Government may I welcome you, and your associate, to Mountfield House.'

Joon-ho smiled, caring not whether his smile would appear genuine or not. He made no attempt to introduce the Russian, and Wellington made no effort to enquire.

'This is Mr Rogers,' said Wellington, indicating the other man.

'Head of Security,' said Rogers. He didn't offer to shake hands, Joon-ho was glad.

The second limousine and the minibuses drew to a halt

behind Joon-ho's limousine, and Joon-ho's staff started to get out, clutching various bags and briefcases.

'As agreed,' said Wellington, 'we have reserved for you the suite on the second floor in the east wing. If you would care to follow me.' Without waiting Wellington started up the steps towards the front door. Rogers waited for a moment and fell in behind Joon-ho and the Russian, Joon-ho's retinue following behind.

Joon-ho was almost disappointed to find a typical grand entrance hall, with a staircase sweeping up one side of it to the upper floors, all too predictable, nothing original. His disappointment was tempered by familiarity, he had studied the plans for the building as soon as the venue had been confirmed. He knew there was a lift at the rear of the building, and his precious equipment cases would be taken up in that lift to the second floor. He didn't want to imagine British servants lifting the case up the stairs.

A wide landing led through the east wing, and at the end were the doors to the suite. Wellington opened the doors with a flourish. A wasted gesture. He beckoned Joon-ho to enter. Joon-ho walked in, making no effort to hurry. The first room was a comfortable lounge, but with too much furniture for Joon-ho's tastes. He stepped further into the room, giving the impression he was weighing up whether it met with approval.

Rogers joined them in the room.

'As you've seen,' said Rogers, 'we have armed police patrolling the grounds. My men monitor the surveillance systems for the grounds and building and will provide you with round the clock close quarter protection.'

Joon-ho continued to wander around the room, as though inspecting his accommodation.

Rogers continued. 'The staff here will ensure your

luggage and equipment are delivered to the suite. There is, of course, full Internet and telephone services, and staff on call twenty-four seven.'

Joon-ho looked out of the window, surveying the grounds. He could see the two lorries starting to make their way up the drive. He turned to face Rogers.

'I thank you for your preparations,' he said. Politeness was always important. 'But they will not be needed. My associates will deliver all my effects to the suite, and will not be hampered in any way by your staff. My associates will be responsible for all aspects of my personal security and for the security of these rooms. I will use my own Internet access, you will disconnect and disable all electronic services to these rooms, I will not need them.'

Rogers stood with his mouth open. Joon-ho was surprised the man had not expected a guest such as himself to be so self-sufficient, and self-secure. But what could you expect? He was pleased to see members of his staff starting to set up in the suite, unplugging the phones and television, beginning an initial sweep with hand-held scanners, searching for the inevitable listening devices.

'Further,' said Joon-ho, 'my chef and her assistants will prepare all my food using the ingredients they have with them. No-one will enter this suite for the duration of my stay, no-one will cross or attempt to cross the perimeter my men will establish.' He looked at Wellington. 'I was promised a detail of your Special Forces soldiers, where are they?'

Wellington seemed to hesitate. 'They are on their way,' he said. 'They have been at their base, preparing, but they...'

Joon-ho interrupted him. 'Good. Your soldiers will ensure no-one attempts to approach this suite or to interfere with my staff. That includes your police or anyone else you have providing security. These arrangements were agreed with your Minister who in turn agreed them with your Prime Minister. I assume I have your assurance you will abide by these agreements?'

Rogers and Wellington looked at each other, speechless.

Two of Joon-ho's men began to push a wheeled flight case through the door and into the suite. Joon-ho felt himself relax a little when he saw the case.

'That case,' he said in Chinese, 'in the office. Leave it there.'

He addressed Rogers and Wellington, in English. 'Thank you, gentlemen, for all your help. I believe everything is under control.' He gave a command in Chinese to his staff. Two of the larger men stepped slightly closer to Wellington and Rogers, almost shepherding them towards the door. The two mumbled some pleasantry as they left, and the door was closed behind them.

'I am sure you will wish to inspect the consignment,' Joon-ho said to the Russian, walking to the small office room. He and the Russian squeezed into the room. With the flight case, the desk and chair and the two of them there was little space left. Joon-ho closed the door.

He slid open a concealed cover on the lid of the case to reveal a numeric keypad and a small display. He tapped in a series of numbers, then placed his thumb on the display. A white light glowed, and his efforts were rewarded by a small green light. There was a dull click as the internal locks disengaged. Joon-ho twisted the two locking catches on the case and lifted open the lid.

Joon-ho and the Russian looked inside. Sitting cradled in the foam padding was a white object, a metallic cone, seventy centimetres in length, a red band around the circumference near the base.

'Could you imagine,' the Russian said, 'the look on some customs officer's face if he had opened this case?' Joon-ho thought it was a stupid question, from a man he increasingly saw as stupid. The case was not only locked but protected by various anti-tampering measures. The point though did prompt some amusement in Joon-ho. What would a customs official have made, had he been able to open the case and find himself face-to-face with a nuclear warhead?

With this, he thought, he will shine a light on the world, a light that will change everything.

THEY HAD GONE straight from the project facility to Stirling Lines Barracks, the main barracks for arguably the most famous Special Forces unit, the original Special Forces unit, the 22nd Regiment of the Special Air Service. Michael always found it amusing that a unit focused on covert and clandestine operations should be so famous.

The entrance to Stirling lines was, in many ways, unremarkable, set back off a sweeping bend on a road that threaded its way through the Herefordshire countryside. The barracks themselves, Michael thought, would probably be a disappointment to the many who were fascinated by the SAS. The barracks had no hi-tech space-age control room, it had no stores of advanced weaponry. It had a mediocre mess which served adequate food. It had uncomfortable accommodation, cold meeting rooms, a gymnasium, and various rooms used for training exercises of one kind or another.

It did, however, have well-stocked stores, able to equip those on rapid deployment who needed to be kitted out for operations in almost any climate or environment, military or civilian. The Head had made arrangements, so when the team arrived a briefing room had already been set up with plans of Mountfield House, details of press conferences and the meetings between visiting dignitaries and government officials and Olympic Games staff. The quartermaster was also ready to hand over, on receipt of signatures on what seemed like a hundred forms, various items of civilian clothing, small arms, larger arms, radio equipment, identity badges, and a Land Rover Discovery.

After two hours of briefings and an hour of signing out and checking equipment, they had set off in the Land Rover, Marshall driving, Michael in the front passenger seat. As usual, as expected, Bullock had shouted "shotgun," and everyone else had told him to piss off.

Motorways had given way to A roads and then to more rural routes. The sky was enjoying the last light of the afternoon as they drove through rolling green landscape into Hampshire. Michael thought it was a good job they'd been assigned a reasonable looking vehicle. Arriving at what they expected to be a very exclusive country mansion in a muddy Army service vehicle would get them noticed. They excelled at not being noticed.

The inspection at the front entrance to the grounds was thorough, Michael couldn't fault them for being suspicious of four unknown men, only recently added to the list of "approved persons," and who (on closer inspection) had a small arsenal in their vehicle. Soon enough they were cleared to proceed and were directed to the rear of the building. Bullock made some quip about only being good enough to use the tradesman's entrance.

Michael guessed the man who greeted them was ex-military but had now spent more than a few years in the private sector, judging by the beer gut. The man introduced himself as Rogers, Head of Security. He directed the team to the outbuilding used by the police, and to the two small rooms assigned to them. Rogers left them, muttering something about 'filling them in later.' One of the rooms had four camp beds, the other had four plastic chairs, the sum total of the furniture at their disposal.

It took them little time to unpack their electronics and personal kit, storing those in the sleeping room. They gathered in the second room, and shut the door.

'Right,' said Michael, 'we need to go and say hello to our visiting dignitary.'

'Remind me,' said Bullock, 'who is he? Really?'

'Who cares?' said Marshall, sighing.

'Visiting Chinese dignitary,' said Michael, 'attached to the Chinese trade mission, beyond that I have no background data on him at all.'

'The only interesting thing is he uses the same jamming system that we came across,' said Singh. 'I'm keen to get a closer look at his set up.'

'I'm not sure he's going to invite us all in and give us a tour of his security arrangements,' said Michael. 'We'll start with a walk around the east wing, see how much we can learn from a visual inspection.'

As they agreed their route around the house and up to and around the east wing, Michael felt his enthusiasm wane. The similarity in the jamming systems was a tenuous link at best, and there were serious issues within the team, issues needing his attention. The last thing he wanted was the team cooped up together on a frivolous assignment. For the moment they seemed focused again, but he was dubious how long this would last.

With radios clipped to inside jacket pockets and

earpieces inserted, the team were ready. Singh had a few additional pieces of electronics with him, 'just for interest' he said. They headed across the rear courtyard and into the main house. British police, some armed, patrolled the house and grounds, as did various Chinese staff. Michael assumed at least some of them were armed.

They did a cursory tour of the ground floor and the first floor, and wasted no more time before heading for the second floor, and particularly the east wing. The carpet was thick and no doubt expensive, thick enough to absorb almost all sound. The east wing was quiet, Michael noticed there were no roaming patrols. They turned into the corridor leading to the suite, and the two gentlemen standing either side of the door, hands clasped in front of them.

As the team approached one of the men took a half step forward.

'I am sorry,' the man said, in good English. 'But I cannot permit you to proceed further.'

'I'm Captain Sanders,' said Michael, 'I and my team are assigned to provide security for Mr Joon-ho.' He hadn't expected to be invited in, but they needed to see more than just the two stooges on front-door duty.

'Mr Joon-ho thanks you for your services, but his security is taken care of. There is no need for you to be here.' The man put on a good show of sounding courteous.

Michael avoided sighing out loud. Diplomacy wasn't his favourite game. 'I have no doubt that Mr Joon-ho's security is taken care of, however we are here on the orders of the Government to assure Mr Joon-ho's safety and security. I would appreciate being able to meet Mr Joon-ho and discuss our arrangements.'

'Again,' said the man, 'Mr Joon-ho thanks you, but your

presence here is not required, and Mr Joon-ho will not be able to meet with you.'

Michael started to take a step forward. In an almost instant response the other guard stepped forward and both dropped their hands to their sides. Michael's three comrades stepped forward, the four of them forming a line across the corridor. Ordinarily, Michael would let things play out, but for now they needed to avoid any confrontation, if possible.

'I suggest you go back to your government,' said the first guard, 'and clarify your role here.' The courtesy had gone from his voice.

'I suggest you remember whose country you're in,' said Marshall.

'Gentlemen,' came a voice from behind, loud enough to attract everyone's attention. None of the team turned around. 'Gentlemen,' came the voice again. Michael recognised it as Rogers, but still wasn't going to turn around. He kept eye contact with the first guard.

'Captain Sanders, I need to talk to you and your men,' said Rogers. He was standing behind them, but none of the four was going to move to let him passed. 'Downstairs please, now.'

Michael held the gaze of the guard, waiting to see who would blink first.

'Captain,' said Rogers again, a sharper edge in his voice. The guard's gaze flicked over Michael's shoulder towards Rogers, just for a moment. Michael thought perhaps he had seen enough, for the moment. Joon-ho's guards were likely armed, well trained, and disciplined. It all indicated Joon-ho had a very professional setup and was dead set on avoiding any intrusion into his affairs. Michael decided intrusion was exactly what he and the team were going to achieve.

Michael turned and followed Rogers, the team falling in behind him. They were led back downstairs to the main entrance hall.

'I'm sorry I didn't have time to brief you when you arrived,' said Rogers, 'but Mr Joon-ho's suite is off limits. To everyone.'

'We're here...' said Michael, but Rogers interrupted.

'I know why you're here, Captain. The government has promised Mr Joon-ho the highest level of service, including his own unit of Special Forces soldiers for his protection. However, as you've seen, Mr Joon-ho has his own security, and we all have orders that Mr Joon-ho is not to be approached, spoken to, or inconvenienced in any way.'

'Then what are we supposed to do?' said Marshall, 'shoe shine service?'

'Mr Joon-ho has his own security staff, I provide the security to the house and grounds. To be frank, you can do whatever you like, but don't get in my way and don't go anywhere near Mr Joon-ho.' Rogers walked off without waiting for any response or agreement.

'This is a shit assignment,' said Marshall, 'that MI5 Head has put us on another shit assignment.'

'This is just a glorified babysitting assignment,' said Bullock.

'We're not even babysitters, we're just patrol-monkeys,' said Marshall, 'we're supposed to walk around just for show.'

'I don't believe there's nothing we can do,' said Michael. 'We need to come up with a plan, but here's not the place.'

He led the team back to their office (Singh's name for the room they weren't sleeping in.) Michael noticed that Singh couldn't wait to pull out a laptop computer and start fiddling with one of the other electronic devices he'd taken with him. He soon had the laptop balanced on his lap, sitting in one of the chairs.

'We can provide patrols,' said Bullock, 'two on, two off.' It was a reasonable suggestion, Michael thought. In any other circumstance it would be the beginning of a plan, and the team would build on it.

'Not this time,' said Michael. 'No-one's going to notice if we're here or not, so we can work together, maximise what we do.'

'I don't want to be defeatist,' said Marshall, 'but what can we do?'

'What we can't do,' said Singh, looking up from his laptop, 'is use the radios anywhere near the target's suite. Mr Joon-ho doesn't just have a jamming device set up, he's got complete electronic counter-surveillance. No form of electronics is going to penetrate those rooms.'

'So Mr Joon-ho is either very, very paranoid,' said Michael, 'or he's doing something that he really doesn't want anyone else being a party to.'

Marshall grinned. 'All of a sudden I find this man more interesting.'

'So do I,' said Michael. 'We need to find a way to see inside that suite.'

'That's the reason we're here,' said Singh, still sitting.

'Yes,' said Marshall, 'we figured that out.'

'No,' said Singh, 'that's the reason we are here.' He emphasised 'we.'

'He's right,' said Michael. 'We've had some weird times over the last few days.' He pulled out his earpiece. 'But we have certain abilities, maybe now's the time we need to use those abilities.'

'How?' said Bullock, mocking. 'I know we can do things, but we can't just see through walls.'

'No,' said Michael, 'we can't. This is a mission like any other. We don't yet know the strength or position of the enemy force, we don't their capabilities or movements. We need intelligence on the enemy, we need to see what we're dealing with.'

'I've tried hacking into the house's CCTV system,' said Singh, 'but with the equipment I have here, I can't.'

'Then we need to go and see Rogers,' said Bullock, 'tell him we need to see the footage.'

'Good idea,' said Marshall, 'because Rogers is going to be ever so keen to let us just play all his security footage.'

'He won't let us,' said Singh, 'which is why we need to persuade him.' Again, the emphasis on 'we.'

'What, just take him to one side and do that weird thing with him?' said Bullock.

'Why not?' said Marshall.

'Because we need to be careful,' said Michael. 'We can't do anything that will make anyone suspicious.'

'So maybe just one of us has to go and have a quiet word with Mr Rogers,' said Singh.

'I will,' said Michael. 'He won't be suspicious of me asking that. I'll have a quiet word with him.'

SEVENTEEN

By the time they'd formulated their plan, Rogers had disappeared for the night. The team retreated to the outbuilding and wasted no time in joining the resident police officers for an evening of microwaved meals and football, streamed onto Singh's laptop.

No doubt the visiting dignitaries would be well catered for, but the catering for the on-site security staff was minimal. At least there had been a plentiful supply of tea. Michael and Julian had gone over the layout of the building, location of the CCTV control room, and what Michael would need from Rogers. Julian had supplied Michael with a USB stick and instructions of where he wanted Rogers to put it, which elicited more schoolboy humour from Bullock.

The next morning Michael set off in search of Rogers. The main building was busy, teaming with people. Many were in more casual dress, and Michael noted the names of various newspapers and media organisations from the ID badges. Having followed one wrong direction after another, Michael finally located Rogers. He was in deep conversation with one of the police officers, who promptly left to accompany one of the Chinese dignitaries to another of the meeting rooms.

'Mr Rogers,' said Michael, loud enough to attract his attention.

Rogers looked at him only long enough to recognise him. 'Not now,' was all he said, before heading off towards another well-dressed individual. Michael assumed the woman he joined in conversation was British Government, but she could just as easily have been from the Games organisers. Michael retreated to a corner, becoming as invisible as he could. The journalists milled around, photographers hurried from one potential photo-opportunity to the next. From further down one of the plush corridors came bright white light, no doubt a TV crew were in residence.

Michael noticed Rogers and the woman making all the right gestures to suggest their conversation was coming to an end. Michael started to move to intercept, and sure enough Rogers turned away from the woman and back towards the centre of the room. He was only yards from Rogers when another man appeared, his press affiliation clear from his ID badge.

'Mr Rogers,' said the man, red shirt and black trousers gave the man a distinctive look, as did his broad smile and hand out to shake. Michael suspected this was a man skilled in using charm to coax an answer out of a reluctant source. He stood back, not wanting to attract the attention of any of the journalists. He was close enough to hear the conversation between Rogers and the journalist.

'Mr Rogers, I'm Grant Bray, Associated News, we spoke recently about the interview,' said the journalist.

'Indeed, Mr Bray,' said Rogers. 'As you can see, things are a bit hectic at the moment, but I can give you a few minutes after lunch if that's okay?'

'That would be fine, thank you,' said the journalist, who then promptly walked away, his eye on his next target.

Michael stepped forward again. 'Mr Rogers,' he said more firmly. Rogers stopped and turned to Michael. Michael wasted no time. 'My team have established a routine patrolling the outside of the house,' he said. It was a complete lie, but he suspected it was something Rogers wouldn't object to. 'And I wanted to thank you for intervening yesterday, it was good to avoid any kind of stand-off with the Chinese security team.' He held his hand out to shake.

Rogers grunted what might have been a thank you, and went to shake Michael's hand, no doubt as briefly as possible. As soon as their hands made contact Michael could feel his thoughts flow through his hand and into Rogers', he felt his thoughts make a connection with Rogers' thoughts. He let a gentle rush of energy flow through the connection, and he conjured within himself thoughts of being friendly, of being helpful.

'Mr Rogers, I'd like a quick word with you, if I may?' He let go of Rogers' hand, not wanting to stand in the pose too long.

Rogers looked slightly vacant, as though he'd lost track of where he was. 'Really? Yes, I suppose...' His voice trailed off.

'Perhaps we could stand over here,' said Michael, leading Rogers away from the crowd and towards the corridor leading to the kitchens. The policeman guarding the door to the corridor eyed their security badges but made no move towards them as they left the main hallway.

Alone in the corridor, Michael again took Rogers' hand, and this time let a fuller flow of mental energy surge through the connection. He noticed Rogers' stagger slightly, he held out his other hand to steady the man.

'Mr Rogers,' said Michael. 'I need your help. You'll help me? Won't you?'

Rogers looked at him for a moment, his eyes taking a moment to focus on Michael. 'Yes. Yes, of course,' he said slowly.

Michael let go of his hand. He couldn't put into words, not even to himself, how it felt to be connected to this man. He could feel the connection between his mind and Rogers'. It was strange, that was certain. It wasn't physical, but it wasn't imagined either, it was very real, almost surreal.

'Why don't we go to the security control room?' said Michael. 'You can give me remote access to the video system, can't you?'

'Yes, of course I can,' said Rogers. He let Rogers lead the way, back through the hallway to the other side, then along a corridor to the furthest side of the house. The police, and presumably MI5, had set up in one of the drawing rooms. The antique paintings on the wall now shared the room with banks of flat-panel computer screens, desks of keyboards and radio systems. Operators sat watching the screens, others talked to colleagues over radio connections, directing teams from one location to another. A couple turned to note Rogers' entry, but otherwise their presence went unnoticed.

Michael stood by the door and watched Rogers walk to a table creaking under the weight of the computers loaded on top of it. Michael had not instructed Rogers on exactly what to do, he had simply held in his mind the idea of what he wanted, and he had felt from Rogers the idea had been understood.

Rogers slipped out of his trouser pocket the USB stick

Michael had given him. He pushed it into one of the computers, then bent down to tap at the keyboard. It took only moments before he'd finished, pulled out the USB stick, and returned it to Michael.

'Mr Rogers,' said Michael. 'I'm sorry for having taken up so much of your time. I'm sure there are lots of things you need to return to organising.' Michael felt the psychic connection fade. It didn't break, it was more like turning down the volume on the radio to the point where it was no longer audible.

Rogers had the expression of someone just waking from a snooze. 'What? Oh. Yes. Of course,' said Rogers, who turned and left the room. Michael followed behind, and in the main hallway parted company with Rogers who made straight for one of the journalists having a discussion with a police officer over the validity of his ID badge.

Michael went straight back to his team in the outbuilding. Singh had the laptop open on the chair in front of him, the other two standing behind him staring at the screen.

As soon as Michael entered the room Bullock looked up, grinning. 'We're in,' he said.

'Mr Rogers must have been a great help,' said Singh.

'He was pleasantly cooperative,' said Michael.

'I can see,' said Singh. 'He's given us full access to the live CCTV feeds and to the stored footage.'

'How far back does it go?' asked Michael. 'Can we see Joon-ho arriving?'

Singh tapped at the keys on the laptop. 'Yes, we can. Here we go.'

They spent the next hour looking over the images of Joon-ho's arrival, his staff ferrying boxes and crates and cases up the stairs and up the freight elevator and into the suite. There were no images from inside the suite, not since

Joon-ho arrived. The team also focused on Joon-ho's guards, where they stood, where they patrolled.

They watched in fascination as Joon-ho joined some of the others for a meeting. He left his suite flanked by four guards, two in front and two behind. Two stood behind him as Joon-ho sat at the table talking with the other Chinese business people. The other two guards stood at the door and the far side of the room. At the conclusion of the meeting, the guards surrounded him as he walked back to his suite.

'There's no way of getting to that guy,' said Marshall. 'I have to admit, his people do a reasonable job of isolating him.'

'Has he left the suite any other time?' asked Michael. It took Singh a few minutes to search through various video files.

'Looking at this, he has left twice more, same arrangements each time. He's completely protected by his men.'

The team turned their attention to Joon-ho's men, who seemed to make almost random patrols of the house and immediate grounds. They saw no predictable timetable, no regularity to their excursions. Joon-ho's team were professional in every way.

'Wait,' said Bullock. 'Back up, that one.' He leaned over Singh's shoulder and pointed at one window of video. Singh clicked with the buttons on the laptop and reversed the video. They watched one of Joon-ho's men walking around the outside of the house, and around a corner.

'There,' said Bullock, 'they patrolled there before, and they go out of sight.'

'How do you know they're out of sight?' asked Marshall.

'Because there's no other picture of them,' said Bullock, sounding like he was pleased to win a point.

'He's right,' said Singh. 'Round that corner is a CCTV dead spot, no coverage. They're out of sight for about half a minute, until they come back into view.'

'That's our way in,' said Michael, 'we have to be ready for one of his men to patrol that way.'

'Then we have a quiet word with him?' said Singh, smiling.

'Indeed we do,' said Michael.

THEIR PLAN WAS SO LOOSE it was hard to call it a plan. The biggest complicating factor was the random timing of Joon-ho's men and their patrols around the house. Michael and Vince walked out of the house, turning right towards the main drive. A few minutes later, Julian and Evan left the house and walked the other way.

There were too many people outside the house for Michael's liking, the press and their various vehicles, but most seemed to be static in the forecourt, leaving the sides of the house clear. There was also the camouflage factor, two more people in amongst the dozens wouldn't stand out.

'Give us a few minutes and we'll be round the back of the house,' came Singh's voice into Michael's mind.

'Okay,' said/thought Michael. 'Vince and I will go down to the drive, then back again, we'll walk around the front grounds. Hopefully we'll spot Joon-ho's man coming out on his patrol.' As plans went, it was flimsy, wandering around hoping to see the man coming out on patrol, then Evan and Julian would intercept him as he entered the CCTV dead spot.

'So what are we going to do after this operation?' asked Marshall, out loud.

It caught Michael by surprise, mainly because he'd not thought about that.

'To be honest,' he said, 'I've no idea.' He turned around to glance at the house. None of Joon-ho's men had left the house, yet.

'Can't say I'm a big fan of going back to that project facility. Conway's a dickhead, no offence to a senior officer, sir, but we weren't exactly achieving much.'

'No, I have to agree, we weren't,' said Michael.

'Can't see how we'll rejoin Special Forces like we were,' said Marshall, 'makes me wonder what someone's plans might be.'

They reached the end of the large forecourt and the beginning of the main driveway. They both turned and started walking around the far side of the ornamental flowerbed.

'I don't even know whose plans we need to worry about,' said Michael. 'Conway just runs the project facility. The MI5 Head of Section might use Special Forces, but we don't report to her.'

'I don't get the sense the Director is in on our little secret,' said Marshall.

'You're thinking what I'm thinking,' said Michael.

'Think I might be, there's someone else in charge of this. That scientist?'

'Can't see how,' said Michael, 'not if he's from outside the Army.'

Their conversation was interrupted as they saw two figures emerge from the main doors of the house. The two were recognisable as the two they first met in the corridor outside Joon-ho's suite. The guards had turned to their left and were walking slowly along the front of the house, as expected. Two guards were not what they had expected.

Michael and Vince picked up their pace and walked as quickly as they dared towards the two Chinese.

'Two of them on their way to you,' Michael thought, intending the other three all hear him.

'Two?' came Bullock's thoughts in the telepathic equivalent of a shout.

'Keep your thoughts down,' said Marshall.

'We'll try and split them up,' thought Michael.

'And how are we going to do that?' came Marshall's voice.

'I have no idea, but I'm sure you'll think of something,' thought Michael, smiling.

They reached the two Chinese, who were deep in conversation.

'Excuse me,' said Michael, out loud. The two Chinese turned around and stopped walking. The two looked at Michael and Vince but said nothing.

'Good morning,' said Michael, trying to sound friendly. 'I think we may have got off on the wrong foot yesterday.'

One of the Chinese frowned. 'Wrong foot?'

'Yes,' said Michael, 'it's a saying, I mean we didn't mean to challenge your authority.'

The two Chinese looked at each other. 'I do not believe my authority was challenged,' said the first guard, the other stayed silent. 'Sorry, please excuse us.' The two turned to resume their patrol.

'I was wondering,' said Michael, 'if I might have a word with you, to discuss how we can work together during your stay.'

'Get the other one to go with you,' Michael thought, aiming his words at Marshall.

Vince eyed the second guard. 'I'd like to talk to you about your military training, share experiences.' Michael

273

almost cringed, but it was probably the best ad lib either of them could come up with.

'So sorry,' said the second guard, 'English not good.' Michael thought that probably buggered that idea.

'Captain Sanders,' came the all too familiar voice of Mr Rogers. Michael had been focused on the two guards and had missed Rogers approaching from the side. Perhaps he'd followed the guards out of the house. In moments Rogers reached them.

Rogers' voice made it clear he was not happy. 'I thought, Captain, I had made your role clear.' He turned to the two guards. 'I apologise, the Captain and his men will not detain you any longer.'

Michael made a concerted effort to keep his face immobile, to give nothing away. He let his mind expand, and felt the familiar connection with Rogers. Michael held in his mind the idea of what he wanted and felt the idea flow through the connection.

Rogers turned to the second guard. 'Please would you convey a message to Mr Joon-ho?' Rogers asked. Michael thought desperately what question he could use to get rid of the second guard. He thought about the only idea that came to mind, and let the idea expand out into the connection with Rogers.

'Please ask Mr Joon-ho if will accept the ambassador's invitation to lunch,' said Rogers.

The two guards exchanged glances, then exchanged words, in Chinese. The second guard gave a perfunctory bow of his head and walked off briskly towards the house. Rogers turned and followed him, at a slower pace. The first guard gave a final look at Michael and resumed his walk along the front of the house.

'What invitation to lunch?' asked Marshall, perhaps out loud, Michael couldn't tell.

'Only thing I could think of,' he said. Then made his words silent. 'One guard, coming your way. We'll be right behind him.'

Michael set off, Marshall with him. They walked slowly enough not to gain any ground on the Chinese, the last thing Michael wanted was to give any impression they were following the man. Soon enough, the guard walked around the side of the house and passed what perhaps used to be stables. Michael knew that in moments the man would reach the area with no security camera coverage.

He and Marshall picked up their pace, but avoided running, they could do without attracting any further unwanted attention. As they rounded the corner the space between the stables and the house was empty, but at the far end were two armed police, standing guard, their backs to Michael and Vince.

'Door on your left,' came Bullock's thoughts. The two turned to the door, Marshall pushed it open and they stepped inside. It was the entrance to a narrow corridor, perhaps a servant's entrance to the house. Singh stood, his left hand resting on the forehead of the guard, who stood in a relaxed posture, his eyes half closed.

Michael felt a growing urge to hurry Singh. He had no doubt Joon-ho was a stickler for punctuality and timetables, and the man would soon be missed. Almost certainly Roger's random enquiry about a lunch invitation was already causing awkward questions.

Singh dropped his hand. He spoke softly to the guard. 'Thank you,' he said, 'for taking the time to talk to me. I'm sorry to have detained you. There's no need to think of our meeting, it was of no concern.'

The guard gave a half-hearted smile, then pushed passed the others and through the narrow space to the door, and was gone.

'You need to contact your MI5 person,' said Singh, 'I think we've got a big problem.'

'Tell me on the way back,' said Michael. They quickly left the corridor and retraced their steps back towards the main entrance. As they walked they kept their conversation to themselves, they were silent to any outside observer, but the words between them were quite clear and audible.

'He didn't know much,' came Singh's words. 'But Joon-ho's got a box, a flight case. It's important, sealed with a lot of hi-tech security, only him and some Russian have access to it.'

'That doesn't sound good,' said Marshall.

'No, it doesn't,' said Singh. 'They're working to a timetable. Joon-ho is doing something and it's going to be soon.'

'Okay, we need to find out what's in that box,' thought Michael. 'We'll get back and I'll update the Head, make sure we've got clearance to find a way in.'

Singh led the way and they marched back towards the front door. As they approached Michael noticed a figure sitting on one of the garden benches around the lawned area beyond the forecourt. The figure had the unmistakable red shirt and black trousers of the journalist, and likely had a clear line of sight to the area at the side of the house.

As THE TEAM walked back into the house they joined the throng in the main hall. The various press interviews were in full flow, journalists and technicians rushing from one room to another.

'Why did we come this way?' asked Michael, silently.

'There's something I want to look at,' said Singh. 'It's just a hunch.'

'Care to give us a clue?' thought Marshall.

Singh stopped and looked around. Michael couldn't think what he was looking for, it was hard to see anything through the mass of people.

'Give us a clue, Julian,' thought Michael.

'The target stopped, yesterday, on his way to the meeting,' said Singh. 'I saw it on the CCTV. He stood and touched something. It looked strange, I just can't remember exactly what it was.'

'So what?' came Bullock's voice in Michael's mind.

'So if it's something he touched then I can touch it,' thought Julian, 'and maybe I can get a connection to him.'

'Come on, man,' said Marshall, 'we don't have time to hang around.'

Michael felt Julian say 'ah ha,' almost as much as he heard it.

'Time,' said Julian. Michael saw Singh move off to the side, towards the bottom of the staircase. He followed, sliding passed guests and officials. He found Singh standing by a wall-mounted clock, an antique no doubt.

'He stopped to change the time on the clock,' said Singh, in a normal voice. 'He opened the face of the clock and touched the hand.'

'Go for it,' said Michael, 'but be quick, we look suspicious.'

The three of them stood with their backs to Singh, trying to look like three security staff, standing around doing security things, hopefully hiding Singh from suspicious gazes. Michael wasn't concerned about the police or any other security staff, their badges made them official. His concern was any domestic staff, they were the ones more likely to complain about Julian interfering with the clock.

Michael was sure his eyes widened as he heard/felt Julian's words of 'oh shit!' come into his mind. 'We need to tell MI5 about this, now.'

Julian pushed passed them and they all made a hasty escape from the hall and through the back of the house. Crossing the courtyard to the outbuilding they spoke in normal voices.

'I couldn't get much,' said Singh, 'domestics touch the clock to change the time, and Joon-ho didn't touch it for long, he didn't leave much of impression, or however it works.'

'You said "oh shit,"' said Marshall, 'so what did you get?'

'This Joon-ho is the one called Shining Light,' said Singh.

'Oh shit indeed,' said Michael.

'It's worse,' said Singh. 'He's planning something massive. I couldn't tell exactly what but it's big, it's nasty and it's very soon.'

Thoughts were racing through Michael's mind as they got back to their room in the outbuilding, possibilities about what Joon-ho might be planning. Michael used the mobile phone he'd been given to call the MI5 Head of Section's number.

He was relieved she answered quickly.

'Captain Sanders,' said the Head, 'please tell me you have something to report.'

'We do,' said Michael. 'We've every reason to believe that Joon-ho is the one they call Shining Light.' He waited for a response, there was none. He continued. 'He's here with a

Russian, we don't know who, and they have a case of equipment with them.'

'A case?' asked the Head.

'Yes, a flight case, an equipment case. We don't know what's in it, could be guns, explosives, we don't know.'

'This doesn't fit,' said the Head.

'What do you mean, doesn't fit?' gasped Michael. The others turned to look at him, no doubt wondering what the Head had said.

'Shining Light is someone we suspect of being one of the biggest financiers of terrorism, most of the action originating from the Middle East,' said the Head. 'Joon-ho is Chinese.'

'Yes,' said Michael, 'we had noticed that. But we're quite certain, he is Shining Light.'

'Someone like that funds terrorism,' said the Head, 'they don't get within a million miles of the actual killing, they maintain absolute deniability.'

'Then I suggest that whatever he's planning is so big he daren't leave it to anyone else.'

'Possible,' said the Head.

'We need to get at the Russian,' said Michael, 'or better still, get at that case.'

'No,' said the Head, 'I can't authorise that, at the moment you have no authority to interfere with Joon-ho, not even to approach him. Diplomatically and politically he's bomb-proof. Any attempt to approach him and the Prime Minister would hear about it personally within minutes, and you'd be out of there on charges.'

'So what do we do? Just hope he goes away?'

'No, Captain,' said the Head. 'I will report what you suspect and try and get you authority for more direct action. In the meantime, you and your men have developed a very particular skill, which is why I had you assigned to this operation. Find a way to use your abilities to learn more, just avoid contact with Joon-ho or compromising his personal security in any way.' She ended the call.

'Well?' said Bullock. 'Now what?'

'Well,' said Michael. 'The bad news is that Joon-ho is so well connected that there's no way we'll get authority to make any move on him.'

'What then?' asked Bullock.

Michael grinned. 'We find a different way in.'

EIGHTEEN

Joon-ho sat with the Russian in the small lounge room of the suite. The room was decorated with a pleasing selection of fake antique furniture and the windows afforded a view of the woods on the far side of the estate. Joon-ho found he sometimes struggled to remember the Russian's name, not that it was of any consequence. He felt quite comfortable in the isolation his men provided. Their electronic counter-measures prevented any eavesdropping by security services or commercial rivals, and the man standing outside the door was one of many whose military skills ensured his physical security.

The Russian sipped quietly on a dainty cup of tea, perhaps the one civilised habit the man had.

'I want to make sure you are clear about the arrangements for tomorrow,' said Joon-ho. He wondered how simple he would have to make things to ensure this man understood and would follow his instructions.

The Russian just stared at him, then spoke. 'They killed your men in Afghanistan,' he said.

'Yes,' said Joon-ho, 'I know. But that does not matter. I

have other contacts, and the people here, in England, are ready. I need to make sure that you are ready.'

'I am here,' said the Russian, 'I am ready to do what you are paying me for. But I am not here for any suicide mission.'

Joon-ho suppressed a laugh. 'No. You are not. After your work tomorrow you are coming back here, and as I explained you would then leave with me. There are others who are intent on killing themselves and will happily do it according to my timetable.'

'They are fools,' said the Russian, turning and looking out of the window.

At last, thought Joon-ho, they agreed on something.

'Tomorrow, you will go with four of my guards, and with the device. You will be taken to a place in the countryside, five miles outside a small town. You will ensure the device is armed and the timer is set for exactly four hours.' Joon-ho leaned closer to the Russian. 'This is important. You will meet men there who will take the case and the device. They must not see the device. They must not see inside the case. They must not see how to open the case.'

'They will not see,' said the Russian.

'Good. My men will make sure they do not try and interfere with you. They have been told to take the cases to a safe-house, close to where they will meet you, and keep the case safe until the following day. They believe someone will contact them the following day. My guards will bring you straight back here.'

'Why tell them that?' asked the Russian. Possibly the first sensible question he'd asked.

'They believe the case contains guns and bombs which they will use to assault a town centre, where they will kill lots of shoppers and tourists. They quite like that idea. They will guard the case with their lives. They have things to do during the morning, so they will not become inquisitive about the case until later in the day. By the end of the day they would probably attempt to open the case, but the device will explode by lunchtime, they will never have time to become inquisitive.'

The Russian smiled, possibly approving of the plan.

'Why a small town?' asked the Russian. 'A very big explosion for a very small target.'

'What would you suggest?' asked Joon-ho, indulging the Russian in a little conversation. 'Would it be better to acquire a larger device, and detonate in somewhere like London?' He didn't give the Russian time to answer. 'That would be almost impossible to achieve. The larger device would be very difficult to acquire without attracting attention, it would be more difficult to move, and the security in London is, I have to admit, very effective.'

Joon-ho looked out of the window. The world outside looked so tranquil, and yet it would take so little to shatter that tranquillity. 'How do you start a stampede in a crowded room? Do you shout obscenities? Do you shout insults about the people? Or do you simply shout one word - FIRE? One drop of vinegar would ruin your tea.' The Russian looked at his teacup.

'Sometimes a smaller gesture, but the right gesture, in the right place, can be just as effective. At the time the device denotes, barely ten kilometres away the Olympic Torch Relay will be passing close to a hospital. The explosion will destroy the town it is near and kill everyone in it. Everyone in and watching the Relay and everyone in the hospital will receive massive radiation burns. Close enough to be destroyed or badly damaged is the main location of their Special Air Service and their Government spy base. All will be irradiated, burned, damaged, with many killed. With so many symbols of the strength of their nation destroyed, so many killed their nation will be shocked to its core. The Olympic Games will die before they even begin. The economy will collapse, the financial markets will implode, and a chain reaction of economic devastation will be triggered which will spread across the western economies.'

He continued. 'During the morning, Arshad's men will have set in motion communications which will identify his groups from the Middle East as those intending to mount an assault on a civilian target. Once it happens, there will be no-one left to try and deny it, and any denial would be deafened by the screams for revenge.'

Joon-ho relaxed back in his chair. Now that he said it out loud he was impressed by his own planning, by the breadth and magnitude of his vision.

'And we leave then?' asked the Russian.

'As I said, the British Government will instantly want to evacuate all high-level foreign dignitaries. They will escort us to my plane, and they will ensure we are allowed to leave quickly. Relax today, and rest. Make sure the arming unit is ready. I have one more arrangement to make today, and then tomorrow we will change the world.'

THE HEAD LOOKED up at the clock on her office wall. She had a few minutes before she needed to be in a meeting, a meeting she couldn't avoid. A few minutes would be enough.

She picked up the phone and dialled a number. Calling the Minister's private mobile phone was a gamble. There was every chance he would be in a meeting, or his aide would answer the phone for him. To her relief, he answered the phone.

'Minister,' she said, 'I hope I'm not interrupting anything too important.' Not that she cared.

'Almost,' said the Minister. 'Just on my way to a Cabinet meeting. I take it this is important?'

'Of course,' she said. 'I assume you're up to date on the Chinese Olympic delegation at Mountfield House?'

'Of course.' He sounded suspicious, but she had no time for games.

'Lee Joon-ho is one of the guests. We have every reason to believe he's involved in laundering funds for international terrorism.'

The Minister barked a laugh at her. She could only imagine the response from anyone close to the Minister. It was also not the most encouraging response.

'Mr Joon-ho,' said the Minister, as though explaining the rules of good behaviour to an errant child, 'is a most important guest of Her Majesty's Government. He is a contributor of significant funds to various commercial enterprises involved in staging the Games and a supporter of many charitable causes in this country.'

'I am fully aware of his financial standing,' said the Head.

The Minister interjected. 'Oh, I doubt that.' It was a curious comment, she thought, as though to imply he had a better understanding of Joon-ho's financial dealings. What else did the Minister think he knew? She filed that for later analysis.

'I have no doubt he has used his considerable influence to ensure his security,' said Head, sailing as close to the wind as she dared. 'I also have strong reasons to believe at least some of his wealth is from money laundering. I need approval to conduct closer surveillance of him.'

'I won't hear of it,' said the Minister. 'I would personally vouch for Mr Joon-ho, and I want to be quite clear that you and your agency are forbidden from interfering with Mr Joon-ho in any way.'

'Minister, it is my responsibility to investigate suspicion and evidence of any threat to the security of this country, or to the security of the Government.' Make it personal, that often rattled cages.

'And do you have evidence?'

'No, Minister, we have strong suspicions.'

'Bring me evidence. If you bring me tangible evidence then I will grant you permission to conduct closer scrutiny.

'With respect, that's a completely Catch 22 offer.'

'No,' said the Minister, 'that's completely your problem. And another thing. The Chancellor of the Exchequer is visiting Mountfield House tomorrow and will be meeting with Mr Joon-ho. I expect your officers to be conspicuous in their guard duties and absolutely nothing else. Is that clear?' The Minister didn't wait for confirmation.

She rested the phone receiver back in its cradle. MI5 and GCHQ had enough computing power and technical expertise to defeat almost any kind of electronic protection, but there was little that could get to someone hiding behind political connections, especially at this level.

She picked up the phone and dialled another number.

'Captain Sanders,' she said. 'As expected, your target has political allies at the highest level. He is completely off the menu.'

She listened for a moment to the inevitable sigh, and then the response.

'I understand. However, there is nothing more I can do.

You should also be aware that tomorrow the Chancellor of the Exchequer is visiting Mountfield House.'

Another pause. 'Yes, I would be grateful if you could avoid shooting the Chancellor.'

Her call was going through the MI5 communications network, protected by GCHQ's encryption and counter-surveillance measures. It was secure, even over the public mobile phone network, yet she couldn't help but choose her words carefully, just in case. Sometimes, though, candour was the only appropriate way forward.

'Captain,' she said. 'Find a way in. Don't touch Joon-ho. Don't go near him, but somehow, find a way in, find a covert way of getting proof of what he's doing.'

The genie was now well and truly out of the bottle. The only problem with that? Genies never wanted to go back in their bottle once they'd tasted freedom.

———

MARSHALL WALKED through the main hallway and out of the front door, away from the remaining bustle of the press conferences. Most of the journalists had departed, the diplomats and VIPs had returned to their rooms and suites, the police retreated to the sanctuary of the outbuildings, or on patrol around the grounds. He noted where security guards were still on duty, where press interviews were still in progress. As he walked out into the forecourt he noted the vehicles still parked there. Each of the team was reconnoitring a part of the house and the grounds, gaining a fuller picture of who was where, trying to gain some idea of where they could make any entry into Joon-ho's security cocoon.

It was good to get away from the rest of the team. There

were times when they each annoyed Marshall, and this was one of those times. Bullock could be an idiot, childish and immature. Singh could over-think things, and Sanders? Sanders could be pompous and self-righteous. What had happened over the last few days was taking some getting used to, but Sanders seemed wilfully blind to just how much they could achieve with what they could now do.

Telepathy. There, he'd said it, even if only to himself. He could communicate mind-to-mind, he could read minds, he could very probably control other people. There was little to notice as he walked around the forecourt, instead he thought back over previous operations, imagining how and where he'd have used his new abilities. It was almost intoxicating. Some of the missions would have become laughably easy, others would have been far quieter and more effective.

As for this current operation? It was obvious. Take control of one of the guards, or two. Use them to get the others away from their master, then take control of them. The team could then just walk into the suite and take control of this Joon-ho character and his pet Russian, and everything would be taken care of.

It didn't take him long to make a circuit of the forecourt and walk back into the house. His route was to go along the first-floor landing, down the staff staircase on the far side, and back to the team in the outbuilding. Child's play. He trudged up the thickly carpeted staircase and onto the first-floor landing. Corridors led away left and right to the various rooms and suites, he headed for the left-hand corridor.

Ahead of him a door opened and a figure walked into the corridor, pulling the door closed behind him. The figure turned and faced him. Marshall stopped eye to eye with Lee Joon-ho. He heard voices behind him on the landing, they weren't completely alone, but the voices faded, they weren't to be intruded upon either.

'Good afternoon,' said Joon-ho, his voice and his manner calm and polite.

'Yeah,' said Marshall, 'afternoon.'

'You are with the soldiers assigned to protect me, yes?'

'Yes, something like that.'

Joon-ho smiled. 'I thank you for your efforts. I hope my men have not hindered you.'

'No,' said Marshall, 'they've been just fine.' He was tempted to make some glib remark about how helpful at least one of them had been, but this was not the time.

'We will be gone soon enough,' said Joon-ho, 'and I'm sure you have better things to do with your time.'

'No,' said Marshall, managing to squeeze out an approximation of a smile, 'guarding you is our pleasure.'

This time Joon-ho did not return the smile. 'Let us be honest,' he said. Marshall thought yes, let's be honest, and you tell me everything you've got planned. 'This assignment is an insult to you, you are soldiers, are you not? You are trained and skilled, sitting around is not the best use of your abilities.'

'We sit around ready to not be needed,' said Marshall, not sure where the conversation might be going.

'Mr Yang does not like you,' said Joon-ho. Marshall had no idea how to react to the statement.

'And who is Mr Yang?' he asked.

'Mr Yang is one of my security detail, you met him earlier, I believe,' said Joon-ho, 'and when we first arrived. He said you were rude, but I confess Mr Yang can be rather abrupt himself, he meant no offence.'

'None taken.'

'Mr Yang wondered where you were from,' said Joon-ho.

'East London,' said Marshall.

'I meant where are your ethnic origins.'

'I know what you meant,' said Marshall, his tone sharpening.

'Let us not hide behind the limp ideas of political correctness,' said Joon-ho, 'I don't believe either of us has time for that particularly Californian ideology.' Marshall had to admit that the man was completely right on that point.

Joon-ho continued. 'I am expanding my activities in Africa, I will need someone to lead my security operation there, someone who will be accepted there, and who has the necessary skill and training.'

'Good luck finding someone,' said Marshall. He eyed Joon-ho. He was supposed to be finding a way of infiltrating this man's operation, not sitting a job interview for him.

'I ensure my men have the best of everything they need,' said Joon-ho, 'the best weapons and equipment, the best accommodation, the best food. An army marches on its stomach, does it not?'

No, it marched in boots, but in the British Army that often meant ill-fitting boots with holes.

'Are you given the best of everything you need?' asked Joon-ho. Marshall resisted the temptation to answer.

'Do not answer that,' said Joon-ho, 'it was rude of me to ask. You are loyal to your men, and to the oath you swore. I understand that.' Marshall wondered just how much this man understood, perhaps more than he was letting on.

'They have given you the rank of Sergeant, yes?' asked Joon-ho. Again, Marshall was taken aback. Joon-ho was indeed very well informed. 'Sergeant Marshall, let me leave you with a question. Do you want to be a Sergeant here, when you can be a General in my organisation?'

Marshall had the sudden desperate thought the conversation was coming to an end, an unprecedented opportunity was about to walk away.

'It's a lot to think about,' said Marshall, holding out his hand.

Joon-ho looked at his hand for a moment and smiled.

'It is,' he said, 'and perhaps we will talk again about this.' Joon-ho reached out to shake hands. As their hands touched Marshall couldn't wait to make the psychic connection. It was like inhaling, drawing in information and ideas and images and impressions. He saw the private jet, an opulent suite overlooking Hong Kong, the sweeping grounds of a private estate in China, another in Brazil. He drew in the impressions of meetings with politicians, with industry leaders, and of wealth, of enormous wealth, and power. He also sensed Joon-ho, an impression of Joon-ho standing looking at him, in awe of what he, Marshall, could do. He realised Joon-ho was aware of the connection.

Like waking from a moment's daydream he heard a stream of language, Chinese. He became aware of someone, Yang, walking along the corridor towards them. The look of concern on Yang's face was unmistakable, regardless of any language barrier. Joon-ho pulled his hand away, a look of mild bemusement on his face. Joon-ho held up a hand to halt Yang and spoke rapidly to him.

'Sergeant Marshall and I were just finishing a conversation,' Joon-ho said in English. 'I am ready to return to the suite, Mr Yang, thank you.' Yang eyed Marshall suspiciously, perhaps not convinced that all was as well as Joon-ho implied. Marshall said nothing, gave no indication of his thoughts, he just stared at Yang, the unblinking stare of two boxers facing off before the bout.

Joon-ho, with Wang in tow, walked passed Marshall to

the staircase, and ascended to the second floor, and were out of sight.

Marshall stood for a moment. He had a decision to make, a big decision, but for the moment he wasn't sure exactly what that decision was. He needed the others. He needed two of the others.

NINETEEN

Marshall opened the door gently and walked into the team's room. He took a moment to push the door closed behind him. Singh and Bullock were huddled around Singh's laptop, they both looked up, and stared at Marshall.

'Since when did you start creeping around?' Bullock asked, grinning.

Marshall looked at him. 'Where's the boss?' he asked. Bullock's grin faded.

'He's out, probably back in a few minutes,' said Singh.

Marshall sank into one of the seats, still not sure how much to divulge, how much to keep private.

'I met Joon-ho,' said Marshall.

'You what?' said Bullock.

Singh checked his laptop, Marshall could see the video images flickering passed on the screen. Singh paused on one particular image, then put the laptop down on the floor.

'And?' asked Singh. 'What's he doing?'

'He offered me a job,' said Marshall. The other two just stared at him.

'This is the same man that is planning some kind of terrorist attack, isn't it?' asked Singh. 'I'm sure we're supposed to be stopping him. Does that ring any bells?'

'Yes,' said Marshall, hesitating, 'but I'm not sure we can stop him. He's everywhere. I mean his operation is huge, it's all over the world.'

'Kill him, kill his operation,' said Bullock.

'Crude, but it sums it up,' said Singh, 'he's only a man, he can be stopped, or killed.'

'Or controlled,' said Marshall, looking each of the two in the eyes. 'We can control him.' He found the more he talked the clearer the possibilities became.

'Control him to do what?' asked Singh.

'What would you do with a man who has that much power?' asked Marshall, his voice becoming a little more animated. 'He offered me a job, heading up his security in Africa. We can get to him, and we can control him, and then we control his operation. All of it. All over the world.' He looked at Julian Singh. 'What would you do with that much power?'

'I'd stop the man who is planning a terrorist attack,' said Singh, feigning a concerned voice. 'Perhaps we should focus on that.'

'If we control him, don't we stop the attack anyway?' said Bullock, his grin gone.

Marshall focused even more on Julian Singh. 'Look me in the eye,' he said, 'and tell me you really believe we're completely safe where we are.' He knew the other two felt the same has he did.

Singh said nothing. The corner of his mouth twitched, he started to inhale, perhaps about to speak, but still he said nothing.

'They've made us this way,' said Marshall, 'either by accident or on purpose. At the moment we're useful to them, but what happens when someone decides we're not useful? Then what?'

'What do you think they would do?' asked Bullock.

Marshall ignored him. 'And what are we going to do?' he asked. 'Are we going to be handsomely rewarded for what they've done to us? For what we can do for them? Or are we going to stay on a regular soldier's pay?'

'How much power does this man have?' asked Bullock, leaning closer to Marshall.

'He's connected to kings, and presidents, and chief executives. He knows everyone in power, and they know him. They will do things for him. He has real power.' If only he could show them what he had seen through his connection with Joon-ho.

'We swore an oath,' said Singh. 'That oath still means something to me. Does it still mean anything to you?'

'It means everything to me,' said Marshall, 'and it will right up to the point where I think the people I should be able to trust are a threat to me. If that time comes, that oath is worthless.'

'Then for now,' said Singh, 'we have a job to do, and that job is to stop Joon-ho from launching his terrorist action. We need to find out what he's got in that case.'

Marshall closed his eyes for a moment. He still wasn't sure how to make it happen. It sort of worked, he just had the idea in his mind and it happened, but it kind of didn't feel like he was doing it. He felt his thoughts shift, move, expand. He sensed something, it had a unique sensation, almost like it had a taste or a smell all of its own. The images he'd seen from Joon-ho came into his mind, but they were more than memories, they were Joon-ho's memories, coming directly into his thoughts.

'You should see the money he has,' said Marshall. 'He has money all over the world.'

'How much?' he heard Bullock ask.

'Billions,' said Marshall, 'billions and billions of pounds.'

'How do you know this?' asked Singh.

'Because I connected with him,' breathed Marshall.

'You connected with him?' said Singh, perhaps louder than he planned. 'You connected with him?' he hissed, sounding like he was forcing himself to be more quiet. 'And when you connected with him, please tell me you did something useful, like see inside that box.'

Marshall opened his eyes, and shook his head slowly, letting go of the connection to Joon-ho's images.. 'We were interrupted,' he said, 'his pet bodyguard came along.'

'Oh great,' said Singh, the anger clear in his voice. 'One perfect chance to find out what he's doing and you just stare at the contents of his wallet.'

'He knew what I was doing,' said Marshall.

'What?' gasped Singh.

'I could feel him, he knew he was connected to me, I knew he could feel it.'

'Oh fucking marvellous,' said Singh, throwing up his hands. He stood up and backed up to the wall, hands over his face. 'Now you've placed us in more danger than ever.'

'Then we'll have to take control of him,' said Marshall. 'If we have control of him it won't matter what he knows, and we'll stop the attack, and we'll have control of his operation.'

Singh dropped his hands from his face. 'Not a word of this to the boss,' he said. 'If anyone, anyone gets wind that we're planning treason we would be in a really bad place.'

Bullock looked at Marshall, then at Singh, then back to Marshall. 'So, what are we going to do?' he asked.

'Exactly what we're supposed to do,' said Singh. 'We find a way in, a way to find out what he's got in that case. Then we get the okay to go in hard and stop whatever he's doing.'

'And when we do we take control of him,' said Marshall, 'then we're safe.'

'And then, only then, do we decide what we're going to do with him.'

The door opened. They all looked round as Michael Sanders walked into the room. Marshall sensed Sanders' entry meant their conversation was over, for the moment.

'Have I missed anything?' Sanders asked.

'Nope,' said Marshall. 'We all came up blank. You?'

Sanders shook his head. 'Nothing useful. Looks like we're no further forward.'

THE FOUR OF them shifted the chairs so they all faced each other. Michael took a deep breath. This was not a time to let his frustration show. This was a time to get his team thinking, being creative. Despite his teenager behaviour, Bullock could sometimes come up with novel ideas for approaching a target or finding an escape route. Singh was intelligent and analytical, and Marshall had a keen military mind. Surely between them they could find a way.

'The way I see it,' said Michael, 'we can't go after Joonho. We know we can get at his guards, but they won't know what's in the case. There's only one other who does.'

'The Russian,' said Singh.

'The Russian,' agreed Michael.

'And on that front, I have made some progress,' said

Singh, turning his laptop around so the others could see the screen. The picture on the screen was a still image of Joon-ho and the man they knew as "the Russian." Next to the image was a window of information.

'He's on our database as Yuri Vostok, but that's probably an alias. Don't know much about him, except that he is Russian, an engineer, spent some time in the Russian air force.'

'Doesn't help much,' said Marshall.

Singh turned the laptop back to himself. 'No,' he said, 'it doesn't, except to confirm that the Russian isn't Joon-ho's man-friend, he is someone we need to talk to.'

'Okay,' said Michael, 'ideas? How do we get to this man? Or how do we make him accessible?'

'Storm the suite,' said Bullock. 'Leave Ho alone but grab the Russian.'

'Simple plan,' said Marshall, 'but can't see us getting away with that.'

'No,' agreed Michael, 'I don't think Joon-ho would keep quiet just because we didn't kidnap him.'

'Smoke grenades, then,' said Bullock, 'smoke them out, literally.'

Michael heard Marshall sigh. He looked at each of them. 'We can't do anything directly while he's still in the suite. Any direct action will get Joon-ho on the phone to his pet politician faster than you can say my-dad's-bigger-than-your-dad.'

'I could hack into the fire alarm system,' said Singh, 'set it off, force them to evacuate, then get to the Russian as they leave the building.'

'They wouldn't,' said Marshall, 'they wouldn't leave. They'd sit there.'

'They would,' Michael had to concede. 'The easiest

thing would be to just grab the Russian for thirty seconds while he's out and about.'

'Except he never leaves the suite,' said Singh, tapping away on the laptop. 'I've not seen him leave the suite since he got here.'

They sat in silence. Michael wracked his brains. Abducting one individual from within a secure environment, without anyone else objecting, seemed to be impossible. All their military training seemed to offer no obvious solution. The next thought was like a light going on in his mind. His eyes must have widened, or his face changed because Bullock asked him what was wrong.

Michael looked at Singh. 'You connected with the guard,' he said to Singh, 'you must still have a connection with him.'

'Yes,' said Singh, 'I probably do, but how do we use that?'

'Have the guard persuade the Russian to go for a walk,' said Bullock. Always the simplest idea, but still not the most workable.

'I doubt my control over him is strong enough to do that,' said Singh. 'He'd resist, doing that is contrary to his duty to Joon-ho. I can influence him, but I can't make him do something like that.'

Michael saw Bullock look across at Marshall. 'Go and tell Ho you want another word with him,' said Bullock. Michael didn't miss that Marshall and Singh both stared at Bullock.

'What do you mean "another" word?' asked Michael.

'I ran into Ho in the corridor,' said Marshall. 'He asked if I wanted to join him, working for him in Africa.'

'And what did you say?' Michael wasn't sure if this was an opportunity or a danger.

'I told him to piss off,' said Marshall, his tone screaming "what did you think I said?"

Michael thought for a moment. Singh had a connection with one of Joon-ho's guards. Marshall had a brief conversation with Joon-ho. If they could put those two conversations together, they might be able to gain enough leverage to somehow move the Russian.

'Ho said I should come back if I wanted to talk about it again,' said Marshall.

Bingo. The pieces fell into place in Michael's mind. His plan had come together.

'Julian,' said Michael. 'If Vince went back and demanded to talk to Joon-ho, could you get the guard to open the door? Even if the other guards said not to?'

Singh was quiet for a moment, perhaps sensing the strength of his connection. 'Yes,' he said. 'Yes, I reckon I could do that much.'

'Vince,' Michael said, turning to Marshall. 'All you have to do is get in and be able to shake hands with the Russian. Get a connection with him, you can use it later to see into his mind, find out what he's doing. We don't have to get the Russian out of the room.'

'No,' said Marshall, 'you just want me to walk into the lion's den.'

'Basically, yes,' said Michael.

'Risky,' said Bullock.

'No,' said Singh. 'Joon-ho's protected by his political connections, but only so long as they can see him as the rich businessman. He can't compromise that by doing anything to Vince, provided you don't do anything aggressive.' He smiled at Marshall.

'Me?' blurted Marshall. 'Aggressive? When am I aggressive?'

'It's the only workable plan we've got,' said Michael. 'Vince, just don't go in and throw any grenades. Get in. Be friendly. Make like you know the Russian and shake hands. Tell Joon-ho you need time to think about his offer, then leave.'

'Simple,' said Marshall. 'What could possibly go wrong?'

MARSHALL WALKED up the stairs towards the second floor. He ran through what he was going to say when he reached the door to Joon-ho's suite and the guards who would be standing there. It was naive to think he would be allowed to just walk up to the door and knock. If he had been planning an armed assault he would have had no problem, or even an unarmed assault. But talking? That had never been his strong suit.

He arrived at the second floor and turned towards the corridor. Michael's words still ran around his head: the man's name is "Joon-ho," not "ho." Marshall had a mischievous temptation to stand outside the door and shout "ho, ho, ho" in a mock Father Christmas voice, but even he realised that might be counterproductive.

He could see the two Chinese guards standing on duty outside Joon-ho's suite. As soon as they were in view he saw the shift in their posture, one unbuttoned his jacket, the other unclasped his hands. Marshall was sure to show his hands as empty, hanging by his side.

As he approached the two he spoke. 'Good afternoon,' he said, no harm in being polite. 'I want to speak to Mr Joon-ho.' He smiled at them, but from the response he wasn't sure his smile was too convincing.

'So sorry,' said one of the guards, 'Mr Joon-ho not available.' The man bowed his head slightly.

Marshall made an effort to keep his next words silent, intended only for Julian Singh. 'Are you ready to get your man to open the door?' he thought.

'I'm ready,' came the silent reply. 'Let me know when you've shouted.'

Marshall spoke to the guards again. 'Mr Joon-ho said I should come back if I wanted to talk to him. I'm back.'

'So sorry,' repeated the guard, 'Mr Joon-ho not available.'

'So you said,' said Marshall, 'but he asked me to come back. So why don't you let me in so I can talk to him like he asked?' He added a note of frustration and emphasised Joon-ho's name.

'So sorry,' the guard said again, 'Mr Joon-ho not—'

'Not available,' Marshall interjected, 'yes, you said.' He raised his voice, almost shouting, focusing on the door. 'Mr Joon-ho, it's Vince Marshall. You said I should come back if I wanted to discuss your offer.' Then he communicated silently with Singh. 'I've shouted.'

He waited. The guards looked at him dispassionately. It was possible their English was limited and they hadn't understood what he had said. He also hoped his shouting at the door and not at them wouldn't provoke any violent reaction. It didn't.

The two guards were caught by surprise when the door opened, and Mr Wang stood in the doorway. He eyed Marshall. 'Why are you shouting?' he asked.

'Mr Joon-ho said I should come back to talk to him,' said Marshall. Wang hesitated, perhaps uncertain whether he should let Marshall in. It was possible Singh's connection with Wang simply wasn't strong enough. If it wasn't, they were back to square one.

Wang stepped backwards. 'You should enter. I will see if Mr Joon-ho wishes to talk with you.'

Marshall took half a step forward, but the two guards blocked his path. Wang spoke rapidly in Chinese, then more slowly in English to Marshall. 'Forgive us, but they must ensure you are not armed.'

Marshall raised his arms and let the guards pat him down. He'd left his sidearm with the team, carrying it would only have created problems. He'd also left the two knives he habitually carried. One of the guards produced a small electronic device with a six-inch antenna and swept it over Marshall's limbs and body. Marshall allowed himself the satisfaction of thinking they could scan him all they liked, they could do nothing to prevent his communication with the team.

Their checks done the two stepped aside, and Marshall walked forwards into the suite. The door was closed behind him.

Marshall flicked his eyes around the room. A guard stood on duty in each corner. Apart from Wang, the only other person in the room was sitting in an easy chair, a pen in one hand and a notepad in the other. The man didn't look up, but Marshall recognised him as Yuri Vostok, or whatever his real name was. A door closed, Wang had left the room.

'Boris,' said Marshall in a loud and friendly way, beaming a big smile and taking a step towards the seated man. He could see the four guards tense, two of them began to step forwards but hesitated, clearly uncertain what to do. Marshall held out his hand to the Russian. 'Boris,' he said again, 'so good to see you again.' He stood there, hand outstretched.

Vostok looked up, his face impassive, his hands unmoving, pen and pad still held firmly. 'I do not know you,' he said and looked back down at his notepad.

A door opened, and Joon-ho entered, followed by Wang.

Marshall had a moment to communicate with Singh. 'Boris won't talk to me, get Wang to do something.' He didn't know if Singh replied, he focused on Joon-ho instead.

'Mr Wang says that you wish to speak with me,' said Joon-ho, intoning it almost as a question.

'Yes,' said Marshall, facing Joon-ho. 'I've thought about what you said.' He hadn't planned what he might say to Joon-ho. He'd hoped to talk to the Russian and then make an excuse to leave.

'And?' said Joon-ho.

'And your offer is interesting,' said Marshall, ad-libbing as best he could. 'What do we do next?' It was all he could think to say.

Joon-ho looked at him for a few moments, but his face gave nothing away. 'We will talk again,' he said, 'and soon. But today I am most busy, and you will have to excuse me.'

Marshall drew breath to reply, but Joon-ho continued. 'Be patient, Sergeant Marshall, all in good time. Please stay and have a drink. My staff will bring you a cup of tea.'

'I need to get back, before anyone asks where I am,' said Marshall.

'I insist,' said Joon-ho, indicating the armchair on the opposite side of the coffee table from the Russian's chair. 'Please take advantage of your Government's generous hospitality.' Marshall could sense the two guards behind him move closer, starting to close off access to the door out of the suite.

Joon-ho turned and left the room, and Marshall found himself staring at Wang, another impassive face. Marshall thought that Joon-ho might have a lot of money, but he didn't seem to have much fun. Marshall would have far more fun with all that wealth.

'Tea? Or coffee?' asked Wang.

Marshall kept his eyes fixed on Wang, he didn't want to give away that he was searching for options, ways to engineer an exit. There was always the old maxim: when in doubt, fight. He'd done alright by that rule over the years. He turned his attention inwards and thought words to Singh.

'They're stopping me leaving. Make this guy wrestle with me, but let me take his gun.'

He hoped Singh got the message, he didn't have time to wait.

'Sorry,' he said to Wang, shrugging his shoulders, 'things to do.' He turned towards the door. He'd barely taken half a step when, as he hoped, Wang reached out and grasped his arm to slow him.

In a whirl Marshall turned on the man, sliding his arm up under Wang's outstretched arm, curving it around Wang's back and turning the man into an armlock. Wang was fast and nimble, it was like trying to grasp hold of a bar of soap. Marshall managed to turn Wang around to slow the advance of the two guards behind. He forced Wang to stumble to the side, and both nearly crashed into the Russian who leapt out of his chair, pen and notepad tumbling from his hands as he dashed behind the guard advancing towards the wrestling men.

They caught the corner of the now vacant chair and crashed to the floor. Marshall pushed himself free and almost floated to his feet, Wang's pistol now in his hand, pointed at Wang. The other guards paused, Marshall noticed them each flick a glance to Wang, they were waiting for his instruction.

'Look,' said Marshall, forcing himself to calm his voice, 'I have jobs to do, so thanks for the offer, but I really do need to leave.'

He checked the safety catch was on and turned the pistol around, offering the grip towards Wang. 'Misunderstanding,' Marshall said, 'it's okay.'

Wang reached out slowly and took the pistol as he stood. He holstered the weapon and uttered a command in Chinese. The other guards backed away, the Russian being shunted into a corner behind the retreating guard.

'Perhaps you should leave now,' said Wang. Marshall heard the door open behind him. He buttoned up his jacket and marched out of the room, the door closed behind him.

'What happened?' came Michael's voice in his head as he marched down the corridor towards the staircase.

'Didn't go according to plan,' said Marshall, 'had to improvise an exit. Julian? Nicely done. Mr Wang was most helpful.'

'Glad to be of service,' came Singh's voice. 'Not sure what you've achieved.'

'We'll see, I'll be back in a minute.'

It took Marshall only minutes to descend the staircase, walk through the house and across the courtyard to the outbuilding. He entered the room to the bemused look of the other three and he closed the door behind him.

'Boris,' said Marshall, 'was in no mood to be friendly, couldn't get to touch him, and the others weren't going to let me wander around, so I had to improvise.'

'So, we're no further forwards,' said Michael.

'Great,' said Bullock, 'now what.'

'All so negative,' said Marshall, grinning. He pulled out

of his pocket, holding it with the end of his thumb and fore-finger, the pen Vostok had dropped.

'Boris was using this, he was holding it while I was there,' said Marshall. He turned to Singh. 'Julian? Can you get anything from this?' He handed the pen to Singh.

Singh sat back in the chair, rolling the pen between his fingers. He closed his eyes.

'I think the pen was used by a lot of people,' said Singh, 'it wasn't Vostok's personal property.' His eyes moved behind the closed lids. 'Difficult, hard to get a sense of just one person.' He paused. 'Ah, there he is. Yes. I can sense him, his conversations with Joon-ho. He's nervous. No, he's afraid. He's out of his depth here, and he's afraid. The case. Joon-ho's case. Yes, they opened it.'

Singh's eyes shot open, wide and staring. 'Oh fuck!' he exclaimed. He looked at Michael. 'Boss, we've got a very big problem. That case contains a nuke.'

'What?' the others said, almost in unison.

'A bomb?' said Marshall.

'No,' said Singh, 'a warhead, a single nuclear warhead. Vostok's the expert, he's got the arming unit, and they plan to use it.'

'When?' asked Michael.

Marshall and everyone looked at Singh. 'Today,' said Singh.

TWENTY

The Head stifled a yawn. The meeting had been tedious, but unavoidable, and now it was over. People filed out of the large conference room, and she gathered her notes and her phone and headed for the door. She heard the muting warbling of her phone, but ignored it until she was out of the room and into the corridor, away from most of the people.

He looked at the phone and the identity of the caller. She answered the call.

'Captain Sanders, please tell me you have something positive to report this time,' she said.

'Yes,' he said abruptly. She tuned out the people in the corridor and focused on the voice on the phone. 'We've no physical evidence, but we know what Joon-ho's got in that flight case he brought with him. It's a nuke, a Russian MIRV warhead, and the Russian he's got with him is a weapons specialist who can arm the bomb and ready it for detonation.'

'Do you know what they're planning to do with it?' she asked.

'No, but I don't think he brought it here as a Christmas present for anyone. We do know whatever he's planning he's going to do it very soon. I need authorisation for immediate action against Joon-ho and anyone and everyone in his team.'

'Wait,' she said, and pre-empted his objection. 'Wait for my call. I need a few moments to let the Minister know first.' She ended the call and began marching back towards her office. As she walked she dialled a number.

It was the Minister's personal assistant who answered.

'I'm sorry, Ma'am, but the Minister is not available at the moment, said the PA, in that I've-got-better-things-to-do-than-talk-to-you tone of voice.

'This is a matter I need to brief the Minister on,' said the Head, quickly, 'then I'm calling the PM and briefing him, and directing him to convene COBRA.' The Head gambled the PA didn't know she didn't actually have the authority to direct the Prime Minister to call an emergency meeting in the Cabinet Office Briefing Rooms, COBRA.

The Head could hear the PA having a conversation with the Minister, presumably with her hand over the phone.

'Please tell me your men haven't been involved in any unpleasantness with Mr Joon-ho's staff,' said the Minister.

'We now have solid intelligence that Mr Joon-ho is in possession of a very significant quantity of arms and explosives and is planning to use those materials in a terrorist action, probably within the next twelve hours.' She decided telling the Minister his favourite VIP had smuggled a nuclear warhead into the country might be too much for him to believe.

She was not surprised when her message was met with silence, no doubt the man was trying to calculate what response would cause him the least personal political damage.

'That's a very serious allegation,' he said. 'But I'd need proof before I could sanction any direct intervention.'

'And what if he launches his assault before you get your proof?' she barked, her patience almost exhausted. 'If I'm wrong I get a telling-off and a black mark on my record. If we wait, hundreds of people could die, and the delay would be political doomsday for anyone who knew and didn't act.' Always hit them where it hurt most.

She didn't wait for his next response. 'I'm ordering my men to take immediate action, then I'm informing the PM and recommending he convenes COBRA.' She pressed the button to end the call.

As she strode down the corridor she spied one of the Operations Team Leaders.

'Lesley,' the Head called to attract the woman's attention. The woman turned around. 'Crisis situation,' said the Head. 'Organise a full police strike force to Mountfield House, liaise with the police commander in situ, and call up a nuclear containment team. I'll brief you with details in five minutes.'

The Head turned into her office and closed the door. She picked up the desk phone and dialled Sanders' number.

'Captain,' she said as soon as he answered. 'I'm authorising you and your team to take whatever action is necessary to stop Joon-ho and any of his men, and to contain that nuke and any other weapons they have.'

'Yes Ma'am,' came Sanders' reply, with enthusiasm.

'And Sanders, try not to kill Joon-ho.' She ended the call, then dialled another number.

Informing the PM was not something she was looking forward to. She'd tried to keep this whole operation away from the most senior politicians, and the less she could say about Sanders and his team the better. The one thing she couldn't contemplate was a nuclear device being detonated somewhere in England. Joon-ho had picked a fight, and she would make sure it was a fight he lost.

THE FOUR SOLDIERS sat in their room in the outbuilding. Three stared at Michael as he took the return call from the Head. He hummed confirmation at the few points of information she gave him, then ended the call. He looked up at them.

'We have a go for direct action against Joon-ho and his men. Objectives are to secure whatever weapon he has in that case and prevent its use. If possible, we need Joon-ho alive.'

He noticed Bullock was grinning and Marshall and Singh both looked satisfied. He had to admit, this was more like what they were trained to do.

'Vince, get the HKs from the Land Rover, get some radio sets, but leave the grenades.' Marshall groaned, a token gesture. Michael continued. 'There are civilians around, lots of them, we need to keep this quiet. The police will help contain the staff, the press and the VIPs, but they won't support us in the action.'

'Why not?' said Bullock, as though he'd been counting on the police making up the numbers.

'I suspect no-one wants PC Plod catching sight of the nuke,' said Singh. 'I'm sure we can rely on our colleagues in Her Majesty's Constabulary, but if they catch sight of a nuclear warhead, I don't think it would stay secret for long.'

'What about Boris?' asked Marshall.

'Vostok?' said Michael. 'Detain if possible, but if he gets anywhere near that equipment case, kill him.'

Singh tapped at the keys of the laptop, still balanced on his lap.

'It looks like they're still in the suite, guards still by the door. No way to approach without being noticed.'

'So we need to find another way into the suite,' said Michael.

'What about your connection with the guard?' asked Marshall, looking at Singh.

Julian defocused his eyes for a moment. 'No,' he said, shaking his head. 'The connection wasn't a strong one, and whatever he's doing he's now focused on Joon-ho, the connection's too weak to make him do anything to help.'

'We could go back to the smoke grenade idea,' said Marshall, 'flush them out.'

'Possible,' said Michael, 'but there's a chance they'll do something with the nuke while we wait for them to come out. No, we need to get in.'

'I think we may have a problem,' said Singh, frowning at the laptop. 'His guards are still outside the door.'

'I think we know that,' said Bullock.

'Yes,' said Singh, 'but I've checked the video, the same two have been outside the door for the last eight hours.'

'Bullshit,' said Marshall.

'Julian, check the time when Vince went into the suite,' said Michael. Singh hammered at the keyboard, bringing up video files as quickly as he could.

'Shit,' said Singh, sharply. 'When Vince went in, the video feed shows the same two just standing there.'

'How come?' asked Marshall.

'They must have hacked the surveillance system, we've been looking at some spoof video they've been feeding us.

When Vince went in I was concentrating on my link with the guard, I never checked the video feed.'

'So there may or may not be guards outside the suite,' said Michael.

'They may have all gone, and taken their toy with them,' said Michael.

With an almost caricature slowness, Singh closed the laptop and put it on the floor beside his chair. 'I can't tell,' he said, 'I can't tell how long they've been feeding us manufactured video.'

'Right,' said Michael, standing up. 'Let's get ready and go and pay them a visit.'

It took only minutes to equip themselves with pistols in shoulder holsters and HK submachine guns, carried in black canvass bags, better not to alarm the VIPs and any press still wandering around. Michael had a word with the police Officer In Charge. He'd been briefed the team were ready for action.

'We'll try and keep it quiet,' Michael said to the OIC, 'but if it gets noisy we need you to keep the staff and the VIPs out of harm's way.' The OIC went to brief his officers, and Michael led his team across the rear courtyard and into the house.

Mercifully there were few press left and only a handful of staff was visible, most clearing away coffee cups from the rooms used for press interviews. As they reached the staircase Michael caught sight of the red shirt. That journalist seemed to have a habit of being in an awkward place at inconvenient times, but they couldn't worry about that now. Michael caught a glimpse of two armed police officers making a good show of wandering calmly into the hallway and placing themselves between the stairs and everyone else on the ground floor.

As the team rounded the corner to the final flight of stairs up to the second floor, Michael pulled out his pistol. The others followed suit, and weapons held in front they cautiously moved up the stairs and onto the second-floor landing.

Michael stepped across the entrance to the corridor, Singh followed, the other two stayed on their side of the corridor.

'No-one outside the suite,' thought Michael, intending his words to be heard by the others.

Keeping their backs to the wall they slid into the corridor, guns held out in front. It was quiet, and for once Michael thought it was too quiet. If Joon-ho's men had hacked into the surveillance system then surely the team would be visible to them. So why hadn't they done anything to prevent their approach? They neared the door to the suite, their footsteps inaudible in the thick pile of the carpet.

Michael heard a door open somewhere behind. The four of them whipped around and saw one of Joon-ho's men step into the corridor from one of the rooms. A look of surprise sprang across the man's face. Unless he was an excellent actor it seemed this individual hadn't expected to see the team. He started speaking, but the Chinese was lost on Michael.

'Kneel,' Marshall commanded, using his free hand to gesture a downward motion. For a moment Michael thought the man might actually comply, but perhaps he had second thoughts. In a smooth and practised motion the man darted back into the room whilst drawing a pistol from a concealed holster. Instinctively Michael and the others each ducked as the man let off two shots, before slamming the door shut.

Instantly there was shouts and voices from the floors

below, followed moments later by the hard and forceful commands from the police officers.

'Vince, Evan,' Michael commanded, 'take care of him.' He motioned at the door concealing the shooter. 'But get him alive if you can, we need to know what Joon-ho's planning. Julian, we need to get into that suite.'

Marshall and Bullock slid slowly towards the door, Marshall muttered something about 'a grenade would be useful.' Michael and Singh approached the door to the suite.

'Booby traps?' asked Michael.

Julian looked at him. 'Possibly. I would. Have we got time to be cautious?'

'No,' said Michael. He looked at the door. At least they could be sure this was still the door the house had when Joon-ho arrived, there had been no time or opportunity for him to reinforce doors or windows. He holstered his pistol, took half a step away from the door and kicked as hard as he could, aiming just below the handle. The wood gave a nasty crack as his foot landed, but refused to give way.

At that moment he heard Marshall (he assumed it was Marshall) give a far more productive kick at the room door he was facing, followed by shouts and gunshots. He focused on the door in front of him, Marshall and Bullock were more than capable of looking after themselves.

Julian stepped to one side, aiming his gun at the handle. 'Need a hand?' he asked. Michael stepped back. Singh shot twice into the door, the lock disintegrated in a shower of splinters. Michael's second kick sent the door crashing inwards. For just an instant Michael caught sight of someone standing in the suite, facing the door, gun drawn. Michael turned away from the door and Julian Singh fell backwards as a double shot echoed around the room beyond.

It took a moment for Michael and Julian to regain their balance and aim into the room. They ducked again as another shot took a chunk out of the wall behind them. Two shots resounded from the room behind them as Marshall and Bullock engaged their target.

As one, Michael and Julian swung around the sides of the door and aimed into the room, the empty room. The gunman had taken cover. From behind them, Michael heard Marshall's unmistakable voice. 'Fuck this,' he said, followed by a burst of submachine gun fire. Michael guessed the attacker was no longer a threat, but also no longer available for questioning.

Michael and Julian stepped into the room, moving forwards slowly, guns held out in front, scanning left and right, aware of furniture which might conceal the gunman, doors through which he might emerge. An eerie silence fell over them.

Michael kept to the left side of the room, Julian crept along the right side. Michael struggled to recall the layout of the rooms, but he did remember the descriptions. The house was old, the doors were old, solid wood, not modern fibreboard, meaning less chance their hidden gunman could shoot at them through a door.

'Vince and Evan,' came Bullock's voice behind them, 'we're coming in behind you.'

'One shooter,' said Michael, 'and he's through one of the doors.'

'Right,' said Marshall, 'let's flush this bugger out and stop messing around.'

MICHAEL SCANNED THE LOUNGE, it was clear the gunman had left this room, but to where? The door to the right led to a small office room and from there to the main guest rooms. The door opposite the entrance led to a drawing room, and the door to the left led to the corridor and the small staff rooms.

'We'll start with the office, sweep anticlockwise through the suite,' thought Michael. At least they could communicate clearly without being heard, and without having to use limited hand gestures. Michael and Julian slid forwards, Julian poised to pull the door open, Michael ready to fire. Marshall was behind them ready to fire from a standing position and Bullock was facing the door on the far side in case the gunman came back around.

Michael gave a telepathic countdown and then Singh pulled the door open. The room beyond was small enough to see it was empty. They moved forward. Clever move on the part of the Chinese, the office was small and cramped the team's movements. Assaulting the main suite from here would be more difficult.

Another countdown and Singh pulled the door open. There was rapid gunfire from the room beyond. Almost in unison Michael and Marshall fired back, Michael firing single shots from his pistol, Marshall firing bursts from the HK submachine gun. Four more shots at them splintered the wood of the door frame.

'Evan,' Michael thought, 'stay there and pin him down if he comes around.'

The three of them pushed through the door and into the palatial bedroom. Gunsmoke hung in the air and plaster debris littered the expensive carpet. Bullet holes peppered the walls and glass from a shattered mirror crunched under Michael's feet as they inched forwards.

The door on the far side was ajar. There was nowhere else the gunman could have gone. They moved more quickly, but the door swung open and shots shattered the quiet. The team fired back.

'I'm out,' thought Michael. Singh and Marshall fired alternately as Michael changed the clip in his pistol and pulled the slide back. He was ready. As they moved towards the door, Michael heard another door open then close.

'Evan,' thought Michael. 'Get into the corridor and come around at him, we can trap him.'

'On it, boss,' came Bullock's reply.

They moved through the door into the dressing room, the door beyond that was where the gunman had gone, and that door led into the corridor now covered by Bullock.

'Evan, we're coming into the corridor,' said Michael.

'I'm covering the corridor,' replied Bullock, 'you're clear.'

Singh pulled the door open and Michael scanned beyond. Even with Bullock's assurance, it was clear it was a habit so ingrained he couldn't overcome it. Always check the way ahead is clear before moving.

The team moved into the corridor. Bullock was crouching further up the corridor, covering the approach from what was now their rear. To their right was the door to the store cupboard.

'This guy's been wasting our time,' came Marshall's words.

'I agree,' Michael heard Singh say. 'He's been keeping us busy.'

'Then let's finish it,' thought Michael.

Before they could move bullets tore through the store-room door, blasting splinters into their confined space. As a reflex they turned their heads away, protecting their eyes. Marshall was the first to return fire, pouring a stream of machine-gun fire into the storeroom door. When his weapon clicked empty Michael and Julian fired a half dozen shots each into the door.

Without giving their quarry time to respond Marshall reached forwards and wrenched open the door. He and Singh stepped forwards ready to fire, Michael crouched slightly behind ready to back them up.

Michael stared into the room. He had to imagine Marshall and Singh were also staring into the room, into the empty room. The walls were lined with shelves on which sat towels and sheets and bedding. Chunks of the wall had been shot away and plaster dust mixed with gun smoke in a blue-grey haze.

A door in the opposite wall of the storeroom had also had holes blown in it by the gunfire. Michael stared at the door.

'That wasn't on the plans,' he thought.

'Let's find where the rabbit-hole goes,' thought Marshall, stepping forwards. With Michael and Julian ready to cover him, Marshall pulled the door open. Beyond the door was a narrow stairwell, the stairs descending steeply away from the second floor.

'Bollocks,' said Marshall, out loud.

It took several more minutes to move through each of the remaining rooms and confirm that their target had indeed escaped.

As the last room was confirmed empty Michael stood up and holstered his weapon. This was not good, not good at all.

'They've gone,' said Bullock, his customary summary of the obvious.

'Yeah,' said Marshall, 'and that last one kept us busy while they got out.'

'Problem is,' said Singh, returning from looking into one of the other rooms, 'we don't know where they've gone, and they've taken the nuke with them.'

'JULIAN,' Michael said, 'we need to find Joon-ho. Find something of his, something you can make a connection with.'

Michael stepped back into the dressing room. There were clothes hung up, clothes in drawers. He brushed them with his fingers but felt nothing specific. He stopped and took hold of a shirt, focused on it and let his mind open. He sensed vague impressions of someone, a woman, a hot room, steam. Laundry. All Joon-ho's clothes were recently laundered, all he would get would be the laundry workers. He guessed he'd likely get a similar result from any item of clothing. He needed to find something more personal to Joon-ho.

He walked into Joon-ho's suite. The gunfire had smashed many of the items on the dressing table. As he looked around he realised Joon-ho had very little in the way of personal possessions. The man had clothes, but he could see no jewellery, no books, no personal electronic devices. Joon-ho likely had his phone with him, and perhaps the few items he valued.

Time was running out. Whatever Joon-ho's escape route he had a head start on Michael and the team. Whatever his plan for the nuke, Joon-ho had the upper hand. Michael stepped towards the door to the small office and felt his foot kick something.

He bent down and picked up a light leather attaché case. He felt something almost the moment he touched it, something personal, something strong. As he let his mind open to the sensations Michael could sense the presence of a man, a strong and imposing character. But this man was not Lee Joon-ho. Perhaps it was whoever had given the case to Joon-ho, perhaps as a gift. Maybe Joon-ho had taken it from this man. Michael let his mind open, become aware of other images, other sensations. He caught the sense of something he recognised, a face, it was Joon-ho. The case did belong to him, it was something that connected Joon-ho to this other person, and it was a direct link to Joon-ho.

Michael focused on the sensation of Joon-ho, like following the memory of a conversation to recall how it started. The sensation changed, it became like being close to Joon-ho, close enough to smell his personal scent. Michael could see something, almost as though through Joon-ho's eyes. He could feel the intensity of Joon-ho's focus, his deter-mination to reach a destination. But where? What destination?

Julian Singh's voice jerked him back into the real world.

'Couldn't find anything, boss,' said Singh, 'and couldn't find anything belonging to the Russian. Whoever he is, he travels light.'

Michael refocused, it felt like waking from a light sleep.

'We found their security room,' Singh went on, 'they've got a laptop plugged into the surveillance system. That's how they were feeding us the fake video.'

Michael focused on Julian's face. 'Good,' he said, 'good. Forensics will want to go over the suite, and I'm sure GCHQ will want the laptop.'

'Did you find anything?' asked Singh, nodding at the attaché case still in Michael's hands.

'Oh. Yes. They're heading for the greenhouses. We need to get after them.'

TWENTY ONE

Joon-ho's guards emerged first from the concealed exit from the staircase. In moments they had scanned the area and beckoned their superior to follow. Joon-ho walked with calm, a man who did not hurry, even when armed soldiers were hunting him and were only yards away. The five guards boxed him in, creating a shield around him. Yuri Vostok followed, looking bewildered and frightened. The group kept close to the side wall of the house, protected from view by the old stable building.

Vostok flinched as the loud pops of gunfire punctured what had been a quiet afternoon. Moments later they heard shouts and screams from the front of the house, then the commanding tones of the police ordering staff and guests to safe areas. Joon-ho had no doubt the police would focus on the safety of the civilians, all at the front of the house, and would not venture further. Sanders and his team were the immediate problem, them and the Russian.

One of the guards left the group and disappeared around the corner of the stable building.

'What are we going to do?' asked Vostok, his voice quivering.

'We are going to do what we came here to do,' said Joon-ho, his voice as calm and measured as always.

'But they're shooting at us,' said Vostok, pointing back at the house.

'No,' said Joon-ho, 'they're shooting at Zhang, and he will keep them occupied while we get away from them.'

The guard returned around the stable and gave the all-clear. The guards and Joon-ho moved as a single coordinated unit, and Vostok shuffled along behind. They walked around the stable building and over the manicured lawn towards the landscaped garden. The ground rose ahead of them with a path leading around the rise. They moved quickly along the path and were soon on the far side of the rise, out of sight of the house. Once behind the rise the sound of the gunfire and the shouting were almost inaudible.

Directly ahead was the imposing glass form of the greenhouse. Standing next to it was a single-storey building. Parked next to the building was one of the lorries and a Transit minibus.

'My friend,' said Joon-ho, placing a hand on Vostok's shoulder. 'You need to be strong. We have nearly completed our mission. Everything now rests on you.' He smiled at the Russian, his best fake-smile.

'What do you mean?' hissed Vostok, as though trying to avoid being heard. 'We have to get out of here.'

'And we will,' said Joon-ho. 'Did you think I had not planned for this eventuality?'

Vostok had no reply to this.

'I have a boat ready to take us to Amsterdam. The British have no idea where we are or where we are going. By the time they discover either the device will have detonated, and they will no longer be a threat to us.'

'Detonated?' gasped Vostok. 'We cannot deliver the device, not now. We have to escape.'

'Yes, we can deliver the device,' said Joon-ho, 'and we must. You must. It all depends on you.'

'And how do I escape? You run to your boat and I go further inland? Do you take me a for a fool?'

'No,' said Joon-ho firmly. 'I take you for a man of your word. You will go with two of my men. They will assure your safety. Arrangements have been made and the men will be ready to receive the device. It has already been loaded on the vehicle, it is ready for you. You need to deliver it to them and ensure the timer is set, as we have discussed. My men will take you to the dock. I will be waiting for you.'

Vostok stared at him. Joon-ho could only imagine the Russian was trying to decide if he really could trust him.

'I have to assure your safety,' said Joon-ho. 'The device has to be set for four hours, to allow us to escape. If you are captured they will soon catch up with me.'

Still the Russian stared at him in silence.

Joon-ho continued. 'Besides. Do you think this is the only device I have? I still have need of your services.'

Vostok took a deep breath. Two of Joon-ho's men stepped forwards.

'I need you, Yuri,' said Joon-ho, trying his best to sound sincere, with a slight hint of pleading. 'Everything I have done depends on you. My men will make sure you're safe. Go now. Go quickly. I will see you at the boat.'

'You had better be waiting for me,' said Vostok.

Joon-ho turned and focused on the guards flanking Vostok. He spoke in Chinese, knowing Vostok would not understand.

'Take him to deliver the device. Protect him. Make sure he delivers it safely and sets the timer. When he has delivered the device, kill him and hide the body. Meet me at the airfield'

The two guards gave a momentary bow, then turned to escort Vostok towards the waiting lorry.

Wang stepped closer to Joon-ho.

'The helicopter is inbound,' said Wang, 'it will be here in four minutes.'

'Be ready,' said Joon-ho, 'the British soldiers may reach us before we leave. If you see them, kill them immediately.'

MICHAEL LED THE TEAM, Heckler Koch submachine guns in hand. They were now fully equipped, although Marshall reminded him that they still had no grenades. They moved cautiously along the path towards the landscaped garden and the greenhouse. To the right were the workman's building and the Ford Transit minibus parked next to it.

The greenhouse's glass panes reflected the beginnings of the sunset, the condensation inside and the reflection hiding whatever, and whoever were within. The greenhouse was big, which made Michael think hiding inside it would not be difficult. What would be difficult would be finding them. Gardening tools littered the path towards the building, as did statues and semi-repaired water features. Michael scanned the landscape ahead of them. Plenty of objects to provide cover, plenty of traps waiting for them to walk into. They were running out of time, he was acutely aware of that, but that didn't mean they could risk rushing into an ambush. He had to assume the guard who'd shot at them in the house had made it outside and joined his employer, but how many others did Joon-ho have protecting him?

He and the team crouched behind a pair of life-sized replicas of Michelangelo's David. Michael cradled his HK, his Heckler Koch submachine gun, feeling the texture of the grip and the weight of the weapon. He looked across the space between them and the entrance to the greenhouse. A tired peeling green door with a crack in its glass pane marked the only apparent way in, or out, of the greenhouse. To the side of the greenhouse was a large pile of gardening supplies and tools.

Michael heard something behind them, he wasn't sure what but something alerted him to a presence. He turned to look, mindful that the others continued to focus on the greenhouse. At the edge of the path by the rise in the land-scaped lawn was the red-shirted journalist. That man seemed to be present whenever Michael really wished there were no witnesses. He furiously waved at the man to get back, indicating the firearm he held to reinforce the danger present. The man narrowed his eyes, but backed away and was quickly out of sight. Michael hoped the man would have the sense to stay out of sight, the last thing he needed was a journalist lurking around.

Michael kept his words voiceless. 'Vince, Julian,' he thought, 'go to the left, get a position to the side of the greenhouse.'

Without reply, the two men started to move forward. Their action was met with a hail of bullets, the rapid cracking from an automatic weapon echoed off the glass and the walls of the nearby building. Stone chips exploded out from the twin Davids and all four of the team ducked and shielded themselves.

Vince leaned forward slightly, his voice appearing in

Michael's mind. 'I'd say there's one shooter, on the left side of that pile.'

'Evan,' thought Michael, 'go around the back side of that building, see if you can get a shot from behind him. We'll guide you in.'

Bullock crept back along the path towards the house. Michael hoped he'd take advantage of the shelter afforded by the rise in the land and run around to the far side of the worker's building.

'Let's keep our friend occupied,' thought Michael. 'Julian, guide Evan in.'

Michael leaned out from behind the statue and let off a short burst of fire towards the location of their adversary. As he pulled back in Marshall leaned forwards and fired. Michael flicked the catch on the side of his submachine gun, then leaned out and fired several single shots. Better to preserve their supply of ammunition at this stage. He and Marshall continued to alternate, keeping their quarry pinned down and under cover.

'I can see the bugger,' came Bullock's voice in Michael's mind. 'There's just one. I can get him from here.'

'No,' thought Michael in reply, 'we need him alive. Force him out, we'll restrain him.'

Without pause Bullock let rip with a burst of gunfire, bullets shattering glass panes, plant pots and kicking up a hail of debris. Almost despite himself the single Chinese guard ran out from his hiding place, clutching a submachine gun. Marshall advanced in a semi-crouched position, his weapon trained on the guard. Singh stepped forward and around to the right, making it clear that the man was covered from several angles and that he had no hope of escape. All Michael could do was hope no-one in the greenhouse had a clear view to shoot at them.

'Drop the gun, drop the gun,' Marshall ordered, keeping his voice firm but measured, avoiding being too audible to anyone inside the greenhouse. In response the guard spread his hands, holding his weapon in only one hand, making it clear the other was empty. Michael motioned at the floor with the barrel of his own gun. The guard bent from the knees and placed his gun on the ground, keeping his hands wide apart and in clear view. The man seemed keen to avoid being shot.

As soon as his gun was on the ground Michael and the others closed in, Bullock approaching from the side. The man's eyes widened as they approached, but he gained a measure of composure as all but Bullock lowered their weapons.

Michael stepped up to the man and in one deft move-ment placed his palm flat on the man's forehead. He felt the man's skin on his hand, and as he opened his mind he felt the man's thoughts. He felt the fear and the desperate struggle for self-control. Michael pushed and let a surge of mental energy flow through the connection. Like warm water flowing through snow, his thoughts rushed into the man's mind and overwhelmed him. His knees buckled and he sank to the floor, kneeling in an almost prayer-like posture at Michael's feet. Michael closed his eyes and focused.

How do you search someone's mind for a specific thought? Michael hadn't asked himself that, and he was suddenly unsure about how to search this man's mind for specific information. He needn't have worried, thoughts about Joon-ho were almost screaming at Michael. The guard was nearly beside himself with a mix of fear and anger and a desperate, painful need to protect his superior. The guard needed to be inside the greenhouse, he needed to be close to Joon-ho, to be with his colleagues and to do his duty. There was something else Michael needed to know. No sooner had Michael thought it than the man's mind reacted. The Russian, Vostok. Thoughts assaulted Michael, thoughts of what the man thought of Vostok, thoughts that were no in any way complimentary. Other thoughts came into Michael's mind, and one thought in particular struck him.

He opened his eyes and let go of the man, who sank forwards until his forehead almost touched Michael's feet.

'Evan, Julian,' said Michael. 'Vostok and two of the guards have taken the nuke.'

'Taken it where?' asked Singh, looking around.

'They're in a dark blue Ford Cargo lorry. They're heading down the access road to the goods entrance of the estate. Find a way, get after them. Do whatever you have to do, but secure that nuke.'

Singh and Bullock turned and left. Michael couldn't waste time watching what they decided to do. He looked at Marshall. 'Joon-ho and his guards are in the greenhouse, we need to get in there and stop them.'

'What about your worshipper?' asked Marshall, looking at the man collapsed at Michael's feet.

'I told him to stay there. He'll stay,' said Michael.

Without communicating they were clear on the only next move available to them. They each stepped back, aimed, and fired a volley of shots into the greenhouse, spraying the gunfire around intending to force everyone inside to take cover. Another short burst into the handle on the door, just to make sure, then they kicked in the door and ducked inside.

With all the focus on the guard, the revelation of the Russian's departure and the need to get inside the greenhouse, Michael and the others had missed the red-shirted journalist cowering behind the David replica, watching the entire episode.

———

As THEY SLIPPED inside the greenhouse the heat and humidity hit Michael. For a brief moment it transported him back to the Brazilian jungle and a mission which had been particularly uncomfortable. He noticed Marshall push the door closed behind him, and thought it an unnecessary act of good manners, then thought it would give them some indication if anyone opened the door to leave. Huge ferns and palms filled the space in the greenhouse, tall and leafy plants sat side by side with trays of smaller blooms. A curious mix of smells filled the air, compost mixed with fragrant orchid scent and spoiled by burned gunpowder.

The guard had given no idea where in the greenhouse Joon-ho might be, the man had had no idea. This was going to be one of those extremely dangerous games of cat and mouse, each side being both cat and mouse.

'You go right,' thought Michael, 'I'll go this way.' Marshall nodded. They split up, creeping in opposite directions, painfully aware of their footsteps crunching in broken glass. Joon-ho's men would have no problem locating them.

Michael moved slowly, his ears straining to hear any sound of Joon-ho's men. No doubt they were also moving, listening for any sound he might make. Once he was away from the front windows there was less debris on the ground to amplify the sound of his steps. He became aware of the low hum of the air circulators, the creaks from the metal structure as it began to cool in the late afternoon air.

Three sharp cracks rattled the glass panes and Michael

heard the smashing glass behind him as he ducked instinctively. Another half dozen shots echoed from the other side of the greenhouse, most likely Marshall's own battle. Perhaps it was a good job Marshall didn't have any grenades with him.

'Mr Joon-ho,' Michael called. 'We could avoid all of this violence.' It was worth a try.

To his surprise Joon-ho replied, but his voice was soft and seemed to drift through the air, giving no indication of the man's position. 'And I suppose I achieve that by surrendering myself to you?'

'Yes, that would be the general idea,' said Michael, scurrying further into the greenhouse, aiming to move away from where he was when he'd spoken, no point giving anyone an easy target. 'Armed police will storm this place sooner or later,' he called out, and scurried again, keeping low.

'And we will be gone, sooner, not later,' came Joon-ho's reply.

'Why the nuke?' asked Michael, not quite a shout, Joon-ho would hear him.

'I have no intention of explaining anything to you.'

'Thousands of innocent people will die,' said Michael.

'And how many hundreds of thousands of innocent people have your soldiers killed across the world? How many have the Americans killed? How many have been poisoned by your depleted uranium shells, starved by your punitive sanctions?'

'But a nuclear device? It will be traced back to you, you must know that?'

Another burst of gunfire from further away announced Marshall's ongoing efforts to corner Joon-ho.

The sound was almost imperceptible, but Michael heard

it, just in time. The slightest sound of a footfall to his right signalled the approach of one of Joon-ho's men. Michael wheeled away as the shot blasted a hole in the glass behind him and he found himself almost face to face with his attacker. Mirroring each other they both raised their guns but changed tactic and tried instead to slap away their opponent's weapon. They each launched a flurry of one-handed strikes and defences as they struggled to gain an advantage or at least some distance, but each kept with the other. Neither could bring their firearm into play at such a close range, but maintaining a grip on the gun made each less effective with the hand-to-hand moves. Michael knew he was in danger of being overrun at any moment, surely Joon-ho's other men would hear the scuffle and come to their colleague's aid.

An arm-deadening strike from the Chinese sent Michael's firearm tumbling from his grasp but at least it turned him so he could punch with his left hand, catching the man a glancing blow under the chin. The blow must have rattled the man's teeth because his gun too fell away, and both men were at each other with closed and open hand strikes. Michael dared not try and grasp the man to assert a telepathic control, such a grip would open him to a punch or a strike. Michael found a grip on the man's sleeved forearm and he wrenched down on it hard, pulling the man's elbow the wrong way. His attacker made no noise despite the move being enough to almost dislocate his elbow. Instead, he pushed Michael hard and Michael launched himself into a forward role heading for cover behind a pile of compost bags. He reached for his submachine gun as he rolled, grasped it and carried it with him as he scurried in a kneeling crouch as quickly as he could deeper into the greenhouse, towards the rear wall.

'Vince,' Michael said silently, 'where are you?'

'Almost back at the front door,' came the silent reply. At least his colleague was still in the game. 'Haven't seen Ho.'

Pain exploded in the small of Michael's back as someone drove a punch hard into his right kidney. Pain erupted through his torso, contorting him and strangling his voice. His weapon disappeared from view as tears flooded his eyes, and his desperate longing to stand and fight was washed away by pain and paralysis and he collapsed forwards onto the ground. He couldn't speak, either silently or out loud. He forced himself to twist onto his back, both arms grasping his stomach to try and contain the pain. Through the tears he saw the slim figure of Lee Joon-ho standing over him.

As MICHAEL and Vince slipped into the greenhouse, Evan made for the drive leading out of the estate, Julian Singh running alongside him.

'We're not going to run after the lorry, are we?' asked Bullock, almost moaning.

'I hope not,' said Singh. Bullock pulled up as Singh stopped at the driver's door of the Transit minibus and pulled it open, not sure what his teammate had in mind. 'It's our lucky day,' said Singh, grinning and climbing into the driver's seat.

'You don't mean they left the keys in?' said Bullock. He didn't think anyone could be that stupid, but maybe they'd left the keys in as another escape option. Singh had already started the engine, so Bullock leapt to the side, hauled open the passenger door and jumped in. Singh put his foot down before Evan had landed in the seat.

'Yeah, I'll have a lift, thanks,' said Bullock, grinning. He heard the click of the radio, Singh had pulled out his transceiver.

'Falcon Lead this is Ghost Two, over,' said Singh handling the radio in one hand and steering with the other. The road was a gravel track marked with potholes. The vehicle bounced and jumped as Singh drove at full speed. 'Falcon Lead, have your men block the lower exit from the estate, stop any vehicles from leaving.'

'Roger, Ghost Two,' crackled the reply from the radio.

'Falcon Lead,' said Singh, 'be advised, your men are to contain any vehicle but do not approach, I repeat, do not approach under any circumstances.'

'Roger, contain but not approach.' Singh clicked off the radio.

The road bent round to the left then again to the right and down an incline towards the high wall enclosing the estate. Bullock could see the electric blue flashes from the two police cars parked across the road, blocking the exit out to the public highway beyond. The brake lights flared on the lorry ahead of them, now visible as it skidded to a halt. Perhaps the driver reckoned crashing a lorry carrying a nuclear bomb wasn't a good move.

'Hold on,' said Singh. Bullock pulled his feet up onto the dashboard and braced himself as Singh braked hard, bringing the vehicle to a stop fifty yards from the lorry. They were out of the vehicle in moments, but Joon-ho's men had already left the lorry and were firing at the police.

As the two men left the road, one to each side of the lorry, Bullock dropped to a crouch and fired a burst of gunfire into the rear tyres of the vehicle. Whatever else happened, they weren't driving out of here, and he felt certain they weren't going to carry the nuke either.

'Try not to hit the nuclear weapon,' came Singh's voice in his mind.

'It's okay,' thought Bullock, 'it won't set it off.'

'Maybe not, but there's a whole world of people who'd wish you didn't risk it,' thought Singh. Bullock avoided his usual insulting thought about Singh's sarcasm, not sure how much of his thoughts anyone else could hear. 'You get the nuke,' Bullock thought, 'I'll take care of these two.'

As Singh cut behind him, making for the back of the lorry, Bullock jumped over the low hedge to the right into the green expanse of the lawn. He found the guard much closer than he expected, he thought the man would have started to run across the lawn. Instead, the guard turned and ran at Bullock his pistol raised, shots cracking. Bullock let rip with a burst of machine gun fire but the man was fast and agile, turning mid-stride and avoiding the bullets. Before he knew it the guard was upon him, knocking the gun out of his hand. The two of them sprawled across the grass, each trying to land a blow as they rolled and separated.

Bullock felt a rush of enthusiasm, keen for a good punch-up, he'd enjoy beating the crap out of one of these men. He lunged forward with a powerful left and right hook, the first missed and the second landed, the Chinese man hardly noticed. A flurry of punches came Bullock's way in return, he only just managed to block them. Maybe this wasn't going to be such fun after all. They were close again and Bullock struck out at his opponent's throat. Again the man twisted and turned, a skilled fighter, he counterattacked, catching a glancing blow on Bullock's chin and a more solid blow to his stomach.

As the man stepped forward to punch, Bullock responded to the momentary opening in his guard and grasped at the man's face. He hadn't practised much in taking telepathic control of someone, so he just let rip with the biggest surge of mental energy he could. He imagined lifting the heaviest weights he could, letting the imagined energy flow through his hand and into the man's face. The guard moaned and staggered, sinking towards the ground.

He stepped back and pulled out his pistol, aiming between the man's eyes. He might have heard them, or he might have seen them in his peripheral vision, but he noticed the police approaching, pistols raised and aimed at the now kneeling individual. Perhaps shooting a kneeling, unarmed man wouldn't be a great idea.

'He's all yours, boys,' he said and turned towards the lorry. The heavy throbbing sound of a helicopter became apparent. Bullock looked up, but couldn't see it. Maybe Julian would need help beating up the other guard.

MICHAEL FORCED HIMSELF TO FOCUS. A figure appeared behind Joon-ho, another of his guards, his pistol aimed at Michael. He flinched as more gunfire burst out from somewhere on the other side of the greenhouse, the tensing causing him more pain in his torso.

'I apologise,' said Joon-ho, bowing his head slightly. 'Your pain will not last long, neither will your inconvenience.'

'Get on with it,' said Michael. The guard stood too far away for Michael to reach him, and he had no strength or opportunity to escape.

'All in good time, Captain Sanders,' said Joon-ho, perhaps boasting about his intelligence on Michael and his team. How little you know, thought Michael. Joon-ho gave an order to his guard. The man stepped closer to Michael and bent down, reaching inside Michael's jacket for his pistol. Michael tried to stop the man, trying to restrain the guard's hand. He held the man's hand for a moment, but the man shook free of Michael's grasp and pulled out his pistol.

A new sound introduced itself into Michael's awareness, a deep thrumming sound, coming from outside the greenhouse. In his shocked state it took Michael a few moments to recognise the sound of an approaching helicopter. More police en-route? Or Joon-ho's men?

'I am curious about you and your team,' said Joon-ho, 'particularly your Sergeant Marshall. But my curiosity is of no importance now. Your interference is at an end.'

'We'll find the lorry with your nuke, and stop it,' Michael said, his strength returning. The pain grew slightly less, he felt he could at least move if needed.

'No, you won't,' said Joon-ho. 'You have no idea where it's going, or what vehicle it is now in. Your police will never find it. But enough of this.'

A sustained burst of machine gun fire echoed off the glass. Michael saw Joon-ho and his guard glance around, and Michael thought it was worry on their faces. The gunfire was from Marshall.

The thought from Marshall wasn't so much words as a feeling of satisfaction. It came into Michael's mind and was enough to let him know that Joon-ho was down to two guards, not that Joon-ho could know that yet.

Michael focused on the guard. The pain made concentration difficult, but he focused as much as he could. His connection with the guard was weak, he'd only briefly had hold of the man's hand and his mind was still a mess of pain and distraction, yet he could feel his mind reach out and make contact with the guard. He had the sensation like he was pushing against a door that was stiff and wouldn't open. For a mad moment Michael wondered if he could project his pain into the guard, but quickly realised it probably wouldn't work. He focused on ordering the guard to lower his weapon. The man's hand wavered, but still it felt like the door wouldn't open. The guard's duty and loyalty to Joon-ho were strong, it provided a barrier to direct control. Michael quickly abandoned the idea of having the guard turn his gun on Joon-ho, but all he had to do was create some space. He willed himself to relax, despite the pain, and let his thoughts flow out through the psychic connection.

Joon-ho barked something in Chinese as the man lowered his weapon and stepped in front of Joon-ho, obscuring his view of Michael. Michael pushed himself to his feet, all he had to do was get the man to let go of his pistol, but without Joon-ho taking it first. He focused, letting as much thought-energy as possible flow through the link, but the link was weak, so weak. If he could get the gun he could get to Joon-ho, and gain control over him.

The sound of the helicopter grew louder, masking the sound of approaching feet from behind Michael.

As BULLOCK HOPPED over the hedge and disappeared into the lawn beyond, Singh crept closer to the back of the now abandoned lorry. The other of Joon-ho's men had made his escape on this side of the road, and Singh was all too aware the man could be anywhere. He held his submachine gun in front, scanning the area around the lorry. He knew he faced a dilemma, take care of the guard first, or make sure the nuke was safe. The dilemma was answered for him.

He heard the crunch of the gravel underfoot, from behind. The man's voice was calm, professional.

'Turn around slowly,' said the voice, a Chinese accent clear but the English was good. 'Keep your hands to the side, finger off the trigger.'

Singh turned around, slowly, spreading his arms out to either side, holding the submachine gun as lightly as he could. As he turned he came face to face with the remaining guard, too far away to attack, close enough for the guard to have a clear shot. Singh recognised him as the guard he'd connected with earlier. He stared at the man. Would he shoot? Did he think he could escape? He heard shots from across the road, Bullock was having fun.

The telepathic connection was still there, weak but it existed. Julian let himself relax, he let himself feel a sense of calm. As he looked at the Chinese man he made himself feel a sensation of closeness, of connection, that they were all friends together. He let the feelings extend out, through the mind-link. He sensed the man's struggle for self-control, his indecision. Singh let waves of calm flow towards his captor, they were all friends together, and friends didn't need guns.

The guard lowered his pistol, and a smile began to form on his face. In a single smooth movement Singh dropped his own gun into position and let rip with a burst of fire. Blood exploded out of the man's chest and mouth and he collapsed into the gravel, still smiling.

In just a few strides he reached the back of the lorry. Holding his gun in one hand he pulled open one of the rear doors with the other.

The flight case was in the middle of the cargo space of the lorry, the lid propped open and a man bent over, leaning into the case. Hearing the door open the man stood up. Singh recognised Yuri Vostok (was that really his name?)

Vostok held a small electronic unit in one hand, a cable trailing into the case. For a lingering moment, Vostok looked at Singh, like the proverbial rabbit caught in the headlights. Singh saw Vostok's eyes drop for a moment as he looked into the case.

Julian fired a burst of bullets directly into Vostok's face. Blood and brains sprayed in all directions, bursting out of the back of his head, splashing onto the back wall of the lorry. Vostok collapsed in a heap without making a sound. Singh waited a moment. He wasn't sure why, perhaps waiting to see if Vostok's device had made anything happen. Nothing happened. He climbed carefully into the lorry and looked into the case.

As he'd seen in his psychic connection with Vostok the nuke was a metallic white cone. It looked impossibly small given what he knew of its explosive power. He looked at the base of the nuke, the cable from Vostok's device lay on the floor of the case, he hadn't plugged it in.

'Looks like you get all the fun,' he heard Bullock say. Singh looked around. Bullock was standing looking into the lorry, at the bloody remains lying on the other side of the case. They both looked up at the rising sound of the helicopter.

'You finished here?' asked Singh.

'Yeah, I'm done,' said Bullock.

'Right, let's get back and give the boss a hand.'

MICHAEL SAW the guard raise the gun slightly, and Joon-ho reached out to take it.

Michael heard the words in his mind, loud and clear and emphatic. 'Get down,' came Marshall's telepathic command.

Instinctively Michael dropped, fighting against the pain flaring in his abdomen. The burst of gunfire followed an instant later, blood exploding out of the back of the guard who collapsed like a puppet whose strings had been cut. Michael caught a glimpse of Joon-ho, his face splattered with blood, dashing to his right, behind shelves of plants and out of sight, glass shattering behind him as more shots rang out.

'Need a hand?' said Marshall out loud. He offered a hand and pulled Michael to his feet.

'We have to stop him,' said Michael, 'if he gets to that helicopter we'll lose him.'

'No we won't,' said Marshall. 'He's still got one guard with him. You take that side, I'll go this way.' Marshall retreated the way he'd come and disappeared back into the depths of the greenhouse.

Conscious of the volume of the helicopter noise Michael retrieved his weapons and followed Joon-ho. He had to move cautiously, turning his mind off to the pain in his back. There was every chance the one remaining guard could lay in wait for him and give his employer time to escape. A single pistol shot cracked and the glass pane behind him shattered. Michael ducked, pain flaring in his kidneys, noting how very close that shot had come. He also noted it came from his left, the guard had moved deeper into the building. The helicopter sound exploded in volume and a rush of air blasted in Michael's face. The door had been opened. Another pistol shot shattered a plant pot on a shelf just ahead of Michael. Where was Marshall? Surely he'd be able to take care of the guard.

The air-blast stopped and the noise abated, the door had been closed.

'Vince,' Michael thought, 'where are you?'

'Approaching the door,' came the reply, 'Ho's just ahead of me, so's his guard.'

Michael scurried forward and as he came to the end of the shelving sheltering him he could see the door. Marshall stepped out from behind a mass of green ferns. Together they pulled open the door and stepped through, guns aimed in the direction of the roaring helicopter. He ran for cover as the inevitable shots landed in the ground behind them and the door frame to their side. They fired back desperately, the blast of air from the helicopter blinding them, the roar of its engines deafening them. In moments the helicopter was airborne and banking away from them. They fired the few shots they had remaining before the aircraft was gone beyond the trees and out of sight.

'Get hold of the police,' Michael said out loud, 'tell them to track that helicopter.'

Michael turned his voice inwards, feeling for the connection with his teammates. He needed to know if the nuke was still a problem.

TWENTY TWO

Michael thought, for a brief moment, about changing clips in his pistol and firing more shots at the retreating helicopter, but soon thought better of it. The aircraft was already out of range, their only hope now was if the police or RAF could track it and locate Joon-ho. He unclipped his radio.

'Falcon Lead, this is Ghost One,' Michael said into the mic.

'Falcon Lead receiving, over,' came the reply.

'Falcon Lead, alert Falcon Command, that helicopter must be tracked and stopped at all costs, confirm.'

'Falcon Lead, confirm, will alert Falcon Command.'

'Ghost One, out.' Michael clicked off the radio and clipped it back inside his jacket.

A whining sound grew louder, heralding the approach of an engine straining and protesting. He and Marshall looked to the road leading down the hill and soon saw the Transit being driven in reverse, as fast as it would go. The vehicle skidded to a halt in front of them, Bullock leaping out before it had stopped.

'Don't tell me he got away,' said Bullock, looking at the disappearing aircraft.

'Tell me the nuke is secure,' said Michael. He was relieved to see Singh getting out of the driver's door.

'It is,' said Singh. 'The police have secured the lorry. Vostok's dead, so's one of the guards, the other's in custody.'

There was no mistaking the awkward silence left by the now almost inaudible sound of the helicopter.

'So I take it Joon-ho's not in custody,' said Singh.

'No, he's not,' said Michael. He forced himself to keep looking at Singh, and not look at Marshall, a glance in that direction might be taken as an accusation.

'His guard kept me pinned down,' said Marshall, in a matter-of-fact way, 'couldn't get to him, couldn't get a clear shot at him.'

'Bugger,' said Bullock.

Michael sensed that the others might believe Marshall's story, but he didn't. There was something missing, something Marshall wasn't saying. Marshall was aggressive and fearless, he didn't believe that just one of Joon-ho's guards could have kept Marshall at bay for that long. For the moment, though, he had other priorities.

'Right,' said Michael. 'Get our gear stowed, we'll be out of here once police have taken initial details.'

'Where to next?' asked Singh.

'That's what I need to find out,' said Michael. 'Keep the guns out, I'm sure the police forensics teams will want them.'

'Then what do we shoot bad guys with?' moaned Bullock.

'Nothing,' said Michael, turning away, 'the shooting's over for today.'

He walked down the path, back towards the house,

taking out his mobile phone. He made sure he was out of hearing range before he dialled the number.

As he expected, the Head answered without greeting or pleasantry.

'I take it your alerting Falcon Command to intercept the helicopter means Joon-ho got away?'

'Yes, he did,' replied Michael. 'But we have the nuke, it's safe, so there's no doubt now he was planning a major atrocity.'

'Some consolation,' said the Head, 'but that doesn't explain how he managed to escape.'

'That's something I need to look into,' said Michael. He really didn't want to speculate about what his team might have done, or might not have done. He needed to talk to them, ask them questions, get their explanations, especially Marshall. It kept coming back to Marshall.

'Keep me updated,' she said and hung up. Michael didn't think the Head needed him to keep her updated, she seemed quite able to keep herself up to date, no doubt plugged directly into the police communications network.

His phone rang. He looked at the display but felt little surprise the caller withheld their number.

'Yes?' he said, answering the call.

'Captain Sanders?' said the caller. 'This is Captain Conway. We need to talk.'

As soon as Sanders was out of sight, Julian and Evan turned to face Vince Marshall. He looked at each of them, staring at them. Try as he might, he couldn't read their thoughts. A pity, that really would be a useful skill.

'So what really happened?' asked Evan.

347

He appreciated Evan's youthful energy and almost childish no-nonsense approach to things, but sometimes it could get waring. At these times he just thought of Bullock as a cocky little twat.

'I get the impression,' said Julian, 'that the boss hasn't got the full picture.'

Singh could be far more diplomatic, but sometimes could be just as annoying. He was, however, quite right.

'No,' said Marshall. 'The boss really was pinned down by one of Ho's men.'

'But you weren't?' asked Singh.

'To begin with, but that problem didn't last long,' said Marshall. 'I caught Ho by surprise. He turned round, but I got hold of him before he could do anything stupid.'

'And when you got hold of him,' said Singh, 'what did you do?'

Marshall looked at Singh, not entirely sure how much to give away. There was a temptation to keep it all to himself. He had thought about it, in the few minutes after Joon-ho escaped and before the questioning started, but he realised he would need help if they chose to go a certain way.

'I have control of him,' Marshall said. The other two looked at him, open-mouthed. Little surprised these two, but it seemed he had. 'I have complete control over Ho. I can make him turn around and come straight back, if I wanted.'

'And what do you want to do?' asked Singh.

'I could make him give us the keys to his entire kingdom,' said Marshall, 'and it's a big fucking kingdom.'

He saw Singh look around, perhaps checking Sanders hadn't returned. 'This is really dangerous,' said Singh.

'What do you mean?' asked Bullock.

Marshall didn't take his eyes off Singh. 'We're now guilty of treason,' said Singh, who glanced at Bullock. 'We're now a party to you deliberately letting a known terrorist escape, a terrorist you're colluding with.'

'Not colluding,' said Marshall. 'Not yet.'

'What then?'

'We have a decision to make,' said Marshall. 'All of us.' This time he looked at Bullock as well.

'We might be about to cross a line,' said Singh, 'and we can only be on one side of this line or the other. There's no halfway.'

Marshall closed his eyes and let his thoughts expand. It was easy now to find the connection to Joon-ho. He could feel the unique sense of the man's thoughts, he could almost see through Joon-ho's eyes.

'He has an escape route planned,' said Marshall, eyes still closed.

'Well of course he does,' said Singh.

'He has a small plane waiting, he's going to fly out. We could tell the police where the plane is. There's still time for them to stop him.'

'Or?' Singh had asked the most relevant question. What was their alternative?

'Or we let him fly out. I'll know where he is, I can always know where he is. We can take advantage of that at any time.'

'If we do that,' said Singh, 'we've crossed the line.'

'Then we need to decide,' said Marshall, 'all of us.'

'All four of us?' asked Bullock. Again, it was the question that now most needed answering.

'No,' said Marshall, 'the three of us. The boss has made his position clear, it's the three of us now, like the three musketeers.'

'We have to be careful,' said Singh, 'that someone doesn't make us the three stooges.'

They heard the sound of footsteps crunching in the gravel. Sanders was on his way back.

MORROW STARED across his desk at Yves Falcone. The afternoon sun was starting to become burned orange in the sky, and sometimes he allowed himself simply to soak up the beauty of the setting sun. Now, he needed to return his thoughts to more pressing matters.

He could sense that Turner had news for him. It was like sitting with someone who was desperate to speak, the desperation was almost palpable. He closed his eyes and opened his mind to the thoughts of Major Liam Turner. The news from Turner didn't take long.

When the telepathic conversation was over, he opened his eyes.

'I take it,' said Falcone, 'that it is not good news.'

Morrow sighed. 'No, it is not.' He looked again at the sunset. All good things have a finite lifetime, he thought. 'The soldiers have used their abilities in combat.'

'Impressive,' said Falcone.

'Impressive, yes,' said Morrow, 'but it also means they are now very strong. If they can use their abilities even in the stress of armed fighting then I suspect they are too strong for me to control them.'

Falcone dropped his gaze. 'So what do we need to do next?'

'It is clear that I cannot risk meeting them,' said Morrow. 'They must now not know of me, or of you.'

'If you can't control them,' said Falcone, sounding like he was searching for the right words. 'They might pose a threat.'

'They do pose a threat,' said Morrow, 'a very great threat. Four uncontrolled, strongly telepathic soldiers, out of our control, able to do whatever they want, with a direct connection to the research facility.'

'And therefore back to us,' said Falcone, finishing Morrow's line of thinking.

'Indeed. This is a very undesirable state of affairs.'

'It's not as if you can simply get rid of them,' said Falcone.

Morrow looked at him, and let the silence speak for him. Falcone returned the stare but soon had to avert his gaze, unable to keep eye contact with Morrow.

'That is exactly what we must now do,' said Morrow. 'It is clear this round of the experiment has failed, but there is much we can learn. We must clear up, remove the evidence, and then plan for the next round of the experiment.'

'But we've failed, we can't control them,' said Falcone.

'No, this is not a failure. This is a setback. This round of the experiment has made it clear, I need to take control of the subjects before they are given the drug, before their abilities emerge.'

'So what do we do about the four soldiers who are out there?'

'We?' asked Morrow, almost mocking. 'You have the contact, Yves. You have the resources to take care of this problem.'

Falcone stood up and walked to the window. Morrow could feel the despair coming from Falcone, he could almost smell it, it had such a distinct note. 'I can't simply call up some pet assassins and have them come and kill those men,' said Falcone.

'I don't mean to be overly simplistic, but why not?'

Falcone continued to stare out of the window, his back to

Morrow. It made no difference, Morrow could feel his fear and reluctance whichever way he was standing. He could feel that Falcone knew exactly what he could do, all he lacked was that last push over the line into action.

'Killing four soldiers would attract a lot of attention,' said Falcone. 'A lot of questions would be asked, questions which would quickly lead back here.'

'But you could arrange individuals who could do the job?' asked Morrow.

He could feel the answer from Falcone, but he needed to hear it, he needed Falcone to say it.

'I could,' said Falcone. 'There are people in South Africa I could contact. There are mercenaries who could be engaged. But it would take them time to get here. I don't know how they'd do it without getting caught, without questions being asked.'

'Perhaps it should not be done here,' said Morrow. He thought through various scenarios, examining the benefits and drawbacks of each option.

'You mean have the soldiers moved?' asked Falcone. He turned around to face Morrow. 'How?'

'First, consider whether that would make it easier,' said Morrow.

Falcone was silent for a moment, then spoke. 'If the soldiers could be sent where there is less awareness of them, somewhere more remote, then yes, it would be easier to deal with them.'

Morrow felt a concern. Falcone still spoke of "dealing with them," he was not yet ready to take decisive action. He let his mind open, and felt the connection with Falcone. He felt the objections almost as a barrier, like walking into a strong wind.

'Yves,' he said, making his voice calm and soothing,

using the psychic connection to enhance the effect. 'We need to protect ourselves, and these men are a danger to us. We have to be strong, and to do dark things to protect the project. You understand that, don't you?'

Falcone nodded slowly.

'I will have Turner arrange for these men to be sent somewhere remote, somewhere where there will be no prying eyes, somewhere out of sight and out of everyone's concern, perhaps somewhere dangerous.'

'If they're sent where there is already danger,' said Falcone, 'it would be easier to have something dangerous happen to them.'

'How quickly can you make arrangements?'

Falcone paused for a moment. 'I can have people in place in forty-eight hours, maybe seventy-two.'

'Good, then it's time for you to get in touch with your South African contact, and I will liaise with Major Turner. He will also need to start work looking for another unit of soldiers we can use.'

MICHAEL SAT with his team staring at the football game streamed onto Singh's laptop. Police still milled around the house, and every so often one or two would come into the police room in the outbuilding, usually for the kettle and a mug of tea.

Each of the team had, at one time or other, got up and gone for a walk, anything to break the monotony. The Head had called Michael to tell him that MI6 and GCHQ were trying to track and locate Joon-ho. If they succeeded the team might be tasked at short notice with "intercepting" him. They had all seemed enthused by this idea. She had also said that they were to stay at Mountfield House until further notice, whenever that might be. The team were much less enthused by that idea. The hours had crept by.

The only truly interesting thing to do had been to watch the police forensics teams set up their lights and little white tents and begin their meticulous analyses of the sites of the shootings. Each of the team had given a very brief statement to the police, longer interviews would have to wait until a Special Forces appointed solicitor was available to accompany them. It took specialist legal training to insist the soldiers answer "no comment" to every question put to them.

Michael couldn't raise any enthusiasm for the game, it provided little more than a distraction, he suspected the others felt the same. They'd each filled a brief time making a round of tea, but even for them there was only so much tea a man could drink in any one evening. The hotel bar was still open, a fact not lost on them, but since they were in theory on standby for immediate action, they gave it a wide berth.

Bullock tapped with his foot, something which often annoyed Michael, but this time he could understand the frustration. They usually filled their waiting time with jokes and banter, but for the moment there was an uncharacteristic quiet between them.

'This is fucking ridiculous,' said Bullock. Michael was almost relieved that one of the others had spoken first.

'It is,' Michael agreed, 'but for the moment we've no choice.'

'I'd rather be back in some dodgy bit of Iraq,' added Marshall.

'Be careful what you wish for,' said Singh, almost smiling.

'That's simple then,' said Marshall, a harsher tone to his voice. 'I wish I was back in some Godforsaken arse-pit in Iraq.'

Michael thought about trying to calm things, but decided if the team was tense it was better they give voice to those tensions. He couldn't make them feel not-tense. He'd not told them about the call from Conway, he wasn't yet certain how they'd react. He sensed a simmering anger at being kept waiting by the MI5 Head of Operations. As soldiers, they didn't report to her and she had no authority over them, but no-one from the Special Forces Directorate had been in touch to give them alternative orders.

Conway's message had been brief, he would be in touch and Sanders was to be available to take his call. Michael could only assume their association with Conway and the project was not over yet.

'I bet we're going back to that miserable place,' said Bullock, 'and more of Conway's stupid tests.'

'Wouldn't surprise me if this MI5 woman has something else planned,' said Marshall.

'Depends if they manage to locate Mr Joon-ho,' said Singh.

Michael kept quiet, he couldn't think of anything constructive to say. They'd spent a lot of time as a team sitting and waiting for orders, waiting for intelligence on a target, or waiting for the weather to clear. Boredom was just a fact of life, another discomfort to moan about or ignore. They'd sat together in rain-soaked ditches and in sun-baked deserts. They'd laughed and joked together, and other times they'd shared the silence with enemies a stone's throw away.

But something was different now, something had changed. Michael couldn't put his finger on it. The bizarre developments at the project facility had certainly changed things. They were different people now, they were different from all other people. But something had changed within the team. There were questions about Joon-ho's escape, and Michael had questions about Marshall's attitude, questions which were becoming doubts.

The warbling of his mobile phone jerked him back into the here-and-now. He recognised the number but said nothing, and answered the call. He listened to the caller, mumbled the occasional acknowledgement, and the call ended.

He looked at the team, and for the first time, he wasn't sure how they were going to react to being given orders to move out.

'That was Captain Conway,' he said, and the three groaned. He'd almost expected that.

'It seems our association with the project isn't over, not yet, but our next round of exercises is going to be in a more challenging environment.'

'And what, exactly, does that mean?' asked Marshall.

'It means we're going back to Afghanistan,' said Michael. 'Conway will contact us there about our next assignments.'

'And when's this all kicking off?' asked Bullock.

'Now,' said Michael. 'We're to drive tonight to the Air Mounting Centre, and fly to Afghanistan tomorrow morning.'

There was a stunned silence in the room.

TWENTY THREE

The Head took her place at the top of the table and was satisfied when the chattering halted. She looked at the assembled team leaders, people representing the military, GCHQ, communications, intelligence, analysis; all the specialities needed to trap a man as well-resourced as Lee Joon-ho.

The first item on the agenda was the fallout from the previous day's excitement at Mountfield House. The media had been in a frenzy, reporting everything from a failed kidnap attempt to a botched antique theft. None of them, to the Head's huge amazement and relief, had mentioned anything about Joon-ho specifically or about any weapons of mass destruction.

More difficult to handle than the media response was the political backlash. The Head was still tired from a late night, and therefore little sleep, fielding calls from the Minister, Chancellor of the Exchequer, the Prime Minister and various other political heavyweights. Most wanted to know first if Mr Joon-ho was safe, and second whose resignation they could expect as a consequence of allowing the debacle to happen.

She dealt with the first agenda item as quickly as possible. They had experts for dealing with the media. What was more important was finding Lee Joon-ho. Whilst they had his Russian nuclear warhead in safe custody (it had been made safe and shipped off to the Atomic Weapons Establishment site at Burnleigh to be dismantled and examined,) the Head had a worrying suspicion that Joon-ho probably possessed other similar items.

The team moved quickly to the second, and only other item on the agenda - locating Lee Joon-ho. The discussion was short; they had no leads.

'We found the helicopter,' said the Police Liaison Officer, 'abandoned at a derelict industrial estate, the pilot had been killed.'

'There were no traffic cameras in the area,' said an analyst from GCHQ, 'so no way of tracking how they moved on from the industrial estate. By the time they came into range of traffic cameras they'd be just one of the traffic stream, no way of picking them out.'

'Exits from the country?' asked the Head.

'Numerous,' said the GCHQ analyst. 'By boat would be the least traceable, they could rendezvous with a larger vessel at sea, maybe head straight for Europe or up to Norway. Either way, like the traffic, they'd be just one of ten thousand vessels.'

'Where might he be heading?'

'The Far East is our estimate,' replied the GCHQ analyst. The Head thought the analyst looked familiar, but his name was not her highest priority. He continued. 'He could head ultimately for Brazil or Mexico, and he has interests in

Africa and India, but we believe his base of operations is in China, and that would put him beyond our reach.'

'Do we still have his aircraft impounded?'

The discussion moved onto what assets they had seized and the police's progress with interviewing Joon-ho's guards who had been arrested. It seemed they were refusing to speak, even with an interpreter and a solicitor present.

The Head looked over at the GCHQ analyst who was tapping furiously at his laptop keyboard. He looked up at the Head.

'We may have a lead on Joon-ho,' he said, sounding almost excited.

'Details?' she asked.

'Flight plans have been logged for private planes, the first one taking off from Southern France, the final one landing at a private airfield in Hong Kong. The plans were all logged at the same time, and together they make a possible escape route for Joon-ho.'

'It's a bit speculative,' said one of the other analysts. The Head ignored the comment.

The GCHQ analyst went on. 'One of the planes belongs to a company we know is owned by Joon-ho.'

'That's good enough,' said the Head. She turned to the Military Liaison Officer.

'I want Captain Sanders' team assigned to capture Joon-ho. Work out where they can intercept him and how quickly they can get there.'

'Yes Ma'am,' said the MLO, and left the room, dialling quickly on his mobile phone.

She turned next to one of the MI5 operational leaders. 'Stand by to set up a Command and Control room, we'll run the intercept and capture from here,' she said. Each nodded confirmation they understood their assignments and responsibilities. 'Dismissed,' she said, addressing the room.

The Head left the room, looking for the MLO. She didn't have to go far, he was at the other end of the corridor, the phone still clamped to his ear. Moments later he lowered the phone. He looked around and made eye contact with the Head. She was sure he shook his head.

'Problem?' she asked.

'It seems Captain Sanders' team is still attached to Special Forces Development,' he said. 'They've been assigned to a training and evaluation exercise, whereabouts unknown.'

She stifled an expletive. Joon-ho had to be stopped. Sanders and his men were the only ones equipped to do it. For a moment she hesitated. She had thought before they were the best ones for the job, and they'd failed, but perhaps no-one else would have succeeded. There was no alternative.

'I need to make a call,' she said and headed for her office.

In the privacy of her office, she knew she could discuss things that no-one else should overhear. She used the desk phone and dialled Major Turner's office. It rang for half a minute before she put the phone down. She tried to contact him again, calling his mobile phone. This time she let it ring for a full minute before abandoning the call.

There were two possibilities remaining. She called Sander's own mobile, but it went straight to voicemail. That left one possibility. After her meeting with him she'd made sure she had a telephone number for Doctor Morrow, just in case she needed to talk to him, and now she did. She rang the number. Again it rang for a full minute before she put the phone down.

That all three should be unreachable was not a coincidence. Turner had put Sanders' team out of reach, back into this project of his. She had no doubt Morrow had a part to play, but her need for the soldiers was greater.

She sat back in her chair and started to ponder other options for intercepting Joon-ho. There were other resources she could bring into play, not least was engaging MI6, and that would be her next call. One thought kept coming back, a thought that troubled her more and more. Where had Turner sent Sanders and his team? And why?

MICHAEL STRETCHED HIS ACHING LIMBS, hours sat in the cramped confines of the C-17 transport aircraft had left him stiff and aching. He closed his eyes and let the hot afternoon sunshine sooth him. The air smelled of aviation fuel and diesel fumes, yet it was a welcome relief from the drab project facility and the mayhem of Mountfield House.

All too soon the team were huddled in the back of a lorry, driving them out of the airfield and towards the Special Forces enclave on the outskirts of the camp. The sense of change and freshness faded quickly, and by the time they reached their destination Michael felt like they'd never been away.

As they jumped down from the lorry and the other soldiers started to carry their kit into the accommodation buildings, Michael found himself face to face with Lieutenant-Colonel Clifton. Marshall and the others grabbed their bags and stood behind Michael.

'Back so soon, lads?' asked Clifton, with a wry smile. 'I can't work out if you're sent here because you're flavour of the month, or because someone wants you as far away as possible.'

'Arsehole,' came Bullock's voice into Michael's mind. He tried hard to stifle a laugh and keep a straight face.

'Anyway,' said Clifton, 'get unpacked, I'll be back to brief you in half an hour. No rest for the wicked.' And he marched off.

'Now what?' said Marshall.

They only had to wait half an hour to find out. Michael and the team sat in the cheap plastic chairs in the briefing room. In some ways it seemed to Michael so much longer than two weeks since he had sat in this same seat as Clifton told them about the project they were being assigned to and all the events that had followed. In a strange way, though, it felt like he had hardly been away.

Clifton marched in, and without ceremony sat down in the remaining vacant chair.

'Right chaps,' said Clifton, sounding almost like a parody of an upper-class officer. 'I've been in touch with a Captain Conway, I believe you know him.'

There was a muted groan from the other three, but Michael heard a much louder response in his mind's ear, the three of them voiced various, and quite vulgar, opinions of Conway.

Clifton continued. 'It seems you're still assigned to that research project, but Captain Conway was quite clear, you're still an active part of Special Forces.'

Michael glanced at each of the team. Their expressions were of uncertainty. They let Clifton speak. 'He's keen that you support local operations, and he and I have agreed that there is one particular mission for you. Captain Conway said it was right up your street.'

Michael looked again at each of the team, psychically

hushing them. Now was not the time for sarcasm or insubordination.

'You'll have tonight to prepare,' said Clifton, 'and you'll be on your way in the morning. We have solid intelligence that the Taliban are using a village as a weapons cache. We need you to get in unseen and place video surveillance devices and a satellite relay. We'll keep tabs on the village. We expect the Taliban will try and deposit a very significant arms delivery there soon, and we'll intercept it. Any questions?'

'Why us?' asked Marshall, 'why not regular troops?'

'The area's hostile,' said Clifton. 'There are Taliban, possibly other Special Forces nearby, mercenaries can't be ruled out, and who knows what the Americans are up to? We need you to stay invisible, get in, place the devices, and get out without anyone knowing you've been there.'

'Sounds like fun,' said Singh.

'You'll have tomorrow to approach the village and arrive by nightfall,' said Clifton.

'Right,' said Michael, 'we'll start planning.'

'Good,' said Clifton, rubbing his hands together. 'I believe Captain Conway will update you when you get back, no doubt explain more about this project of yours.'

'Why doesn't Captain Conway come out here and do some proper soldiering?' asked Marshall.

The others, Clifton included, looked at him. Michael still wasn't sure about Clifton's sense of humour.

'Did I say that out loud?' said Marshall, 'sorry.'

'Let's get this over and done with,' said Michael, 'then we can get back. I'm sure we've all got some questions for Captain Conway.'

THE APPROACH to the village had been tiring, boring and uneventful. Boulders and gullies marked out the landscape, peppered with bushes and scrub. As planned, they'd walked for the best part of the day from the helicopter drop-off. As missions went, Michael thought, this one should provide no trouble. There again, every mission was easy and no trouble, until it went badly horribly wrong.

The four of them had parted company after the helicopter had left them, each setting off to approach the village from a different direction. Four solitary figures would be less visible than one group of four. That was the theory.

As usual, the 'intelligence' available to them consisted of little more than maps and satellite photographs of the village and the surrounding area. Collectively it didn't say any more than Clifton had told them.

Ahead of him, Michael could see the ground twisted and turned and then rose up. Beyond the rise was the village. At least the day had been, relatively speaking, a mild one, temperatures down from recent levels. This meant the night would be colder.

The words came into his mind, Bullock's timbre and intonation unmistakable. 'I'm having a look around,' he said, 'and I can't see anyone. Not a single person or camel.'

'They don't have camels in this part of the world, dickhead,' came Marshall's voice.

'No,' said Bullock, 'but I'm fairly sure they have people, and I don't see any.'

'Can you see the village?' came Singh's voice.

'Yes, I can see the village,' replied Bullock. 'A bunch of ropey huts, but no people.'

'Try using your binoculars,' said Marshall.

'What the fuck do you think I'm using? I'm telling you, this place looks empty. What are we doing here?'

'We're following orders,' said Michael, 'it's what we do.'

'This isn't what I signed up for,' said Bullock.

'What did you sign up for?' said Singh. 'Nice cushy office job? Sitting behind a desk? Someone bringing you cups of china tea and cucumber sandwiches?'

Michael had to laugh, to himself if not to the others. He got the sense that Marshall and Singh were also laughing, but not Bullock.

'If you wanted a job like that you should have gone for Conway's job,' said Marshall.

'Is he behind all this?' said Bullock. Michael could hear the change in tone, even in the silent thought-voice.

'Conway gave us the orders to come out here,' said Michael, 'but I don't know if he runs the project.'

'I reckon it's that MI5 woman who's behind all this,' said Marshall.

'Well, whoever it is, we'll ask Conway when we get back,' said Michael. 'For the moment, we're here, and we have a job to do. Stay out of sight, we've three hours before it's dark. We'll move into the village then.'

He felt the mind-voices go quiet. He reached the rise and sat down between some rocks. In a few hours he'd lead the team into the village. He'd been in this position so many times, ready to lead the team into action. This time it felt different, something had changed. He had to rely on his men, but could he? Were they a team anymore? He'd find out.

MARSHALL LAY ON HIS FRONT, hidden by bushes and rocks. He looked at the village through his binoculars. Even in the fading half-light of the evening he could see, Bullock was right, there was no-one in sight.

He felt Singh's voice come into his mind. 'Just out of interest,' said Singh, 'where has our Mr Joon-ho got to?'

Marshall closed his eyes for a moment and concentrated. As he answered he felt Bullock's mental presence.

'Joon-ho's in an aircraft, somewhere over Russia,' said Marshall. 'I think he's on his way to China.'

'What's he going to do?' asked Bullock.

'Can't tell,' said Marshall, 'but man, is he cross? He's one very angry man, and mainly at us.'

'Tell him sorry, from the three of us,' said Bullock. He 'heard' Singh's laugh.

'What are we going to do?' asked Bullock.

'In an hour,' said Marshall, 'we're going to creep into that village and plant some video cameras, then we're going to creep out and fuck off back to camp.'

'I meant...' began Bullock, but Marshall cut him off.

'I know what you meant. I'm not thinking about that, not yet. Let's get this bullshit mission over and done with first.'

The next hour dragged by, the passage of time marked by the drop in temperature. He had to move between squatting and crouching and kneeling, the ground was too cold to lie on. He checked his watch. Right on cue, he heard Sanders' voice in his head give the order to move in.

Marshall slipped on the night vision goggles and turned them on. The world lit up in a sparkling green haze. He crept forward, moving slowly over the final few hundred yards to the first hut. The rough mud-brick buildings were crude and simple. He moved and checked for anyone else, moved and checked, always slowly and carefully. He reached the first position and slipped the pack off his back.

The cameras were thin black cylinders, reminding him

of a miniature flashlight, but no doubt much more expensive. He slipped the device out of his pack and into a crevice in the dry stone wall, its lens looking straight down the rough track running through the centre of the village.

He crept passed the first hut and on towards the second, crouching by the wall. There was no movement. There were no lights, no animal noises. There was nothing here. 'This place is dead,' said Marshall, thinking his words to the others. 'There's no-one here.' He looked around.

Something was very wrong, this looked too much like the bad-news side of an ambush. One thing he was sure of, they were alone here. He stood up and pulled off his goggles. His eyes started to adjust to the darkness, the dim starlight providing just the barest illumination.

He heard Sanders' voice. 'The village is abandoned. RV, position one.' Then he heard Singh's voice, 'coming in from your left.' He looked and saw the slim man walking towards him, also pulling off his goggles.

From further up the path, Sanders and Bullock walked towards them.

'What's the point putting out the cameras? said Bullock out loud. 'There's no-one here to watch.'

'There's no weapons cache here, this is a bullshit mission,' said Singh, not quite as loudly as Bullock.

'Did I miss something?' said Bullock, 'but I'm sure the briefing said there were people here.'

'Intel' was wrong,' said Marshall, resisting the temptation to add 'again.'

'No, something else is going on,' said Singh. 'This place looks like it's lived in, it's just all the people have left.'

'Why? There's nowhere to go,' said Bullock. That was quite true. None of them had seen a living soul all day. They'd passed no other villages, seen no vehicle tracks, nothing to suggest how the occupants of this place had made their exodus.

Sanders turned to Singh. 'Find something and get a sense of what happened.'

Marshall wondered about this business of being able to connect with things, with objects. He could sort of get his head around mind to mind communication. Why not? He had thoughts. Other people had thoughts. Even Bullock had to have something going on between his ears. Radios worked, machines could communicate over a distance, so why not brains? But creating a connection with a dead object just didn't make sense.

He watched Singh drag a blanket out of a hut and turn it over in his hands. Even in the dim starlight, he could see the man had his eyes half closed.

Singh spoke. 'They were sent away, all of them, ordered out. Men with guns, soldiers, like us.'

'Why?' asked Marshall.

'Can't tell,' said Singh, running his fingers over the blanket. 'All I can sense is they were ordered out.'

'This is wrong, very wrong,' said Bullock. For once, Marshall had to agree with him.

Singh's next words surprised him. 'But one stayed, he's still here.'

Marshall lifted his submachine gun and flicked off the safety catch. The others did the same in a single simultaneous motion. He scanned the area, listening for anything that might betray the location of a person. In a flash, the mission took on a different feel in his mind. This was no longer surveillance. This was hunt-or-be-hunted.

Marshall crouched, as did each of the others, and they started to move away from each other, spreading out. He saw Singh motion with his hand, towards one of the huts on the other side of the track. He stepped carefully towards the hut, Bullock coming in to cover the other side of the entrance.

A single rough blanket hung in the entrance to the hut. Marshall took up a position to the side of the entrance, Bullock on the other side, Sanders and Singh standing further back, weapons ready to fire.

He heard Singh's mental voice. 'He's in the hut, just inside. He's listening to us.'

With almost frightening swiftness Bullock pulled away the blanket covering the door. Holding his gun in his right hand, Marshall reached in with his left and pulled out the man cowering just inside. The man let out an involuntary yelp, shaking with fear kneeling at Marshall's feet. He clasped in prayer then opened them out towards Marshall, perhaps trying to show he was unarmed, then clasped them in prayer again, chattering away in some dialect of Pashto.

Sanders looked at Singh. 'Why's he still here?'

'Don't know,' said Singh, 'all I saw was the villagers being ordered out by the soldiers.'

Marshall could feel the anger rising in him. He needed to know what was going on. 'I'll find out,' he said. He swung his weapon behind his back and pulled off his gloves. He reached for the begging villager and slapped away the man's hands as he tried to defend himself. He clamped his hands on the man's head, one on either side.

'Marshall, no,' he heard Sanders hiss. All he could think was; Marshall, yes. He opened his mind and let the full force of his thoughts and his anger rush into the man at his feet. He could feel the man's mind crumble under the telepathic onslaught, a torrent of images rushing into his mind as the man's consciousness fell to pieces.

'Four of them came here, boss,' he said. 'One of them

spoke Pashto. Ordered the villagers to leave.' He could see the images, he could see the other soldiers. Modern combat dress, modern weapons, they were not locals.

'Why?' asked Singh.

'He said others would come, to hurt the villagers,' said Marshall, 'but the soldiers would stop them, kill them, there'd be lots of shooting. This one was to tell them when the others came.'

Bullock shook his head. 'What is going on here?'

'So soldiers are coming here, and we must be the "others" he was warned about,' said Singh.

'So who's coming? Who else knows we're here?' asked Bullock.

Marshall focused harder on the man, who let out a whimper as he succumbed to the psychic onslaught of Marshall's mental interrogation. He let go of the man, who sank into a whimpering heap on the ground.

'He doesn't know who the soldiers are, but he is clear they're coming to kill us.'

'Bastards,' said Singh, 'this isn't a surveillance mission, it's a fucking ambush.'

'How?' said Sanders. 'How was he to tell them?'

Almost in response the man on the floor took something out from under his jacket, a small black device, sleek and modern, a single red button set in the centre of it.

'Bastard,' said Bullock, 'radio beacon, they know we're here.'

'We need to get ready,' said Sanders, 'surprise them before they surprise us.'

'What about him?' asked Bullock, nodding at the whimpering villager.

The man on the floor looked up, the fear shining in his

eyes, the look of a man who knew his life could end at any moment.

'We take him with us,' said Michael.

Weakness. That's all Marshall could think about Sanders' approach to this situation, to their general situation. He was weak, he was never willing to do the hard things. Marshall reached down and again took hold of the man's head. There was an unpleasant wet crack as Marshall twisted the man's head violently. The man crumpled, motionless. 'Problem solved,' he said.

Even in the dimness, he could see the anger in Sanders' eyes, but he knew the officer wouldn't act on it. The man probably still thought he was the leader here, probably still thought they were a team of four. He watched as Bullock dragged the dead Afghan back into the hut.

'So where are they?' Did you find out before you broke his neck?' said Sanders, the barely controlled anger clear in his voice.

'Yeah, they're close and moving in, one from each point.'

They each looked at Michael.

'We'll form a perimeter,' said Sanders. 'Let them enter the village, then we trap them and subdue them.'

'What! Fuck that, we let them enter the village then we kill them.' The words were out of Marshall's mouth before he could stop them.

'No, we don't. They're four of our own, they don't know what we can do, we can do this without killing them.' Marshall stared at Sanders.

'I don't know,' said Singh. 'It's a nice idea, but they're not here to play nice, they aren't simply going to give up to us.'

'He's right,' said Bullock, 'they're not going to let us get close enough to subdue them.'

Sanders looked around at each of them. 'Look, they're not here because of some personal grudge, we know there's just one person who's ordered them here, our fight is with him.'

Marshall wondered if it had been Conway who'd ordered them here, ordered in a hit squad to get rid of them. Maybe it had been that MI5 woman, maybe she really was behind this whole thing. It really didn't matter. All that mattered was they were in a to-the-death fight, and Marshall had no doubt that his death wasn't an acceptable outcome.

'My fight's with anyone who wants to kill me,' he said to Sanders. 'You stay and have a friendly chat if you want, I'm going to stop them.'

Michael faced him, looking up into his eyes, shoulders square on. Marshall looked down at Sanders, he was a head taller than Michael, they both knew who was the naturally more violent. They used to know who was the superior officer. That didn't seem to matter now.

'You'll follow orders, we trap them and subdue them,' said Sanders.

'My following orders stopped when someone gave the order to have me killed,' said Marshall. He lifted his submachine gun to his chest. He was aware of the movement almost behind him as the other two lifted their weapons, a visual sign, "we're with you."

'Sorry boss,' said Bullock, 'but if they're here to kill us then that's just bad luck, we stop them, end of discussion.'

Marshall never broke his stare into Michael's eyes as he gave his own orders. With an attacker approaching from each point they'd need to find the best place to ambush each one. Three of them, three attackers. Sanders could look after himself, maybe.

'East and west access is this track, south is up that stream bed. Best ambush is the north approach, he's going to have to come between those rocks, it's a natural pinch point. Trap him there, suck his brain dry, kill him, pick the others off.'

Marshall pushed passed Sanders, Bullock and Singh walked with him. They headed for the rocky crag on the north side of the village, and Sanders was soon lost in the blackness.

TWENTY FOUR

The crag on the north side of the village was the most significant geological feature in the area. The land rose gently, then a rocky face thrust thirty feet upwards. Marshall crouched in the darkness, knowing the would-be assassin would be creeping along the base of the rock wall, hidden in the shadows.

Singh and Bullock were each in position ready to intercept the other two soldiers. He was no longer sure what Sanders was doing. He still cared. He'd served for too long with the man, been through too much to simply cut him out. How had this divide happened? He hadn't planned for it, hadn't wanted it. Everything had been fine until that cursed project until Conway filled them with that wretched drug.

The more he thought about it the more he realised, it went back further. It all started when the MI5 woman ordered them into the surveillance of the meeting, despite the total lack of intelligence. That had been the start of all this, she had been the start.

A blast of automatic gunfire jerked him back to the present moment.

Bullock could hardly contain his enthusiasm, even through the telepathic communication. 'Got him,' said Bullock, 'got the bastard.'

'Very good,' thought Marshall, 'now sit tight while we deal with the others.'

Maybe Joon-ho's African option wasn't such a bad idea. Maybe he could do a whole lot more with Joon-ho than just work for him. Perhaps he'd have Joon-ho put them up in a very nice apartment somewhere, while he found out more about Joon-ho's operations, and how he could use them.

Whichever way he thought about it, going back to Camp Bastion, back to the British Army, was seeming like a less workable option. What had happened could, he imagined, be seen as mutiny. That would be a difficult thing to get out of. Special Forces had little tolerance for soldiers who made basic mistakes, and mutiny was unlikely to further his career.

Another burst of submachine gun fire echoed off the rocks. Singh's voice came into his mind. 'Number two is taken care of.' No celebration in his voice, no enthusiasm, just matter-of-fact.

A movement caught his eye. Creeping out from the cover of the rocks, a man in black combat dress, the night vision goggles fixed in place. Marshall could tell from the man's posture and gait he was well trained. Marshall lifted his weapon to the firing position.

'Don't move,' he said, calmly. The man froze. 'I'm behind you, I will kill you if you don't do exactly as I tell you. Arms outstretched.'

The man stretched his arms out to the sides. Marshall moved forward, reaching out with his bare hand, and took a grip of the man's neck. He let a rush of psychic energy blast into the man's mind. The man staggered, his knees buckled and he dropped to the floor.

'Meet me in the centre of the village,' Marshall thought to the others.

He had the man march ahead of him back to the village. In minutes the three of them were together. The captured soldier knelt at Marshall's feet. He reached forwards and unclipped the radio unit from the man's jacket. No doubt Sanders had intercepted the fourth, and there was no way Sanders would have killed him.

He pressed the transmit button. 'Sanders, where are you going?'

There was no reply. He hadn't expected one, but he had to try, one last time.

'Michael, we need to talk about this,' he said into the radio.

It was worth trying to use their captive. 'We've got another of them here. He wants to talk to his friend.'

He bent down and held the radio to their captive's face. He reached out with his mind and gave a telepathic instruction. The man spoke, slowly, as though half asleep.

'Dave, Dave, you need to come back.'

Marshall stood up. How long to give it? He waited. He looked at the others. Singh looked at him, Bullock shrugged his shoulders. Marshall tossed the radio aside.

Enough. They were each now so far on opposite sides of the line there could be no going back. He pulled out his pistol and put it to the back of the man's head. He wondered for a moment what it would be like to be telepathically linked to someone when they die. Perhaps now wasn't the time to find out.

A single shot and there was a wet splashing sound as

blood and brains sprayed the frozen ground and the man fell forwards, his legs twitching slightly. Then he was still.

Marshall let his thoughts open out, connecting with Sanders. 'Michael, we're a team, don't do this. They won't have you back. They sent them to kill us, all of us, you too. You think they're going to welcome you back? Forgive and forget? Won't happen man.'

Surely he'd come back. Surely they'd stay as a team. Wouldn't they? He felt more angry, angry at Sanders, angry at him for walking away from them.

'We're supposed to be a team, Michael. Don't do this. If you turn against us Michael, we'll come for you, I promise man, we'll come for you.'

He let his mind be quiet, but there was nothing. Sanders was blocking him. Now he was truly gone.

'Now what?' said Bullock, sharply.

'It is a good question,' said Singh, his voice rising in volume as he spoke. 'We're in the middle of Afghanistan, no food, no water, and very soon the whole of the British Army will have orders to arrest us for treason and murder, as well as other people simply wanting to kill us.'

Now that he put it like that, it didn't seem a very good situation. Marshall let his thoughts turn inwards for a moment. There were always options.

'What are we going to do?' asked Bullock, urgency creeping into his voice.

Marshall held up his hand to silence him. He needed a few more moments of quiet.

He opened his eyes. 'Joon-ho can organise a plane. We have to get across the border, to Pakistan.'

'That's a long way,' said Bullock.

'I'm sure the Army will give you a lift somewhere if you'd like,' said Singh.

'Enough,' said Marshall. He'd had enough of joking and of banter and of sarcasm. Now they had to survive. Michael had betrayed them. The Head had betrayed them. Conway and the army had betrayed them. Joon-ho had unlimited resources, he had a business empire that could give them anything they want. From his connection with Joon-ho, he got the sense the man was skilled in the business of revenge. That sounded a fine idea.

MICHAEL KICKED another rock and cursed under his breath. Progress was slow across the uneven terrain. The starlight wasn't bright enough to walk by, and the night vision goggles gave no depth perception, making it easy to miss a footing. He found it curious that his captive seemed to walk without effort. Michael did not need to hold the man at gunpoint, the telepathic control ensured his obedience, but neither did he need to direct the man's every step.

'Where are you from?' Michael asked, out loud. He supposed when they got back to Camp Bastion, if they got back, the man would likely be interviewed at length. The more this man, Dave, behaved normally the better, so Michael had decided to use as little psychic control as he could.

'Cape Town,' replied Dave, although his accent was faint.

'Who do you work for?'

Dave paused. 'A group of us. We work together. People hire us.'

'What do they hire you to do?'

'Bodyguard work,' said Dave. 'Sometimes they need

someone taking care of.' Michael assumed this meant contract killing. He didn't bother to clarify.

'Who hired you?'

'We have a representative,' said Dave. 'He does the deals, passes on the orders.'

So Dave and his friends would never know the identity of the customer, and the customer likely wouldn't know Dave's and friends' identities; security all around.

'When were you given your orders to come here?'

'Two days ago,' said Dave. So Dave and his team were ordered here at the same time as Michael and his team. It left no doubt in Michael's mind that he and his team had been sent here, sent out into the desert, so Dave and his team could kill them. Someone had wanted them taken care of, in Dave's words. Marshall had been right to be suspicious.

What else had Marshall been right about? Was it the MI5 woman behind this? Michael wasn't so sure. The project facility was a joint venture between the Ministry of Defence and a private contractor, who supplied the drug. That didn't suggest an MI5 run project. Perhaps MI5 had some other role?

A more pressing problem was how he was going to get back to Camp Bastion. It was unlikely Dave's helicopter team-mates would just oblige and give him a lift back to camp. Taking control of the helicopter's crew would be essential, but not easy. His next problem was getting an unidentified aircraft cleared to enter Bastion airspace without being shot down as a hostile. So far, this had not been a good day.

His day, possibly, was better than Marshall's and Bullock's and Singh's. At least he knew a helicopter was a possibility. As soon as he got back to Camp Bastion he'd make sure the helicopter scheduled to pick up him and his team was cancelled, abandoning Marshall and the others in the Afghan desert. Marshall would know he and the others would never make it to the rendezvous site before the helicopter was grounded. What would they do?

Michael forced himself to turn his thoughts away from that line of thinking. Marshall had made his choice, as had the others. They would have to live with that choice, or die because of it. One thing was clear, their team was no more.

'Why did someone want us dead?' Michael asked.

'They said you were intercepting Taliban weapons stores, selling the guns for your own profit,' said Dave. 'We said we didn't care. We were paid to do a job.'

Michael made a mental note, before the helicopter arrived he'd use the telepathic link to find the identity of Dave's manager.

The faint but deep thrumming of a helicopter's rota became apparent in the darkness. Dave stopped walking and stood still. Now it was time to see how good his control over Dave really was.

MICHAEL THOUGHT Lieutenant-Colonel Clifton had a very small office for his rank, and for the importance of his role, but then maybe he didn't need much of an office. The small and cramped room had yellow sticky notes decorating the desk and computer monitor. A single battered filing cabinet stood in the corner, next to the maps and photographs pinned to the wall.

Clifton had gone off to ensure the cancellation of the helicopter scheduled to pick up Michael and his team. He and Michael hadn't yet established a clear explanation for what had happened to his team, at least not an explanation which could be put in a report and sent up the chain of command. They had discussed it briefly, established that Marshall and the others were likely dead, and that hostile forces had been operating in the area. Clifton hadn't yet pressed him on who his 'captive' might be, nor for the identity of the helicopter crew. No doubt an awkward conversation lay ahead.

Michael mused that his return trip had been far less difficult than he had imagined. Taking control of the helicopter pilot and co-pilot had been straightforward. Even getting into Camp Bastion airspace with his short-range radio and call-sign had been pleasantly uneventful. Armed troops had surrounded the aircraft as soon as it touched down, and people had insisted on pointing guns at him while his identity was confirmed. But after that, he had had no further trouble.

Now he sat in Clifton's office, staring at the telephone. There were only a few people he could think to call, and now he thought about it he didn't actually have a number for any of them. No matter, he picked up the phone and started making enquiries as to how to reach certain people.

Dialling the numbers was the easy bit, actually reaching people was a lot less productive. He reached the switchboard of the project facility, but Captain Conway wasn't available, and the operator couldn't (or wouldn't) give him any further information. The duty officer in the Special Forces Directorate denied all knowledge of his team's assignment, saying that was a matter for Special Forces Development but he couldn't divulge any details of any senior officers involved. Instead, the individual referred Sanders to the officer running the project.

Michael had one last number to call. He checked his

watch. It would be right at the start of the working day in London. Having acquired a phone number, Michael dialled.

Perhaps he shouldn't have been surprised when she answered.

'Head of Operations,' said the woman in a no-nonsense tone of voice.

'Good morning,' said Michael.

'Captain Sanders,' said the Head, 'I was beginning to think you'd disappeared off the face of the Earth.'

'Someone did try to make that happen,' he said and proceeded to give her a brief summary of his night's activities.

'Did you know?' Michael asked, the question he needed to ask.

'Did I know what, Captain?' asked the Head. 'What specifically are you asking me?'

'Do you know who sent us here? And why?'

'I had no idea where you'd been sent, and no, I have no idea who sent you.'

'It was a very big coincidence. Captain Conway told us we were being sent to Afghanistan, still as part of his project, at the same time this unit of mercenaries was dispatched from South Africa.'

'We both know that's not a coincidence,' said the Head. 'But I had no part in that.'

'Forgive me for being blunt,' said Michael, ready to ask a question which could prompt the ending of the call. 'But how do I know you're not behind all this?'

'I'm willing to bet, Captain,' said the Head, 'that I'm the only person who's answered your call.'

Sanders paused. Ghosts tended to disappear into the dark and the shadows if you tried to shine a light on them.

'Yes,' he said, 'yes, you are.'

'So what are you going to do now?' she asked.

It was a good question and one to which he had no good answer.

'I don't know, but what I do know is someone clearly wanted us dead, and that can only be whoever is behind this project. What happened to us was no accident. Someone knew what that drug would do to us, this whole thing has been planned all along.'

'Before you ask your next question,' she said, 'let me say this. I'm not going to tell you anything else. Before you protest, consider this. The less you know, the safer you'll be. A little knowledge can be a dangerous thing. If you knew a little more than you know now, someone might have a strong enough reason to make further attempts to get rid of you.'

'I know enough,' said Sanders.

'Enough to do what?' asked the Head, sharply. 'If you're out on your own then you're a target, you have no cover. I don't imagine you can return to your previous role in Special Forces?'

'I can't see that happening, somehow,' he said. 'It seems I have enemies on all fronts.'

'Meaning?'

'Marshall, Bullock, and Singh,' he said. 'They're still out there. It's unlikely they'll survive, abandoned in the desert, but then again, they're specialists in surviving hostile environments against overwhelming odds.'

'So they remain a problem?' she asked.

'Oh yes. Marshall will be angry, very angry, they all will. They'll want revenge.'

'And what do you think they'll actually be able to do?'

'It's possible,' said Michael, thinking through recent events, 'that Marshall had some time alone with Joon-ho. If he did, it's more than likely that Marshall has a strong telepathic control over Joon-ho. What do you think Marshall would do if he could reach out with his mind and make Joon-ho do whatever he wanted?'

'I think his chances of escaping Afghanistan increase significantly, as do the chances of him acquiring the resources to set about exacting revenge,' said the Head. 'If you can't go back to the Army, then you have no cover from enemies coming at you from two fronts.'

'Then what do you suggest?' asked Michael.

'We will all need protection if, and when, Marshall and the others return,' said the Head. 'You need protection until that time. I could use someone with your very unique abilities.'

'That sounds worryingly like a job offer,' said Michael.

'It is,' said the Head. 'Work for me, at MI5. I guarantee you work that you will find challenging and rewarding.'

'I don't think I'm quite cut out to be a spook.'

'I think you're exactly the kind of person whose cut out to be a spook, and I have more experience in judging that than you do. Unless you have a better idea.'

Michael had to concede, he did not. The idea didn't immediately appeal, he felt there was too much of his Army life he'd be giving up.

'What about Captain Conway?' asked Michael, thinking about other avenues of enquiry.

He caught the pause before the Head replied, a moment of silence which spoke volumes. 'It seems,' she said, 'that Captain Conway cannot be contacted, and no-one will admit to knowing his whereabouts.'

'Maybe he's been reassigned?'

'Possibly,' said the Head, 'but we do have some considerable resources to draw on when it comes to finding people, and we can't find him, nor can GCHQ.'

Michael felt sad. Conway was a soldier, but an office-soldier. He and the team had had a less than complimentary opinion of Conway, but he hadn't deserved to be killed, not simply for being inconvenient. The Head had said something which made Michael think. How would he know if Marshall and the others had come back? How would he get any early warnings of their return, before it was too late? How, unless he had access to the kind of resources that MI5 and GCHQ had?

It also made him think such resources might, in time, be useful in tracing who was behind all this. Not to begin with, but when life for everyone had returned to normal, perhaps then he could begin shining lights in dark corners.

'Captain Sanders?' said the Head. Michael realised he'd been silent for a while.

'Still here,' he said.

Dangerous missions and assignments were what he and his team did, or used to do. But someone had betrayed them, and that felt personal. Michael felt a need to find them, he would make it his business to find them. No doubt Marshall would make it his business to take revenge on everyone he thought had betrayed him, and that probably included Michael.

He had no doubt his path would again cross Marshall's, and the others'. He would need to be ready. He would need to be prepared.

'Very well,' he said. 'I'm in. Where do we start?'

EPILOGUE

Michael stood and stared through the window, watching the lights of the London skyline twinkle in the cool small hours of the morning. He cast a glance at the clock on the wall. It had taken them longer to piece together the story of the Psiclone Project than he'd expected. Coming back to the present moment he realised how much he ached after the intense action at the farmhouse.

He turned around to face the others. He could see the fatigue on their faces, the tiredness visible in their postures. He had no doubt Eric ached as much as he did, his throat no doubt still painful from where Marshall's man had almost strangled him. The Head sat back in her chair, and he was sure he saw he stifle a yawn.

'I didn't feature much,' said Eric, stretching his arms as he made no attempt to stifle a large and protracted yawn.

'Be thankful for small mercies,' said Michael, 'but you're well involved in the current part of the story.'

'Don't I know it?'

Silence returned. Michael had talked for so long he felt he had run out of words.

'So they obviously got away,' said Anna, finally breaking the silence.

'Yes,' said the Head, glancing at her screen, perhaps checking an update. 'Since your little confrontation at the farmhouse the police haven't yet traced the helicopter, so Marshall and Singh are still on the run.'

'And Bullock's lying on a slab,' said Eric, half smiling. 'At least you've cut our problems down a bit.'

'It's not that big a victory,' said the Head, leaning forwards. 'You may have killed the buffoon of their operation, but the brains and the brawn are still very much alive.'

'I meant they escaped from Afghanistan,' said Anna.

Michael looked at her. It was an obvious question, but at its core it was a reasonable one. At the time he hadn't expected Marshall, Bullock and Singh to make it out of Afghanistan alive. He thought they might, a small part of him even hoped they would, but he just hadn't been able to bring himself to believe that they would.

'Against all expectation,' he said, 'yes. I assume they were able to walk far enough to make contact with some of Joon-ho's men, or maybe his men got to them sooner than we thought.'

'So what happened to them after that?' asked Anna.

'They pretty much disappeared,' said the Head. 'We kept tabs on Joon-ho, and we kept an active watch for Marshall and his friends. Eventually they were spotted in Hong Kong, after that we caught sight of them once in a while in various places in the Far East.'

'What about Joon-ho?'

The Head sighed. 'We had to keep the existence of the nuclear weapon a complete secret, so we could never make any direct accusations against him. That and his political connections have kept him free to carry on his business, although he's never since tried to visit the UK.'

'So why don't we just go and get him?' said Eric.

'An assassination of a prominent business leader in a foreign country, especially a country like China? It could start a war, never mind the practicalities of getting passed Joon-ho's own security, which does seem to have become a lot closer over the last three years.'

'I can imagine the three of them spent the last three years enjoying themselves spending Joon-ho's money and using some of it to prepare for their return here,' said Michael. 'No doubt Marshall will have summoned Joon-ho to come and rescue him again.'

'I think that would be a safe assumption,' said the Head. 'Joon-ho has supporters, operatives and affiliates in almost every country, no doubt he will dispatch people from somewhere close, but who or where they might be we don't know.'

'But they did get away with more of the drug,' said Anna. The room fell silent again. Michael had been pondering that very point. What might Marshall and Singh do with more of the drug? Become more powerfully telepathic was the obvious answer. But to what end? What was their plan? The drug was a means to an end, they knew the means, they didn't know the end goal.

'I think,' said the Head, 'that is probably enough for tonight. The police and MI5 are continuing the search for Marshall and Singh.' She stood.

'There's just one bit I don't understand,' said Eric. He looked at the Head and fixed her with a stare. Michael hadn't seen Eric look so serious, nor had he seen the Head stopped in her tracks like that.

'Which bit is that Mr Braithwaite?' she said.

'All of it,' said Eric. Michael, Anna, the Head, they all drew breath simultaneously to answer Eric's seemingly flippant comment, but his next question silenced them all. 'What was that Psiclone Project all for?'

Michael thought about the obvious answer, but he had a sense that Eric had picked up on something important. The obvious answer wasn't the important answer. Perhaps they had missed something. But how could they have missed it for three years?

'Why did Morrow go to all the trouble of trying to create a unit of Special Forces soldiers?' said Eric. 'If he wanted personal protection a couple of bodyguards would have done. Going to all that trouble to get control of the military project, hijack a unit of soldiers, turn them into his own private, if very small army. Why? What's he been doing for the last three years?'

The Head sat back down.

'You have been keeping track of him, haven't you?' said Eric, with a tone Michael hadn't heard many people use to the Head.

'Thank you, Mr Braithwaite,' said the Head, her voice hardening. 'We have indeed kept eyes on Doctor Morrow. He's done very little. He turned his special projects building into his own fortress and he has ventured outside its walls very little over the last three years.'

'But he has telepathic control of lots of people,' said Eric. 'He doesn't need to go out, he can just do his astral-projection-woo-woo thing.'

Michael had to stifle a laugh. The Head didn't laugh.

It was Anna who spoke next. 'I didn't have any involvement after that second visit to the project facility, but I assume the project's IT was all secured after that?'

'It was Miss Hendrickson,' said the Head. 'And we used our newly installed security measures to keep an eye on what was going on, but after Captain Conway disappeared nothing happened at the facility.'

'And at PanMedic's facility?' asked Michael.

'Morrow continued to work on a range of projects, he did further research into the telepathy drug, but hasn't done much with it,' said the Head.

'So what happened last night to that Falcone character?' asked Eric.

'It seems not long after Captain Sanders left, he threw himself off the roof of his office building,' said the Head.

Eric looked at Michael, and Michael flashed his don't-say-a-word stare. Eric didn't say anything, not to Michael.

Eric spoke to the Head. 'So we've all just assumed that after his little project went pear-shaped, he gave up? A man who has telepathic control over other people, including at least one senior military officer that we know about, who can have other people run around and follow his orders. Everyone's assumed he's not been up to anything.'

'So what do you think he might have been up to?' asked the Head, her tone making it more of a challenge than a question.

'Well,' said Eric, 'we've met this mysterious bunch of soldiers twice, and they've nearly killed us twice. So it may be a daft question, but where did they come from?'

They all looked at the Head.

'We've not yet had time to investigate them,' she said. 'My working assumption was they were a unit ordered in by Major Turner.'

'Turner?' said Eric, 'the man who's under telepathic control of Morrow?'

'Turner is a senior military officer,' said the Head, 'and

one who works in a part of the military which makes it extremely difficult to monitor his activities.'

'I think Eric's right,' said Michael. 'It's quite possible Morrow hasn't been quiet for three years, and it's quite possible he's still working with Major Turner.'

The Head was silent for a moment. Then she spoke. 'Later. Marshall and Singh are our first and highest priority. Tomorrow morning you'll join the search for them.'

'I'm sorry,' said Eric, 'but with respect, they're on the run. We've destroyed almost all their assets, they're no threat.'

'They still pose a clear threat, and with their additional supply of the drug we have no way of knowing how powerful they can become or what they will be able to do.'

'But Morrow is the unknown,' said Michael, 'he's ultimately the one behind all this, he's the biggest danger. Marshall and Singh have a small amount of the drug, Morrow could have an entire lake of it.'

'I agree,' said the Head, 'Morrow warrants further investigation, but not as a priority.'

'Then for the moment, why don't we just close him down, make sure he can't do any more of whatever it is we don't know he's doing,' said Eric.

'That's more easily said than done,' said the Head. The following silence prompted her to say more. 'PanMedic has become something of a darling of British industry, and their Chief Executive is a close friend of the Prime Minister.'

'Oh that doesn't smack of telepathic manipulation,' said Eric, not disguising his sarcasm.

'From everything we've heard this evening, someone enjoying political protection is not one of the good-guys,' said Michael.

'I could dig into their systems,' said Anna, 'see if they've been trying to hide anything.'

'Yes,' said the Head, 'but only after we've found our two fugitives.'

'So what about these mysterious soldiers we keep running into?' said Eric. 'First time they almost executed us along with those Serb mercenaries.'

Michael's mind was taken straight back to the moment he and Eric had been ambushed by the unknown soldiers. Marshall and the others had led them on a wild goose chase, having them think they were pursuing Marshall and friends when in fact they were pursuing the three Serbian mercenaries. The unknown soldiers had executed the mercenaries, but probably because they too believed them to be Marshall, Bullock and Singh. Michael had never been certain who the lead soldier had been in contact with, who it was had decided whether Michael and Eric should also be killed. He hadn't seen the lead soldier's face clearly, but he had looked into his eyes. It was only now that recognition flashed into Michael's mind.

The others were still talking, Michael had zoned out for a moment.

'Conway,' he said. The saying of that name brought quiet to the room.

'He's dead, isn't he?' said Anna.

'No,' said the Head. 'I said he had disappeared. Once Captain Sanders and the others had been dispatched to Afghanistan we lost track of Captain Conway and couldn't locate him, not a trace of him.'

'I didn't see his face clearly,' said Michael. 'But now that I think about it, it was Conway.'

'Who was?' said Eric.

'The team who killed the Serb mercenaries. Conway was their team leader.' He saw the Head sit back in her chair, into her thinking pose.

'It seems our friends Morrow and Turner have been busy boys,' said Eric. 'Pity we've not a clue what they've been up to.'

'One more sarcastic comment Mister Braithwaite and I'll have you put on desk duties.' The Head's tone was not a joking one. Eric too sank back into his chair, but into more of a sulking pose. Michael knew the threat of desk-work was a most serious threat to a field officer.

'It does change things,' said the Head. 'You're sure it was Conway?'

'Not a hundred percent, but sure enough that I really want to know what they've been up to.'

'Very well,' said the Head. 'First, we all need rest, and that is an order. Tomorrow morning we start a deep dive into Morrow and Turner. Miss Hendrickson, your skills will be essential in penetrating the security we put around PanMedic's systems.'

'Yes Ma'am,' said Anna with enthusiasm.

'We'll leave the police and other agencies to pursue Marshall and Singh, but if they find them you may be needed.' She directed her last comment to Michael.

'Yes Ma'am.'

'But until then, I want every effort made to find out exactly what Morrow is planning. And stop him.'

OCCASIONALLY, but not often, Morrow found he could let go of the voices, he could let them all fade so far into the background his mind became quiet. He relished such times. He had tried to develop it as a skill, and had made some progress. Early on there were times when the voices were so many and so loud he thought he was going mad. He couldn't hear his own thoughts above the cacophony of telepathic shouting.

Now he liked to simply bask in the psychic solitude but no sooner had he settled back in his chair than he felt the urgency in Turner's thoughts as they reached out to him. Turner couldn't force his way into a telepathic conversation, but Morrow could hear when Turner was particularly agitated and wanted to communicate.

'Liam,' Morrow said in his silent psychic way, 'I hear you.' He made his words soothing, calming.

'Things have not gone according to plan,' came Turner's voice.

'When do they ever?' replied Morrow.

'What?' Turner, it seemed, was not in the mood for philosophising.

'What specifically did not go according to plan?'

'Marshall and Singh escaped, Sanders failed to stop them.'

'From that I take it Bullock did not escape?'

'No, they managed to kill him.'

'That is no great loss, but no great victory either. Did your men take care of Sanders?'

'No,' said Turner. 'Marshall and Singh are still at large, there is a chance Sanders will find them.'

Morrow was quiet for a moment as he mulled things over, but he could sense Turner's anxiety at the silence.

'I am less convinced Captain Sanders and his people are an asset, they have failed in every attempt to stop Marshall and his colleagues.' He paused, not entirely sure how to phrase his next admission. 'There is further news,' he said finally.

Turner was quiet, perhaps waiting. Morrow continued. 'Yves Falcone is dead,' he said. 'He took his own life.'

'Why?'

'I'm not sure, Liam, I'm not sure. I knew Yves very well, but I couldn't know every thought in his mind.' Morrow thought maybe this admission might be some comfort to Turner, even though it was bordering on a lie.

'I am sad to hear that news,' said Turner. Morrow believed him, he could feel the sadness deepening in Turner's mind, but then it changed, his thoughts took on a different quality. 'We need to press on.'

'We do, Liam. Yves' death has left a problem. He was a personal friend of Commander Halbern. Without Yves to introduce us, it will be difficult to get access to the Commander.'

'Is there an alternative?' asked Turner.

'No,' said Morrow. 'I need control of the Commander, I need direct control of the police firearms unit, it is crucial to the plan.'

'Then we must arrange a meeting with Commander Halbern another way.'

'I agree,' said Morrow. 'I must meet with Commander Halbern, and you must arrange it. But it must be discreet. We've stayed out of the gaze of MI5 so far, it would be unfortunate to pique their curiosity at this late stage.'

'I will see what I can do.'

'Make the introduction happen, Liam. I need to have control over the police, over their firearms officers, it is key to everything.' He paused for a moment. 'Liam? One more thing.'

'Yes?'

'When the police or MI5 find Marshall and Singh, make sure that your men are there to kill them.'

'I will, they won't be a problem any longer.'

'Good, and one more thing. I think Captain Sanders has

outlived any potential usefulness. Find a way to do it quietly, but it's time to kill Sanders and his team. We've a lot to do, we're going to change the world, and I don't want Sanders or his people getting in the way.'

Turner's thoughts faded, and Morrow returned to his quiet. He stared out of the window of his office. He couldn't risk Sanders or anyone else getting in the way. There was so much to do, there was so much to achieve. He would change the world in ways that few could imagine, he would change the world forever.

To be continued in ... **Power In Mind**

POWER IN MIND

Power In Mind

Michael Sanders and his team have finally unmasked the force behind the Psiclone project, and now they realise the true scale of the threat, but in a violent attack in broad daylight, Sanders is kidnapped. Stripped of their leader and their most powerful weapon, Anna and Eric take the lead and team up with an unlikely ally as they face their greatest dilemma - stop Morrow, or save Michael Sanders.

ABOUT SIMON STANTON

Simon Stanton fell in love with stories at an early age, reading and writing science fiction. Despite the best efforts of parents and teachers to broaden his horizons, Simon remained obsessed with sci-fi. Teaching himself to touch-type so he could get his thoughts on paper quicker, Simon wrote shorts stories, ideas for bigger works, and finally his first novel length work - a piece which remains safely locked away. Then he stopped writing, and after a thirty year hiatus (which not even he can adequately explain) he began writing again, first short stories and then his first novel, A Mind To Kill. The first book in The Psiclone Series is now followed by Force Of Mind and by this third book, with the fourth (Power In Mind) well under way.

Simon lives in West Yorkshire, UK, and balances his writing with home life, a job in project management, and his practise of Aikido (a Japanese martial art.)

To find out more about Simon and the Psiclone novels (but, to be fair, not much about Yorkshire), visit his website at:

About Simon Stanton

www.simonstanton.com

or on Facebook at:

www.facebook.com/simonstantonwriter

Printed in Great Britain
by Amazon